'At the end of its five hundred year life, the Phoenix builds a nest of spices, perches on it, and sings until the sunlight sets it alight; both nest and bird burn completely away and a new young Phoenix bird arises from the ashes.'

The consequences of a mother taking the secret of her new-born child's paternity to the grave, are grave indeed.

Joseph Elliot, Lizzibeth Buxton and Henry Ferguson, are unlikely childhood soul-mates through a fortuitous, yet near tragic, twist of fate on Henry's father's Dorset estate in the autumn of 1843.

When Lizzibeth invites one of her two friends, as she surely must, to explore the adult world of physical pleasure, she could not know that this momentous and mutual right of passage, would share the same moment in their history as her brother's crime. As Joseph begins to build his family life far away from the Dorset coast amidst the events and establishment of Scarborough as a successful Victorian seaside resort, Henry settles for a career in the army. They could not have known how both these past events would riddle the embers of their lives, as history begins to taunt them in their new situations.

Joseph and his wife graciously struggle to cope with these intermittent and sometimes malevolent flickers of the emerging truth from not only their own and Henry's past, but also the Buxtons. Secrets spark from subsequent generations fueling this otherwise benign yet glimmering glow of deceit from the Elliot women.

Absolution for them all, arrives in an engulfing blaze of revelation to Lizzibeth's daughter Betsy Agatha, almost seventy years after her birth. Only then, like the phoenix in the Dorset town where her life began, can she openly bequeath a bright new dawn to her family, in her own enlightened dusk.

Nest of Spices

Linda Sidgwick

authorHOUSE®

AuthorHouse™ UK Ltd.
500 Avebury Boulevard
Central Milton Keynes, MK9 2BE
www.authorhouse.co.uk
Phone: 08001974150

First published by AuthorHouse 3/5/2010

ISBN: 978-1-4490-6455-6 (sc)

This book is printed on acid-free paper.

Acknowledgements

I could not have achieved the completion of this project if it had not been for the unconditional love, support, and encouragement together with some pride in my endeavours from my husband Steve, my children Gemma and James, and my Mum. Thank you also James for the regular, timely, constructive criticism that I valued more than you know, as well as the design for my 'pink' cover. Also for the support from family, friends and colleagues who perhaps thought I was a little deranged in even attempting to write a book in my already hectic schedule.

Contents

Character List

Thomas Elliot – Head Coachman to Charles Ferguson
Mary Elliot – Thomas' Wife
Joseph Elliot – His son
Louisa Elliot - His daughter
Benjamin Elliot - His son
Rose Elliot - His daughter

Jake - Head Coachman at Bramble House

Agatha Buxton – Mary Elliot's friend
Bill Buxton – her son
Lizzibeth Buxton – her daughter
Arthur Brown – Bill Buxton's friend

Charles Ferguson – Master of Bramble House
Henrietta Ferguson – His Wife
Henry Ferguson – His son
Charlotte Ferguson - His Daughter
Amelia Ferguson – Henry's wife

Mrs Brookes and Mr Simms – Housekeeper and Butler at Bramble House

Jacob Thackery – Cabinet Maker
Kate Thackery – Jacob's wife
HannahThackery – Their daughter, then Joseph Elliot's wife

Betsy Agatha Elliot – Lizzibeth's daughter –brought up by Joseph and Hannah

Thomas Henry Elliot – Joseph and Hannah's son

Kathy   Louiza   - Joseph and Hannah's daughter –

Albert Edgar   - Joseph and Hannah's son

Eliza Henrietta – Foundling baby brought up by Joseph and Hannah

John Hetherington – Local Doctor in Scarborough

Mary Hetherington   - His wife

Edward Hetherington – His son

Beatrice Hetherington- His daughter

Henry Hetherington – His younger son

William   Robinson   –   Neighbour   of   the   Elliot's   in Scarborough

Jane   Robinson – His Wife

Peter   Robinson – His son

Johnny Robinson - His son

Annie   Robinson - His daughter

Mr Wilson - Kate's 2nd Husband

Mr and Mrs Hudson – Neighbours of the Elliot's

Michael Hudson – Their son

Mrs Jones - Neighbour of the Elliot's
Miss Briggs – Neighbour of the Elliot's

Micky Walker – Local Fisherman

Charles Walker – His son – thought to be his nephew

Beth Walker   - His daughter

Edith – His sister

Thom and Annie Elliot's children:-

Alice Jane Elliot -

William Thomas Elliot
Little Joe Elliot

Arthur Jones – Bill Buxton's son

Arthur and Kathy Jones' Children
Emily
Billy
Twins (Thomas and Mary)
Hannah

Lottie Elliot – Albert's wife

Albert John (Bertie) Elliot - Albert and Lottie's Son

Norah – Friend of Beth's

Sidney Ramsbottom– Friend of Charlie's

Mr Chapman – Neighbour to Betsy

Charlotte – Beth's daughter

Mr and Mrs Bagshaw – Neighbours to Albert Elliot

Part 1

Lizzibeth

1844 - 1858

Chapter 1

Dorset, Oct 1853

"What's a Phoenix?" she said gazing over his shoulder from the step below him at the words carved so uniformly in the monument above their heads. Startled by the question, he turned to look at the moonlit words she appeared to have read.

"Oh, don't get excited, I didn't really read it. Mr Simms told me the other day that the inscription on here reads." - She paused to gather herself and began slowly,- "In grateful acknowledgement of the Divine Mercy, that has raised this town like a Phoenix from its ashes, to its present beautiful and flourishing state." Self-satisfied at her impressive recall; she looked back at him from the inscription, punctuating the end of her quote with a decisive nod of her head.

"I'm sure that's right, but I didn't like to ask 'im what a Phoenix was. 'E's always laughing at me. I do try so hard to make sense of the books you give me, but the bigger words are so hard to work out." She hung her head in mock shame at her ignorance.

He suddenly sat up very tall and away from the stone pillar that had been his prop. Adopting a professorial pose, arms in an open, if slightly shaky, gesture of knowledge, enthusiasm spilling his liquor from his bottle, he lowered his chin, and paused for the revelry in the nearby Ferguson Arms to abate. Then deepening his reply, he began. "A Phoenix, my dear

3

Lizzibeth, is a mythical bird, Greek I think; or is it Egyptian, I can't remember; with bright gold and red feathers. At the end of its five hundred year life, the Phoenix builds a nest of spices, perches on it, and sings until the sunlight sets it alight; both nest and bird burn completely away and a new young Phoenix bird arises from the ashes."

A little smug in his own echelon of knowledge, he took another mouthful of whisky from his bottle, Lizzibeth snuggled up close to him trying to warm herself.

"That explains why the town is likened to it, following the big fire. It's hard to believe a fire could almost completely destroy a whole town. How long ago is it now, I can never remember?"

"1731, more than a century ago, but so many lives were lost, that every family was affected in some way, hence the stories of the tragedies have passed down with such vividness that everyone feels it was not that long ago. The new buildings are much better built, it would never happen in such a way again. The church apparently held out for a long time, the townspeople quenching the flames many times before the fire became so powerful that it melted the lead and dissolved the bells until they purportedly, ran as a river."

"Goodness me! You're so clever, I wish I knew things, I want to ask and know more but everyone teases me for not knowing – so how can I ever learn?" He playfully tweaked her nose, smiling at both her sincerity and candour. An affectionate smile. It held and reflected his sincere admiration for the efforts he had watched her make through her uneducated childhood in pursuit of a knowledge and understanding of the world around her.

"Maybe they don't know either, Lizzibeth, and laughing at you is a way of covering their own ignorance. Attained knowledge, if indeed it genuinely exists, should be shared and not jealously guarded."

Feeling her shiver, he pulled her closer to warm her, contemplating briefly if the two of them could have done more to help her in this thirsty quest for knowledge.

"Ugh, stop it, Lizzibeth, you're tickling my neck." He cringed as her warm breath flew back and forth within his ear.

"I was only rubbing my nose on you. It's freezing tonight." Her words were lost in the raucous din coming from the local hostelry, a mixture of singing and good natured, though drunken high spirits.

"Our Bill's in there again tonight," she continued, "he was going with a crowd to drink to his friend Arthur Brown who's getting married tomorrow. I hope Arthur'll still be capable of turning up at the altar after the amount that's obviously being drunk in there, 'cause Molly Jones is already starting to show and needs a respectable ring on her finger. They'll miss spending so much time together once Arthur's wed, Bill 'n him have been inseparable since childhood, Ma often joked they'd 'av to share a wife just like they shared everything else!" They both laughed at such absurdity.

Without disturbing her, and as if prompted by the noise, he reached out with his foot and nudged the unresponsive body propped up by the cold, unyielding pillar to his left.

"Hoy, come on, wake up, we need to all get back before we're in trouble. Or possibly freeze to death."

"Aw, leave 'im to sleep it off, don't kick 'im. He'll be dreaming there's another one of them earthquakes. Remember at Easter 'e kept going on about how we could possibly have slept through it when the shakes were felt so violently on the coast 'ere. He should go to sleep on a night 'imself instead of lying awake waiting for earthquakes. It was a long way from here wasn't it?"

"In Coutances, France, but they can be felt very great distances away from the centre of them." This knowledge of his was so wondrous. She was so much in awe of what destiny had so easily done for him, she wanted to bleed it into her, drop by drop.

"Don't let's go back yet, please. I've 'ad so much fun tonight I don't want it to end, they'll all be asleep now anyway at this hour of the night. And please don't drink anymore, 'e's out cold already. If it don't do the same to you it'll 'ave you chucking up soon, then what shall I do with the pair of you? I've only 'ad a bit, and I feel real funny, I always hated the effect it had on my Pa, even before it made him so ill."

They sat motionless and quiet for a moment, as if considering what she would do in such circumstances. She wanted to savour the moments of this spontaneous and adult evening with her two greatest friends, it was as if it had sealed and underlined the very essence of their childhood friendship. How could she have known, that by the end of this night, the fateful downfall of their young triumvirate would be sealed?

"Don't worry, I haven't drunk anything like as much as he has, Lizzibeth, or as much as that lot in the Inn. Good thing we came across you tonight on your way back to the house, else we would surely have gone in there and indulged further. Besides, I am used to a little of my father's poison!"

He thought for a moment that many might have resented the curtailment of a night at the Inn, but they were always so pleased to have Lizzibeth's company that they were more than happy to spend the time with her. They had wandered the town, and sat by the bridge over the river, reminiscing over previous adventures and catching up with each other's thoughts, hopes and plans. Despite the cold, the night had been crisp and clear, with a full bright moon levitating in the cloudless sky, leading them by an invisible rein and illuminating their progress.

This unlikely friendship between the three of them had spanned many of their early years. It made holidays glorious and companionable, as well as subliminally enlightening the three of them to societal diversity in Victorian England. But with their adulthood would come inevitable separation, diverse aspirations defining the parting of their ways and an end to the unity they childishly enjoyed.

Lizzibeth already knew she would grieve for the loss of them both. She resented the appearance of Hannah on the scene for some of their exploits and had noticed she was around more and more. The day either of them took a wife, would be a difficult, yet foreseeable day for her.

Suddenly, she turned his face to hers, and as though obeying an ethereal instruction to attempt to pursue him into his future and abandon her own; she climbed astride his knees, held the bottle away from him, and began kissing his mouth.

"What are you doing?" He pulled away soberly, just a little too late to convincingly illustrate displeasure, but showed genuine astonishment and shock, not only at her action, but at his own reaction to it. He looked into her moonlit face and found it hard to believe in this bizarre moment, that he had never before noticed the pretty young woman their 'little Lizzibeth' had grown into. She had always just been so much fun and the willing butt of many of their teasing games, but she was surely just a childhood friend to him. Wasn't she?

Embarrassed by his scrutiny, and then nervously giggling at his hesitancy to speak further, she turned back and cuddled into his shoulder, wounded by a rejection she did not really understand. His chivalrous protective and warming arm tightened around her as if to negate the sadness he had caused, yet strangely shared.

They sat as if cast as one with the pillar of the monument, Lizzibeth, filled with regrets and embarrassment despite the excitement of that momentary kiss. Icy air chilled their hazy thoughts as his right hand played subconsciously with her hair, thick ebony curls falling sensuously between his fingers, soft and yielding to his touch. Straining to pull the right words together to annul the situation she had naively created, he brought his other hand round towards her still holding tight to his liquor bottle as he tilted her chin up to his face to speak.

"I am so close to you, Lizzibeth, and I would do anything for you, but my feelings are more like those for a little sister or cousin you know that." She stared up at him with an innocence which belied the forwardness of a few moments ago. They held each other in a gaze which seemed to thaw their frozen senses and yet confound them both. He kept hold of her chin comfortingly, and though sharing his hand with the bottle, its very presence soothed his rejection. His thumb began stroking up towards her cheek and back again in cadence with her quickening heart. The sensations in her face seemed connected to faraway parts of her and she wanted him to stop and yet go on at the same time. A light, enticing groan escaped her throat as she pulled back her head and momentarily fluttered her eyes shut, fastening him inside. He flinched, amazed, afraid and confused at her response to the innocent intention of his touch, and then at his own involuntary yet powerful physical response to it. Big appealing brown eyes appeared to grow and flicker in the intensity of his inspection, as if lit by candles from within, reflecting back his own image. Her lips, slightly parted and down turned, hinting at repentance, but so blue with cold. He suddenly had no choice but to rescue them with his own. Barely in contact at first, he lightly brushed warmth into them, moving over them from side to side, then paused midway. They both opened their eyes and watched the other's soul as they breathed intimate air into their relationship setting it alight. His kiss then took hold with such urgency, that he sensed the uneasiness at the loss of initiative, which had first belonged to her.

Another wave of carousing traversed the frosty atmosphere towards the monument causing a stirring beside them, they paused momentarily. Attempting to conspire silence, each raised an inebriated finger towards their lips amidst merging frost clouds of their silent giggles. He gently adjusted their position on the steps of the Monument and continued their kiss. Eager now to explore the awareness that Lizzibeth had begun to stir in him and buoyant with her ardent response.

Still uncomfortable, he eased Lizzibeth away from him, never leaving her eyes. He snatched the wool coat draped over the motionless form beside them. He laid it down on the cold slabs at the other side of the pillar against the central stone, affording shelter under the small stone canopy and at least symbolic privacy from their sleeping company. He tenderly helped her to lay herself down on it. Neither said a word. The light mood of frivolity had given way to a serious yet precious silent moment, suspended in this bleak autumnal night. The spell of which neither wanted to break, for fear of the other's change of heart. He heard the bottle smash as it rolled down the stone steps onto the road, and he knew the liquor would be trickling away. He did not care, any more than he had been aware of when it had left his hand. He only knew that Lizzibeth's warm soft form, now in its place, was so much more intoxicating.

Time stood endlessly still as they allowed their affection for each other to enter a new and forbidden era, the tenderness in unfastening another's buttons, the warmth of skin on skin replacing any need for cloth, and the closeness of such unimaginable intimacy.

He felt he would love Lizzibeth forever, her heat conducting into his own body, swiftly wracking as it was, in silent uncontrollable paroxysms of pleasure far beyond his imaginings. This moment was so precious, yet it was pooled with his friend beside him puking his excesses all over the fire monument. His aim fell short of the unlikely lovers, but splattered their makeshift mattress. The tranquillity of this perfect moment was gone. They rolled away from him with disgusted yet nervous whispered exclamations. They held each other tight, too shy now to pull away and face the judgment in each other's eyes, which only a few short moments ago, had held only compelling and undeniable desire.

Lizzibeth, cold and coy, awkwardly dragged her dress back around her beneath his embrace, and tried to push it down over her legs. He tried to help without moving from their adopted defence. He loved this intimacy, the softness, the smell of her. He felt he could have stayed there forever in her arms until suddenly, the stench from his friend registered in his nostrils, forcing the instant sobering and fading of this indulgence.

What had he done?

Whilst clearly aware of such physical pleasures, he was not given to idle thoughts and preoccupations. This was not how he imagined it would be, intoxicated, and in a public place. What about Lizzibeth, his childhood soul-mate, they had shared so much, but was it now, too much? Things would surely change forever. He could regret this always. And so could she. This could never happen again, however special she, and this night, would always be for both of them.

The coughing, spluttering figure beside them was slowly rousing. Lizzibeth, feeling mysteriously disappointed, yet strangely elated, eased herself clear of her lover, interrupting his restless regrets as he lay buttoning his clothing. He watched anxiously as she went towards their friend. She helped him to sit forwards clear of the mess, wiping his mouth with her handkerchief. Speaking soothing words to him, and ruffling his hair affectionately, she smiled at him as he staggered successfully to his feet using her shoulders to lever himself up. He propped himself against the stone column which until a moment ago had been his unforgiving pillow. He rubbed his head and pulled a face at her as if acknowledging the self-inflicted nature of his discomfort. She followed him onto her feet and was straightening and checking her crumpled clothing when their private, treasured tryst was shattered.

"Oy, you two toffs had better not be messing with my sister, what's going on?" Lizzibeth's huge brute of a brother was staggering drunkenly towards them from the Inn. "Looks very suspicious to me, I always knew you being friendly with them would lead to trouble, they're not like us, Lizzibeth, not even 'im, I've warned you, Pa used to warn you. Have these villains interfered with you, or hurt you?"

"Don't be foolish Bill, can't you see they're more drunk than you are, and he's just chucked his guts up." She then looked pleadingly back at her fellow conspirator, who, raising himself from the ground, wavered slightly to illustrate and exaggerate his drunkenness. Her protective brother continued,

"Shouldn't you be back at the house. You told mother your

day off finished hours ago, she thinks you're safely tucked up in bed, and I find you playing nursemaid to these two spoilt toffs." He venomously spat the last few words to show his loathing of those with more privilege than himself. One of his antagonists bent to retrieve Lizzibeth's 'bed' from the cold concrete of the monument, he placed it gently around her shoulders to suggest they should get moving. The irony of this fashionable new beige wool coat as protection, stained as it now was, by all of the three friends, was lost on them all. Not only from vomit, but also from the rites of passage of both lovers tonight, providing the proof of Bill's suspicions, and binding them together more tightly now and beyond, than their alliance alone could ever do.

As they turned to walk away, Bill's companion staggered towards them from across the marketplace. He was much shorter than Bill, and slightly built. In the twinkling darkness, his outline behind his friend mimicked Bill's own shadow from a high midday sun. The shady figure spoke loudly,

"Hey Bill just leave 'em alone, it's too late anyway, the whole town knows she has already become their personal whore."

The words hung in the night air like silent sirens, blasting the childhood friends brutally into sobriety and halting their departure. Shock at the words caused momentary paralysis as they looked from one to the other. Lizzibeth recovered first when she saw Bill's look of concern for her, turn to livid anger at his friend. "Bill, no, leave it, he's wrong, what does it matter what people think, they're all wrong, leave it, please, please, Bill."

But Bill had already picked up the discarded whisky bottle by the steps of the monument and was heading towards the proprietor of those fateful words, family pride paramount in his unreasoning rage.

"No, Bill, please," Lizzibeth was by his side now pulling at his sleeve, he waved his arm flicking her as if she was an annoying thorn threatening to tear his flesh. It was the same flick of his hefty arm which succeeded both in releasing Lizzibeth, depositing her callously on the road, and on its return, having unexpectedly off-loaded its cargo, rapidly propelled itself forwards, driving the shattered end of the bottle deep into the bewildered bridegroom's neck.

The moonlit night became mute and stretched as it watched Bill's stunned friend slump slowly to his knees and then quickly to the ground, his blood intermittently spurting across the market cobbles in perfect time with his slowing heart, until the beat, along with its crimson flow, ebbed away, and in moments he was gone. His essence, trickling down the market street, snaking short cuts round the cobbles to speed its journey.

The friends' shock was palpable, a few short minutes ago, the mood had been one of merriment. Now there was horror and disbelief at the scene which had just played out in front of their wide eyes.

Bill was on his knees beside his friend. "Arthur, I'm sorry, I didn't mean it, you just don't go callin' my sister a whore, you just don't do that. Oh God, Lizzibeth, what've I done?" Lizzibeth dropped down beside him, her strapping older brother had shrunk before her eyes. She put her arm through his, he looked small and vulnerable and so reminiscent of her Pa on his death bed. "It was an accident Bill, you didn't know the bottle was broken, I know you would never hurt poor Arthur, but this is trouble a'right now."

She straightened herself up, and turned back towards the monument where her two boys stood together, cast in its very stone, as though beholding Medusa herself. "Henry, Joseph, what shall we do?" Taking the coat from her shoulders she draped it around Bill, tenderly rubbing his back attempting to ease their anguish with each stroke. Her eyes silently appealed to her friends for a solution, and in response, miraculously resurrected by Perseus, they came swiftly to her side. Peering over the gruesome irrevocable scene, they looked questioningly at each other, this was not within their experience, but they did not wish to see Bill in trouble. He was Lizzibeth's brother after all, and they all knew his mother Mrs Buxton well, she would be distraught. As if their family had not suffered enough. Henry spoke first, quietly and quickly.

"Did everyone see you leave the Inn together Bill, or could you have left separately?"

"We did leave separately, 'coz he wanted to use the midden, but he wasn't far behind me, as you saw."

"I think we must all get swiftly on our way. You go the same direction as us anyway, you could have caught us up, none of us saw anything. We can be each other's witnesses." Henry looked at Joseph to ensure collaborative approval and continued, "By the time he's found, if questioned, we can claim that we know nothing about it and everyone will assume that he must have been pounced on as he left the Inn after you. Maybe by one of the vagabonds that often shelter in the church here."

"Henry's right Bill, come on let's get away before anyone else decides it's time to go home tonight and catches us here." Joseph spoke as Henry bent down towards Lizzibeth. She was now on her knees at Arthur's head, tears were rolling down her face as she stroked his hair. Her horror and concern for her brother, had given way to an overwhelming sadness for the betrothed, the unborn child and family of her brother's friend. She could only see the right side of his face, but his right eye still captured the look of utter disbelief that he wore as the bottle had struck him, but his mouth was now open as if gasping for the air that was no longer any use to his body.

He had been guilty only of tormenting Bill when he wasn't in total control of his actions. Not a crime to die for, but Bill's anger had already been groomed by what he thought he had witnessed on the fire monument before Arthur appeared. She had to take some responsibility for this, some would even point the finger and say it was all her fault. Her brother had only been defending her honour, but yet she had hardly even tried to defend it for herself tonight.

But had they been so wrong? With so much death and disease claiming the young, both at home and on the battlefields, surely they were entitled to some pleasures and fulfilment in life before death claimed them. She also knew that for her it went deeper than an entitlement to pleasure, or fulfilment of need, but she knew she was almost certainly alone in this. Tomorrow would bring sober reality to what they had done.

Henry put a hand under her elbow now and tenderly helped her to stand. Joseph wiped the tears from her cheeks gently with his thumbs, and put an affectionate arm around her, leading her away. Henry fell in step alongside saying,

"Come on now, let's get back quickly, try our best to forget what we've just seen and sleep without nightmares." With a glance over his shoulder at Bill, he chivied in a deafening whisper, "You too Bill, you can do nothing for him now. Though why we are helping you after what you accused us of is beyond me. You should think about what you say to people in future, especially to your own kin. It's too late now for your friend to learn that, but perhaps you will have learnt a valuable lesson tonight." He paused.

"If anyone asks any one of us anything, we know nothing, right?"

But Bill was already out of earshot in the opposite direction.

9 Years Earlier

Chapter 2

Dorset, October 1844

"Master Henry, what are you doing, come down from there at once before you fall."

Thomas Elliot was riding the new carriage horse around the grounds of Bramble House to get the feel of how he responded to commands before trying him with the harnesses. Nine year old Joseph was perched as he often was, on the front of the saddle with his father.

Thomas hadn't really been paying attention to Joseph's excited chatter about the stilts Lizzibeth's father had made them at the forge, or how he could stay up on them so much longer than Lizzibeth. Thomas was far too pre-occupied thinking about head coachman Jack who hadn't been himself of late, and was genuinely concerned for his good friend and mentor.

"Master Henry, did you hear me, what are you doing up there?" He was perched on a large anomalous branch of the huge sycamore tree set back from, yet reaching over the edge of the lake, and next to the jetty where the Gamekeeper kept his boat for fishing.

"Good morning Mr Elliot", Henry shouted back, "Nanny isn't far away, she asked me to look for some sycamore wings, but when I found them here, I saw my kitten up this tree. Well he's really a cat now, but he must have got himself down on his own, I can't see him now – he was on that branch over there, can you see him?"

"No I can't", replied Thomas sternly, "and I'm not wasting my time looking for him either. Cats'll always find their way down on their own, they don't need little boys risking their lives over them. Now you come down this instant before I tell your mother and father what you've been up to."

His son sat quietly on the horse watching his father deal with the wilful but compassionate son of the house, who was now looking a little shamefaced having realised his mother would scold him about this. Especially as Bertie the black and white cat, was nowhere to be seen. Suddenly Joseph's gaze widened in the direction of the lower part of the tree where the large branch supporting Master Henry took its early leave of the main trunk. It seemed to be leaning gently but purposefully towards the lake, as if unable to resist a taste of the cool clear water. He slapped his father's leg and pointed, "Pa look, the branch is breaking, he's going to fall in!" Thomas swung his leg over the horse's back and was at the jetty in a second. Henry, sensing the branch release its support from under him, began wildly grabbing at the branches above. For a moment, it was as if Henry's tight hold on the flimsy kindling relieved his weight somewhat and distracted the branch, pausing its thirst. But then a snapping sound left him proffering a few small twigs, and the main branch impatiently cracked loudly under him and dived desperately for its first gulp.

Henry appeared fleetingly suspended in the air, before screaming loudly and following the branch through the jetty and into the lake.

In the eerie hush that followed, the irritated lake calmed, and Joseph watched helplessly as Henry didn't immediately re-appear. He saw his father jump off the remains of the jetty and vanish. Joseph slid silently down from the unperturbed horse and quickly tied him to the nearest tree. Running to where he had seen his father go into the lake, he saw the damage wreaked on the jetty by the giant branch, some of which had recoiled upwards, as if to refurbish its own destruction. He broke the quiet stillness by yelling to his father, panic welling up inside him as he tried to make out any movement under the water.

The surface opened and Thomas' head re-appeared, "Joseph, come down here and see if you can reach Master Henry's head. He's been knocked out and his face has just gone under the water. He's between the posts of the jetty and I can't fit through."

Joseph, a reluctant swimmer with little confidence in water, sensed the urgency in his father's voice. Kicking off his shoes, he sat on the edge of the jetty as Thomas snatched him quickly down into the cold water, turning him swiftly to face his predicament. The water level was high, and the surface of the water was only just visible under the remaining platform of the jetty. Joseph looked to where his father indicated. He could see the back of Master Henry's head floating near the surface amongst the branches in front of him, but between the narrow posts. He stretched between them, but whenever he grabbed for Master Henry, the movement of the water took him out of reach. He knew Master Henry couldn't go long without air inside him. Heaving himself up onto the cross struts of the wooden posts, his slight frame was supported by them and aided by the buoyancy of the water, no longer his foe in this onerous task. Now he was able to reach, and turn Master Henry's head around so his face was uppermost, but something was stopping his body from following his head, and Joseph had to strain to keep him from turning back. "Well done, Joseph, can you pull him towards us?"

"I can't Pa, he's caught on something."

"Keep his head up then, I'll see if I can make out what it is."

Thomas disappeared under the water and swam around the other side of the jetty. Joseph felt Master Henry's body being moved as if something was tugging at it from the other side, but still he didn't come loose. Thomas reappeared, "Joseph, I am going to have to get help and some tools to cut Master Henry free. He's tangled up with the branch where it has wedged itself into the jetty supports down there, and I'm afraid that it has broken Master Henry's leg. We can't just pull him free. Can you hold his head while I am gone, I would send you but I can't fit in there to keep him safe, will you be a'right there?" Joseph nodded weakly, he was troubled that he might have to let go. He wasn't sure he could keep reaching this far for any length of time, let alone while his father rode to Bramble House and back.

"Hurry Pa, hurry."

Joseph had no idea how long his father had been gone, but at one point he had let go of Master Henry when he started to cough and splutter and vomited all over his hand. He quickly regained his hold on him, but now his whole arm was rigid with cramp. Fatigue was causing his own head to droop into the water, he knew if he lost concentration, Master Henry's head would sink back under the surface, but he couldn't hold on much longer. To keep himself distracted, he started to yell for his father,

"Pa, Pa, where are you, Pa. Pa." His shouts seemed to echo around the confined space under the jetty, and Henry started to groan, "You're alright, Master Henry. You fell. My Pa has gone for help, just keep still, can you hold your own head up now?" Henry struggled to free himself, then immediately passed out with the pain from his movement. Disturbing the branch rocked the unstable jetty, and the posts slipped slightly, just enough to narrow the space propping Joseph's chest. His hold of Henry was secured by his cramped muscles, but the pain as he felt his ribs crushed made him scream long and loud drowning out the sound of his father's return.

The lake was suddenly teaming with life, men were all around them securing the posts, and releasing his load. Strong soothing safe arms seemed to part the vice around his body and lift him clear and onto the lakeside. His father was talking to him and trying to get him to reply, but he just wanted to sleep, he was so exhausted, and he wondered why they had left his right arm in the lake with Master Henry's head.

* * *

Joseph awoke in a vast bed, enveloped and propped by lace pillows, there was a 'clean' smell all around, but his body seemed to ache all over. The flicker of his eyelids alerted his dozing mother, she was immediately at his side, stroking his face.

"Oh, Joseph, you're awake, how do you feel? You were a very brave boy yesterday, and everyone is so proud of you."

"Where am I, Ma?"

"You're in the big house, the Master insisted that you be brought here to recover so the doctor could keep an eye on both of you. You were exhausted, your Pa reckons you must've held Master Henry's head for almost twenty minutes while he found the Master and some tools."

"My side hurts, Ma, and I can't feel my arm, did it come off?"

Mary laughed,

"No it didn't, you silly boy, the doctor says you 'ave two broken ribs, but he didn't mention your arm, which one, can you move it?" She pulled free the bed covers that had swaddled him in his sleep. Joseph lifted his right arm slowly and weakly. He looked at it as if it was totally unfamiliar to him, he feebly clenched and unclenched his fist, "It works, Ma, not as well as usual, but I can't feel it, can you feel it, is it real?"

Mary Elliot fought the panic rising in her throat as she took in her son's concerned face. Haloed as always by his abundant dark curly hair, yet it was bereft of his usual cheeky grin which always incorporated twinkling emerald eyes, and endeared him to all who knew him. She stroked her son's arm, "It feels a'right to me Dear, yes definitely my first born's arm!"

"But I can't feel you doing that, Ma, it doesn't feel like mine."

"Hush now, it'll be fine, you get some more sleep and I'll get the doctor to come and take another look at you when you wake up." She bent over the bed and gave her precious son a gentle hug, placing a tender kiss on his forehead. This was becoming a luxury to her lately as he had begun to tell her she was soppy when she tried to embrace him now, he felt he was too old and grown up for all that.

"Ma,"

"Yes Dear,"

"Is Master Henry alright."

"Thanks to you he will be in time. he was concussed, has badly damaged his pelvis which may be broken, has a broken leg bone, which'll take a long time to heal, and a broken wrist. He won't be climbing any trees for a long time to come. Now you get some more sleep, I'll be here all the time."

She looked around the grandeur of the room in an attempt to distract her anxieties. The drapes at the window were a heavy plush burgundy damask; the shade successfully picked to enhance the roses in the thick rugs which scattered the polished floor like ordered gardens. The large furniture was of a heavy mahogany, wardrobes built for blissful carefree games of hide and seek. The chests held a mix of both toys and sober ornate curios, enlightening and informing of a more sombre world of Victorian adulthood, amidst childish frivolities.

The bed cocooning her first born child, cherubic in his restless slumber, seemed unnecessarily large. Its canopy was supported at each corner by a large mahogany post, each one reluctantly hugged by burgundy damask to match the window drapes, and bound to it with decorative cord. Additional swathes of burgundy superfluously fringed the canopy as if there was an abundance that had to have its place.

As soon as Mary knew her son was fast asleep, she crept out of the room to find someone. She was familiar with the layout of the house, she had been a chambermaid here before her marriage to Thomas. How unbefitting she felt now walking these corridors, with her own son occupying one of the main bedrooms. One she had prepared many times before, but then for only very important guests.

She reached the top of the stairs and was about to descend, when she heard her name being whispered from along the landing. A sweet lilting voice, gaining in volume as it floated towards her. It was accompanied by the rhythmic soft swishing of Henrietta Ferguson's numerous petticoats secreted beneath, yet sustaining her bell shaped crimson gown. The lady of the house was a vision of milky fair, womanly perfection. She moved so delicately, that she reminded Mary of a fuchsia flower, dancing effortlessly in a gentle breeze across the rays of autumn sunshine as they streamed through the gallery window.

"Mary. Excuse me, Mary. How is Joseph? Charles has told me all about what he did, how can we ever thank you. Our sons are so precious to us, how could I have coped if your son had not saved mine, we owe him so much, how is he?"

"Oh, M'Lady", Mary replied, bobbing a curtsey and ineffectually straightening her grey worn serge skirt and taming stray curls as she spoke. "I was just looking for someone, he 'as woken up once, but 'as gone off to sleep again. It is so kind of you to 'ave him here, but I must confess M'Lady, I have a new concern. He says he can't feel his right arm and it doesn't work as well as his left. I wondered if I could trouble the Doctor to take another look at him? How is Master Henry, I heard he'll 'ave to spend months in his bed until his leg is healed?"

"Yes, he will, and he has had a lot of pain poor thing. A small price to pay though for his life, Mary." She paused to accept Mary's nod of concurrence, then hurried on empathically.

"But of course we must get the Doctor back to check on Joseph, he must be so exhausted poor dear, sleep is the best thing for him. Come down to the drawing room with me and have some tea and we can send Edward to get the Doctor for when he awakes."

Mary pinched herself, tea in the drawing room, what would Thomas say if he could see her chatting away to the Mistress as if they were pals. She chided herself for savouring the moment. She knew she would just as soon have tea in her cottage with Aggie, and not have Joseph upstairs with broken ribs and a 'dead' arm.

* * *

Thomas let himself in to the bedroom, Joseph was seated in the chair by the window, he kept rubbing his arm as if to remind him it was his own, but he was beginning to feel a little better. The doctor had reassured him that both the strength and the feeling should come back in his arm but may take quite a time. He had badly damaged the nerves by leaning on his arm pit for so long under the water, and they would have to grow back. He warned him that he would have to be careful to make sure he didn't badly injure it whilst it was numb. Doctor Bridges had explained to him about how the ability to feel things stopped the body from doing all sorts of damage to itself, like burning, grazing and cutting. Joseph felt anxiously that he was going to have to be vigilant if his arm was to survive until these lost 'feelings' returned. At the moment someone could hack it off in his sleep and he would not know.

His ribs were still sore, especially if he coughed or sneezed. He had been very cross with his little sister Louiza when she tried to tickle him yesterday, that had hurt.

Thomas' heart ached at the sight of his normally carefree happy son gazing fretfully out across the lawns, his left fist now was rubbing his left eye so hard as if to burrow it through into his brain. Thomas knew this was Joseph's mannerism if he was anxious about something. He considered whether his son may have overheard his own conversation with the Doctor. Although what Joseph had been told, could be true, little was known about nerve injuries and their recovery. They actually had no way of knowing how well Joseph's arm would recover, they would just have to wait and see.

"You're going home today, Joseph, three days of being spoilt in the Master's house is more than enough for you young man! Now, the Master wondered if you would like to 'ave a talk with Master Henry in his room before we take you home. Then he's given us permission to use the brand new Landau carriage to transport our little hero home!"

"In the new Landau really, Pa, all the way back to the cottage – just for me, what'll Ma say when we pull up in that." He paused in his excitement, "But I don't know about visiting Master Henry, Pa, do you think he'd like to see me? He must be very unhappy about having to stay in bed for a long time. Does anything hurt him? Does he know I let him go once when he puked on me?"

"That's a lot of questions, Joseph. I think he has had a lot of pain over the last few days as the Doctor had to set his bones into a good position for healing. Now he has to lay still until they have set. The Doctor is giving him something for the pain though. And yes, he must be very fed up about having to stay in bed for a long time, it's a hard way to learn about the dangers of climbing trees. And yes, I think he must want to see you or the Master wouldn't 'ave suggested it, although I'm not sure he knows about the 'puking' bit, the main thing is you grabbed him again and no harm was done!"

Thomas tried to hide the teasing tone of his last remark and suspected that it was this incident that was the cause of Joseph's melancholy, and not concern for his own afflictions.

Thomas, protectively carrying his young son, knocked on Master Henry's door carefully so as not to cause Joseph's ribs any unnecessary discomfort. Sarah the chambermaid opened the door and smiled warmly and sympathetically at Joseph, grateful for his bravery. The household were all very fond of Master Henry, he was a very pleasant, caring and often amusing child. She scurried ahead of Thomas and pulled a chair up next to Master Henry's bed for Thomas to deposit his load with ease. Once assured of Joseph's comfort, he turned his attention to Henry,

"Now then, Master Henry, you look a lot better than the last time I saw you, dripping wet and completely lifeless you were. I've brought Joseph to visit you before he goes home to the cottage with me today. Your father told me you wanted to see him." He paused as Henry smiled at them both in acknowledgement. "Well, I have to go and bring the carriage round to the front of the house for this young man here, so I'll leave you two together for a little while. Get well soon, Master Henry, I expect to see you helping me with those horses again before you know it." He gave Henry a wink and a grin, then turning to Joseph he said, "I'll be back up to collect you soon son, don't tire Master Henry too much."

"Would you like some lemonade, Joseph, Master Henry already has a glass?"

"No thank you Sarah, I've just had one before I left my room."

"Well I'll go and take these things down to the wash house but I'll be back in a jiffy, will you be a'right while I'm gone, Master Henry?"

"Yes Sarah, thank you."

Henry was an attractive looking child, he looked none the worse for his ordeal although a little pale with pain, and abashed now in Joseph's company. There was a mound in the bed which appeared as if someone was hiding there, charged with the responsibility of restraining and protecting Henry's broken leg and pelvis. His left arm was wrapped in a sling and looped around his neck to limit its movement. He had his father's striking colouring, but his mother's gentle features. He always looked to Joseph a trifle small for his age, which he guessed would now be either seven or eight, a little younger than himself. He reminded him of the angelic boys so often portrayed in paintings wearing velvet suits, hair too long and buckles on their shoes. Henry had an added innocence with his golden hair and large baby blue eyes. A look that was a little too 'girlie' for Joseph, but he always seemed friendly enough when they had occasionally exchanged greetings at the stables or the coach house. Today the two boys looked uneasily at each other for a few seconds; then Joseph, feeling the responsibility as the elder of the two, despite an awareness of his lowly position, opened the conversation.

"Did your cat turn up, Master Henry, or did it fall in the lake and drown like you nearly did?"

"No." Henry paused as if wondering whether to admit his mission had been futile. "Mama said he was curled up on the library floor in front of the fire when they brought us back into the house, I am never going to try to save him again, he can look after himself from now on and just get on with the job of catching mice. But, I am jolly glad you didn't think like that, and you hung onto me in the lake, you were very brave, Father told me you got hurt too."

"My chest hurts a lot if I laugh or cough or sneeze, but I've hurt the nerves in my arm, which is funny 'coz they don't hurt at all. I just can't feel anything, here you can nip me, and I can't feel a thing."

"Really, if I do that hard can't you feel it?" Henry leant slightly forwards in his bed flinching as he did so, and pinched a little of Joseph's skin on his right forearm, between the thumb and finger of his good right hand. He watched amazed as Joseph did not recoil, or snatch has arm away. Henry spoke as he gently eased his weight back into the imprint on his pillows, unable to prevent the flesh in his face performing a contorted grimace. "How funny, will it get better?"

"The doctor says so, but it'll take a long time."

"But you are still using it, aren't you? It is moving alright?." Joseph felt embarrassed yet strangely elated at all this attention from Master Henry.

"Yes. When I remember to, it's very weak, and I keep forgetting it's there! Anyway, what about you, I thought you might be dead when they got you out of the water, does anything hurt still?"

"A little, well a lot really, especially around my middle here." He pointed clumsily towards his lower abdomen and winced. "Ooh, that hurt. But I am more worried about having to stay in bed for so long, how boring it will be. I love to watch your Pa and Jack with the horses. Even my lessons will be boring if I can't go and find things in the garden to draw and write about. Nanny always thinks of fun things to do."

"I'm sure she'll still try to do that, Master Henry, it must be fun to be able to learn so much, my Pa is trying to teach me to read with him. He knew a little before he came to work here, and Jack has taught him a little more, but he wants to be able to read the newspapers and know what's going on in the world. He wants us all to be able to do that too when we're grown up. Anyway, he's started to teach me what he knows." Henry looked quizzically at Joseph,

"Can't you read, don't you have books? I have loads, and Nanny makes us read all the time, even my little sister Charlotte reads well now."

Joseph found this hard to understand, how different life was if you lived in a big house, he found himself lost for comforting words for Master Henry, and a little sorry for himself instead. Naïve to the subtle change he had unknowingly induced in his audience, Henry continued, "I was supposed to go off to school soon too. Mama says she is pleased that I can't go now, she thought I was too young, but I don't think Father is pleased, he is going to have to get a governess to teach me at home now, so I don't fall behind what I should know at my age. He is very cross about me climbing a tree so close to the lake. He keeps saying if you and your father had not been passing, I would be dead now." He paused as if remembering something.

"How can Jack read better than your father?" Joseph realised that Henry had been taken aback to learn that reading wasn't the birthright of everyone, and this obvious innocence provoked an instant release from the self indulgent resentment of a few moments ago for this boy who's life he had indubitably saved. "Pa says that Jack's mother had been a nanny in a big house in Yorkshire before he was born, it's a long way from here, and he still has family there. Anyway, she taught him to read."

"Oh, I see." He looked down at his book pensively contemplating this information, there seemed to be no rule about who could read and who could not; that didn't seem right. He lifted his head to Joseph decisively. "Will you come and visit me again, Joseph, I would like that?"

"If your father'll allow it, Master Henry, then I would like it too."

They were both smiling to silently seal this arrangement, when Sarah returned to the room, balancing a tray with some broth for Henry's lunch, she was closely followed by Henry's father.

"Now then, Joseph, your father is waiting for you in the Landau outside the front door to escort our young hero home to his cottage. I hope you have enjoyed being here, we have certainly been very happy to have you after everything you did for this little scallywag."

Charles Ferguson had been to see Joseph a few times during his stay, always making reference to this gratitude. He was a gentle man. Joseph had always liked him, and knew his father had a lot of respect and admiration for him. He always appeared very similar to his father in his commanding stature and he supposed in age. But where his father had dark curls much like his own, Master Henry's father had fine golden hair, which gave the appearance of shrinking away from his face at quite a pace. Yet it had no difficulty in boldly residing on his top lip, as if made of sterner stuff.

"Come along now, Joseph, let me carry you downstairs, your carriage awaits."

Chapter 3

Dorset, October 1844

"Papa, can I talk to you?" Charles Ferguson moved to the side of his son's bed and perched on the side. "Of course, Henry, what's troubling you?"

Henry looked very seriously at his father and half whispered as if he was about to divulge a secret that he certainly did not want the chambermaid Sarah to overhear. "Did you know that Joseph and his father can't read!"

Charles laughed aloud, then catching his son's puzzled expression, he added "Is that all, of course they can't, Henry, education is a privilege you know, not everyone can afford it." He picked up the book Henry was reading and replaced it with an approving nod. "Why did he tell you that?"

"Well" Henry replied, "We were talking about me having to stay at home for lessons, and he told me his father and him were trying to learn to read together. He wants them to be able to read newspapers and things."

"Well that's very commendable, Henry, and he is a bright lad, I'm sure he will succeed if he is anything like his father."

"I was wondering, erm, I was wondering, Papa, I want to lend him some of the books that Charlotte has finished with, and try to help him myself. Would that be alright with you? I am going to be very bored when I have finished lessons each day, and it will give me something to do. Sarah says Joseph hasn't got much time before he will have to go out to work, some of

the town boys start to work at eleven, and he is already nine!"
Charles was gazing out of the window as if distracted, but in
fact seriously considering his son's suggestion. How to occupy
Henry over the coming months had caused both him and his
wife considerable concern.

"You know what, Henry, I think it is a splendid idea. I will
have to see what your mother says to one of the estate lads
coming up to your room regularly. But they are a meticulous
family, I can't see her having any objections, she always liked
his mother when she worked here. And it will be good for you,
as well as an excellent way for you to show your gratitude to
him. There is no greater deed that anyone can do than to save
another's life. He may end up with much better employment
if he can read too, and write of course. First-rate idea my boy,
well done."

Thomas entered their tiny cottage in time for lunch. It was
the middle one of the row, built specially for married workers
on the Bramble House estate. Mary had the inviting smell of
broth and fresh bread waiting for her family at mid-day, as she
did everyday. At the sight of her husband, she shouted at her
two younger children playing in the yard to come inside, and
get up to the table to eat. Joseph was sitting by the fireside
already tucking into his. In the week since the accident his
mother had been spoiling him, although he was now able to
move around a little less guardedly. He still tended to either
forget about his right arm completely, or was so conscious of
not feeling it that he carried it protectively as if limp. He had
stayed within the cramped confines of the cottage to please his
mother. He knew she should be forgiven for wanting to keep
him safe from further harm, but he was beginning to crave the
outdoors again, and he was actually much more comfortable
standing up and walking around than being carried or seated.
Mrs Buxton and her daughter Lizzibeth had been to visit him
once, and that had been the only highlight of the week. Mrs

Aggie Buxton and his Mother had been friends since they both worked at the big house when they were girls. His Ma had been a chambermaid and she had taken pity initially on little young Aggie the kitchen maid. As time went on they had become firm friends, both marrying their first loves. When their families came along, they shared experiences and supported each other along the way. Aggie's husband was the local farrier in the town, and was always making Lizzibeth and him things to play with out of old ironwork. They had an older son, Bill, a gentle giant. Although only twelve years old he was very tall for his age and could shoe a horse and wield the tools in the smithy with no problem at all. Lizzibeth, only one year younger than Joseph, at eight years old was always so full of mischief and fun. He hadn't even minded the pain when she made him laugh on her visit. He couldn't wait to get back out enjoying their escapades together, although he was sure she would've been practicing on her stilts. He looked longingly at his own standing idle in the yard and supposed she would now be able to walk further than him on them. He felt angry at this fireside chair. It was a cast-off his Pa had repaired from the big house. Subconsciously he now knew every inch of the marquetry patterns and carvings on it, he had traced them so often with his fingers in his boredom, yet he was curiously fascinated by them. Moving out of the chair caused him physical pain, but staying in it was so tedious. He had even slept downstairs in it all week, not wanting to risk his young sister and brother kicking him in the ribs overnight. These four walls had been his loving gaol. He was desperate for his release.

Mary noticed the absence of her husband's usual wifely greeting of the cheeky pat on her generous behind, and turned to look at her husband as she poured him some broth. "Is there something troubling you, Thomas?" He looked up from tearing himself a large piece of bread, and his preoccupation showed in the eyes that travelled through her as if she was made of glass. He shook his head and re-focused on his adoring wife.

"Errm. Err, sorry Love, I've a couple of things on my mind that I have unease about, one as you know is Jack." Jack had been respected in his position as head coachman within the household for more years than anyone could remember. He had lost his wife suddenly one morning. When he had awoken, she had been gone beside him for hours, icy cold. He had never really recovered his contagious zest for life that had made everyone find his company irresistible. Thomas continued,

"Well, he dropped the harness again today when we were preparing to take the Mistress out to visit her sister. It just isn't like him, and one of the stable hands called to the head coachman's cottage to take him some left over pie from Cook the other day. She thinks he isn't eating properly. He returned saying the cottage was such a mess, as if things are being spilt constantly. Cathy'll be turning in her grave poor soul."

Mary paused in pouring out the broth into Louiza's bowl to consider this news, "Poor Jack, perhaps I should go over there and give him a hand with cleaning his cottage if he'll let me. Can he afford to see a doctor?"

"I don't know, I was going to have a word with the Master, but I'll have Jack to deal with if I do, he needs the work and couldn't afford to lose his job, or his home. I'll just keep my eye on him for a little longer perhaps, but even when he's all right and working well, there's a shake in all he does."

Five year old Louiza started to giggle, Joseph looked up from his fireside chair. "Ma, Louiza needs her broth, you've only given her a drop so far, and some has gone on the table!"

"Oh I'm sorry Louiza, there you are." She poured a bowlful, then wiped the broth on the table with her apron and moved on to fill little two year old Benjamin's bowl. "Be careful, Benjamin dear, its hot!" She sat down at the table pouring the remaining broth into her bowl and leaning over to replace the pan on the fireside, winking comfortingly to Joseph as she did so. "And what's the other thing on your mind, Thomas?"

Thomas looked up, he had forgotten that he had indicated that he had two troubled thoughts.

"Oh yes. Well, the Master called me into his study today with what he called a 'proposition'. I was worried he was going to finish me as he looked so serious."

"What did he want, Thomas? He needs and respects you too much to finish you, but you have us all listening. What's a proposition?" Without realising the whole family had stopped eating and were waiting for Thomas to go on.

"Young Joseph here has impressed both him and Master Henry so much, that they're inviting him to go up to the boy's room in the big house, three times a week after Master Henry's lessons. He can then be taught by the boy himself to read and write, and then to spend some time playing games to amuse him if you please!" He paused to allow the astonishing proposal to be properly absorbed by them all, then he continued. "The Master said it would be doing them a favour in keeping young Master Henry occupied, and they would give Joseph some pocket money for his trouble! I think they're over-doing their gratitude, Joseph only did what anyone would've done."

Joseph's eyes had widened, his head turned smoothly away from the rest of the family to nowhere in particular, like a watchful owl sensing danger from behind. The very idea of being taught to read and write by Master Henry from the big house seemed very uncomfortable, and he must be more than a year his junior. Yet part of him was eager for the chance, not to mention having some pocket money, he could give some to his Ma, but he could also save some, it would mount up if he kept going for a little while! Pa had always said he could maybe get a better apprenticeship if he could read and write. Perhaps if it was doing them a favour too, then he could do it to help out Master Henry, not to mention getting out of the cottage! He turned back round to meet the four pairs of eyes all fixed on him.

"Well, Joseph, what do you think to the Master's suggestion?"

"Well I'm not sure, Pa, I am quite happy learning to read with you, but I suppose if it'll help to pass some time for Master Henry, then I can't really refuse can I? I don't want to make the Master angry by turning him down."

"That's very grown up of you, Joseph, I felt the same, we were doing alright between us, weren't we? But helping Master Henry out'll be good for him, and you might learn something after all. Are you sure you don't mind?"

Joseph indicated nonchalantly with a mouthful of broth, that he was agreeable.

They both knew they had not spoken the whole truth, they weren't getting any further with their own attempts at self-educating. This was principally as their only source of reading material was the newspapers discarded by Bramble House. Often the words in them were too long for either of them to make sense of, and Jack was too old now to bother him much for his help. However, their mutually conspired conversation had successfully convinced the remaining Elliot family as well as themselves, that yet another favour was being bestowed upon Master Henry.

"That's settled then, I'll tell the Master this afternoon, he wanted you to start tomorrow at two-o-clock. Do you think you'll manage to walk up to the house on your own? No more front entrance though do you hear, go round to the kitchens and Cook'll let you in the back, you can then wait and walk back with me at the end of the day."

Joseph sauntered from their row of cottages, planted discretely within a copse of trees, and followed the winding path up towards Bramble House. He felt excited, yet a little apprehensive about this new adventure. He had set off early, not really to be prompt, but rather in not wanting to speed his journey. He wanted to savour the fresh air and surroundings that he couldn't believe he had missed so much in only eight days. He kicked at stones gently within the limits of his painful ribs, and subconsciously but repeatedly tested his hand sensation by feeling different textures of foliage as if badgering nature itself to cure his infirmity.

He reached the kitchen door of Bramble House and was met by Cook. No-one ever knew her name, she was just 'Cook', she enveloped him in her ample bosom, squeezing him as if he were a long lost relative. Joseph nearly collapsed with the pain, but she was oblivious to his plight in her enthusiasm to exult his bravery, and the remarkable survival of both boys.

"Now, Joseph, when you and Master Henry have finished your lessons and games, you come down to me and I'll give you some treats to take home to those little ones. How are they? When is your Ma going to bring them over to see us? We haven't seen little Benjamin since he was still in that fancy perambulator your Ma got from your Aunt. He must be walking all over by now?"

Joseph extricated himself from her lessening embrace, and presented his dimpled winning smile to her through the pain, he assured her he would chastise his Ma and they would visit soon. He took his leave and quickly made for the staircase in the hall. He hoped he could remember which room was Master Henry's once he was up on the next level. The staircase yawned into a grand bifurcation halfway up, but he knew the Master had carried him down from the right hand side. At the top, he turned to look down the stairwell. With an appreciation which belied his years, he took in the splendour, intricacies and skilled craftsmanship of the wood, smoothing it with his left hand. He had never touched wood so magnificent and highly polished. But oh how the child in him would love to fling his leg over the banister and slide down. Lizzibeth would've done. She wouldn't care about decorum in the big house, she would've just done it, taken the punishment afterwards, and would've always believed that it was worth it. Joseph had never been as mischievous, but he supposed he was also not as much fun. He loved being around when Lizzibeth did things, she made their days so amusing, he must let her know that he was out and about again so she could come over and play.

Luckily, just as Joseph was looking helplessly at the doors which all appeared to be the same, and wishing he had asked to be shown up to Master Henry's room; Sarah the chambermaid emerged with a chamber pot covered in a cloth. Ugh, he hadn't thought through all the inconveniences of having to stay in bed!

"Aah, Joseph, there you are, Master Henry was just hoping you had remembered about today." She spoke as she leant back keeping the door open for Joseph to enter. "Master Henry, young Joseph Elliot is here."

"Joseph, how are you? Can you feel your arm yet, or can I pinch you again? It was funny doing that knowing it wasn't hurting you, my cousins often do that to me, but I always want to squeal as it hurts so much."

Joseph slowly entered the room taking in its contents that had been hazy to him last week. He could see at the side of Henry's bed, as if on its way to the window, was a very grand and arrogant rocking horse. Sparse scratches on its fine polished oak surface served only to accentuate its very perfection. The brown leather saddle and bridle were worn from the many miles travelled over the generations with its small riders. On a table by the side of the huge window was a large wooden Ark with pairs of animals lined up awaiting their embarkation instructions from Noah. He was standing commandingly on the bow of the vessel with his wife tidily by his side. Scattered across the window seat was an army of toy soldiers as though decimated by their foe and left forgotten.

"Good afternoon, Master Henry. No, I still can't feel my arm and it's still very weak, but from what the Doctor said, I don't think I can expect anything back just yet."

"Oh well, it might be funny writing with it though. You will have to write with your right hand no matter what, I always want to put the pen in my left hand, but Nanny will not let me, she says I have to do it with my right, so you must too. Now, Joseph, I think to begin, I need to know how much you can read so that we know where to start with your learning.

So, I got Sarah to pass me this pile of books to find out how far you have already got with your Pa. After that we can do some practice writing of some of the letters, and then I have a new game we can play, its called draughts. Father brought it from the town the other day, but playing it with Sarah was not much fun!

Henry picked up a colourful book from the side of the bed. "Come on then, Joseph, show me what you can read in this book."

* * *

Lizzibeth was disappointed as she skipped back down the road to her father's forge, she had been sure Joseph would've been at home and pleased to see her today. Mrs Elliot had said that he was having lessons at the big house, how had he managed that she wondered? She had always wanted to learn to read since the day she had watched a girl reading a book as she was waiting for her mother in an open carriage. She looked very dainty and pretty, sat in the fancy carriage, wearing a green coat and hat with white fur trim and a matching muff upon which rested her book. Lizzibeth had stopped to talk to her and the little girl had told her she couldn't put the book down, she was so engrossed in the story. She said it was about a little girl who went to live in America and then got separated from her mother. Ever since then Lizzibeth had been aware of reading being a skill she unfairly couldn't possess. It was consigned to being an unachievable but longed for pastime. Perhaps Joseph would be able to teach her. Maybe she would get to meet Master Henry too.

"Pa, can I help you, I could comb the horses mane if you sit me up on its back." Mr Buxton turned and smiled at his daughter as she squeezed through to him between the queue of black shiny carriage horses.

"Not today Lizzibeth, we're really busy, Bill and I have to get all of this lot sorted tonight before we can get home for a meal. Thought you were spending the afternoon with Joseph today?"

"Oh, he's not home, he's up at the big house again, I think the Master's son is his new friend, maybe he won't want to play with me anymore." Seeing the disappointed look on his beloved daughters face, he put down his tools, and picking her up as if she was no more than a feather, he swung her onto the horses back and handed her a brush. "Rubbish my dear, people who live in big houses can never be friends with those that don't, that's just the way it is."

"Now, Joseph, you will practice those letters before Wednesday won't you, I had to do them again and again before I could get them as even as I do now."

Joseph had thoroughly enjoyed himself this afternoon and the time had flown by. His mind was like a warm cloth eager to absorb a spillage of ice cold lemonade on a hot summers day. He had only concentrated on the reading with his Pa, not on how to write something himself. He had learnt so much, he must remember to tell his Pa about the way the letter 'e' on the end of a word, could change the whole sound of it. He was sure that was going to help them with the newspapers. His head was brimming with it all, when Henry suggested they finish their afternoon with a game of draughts.

"Joseph, are you very tired tonight, was the walk a'right, it's still early days for your broken ribs you know?"

"No, Pa, I'm fine thank you, you did walk a bit fast though on the way home, that hurt a bit."

"I'm sorry son, you should've said, but if you're not tired, do you fancy having a go at this newspaper with me? I picked a discarded one up from outside the house, it's a brand new paper called the 'News of the World'. It's apparently for the likes of us, working people who are beginning to learn to read. I think the Master must have bought it out of curiosity. It still cost him thru'pence though, see it says the price on the top corner there."

Joseph pulled an incredulous look of disbelief.

Thomas lit the oil lamp and placed it cautiously on the table where Mary had just finished clearing the remnants of the supper away. They had all enjoyed the cakes that Cook had bestowed upon Joseph. Then he spread out his newspaper carefully, smoothing the creases so that the words were clear to see. "Which bit shall we read, Joseph, find something where you can show me what you've learnt today." Joseph leant over the paper, straining to see the bits lit by the lamp light.

"Oh look there's one of the words Henry told me about, see it has an 'e' on the end of fat, and that makes it sound like fayt – fate, but it means something completely different. Master Henry gave me loads of words like that, there's pan, that when you add an 'e' becomes payn – pane, like in a window, nothing like a pan, and hat becomes hayt – hate. See?"

"I do see, Joseph. That is a good trick to learn about, now see if you can read this bit here."

Joseph looked to where his father pointed, and started to read aloud very slowly and very hesitantly, with some prompting from his father.

"Charles, 5th Duke of Dorset died with no wife or children in July, and all of his titles became ext…, I don't know that last word, Pa."

"That was very good though, Joseph, I couldn't 'ave worked that one out either, but when I looked at the paper earlier I did ask Jack what it said and he said it was 'extinct', do you know what that means, Joseph?"

"No, Pa, it's a funny word."

"It means that something dies out and doesn't exist anymore. Like some types of animals that are weak and so don't survive, they die out, and so the Dukes title'll die with him on account of him not 'aving any sons."

Thomas straightened up from the table stretching and arching his back. Joseph was still digesting this information.

"Does that mean that if you had no children, Pa, the name

Elliot would be – extinct - when you die?"

"No. That's not quite the same son. You see, there are other Elliots in the world. Your Aunts, Uncles and cousins in Bristol for a start, but there are also lots of other people called Elliot, and they may or not be any relation at all to us. Do you see the difference?"

"Yes I think so, Pa."

"Did you enjoy your afternoon though Joseph, you haven't really said, I don't want you to be uncomfortable about it."

Joseph's face lit up, he had been quiet in trying to go over all he had learnt so he didn't forget anything. But moreover he didn't want to hurt his father's feelings by appearing to have learnt more from Master Henry than he had at home with him. He suddenly realised that he was in danger of conveying no enjoyment at all, and risked jeopardising this whole opportunity. He replied excitedly.

"Oh yes, Pa. Master Henry is really nice and he has lent me one of his old books. It's quite easy to read, but he wants me to copy the letters so I can write the words myself, I've to practice them before Wednesday."

"Homework eh, you're getting very grand, my boy." Thomas spoke, imitating the Master's accent and the whole family laughed. It was as if their father's humour had broken the spell of the moment. The father and son had not been aware of Mary, Louiza and Benjamin sitting quietly by the fire, in awe of the scholarly presence they were in. "Seriously, Joseph, being able to write'll get you an apprenticeship, and it'll give you a bigger choice of them too, I hadn't expected that Master Henry would also teach you to write." He hid his benign resentment well, amidst pride for his eldest child.

Joseph looked nervous, "Don't expect too much, Pa, I've only had one lesson so far, maybe I won't be able to." Thomas, encouraged by his previous reception from this adoring audience, again made the Master reply for him.

"Nonsense my boy, you can do anything you set your mind to!" They all laughed together but Louiza looked concerned that her world may change with this new development in their lives. "You won't start to talk funny like that will you, Joseph?" He tweaked his little sister's nose and reassured her as his Ma banished the two young ones off to bed.

"I think I'll come upstairs tonight too." said Joseph. "I'll tuck you in, come on I'll chase you both up those stairs." Mary and Thomas smiled at each other confirming their tacit worries were unfounded. Their spirited and resolute son had returned and was on the mend at last.

"I think tonight calls for a little drop of the whisky the Master gave me as a gift when Benjamin was born, Mary. Who'd have thought it, a son of ours, educated in a big house."

Chapter 4

Dorset, April 1845

Thomas stood facing the heavy wooden door to the Master's study as though it were a looking glass. Holding his top hat under his arm, he straightened his gold waistcoat and adjusted first his black jacket with its polished gold buttons, and next his gold and black striped cravat. He was a very dashing handsome figure in his coachman's uniform. He knocked firmly with his knuckles at shoulder height and paused awaiting further instructions.

"Come in".

Thomas tried to open the door confidently, but being summoned wasn't a regular occurrence so naturally carried a degree of unease.

"You wanted to see me, Sir." Thomas closed the door behind him and walked to the large ornate wooden desk at which Charles Ferguson was seated, ledgers sprawled across its full width. He pushed his work towards the front of the desk, and resting his arms on the leather inlay, he looked up at the man he had learned so much about this morning.

"Yes I did, Thomas. I trust the Mistress is returned safely from the town?" Thomas nodded as the Master continued. "Tell me, Thomas, why was it that you told the Mistress that you, rather than Jack would take her today?"

Thomas' initially hesitant, but then festinating reply, bellowed out his discomfort. "Er, Jack had a lot to do, Sir, and was relieved when I said I could take the Mistress to town for him, I can still get my other jobs done, Sir, I worked late last night and was ahead of myself so it was no trouble. The carriages'll still be ready for your journey tomorrow."

"I'm sure they will be, Thomas, I don't doubt it. However I do doubt that Jack was busy this morning, as your wife found him at the bottom of his stairs in his cottage when she went to clean for him."

Thomas' head dropped in shame at the discovery of his deceit. He contemplated his highly polished boots, then slowly raised his head making direct eye contact with his Master. In a quiet concerned tone he replied.

"What can I say, Sir. Sorry, Sir, is he a'right? He's struggled recently, but he needs his wages. And his house. He was afraid of losing both. Is he alive? Had he fallen, is Mary a'right?"

"As I am sure you are well aware, Thomas, he is not well. However, why in God's name did you choose not to inform me? Do you honestly think I would throw loyal and respected elderly staff out onto the streets? I am disappointed that you did not feel you could confide your concerns to me. How long has your wife been covering for him too? Am I to be the last to know about everything on my own estate?"

Thomas looked beseechingly at Charles Ferguson, and felt shame at a disloyalty to his employer that until now he had perceived only as loyalty to Jack.

"I'm so sorry, Sir, I thought we were helping him. He's always been so good to us, and so was his wife Cathy too before she died. Please tell me how he is?"

Charles gave a long deep sigh and replied sympathetically,

"The Doctor has been to see him, Thomas, and he will recover from the nasty ankle strain and the bump on the head he acquired in his fall today. However, the Doctor says that unfortunately, he will not recover form the Shaking Palsy that he has been suffering from for some time now. He has been reading up on this condition recently described by a Dr Parkinson, and thinks perhaps it could have started even before Cathy died. There is absolutely no way that Jack can be allowed to work on the horses and carriages anymore. He knows that. I suspect he has known for some time. I have spoken to him, and he agrees that he could have put lives at risk if he had not tightened or connected up the harnesses properly."

"Oh no, Sir, I always went round everything again after him of late, Sir. I would never have allowed anyone to go out in the carriages without doing that for some time now."

"And exactly how long did you think you could go on doing the work of two men, Thomas?" Charles fought hard not to smile as he watched Thomas struggle to know whether a reply to this rhetorical question was required. He knew Thomas had a kind heart, and had done what he thought was best for Jack. He was even perversely moved by the extent to which he had covered for and abetted his mentor. But estate tradition and etiquette dictated an air of authority over errant employees, whatever the motivation behind their transgression, and especially in view of what he was about to do. He certainly didn't want to encourage such behaviour in the future; he expected total honesty from all his workers. He upheld his formal performance and continued.

"Not much longer I suspect is the answer, Thomas. Jack can no longer work, that much is clear. The position of Head Coachman is therefore vacant. As you appear to have been doing it for Jack as well as doing your own work for sometime, and as Jack recommends you very highly, you will take over his position. I expect you to appoint another coachman to take your place. Mr Simms will help you to draft something to post up in the town by way of an advertisement, is that clear?"

"Certainly, Sir, thank you very much, Sir, but what'll happen to Jack?"

"Jack is a very lucky fellow, Thomas. As your wife has been secretly looking after him for a while, and from what she told me earlier, is prepared to carry on doing so for the short time he will have left with us, - this Shaking Palsy is a cruel disease-then he can stay where he is. The difference is that he will be cared for now in the parlour of the cottage. I have had two men bring his bed downstairs for him this afternoon. Today has shown that he is no longer safe using a staircase, and it would be even more difficult with a painful ankle. You and your family can manage in the other room for your meals. I'm sure by the look of that young wife of yours, the extra rooms that go with the head coachman's cottage, especially upstairs, will be put to good use very soon. The position of head coachman, with all the responsibility it carries, also includes a salary increase of one quarter more than you currently earn. It will be a good idea to talk through the whole job with Jack while you still can, there may be some issues you have not yet dealt with."

He paused to savour the look of amazement on Thomas' face. Benevolence was a privilege of the privileged according to Charles Ferguson which he personally relished. To make a difference to the lives of those with less than us is an honour, he had frequently informed his wife. She had seen the respect the workers on the estate had for her husband, and she now generally, if a little reservedly agreed with him. Her father had ruled his own estate with an iron rod, but Henrietta had noticed that his way lacked the infectious smiles and laughter around the home and grounds that she had come to so enjoy at Bramble House. She loved her husband all the more for his wise ways.

"That will be all, Thomas, you can take the rest of the day off to sort your belongings and move them into your new home. Your wife has begun the packing. Jack will be better off the sooner you move in with him. My family too, have appreciated his long and dedicated service. You will be helping us all by serving him on our behalf in his last days. Let me know if you need anything that would be of any assistance in this task, Thomas."

Thomas collected himself, thanked the Master profusely and was heading for the door, when Charles remembered something. "Oh I nearly forgot, with everything that has happened today. You can tell that cheeky little upstart of a son of yours that I have located a bath chair of the type he requested! It is being sent from London. Master Henry should be able to go outside for these nature lessons by next week. But only if the Doctor approves the chair. I don't want any chances being taken, that leg has been the very devil to persuade to heal, nothing must jeopardize it now or we will never get Master Henry off to School." Not for the first time in this discussion, Charles enjoyed the look of astonishment on his employees face. He smiled inwardly and continued.

"Oh, and, Thomas, I shall ask the housekeeper Mrs Brookes to come over and get some measurements from you. You will be required to wear the burgundy frock coat and cravat befitting the position of head coachman from now on."

Thomas left the house feeling ten feet tall and as if he were walking on air. He wasn't only bursting with pride for his own improved position, but that his son had the respect of the Master too. Only his sadness for Jack spoilt what would've been a wonderful change in position for the Elliot family today.

"Joseph, I am well aware of how bored Master Henry is, but this chair does not support the whole of his leg." The Doctor paused as if to accentuate the point as he gestured towards the part of the chair where support was lacking. They were all gathered around the London delivery in the front hall. A 'picnic basket on wheels' according to Charlotte.

Henry's sister, now seven years old, was currently disparaging about everything, so the comment was dutifully ignored. The chair was made of wicker to explain her analogy, with a very high back which made it look far too big for Master Henry. Two large wheels occupied each side of the chair towards the front and a small wheel was in the middle and behind the seat at the back. On each side of the back-rest was a handle with which the chair could be pushed by an attendant. The doctor continued, "The leg bone is mending nicely after such a difficult beginning. Indeed I seriously wondered if Master Henry might even lose his leg as it seemed so slow to begin the healing process. Now it is so close to taking his weight again, the chances of it breaking if it is not supported in a straight position are too great."

Henry's voice shouted from upstairs, "Has it come, can I go outside? Someone come and tell me what is going on."

Joseph looked appealingly at the Doctor, his fist anxiously burrowing a niche for his eye. "What if I make a strong wooden 'bed' for his leg to rest upon, we can keep it straight then, I've got some wood back at the cottage."

"I don't know, Joseph, you could try it. Then when I come back next week I will see if it does the job."

Joseph moved to the bottom of the stairwell and shouted upwards to Henry. "Sorry, Master Henry, it isn't as straight forward as we thought, I'll come up now and explain."

"Joseph, it's me!"

Joseph looked up from his task and beamed when he saw Lizzibeth skipping along the road towards the cottage.

The head coachman's cottage was really a gatehouse for Bramble House situated as it was at the entrance to the mile long driveway. They had settled well into their new home and Joseph had the luxury of his own bedroom which he knew he would have to share eventually as their family grew. His mother was due to have the new baby any day now.

Joseph loved the extra land around the cottage that they were able to use. He had a small workbench at the side next to the privy, where he liked to make things with wood. He had made his mother a new pestle last week and she had said it was smoother than a baby's bottom. He assumed this was a compliment. She couldn't believe it had been made from the old bit of tree trunk that had been lying around outside the cottage. He sometimes put the results of his labours on a little table outside the house and sold them for coppers to passers-by. He was beginning to have quite a little nest-egg under his bed, together with the pocket money from Charles Ferguson. Today Joseph was working on a plank of wood, smoothing it and shaping it as if it's very existence was crucial to his day.

"Hi, Lizzibeth, what're you doing today, not helping your Ma?"

"No, we've finished all the chores, and now Ma is just sewing something for your new baby. So I sneaked out!"

"You couldn't sneak anywhere, Lizzibeth Buxton, everyone can hear you from a mile away!"

"What shall we do then? Shall we race across the stepping stones on the river, bet I can still beat you."

"I'm sure you can, you've more time to practice than me, I've to get this finished before tomorrow otherwise Henry can't use the bath chair his father got for him, and he's so desperate to get out of the house." Joseph worked on the wood throughout the conversation making Lizzibeth realize that playing today was not for debate.

"Ooh, Henry now is it, what happened to the 'Master' bit?" She paused as Joseph pulled a face at her. "I wouldn't call him 'Master', he's no older than me, he wouldn't call me 'Miss' so why should I call him Master?"

Lizzibeth gave a defiant nod of her head, propped as she was on the work-bench, her green serge pinafore was caught on the edge displaying her torn pantaloons. Joseph smiled at the sight of her, she had never been a feminine child, despite her prettiness. Always rather boyish, very competitive, and wanted to be better than him in everything they did.

"It's a good job you don't have to address him then isn't it? Henry has told me to stop using it when we're by ourselves, he says it is silly, but we both know that others wouldn't like it, so I still say 'Master' in public, and Henry always winks at me!" She continued as if he hadn't spoken. "Is he your best friend now, better than me? My Pa says we can never be friends with people in big houses, it just isn't done."

"Don't be silly, Lizzibeth, we can be friends with who we like, it's just difficult sometimes on account of our lives not being the same. But of course he's not a better friend than you, it's different with a boy, that's all." Lizzibeth contemplated this, then seemed to accept his explanation, she would explain it later to her Pa. She hoped he wouldn't go to the local hostelry again tonight, she hated him when he was full of ale, it changed him.

"I don't know how your 'Master Henry' has stood being in bed for this long though, I would've died of boredom by now. Why are you always playing with wood?"

Joseph looked up at her and smiled, pleased with her compassion for a total stranger, and thought how wonderful it would be for Lizzibeth to join their lessons. Unspoken yet congenitally ingrained taboos told him that could never happen, indeed he often pinched himself to reassure his own good fortune. As if reading his thoughts, she added,

"He does sound really nice though, this Henry, can I meet him sometime?"

"I would love you two to meet. You would like each other I know you would, he knows all about you, but I've a feeling that none of the grown-ups would like it to happen. Not because of you Lizzibeth, but I often hear the servants talking about Henry needing to go off to school to mix with his own sort. I suppose that's what your Pa means too, and you would just be another of my sort!" He flinched as she flicked the back of her hand across his arm distracting his rhythm of work on the wood and taking the opportunity to snatch the piece of wood away from his grasp. "Oy, don't wack me you little vagabond, you know exactly what I mean. You're definitely a 'sort' alright, come here with that piece of wood, now!"

Joseph took the wood back from her and continued to work with it, feeling it all the time with his left hand to reassure the work of his right. His right arm was recovering its power, and was useful again, but he still lacked confidence in its ability. The feeling hadn't recovered at the same rate and was still a hindrance to him; he couldn't gauge the amount of pressure he was applying to anything. Everything felt woolly and spongy on his arm as if it was permanently wrapped in a thick soft winter blanket. He managed well and never moaned, and it seemed such an insignificant ailment in comparison to Henry's.

"I do seem to be good at working with wood though, Lizzibeth, and I love making things with it. I've to start to think of apprenticeships very soon, I'll be eleven in less than a year. I haven't mentioned it to my Pa yet, but I would really like to work with a cabinet maker, I might go along to speak to old Mr Thackery in the town to see if he's thinking of taking anyone on." He paused to inspect the effect of his latest efforts. Clearly satisfied, he continued. "He makes some fancy pieces of furniture, the Master has some of it around the big house. I could take him some of the things I've made to show I can work with wood, and I can show him that I can read and write lots of things now, I'm sure that would help. The Master says it should broaden my opportunities as well as my expectations in life."

Lizzibeth looked adoringly at Joseph. How clever he was, she couldn't imagine being able to make sense of all those little squiggles she had seen in newspapers. She only looked at the drawings in newspapers, or more recently sometimes there were photographic pictures which she loved to look at, especially of the new young Queen. Master Henry had sent a very basic book for her one day, and although Joseph had taught her all the words in it, she had learnt them all from memory prompted by the pictures. She knew she would not be able to make sense of them if their context was changed. Joseph's pause gave her an opportunity to chatter again.

"I know Mr Thackery's daughter Hannah, she's a bit older than me, but a little stuck up, her Ma's a'right, she always has a bag of boiled humbugs that she offers round if you pass by. She makes fancy dresses for people that can afford it." As she spoke, she began picking daisies round about her and put them all in a pile on Joseph's work bench.

"Aren't you going to work with the horses and carriages like your Pa? Ma says I'll go to work in the kitchen of the big house when I'm eleven, just like she did. That's only a year and a bit away, my Pa doesn't want me to. But, lots of fun and adventures around the countryside to be done first eh, Joseph? Cook is very nice though, I shan't mind working with her, and I'll work hard. P'raps then I'll get to meet Master Henry."

Joseph paused in his toil and watched Lizzibeth; she had picked up a blade of grass and was positioning it between her thumbs to whistle through. He returned to his task, the smoothing sounds of wood accompanied by Lizzibeth's high pitched screeching sounds, shattered the once peaceful countryside. Pensively, he considered how he now wanted more from life. His education, however short lived it may be, had motivated an ambition in him, and he realized they now had diverging expectations. Saving most of his pocket money, he was accused by his family of being quite thrifty, even frugal with it, but he wanted to have something to show for his twist of fate, he knew it could not last forever. He must spend more time with Lizzibeth though, she could learn to read and aspire to being an upstairs or ladies maid, her life then wouldn't be so hard. He watched her again now as, tired of her musical reed, she had chained the stalks of the daisies through each other to make a floral halo from the pile. Excitedly she placed it amongst her dark curls. Fluttering her lids at him she came to Joseph's side holding the remaining daisies in her right hand, and put her left arm through his. "What do you think then, Joseph Elliot, will I make a beautiful bride for you, do I look just as pretty as the Queen looked on her wedding day?"

"Phugh, get away, you are such an actress Lizzibeth. You might do in time I suppose, for someone. Thankfully, you are so much like a sister to me, that you could never, ever be my bride. It'll be a brave fellow indeed that'll take you on though, Lizzibeth Buxton!"

The words pricked brutally at her dream bubbles but she recovered quickly.

"Chase you over the river, come on, Joseph, lets 'ave some fun. Catch me if you can." She lilted the last sentence to feign irresistible, companionable jollity and conceal her injured childish pride. He would change his mind. Her Ma had said that Joseph would make the perfect match for her in time. And she agreed.

"Well, young Joseph, I have to concede that you have made the chair very acceptable for Master Henry's leg. I cannot see any reason why he should not go out in this. I must stress though, Sir, as his Physician, that it must be only pushed very slowly and on flat ground. On no account must there be any escapades that could result in Master Henry toppling out of the contraption. He is so close now to being able to gradually stand again that we must not jeopardise this with any mishap."

Charles Ferguson looked at Joseph, "I sincerely hope there is no question of any such 'escapades' in the chair, eh, Joseph?"

"Oh certainly not, Sir, but surely the fresh air'll be good for Master Henry, it'll put some colour in his pale cheeks and make him healthier and more prepared for school when his leg is better."

"Err, yes quite, Joseph."

Henry looked at his father and then winked at Joseph's diplomacy; he could not wait to be outside again. The chair was not the most comfortable he could imagine, but that was a small price to pay for a break in the monotony he had come to know over the last few months. Joseph had fixed a piece of wood to the seat of the bath chair. It was so secure it felt as though it had been made as one with the seat. It was also so smooth and polished that there was no risk of splinters to damage the delicate sun-bleached and vulnerable skin encasing the withered limb. Henry's mother stood behind the chair, a protective hand on his shoulder, her other hand holding tight to Charlotte in an effort to restrain her unruly daughter.

She had continually tried to perch on the end of Henry's leg support which could threaten to snap anything less sturdy.

"Meanwhile, Henry, I have a new Governess arriving tomorrow. We must step up your rate of learning or you may find yourself in a class with younger boys when we get you off to school. When I was your age I was already studying Algebra and the Classics. You are falling behind my boy. Sarah, I presume you have a room prepared for the new governess?"

Sarah bobbed a respectful curtsey to accompany the nod of her head in affirming that the work was done. Henry had already begun to implore his father.

"Oh but, Papa, can Joseph still learn with me, Nanny has been teaching both of us and Joseph helps me to understand so much better, it's a bit like being at school when he is with me? Oh please, please say yes, Papa. It won't be for long now, and the governess won't be able to push this thing around either, so Joseph could do that for her, please, Papa?"

Charles turned away from his son, encircled as he was by the group gathered around him at the bottom of the grand staircase. Hands behind his back, head bowed, he stomped back to his study. Muttering as he went amongst his squeaky leather footsteps on the polished floor, about no longer being the head of his own household and everyone just manipulated him into doing what they wanted.

Henrietta winked at Joseph, she loved the effect spending time with him had on her son. He was much more animated, less shy, and she believed from Nanny, also much more learned since Joseph had been with him. Henry would have her support in this if Charles needed further persuasion. She would rather keep him at home a little longer too. At least until his leg was back to normal, which the Doctor assured her would happen in time, despite his frequent misgivings over the past months.

"Mama, can we go to Joseph's new house after lessons today, he will take great care of me, he promises don't you, Joseph?

We can go in the bath chair, and I will just use the crutches when we get there, I won't stand or walk any more than if I was at home I promise. I can take the gift you have for his baby sister Rose, if I don't take it soon it will be too small, Joseph says she is growing fast. It is only a mile down the driveway. It will give Joseph a chance to check his mother is alright, she has been very sad about Jack's death, and I need to get used to being out of the house ready for being away at school. Please say I can, Mama?"

Henry's non stop rhetoric was punctuated only by Henrietta's changing facial expressions. Indications of negativity from her, inspired further pleading and justifications from Henry. He longed to get away from Bramble House if only for a short time, his internment had been endless.

They were approaching Joseph's cottage at the end of the driveway, with Joseph swishing the chair from side to side to amuse Henry. Spring was fusing into summer and the blossom was falling from the trees like a frivolous snow storm in a light breeze. The distinctive smell of newly hatched bird's eggs hung in the air above the empty shells.

"Did you know that the railways now go from Bristol, to all the way up the country to the north now?" Joseph asked, "A relative of Jack's came all the way down from Yorkshire to collect some family belongings after the funeral. He lived in a place called Scarborough, like in the song Scarborough Fair. It's supposed to be turning into a seaside resort popular with people who take holidays in the summer. It has special waters there that are good for healing people that have diseases."

Henry was losing his pallor and gaining a healthy glow from some regular fresh air and sunshine. His parents were beginning to worry less about his recovery and were more and more accepting of his friendship with Joseph. They had noticed and ignored the change in Joseph's mode of address to him, feeling it was suitable under the unusual circumstances, if a little inappropriate. Joseph had been the one who had supervised, encouraged and sometimes had to cajole Henry in taking weight through his healed leg, to aid this recovery, and his doting parents would always be grateful.

He considered Joseph's information and added, "Papa says they will be connecting Dorset to Bristol by railway soon too, what an adventure to be able to travel around the country and see so many different places. Travelling by coach and horses is fun but it is so slow, railway trains will be so much quicker."

They were just reaching the small vegetable garden outside the cottage when Joseph leant towards Henry's ear and spoke quietly.

"Henry, do you believe in ghosts?"

"I'm not sure, Joseph, why?"

"Ma said that just before Jack died, he was talking to the window, and when she asked him who he was talking to, he said that Cathy – that's his wife that died a while ago, - was there waiting for him. He said to Ma that he had told her he would just finish the cup of tea Mary had kindly brought him, and then he would join her. Ma was a little worried, but when she went back to fetch his empty cup, he had passed, gone! She said his face was set with the loving smiling mask of someone so pleased to greet their very last cherished image. Strange isn't it, but nice too I suppose." Henry nodded in agreement, and both boys fell subconsciously into a moment's silence in respectful contemplation of this strange phenomenon. Their thoughts were abruptly broken, by an eerie wail.

"Joooseph, Joooseph"

"Where's that coming from, Joseph, it sounds like it is up in the sky, who is it, are you expecting any ghosts? I'd much rather you didn't die, not just yet anyway!"

They both chuckled and listened intently.

"Joooseph"

"It's Lizzibeth, Henry, you'll get to meet her."

"But where is she, Joseph, I can't see anyone."

"She's up on her stilts behind the hedge over there, but pretend you can't see her!"

"Joooseph, where are you?"

"Oh don't be so silly, Lizzibeth, I know exactly where you are, get down here this instant if you want to meet Master Henry!"

They heard a clatter of ironmongery and a tearing of foliage from behind the leafy screen. Birds deserted their hedgerow nests as Lizzibeth tumbled from her stilts in her desperation to meet the famous Master Henry. Joseph and Henry laughed so hard when Lizzibeth emerged like a scowling scarecrow with bits of fern and leaves sticking out from her clothing and hair. She was rubbing her arm and leg where she would no doubt be bruised tomorrow for her carelessness.

"Well you aren't very nice, I've hurt myself, it's not funny."

Henry straightened his face with some difficulty and Joseph pushed the bath chair over towards Lizzibeth. "Master Henry, may I introduce you to Miss Elizabeth Buxton." Henry extended his hand towards Lizzibeth as he raised up onto his left foot using one of his crutches.

"Charmed I am sure, Miss Buxton. You may call me Henry." Lizzibeth pumped his hand vigorously. "Careful, that is my broken wrist, it was mended, but I'm not so sure now!"

"Really," she said, "Don't I 'ave to say 'Master' Henry for a little while first like Joseph did? Oh I'm so sorry about your wrist, is it a'right?"

"Well, yes it will be fine, and as far as addressing me is concerned, better to stick to the 'Master' bit when anyone is listening, otherwise just Henry is fine, Miss Elizabeth."

"Aw," Lizzibeth giggled coquettishly, clutching her hands and arms close in to her and swaying from side to side. "You know you can call me Lizzibeth, Master Henry, everyone else does."

Chapter 5

Dorset, September 1847

Thomas walked into Thackery's workshop. "Excuse me, Mr Thackery, but Joseph forgot his lunch this morning, he left in such a hurry."

Jacob Thackery looked up from the planing he was doing to a table top using his treasured new Spiers plane.

"Well good-day there, Mr Elliot. How are you. It was a great day for me when you brought me your son, he is such a natural carpenter, I'm hoping he'll make me my fortune for my old age." The two men shook hands laughing at his remarks.

"Glad he's working hard, Mr Thackery, that's what he has been taught to do, to give his best to his work."

"No doubt about it, it shows well in the quality of his work too. Why don't you take him off for half an hour to eat his lunch if you can spare the time. He deserves a break, he's worked without stopping since early this morning. We just 'ave to get this dining set out before the end of the month, a lot to do yet, but we can't afford not to eat. Joseph, Joseph." He shouted out to nowhere in particular behind him, "your Pa's here with your lunch."

Joseph emerged from behind a curtain holding what appeared to be a chair leg. "See, I'm trusting him with orders already, he can turn those legs as well as I can."

"Oh but, Mr Thackery, I can't do the finishing off yet."

"I should hope not yet, Joseph, it's taken me a lifetime to

perfect, I don't want you doing it in the blink of an eye, showing me up! Now be off with you and eat your lunch with your Pa."

"Oh Pa, I realised I'd left my lunch, I thought I'd go hungry today."

"Do you think your Ma would let that happen, come on, lets find somewhere for you to sit and eat this?"

They ambled across the main road into the town, and across to the bustling marketplace, Joseph eating his homemade crusty bread and cheese as they walked. At the fire monument Thomas stopped and sat down on the steps scattering hens as he did so.

"Tell me, Joseph, are you happy in this apprenticeship, it appears you've a natural ability with wood, are you sure you don't want to be a coachman at all, it feels wrong not to be passing on my own trade to you, my first born son."

"Oh no. No Pa really, I love what I'm doing now, and I was never really much good with the horses, not like you are, maybe Benjamin'll want to follow on from you. Do you think so?"

"I don't know, Joseph, but it's important to feel happy in your work, you'll spend a lot of years working at whatever you have chosen to do, God willing. I didn't follow my father either, do you remember the story? My father was a trunk and portmanteau maker in Bristol, but that didn't interest me at all and your Uncle Robert has followed him in that trade. I met the Master one day in Bristol and was so interested in his carriage and the horses, that he offered me the job here, and the rest you know. Fate plays a big part in what we do with our lives."

Joseph was leaning against a column of the fire monument and nodded at his father's vision. He finished his apple, and tucked the clean rag which had served as a lunch container into his pocket. He turned to look at the monument.

"That must've been a huge fire to destroy a whole town, Pa?"

"I'm sure it must 'ave been, but you would've thought they

could've written a better tribute to the revival of a town than that." Thomas didn't get up, but just waved his hand disparagingly in the direction of the inscription.

"What bit don't you like, Pa, I think it sounds rather grand."

"My boy, I don't think the magnificent rising of a whole town and all that the rebuilding would've entailed is anything like the rising of erm, you know, erm men's erm…., its totally disrespectful."

"I don't know what you mean, Pa, a Phoenix is a Greek mythological bird, as one dies, another rises from the ashes, I think it's a very good comparison."

"How do you get it being a fenix or whatever you called it, it starts with a 'p'."

Slowly Joseph realised what his Pa had thought the inscription had read and was overcome with a mixture of such emotions that he was unsure of how to proceed. Sadness for his father's enduring misunderstanding, anger at his lack of opportunity, guilt for his own schooling, but shamefully, not without a hint of amusement too. Nonchalantly he responded,

"Oh I can see how you might think that, Pa, but a 'p' and an 'h' put together make the same sound as an 'f'. I can't believe we've never come across that in our reading, Pa." He had begun to kick a few stones around the steps, minimising his father's error. He resisted any temptation to offer either physical comfort or humour to his father's fault. He could bodily feel the blast from the shattered pride that his revelation had exposed, and was never more uncomfortable in his life, than at this moment.

Thomas' humiliation was neither intended, nor deserved. Nonetheless, it hung pendant in the air above the noise of the busy marketplace parting the father further from the son than if he had been on the moon. He was torn between feeling so proud of his child with his unquestionable abundant knowledge, and feeling utterly ashamed and degraded. More so on account of the nature of his misunderstanding. He snapped himself back around to face Joseph and smiled.

"Well, we haven't had much time for reading recently, have we? It's maybe a little late for me Joseph, but I would appreciate you spending some time with your brother and sisters. I want them to know everything that you do, and share in the opportunities that being learned brings and that you've so much enjoyed. Right. Time to get back to work, see you at home tonight, Joseph, work hard for Mr Thackery."

"I will, Pa, and of course I'll help Louiza and Benjamin, and Rose when she's old enough. Thank you for bringing my lunch."

But Thomas had gone before Joseph had finished his reply.

"Henry, you can't be serious about wearing this uniform, you'll look such a fool." She pranced around his room with his cap over the top of her maid's lace bonnet and holding his short trousers up against her apron. "I'm really going to miss you. Don't get big-headed, it's just that with Joseph and I working, we don't get to see much of each other now, even on his day off he likes to play with his wood. He sees more of that Hannah Thackery than he does me. It's been a'right 'til now, 'coz I get to see you, but when you leave it'll be so, so boring!"

"It will be fine, Lizzibeth, you fit in well here, all the other staff like you, and I will be home for the Christmas holiday. I have asked Mama for a copy of Charles Dickens' new book 'A Christmas Carol' for Christmas, he does write a very good story. Oh and I have left my copy of 'Oliver Twist' with Joseph, and I have asked him to go through it with you. It is quite a hard book to read, but a great story, it should motivate you to learn more words. Perhaps if you are bored, you could work more with Charlotte." His talking was punctuated by rhythmic leaps over the corner of his bed by swinging around the bed post.

"You mean 'Miss' Charlotte to me don't you, Henry? Do you 'ave to do things like that, you'll break your other leg. The book sounds good if Joseph can find the time f….."

"Ssh, Lizzibeth, someone's coming." She quickly busied herself packing together Henry's uniform as Henrietta swept into his room.

"Lizzibeth, go and ask Cook if she has remembered to put the food parcel together that I asked her to. Master Henry can't be without good food, he might not like what they give him at Moorcliffe.

"Yes, M'Lady." She bobbed a curtsey and turned to Henry with a superficial subservient sycophantic smile knowing she was being watched by Henrietta. "Would you like anything to drink Master Henry, or will that be all?"

"No thank you, Lizzibeth, just make sure I have some good food in that parcel won't you!" He winked at her knowing his mother had now turned to look in his closets to see if there was anything that had been forgotten in his packing.

"Oh and, Lizzibeth, I keep meaning to ask Cook, has Sarah had her baby yet?"

"Not that I know of, M'Lady."

"Is David around today if it arrives?"

"David told Mr Simms this morning that he hoped it wouldn't be today on account of Mr Elliot and 'im being away most of the day taking Master Henry off to school."

"Did he say what time they expected to be back?"

"Quite late I think, M'Lady, since Mr Simms said that by the time they bed the horses and sort the Landau on their return, it'll be very late before he gets back to the cottage."

"Does she have anyone with her? I'm sure the women at the cottages would give her all the help she needs. But tell Mrs Brookes to let me know when anything happens, or if any help is needed, the first child can be a little frightening, you don't want to be alone."

"Yes, M'Lady, excuse me, M'Lady." She curtsied again and set off down the stairs leaving Henry with his mother.

"You are far too familiar with that chambermaid Henry, just as a consequence of her mother being friendly with Joseph's mother does not give her the right to take liberties."

"Oh but she does not, Mama, really. It is just that she is so much younger than Sarah, we 'ave much more in common."

"You h..h..have nothing at all in common with that girl, Henry, I'll thank you to remember that. As well as pronouncing your 'h's. See what you are picking up from her, your father is right, it is time you went off to school!" She had bellowed 'nothing' so loudly to emphasise her point that Henry looked away embarrassed lest anyone else had heard her.

Her stern tone caused them both to busy themselves inanely for a few minutes. Henrietta had meant what she said, but did not want an atmosphere between them when she would not see Henry again now until the Christmas end of term. They must get a tree again this year for the big hall, they had so enjoyed dancing around it last year. She pictured that their family had looked just like Queen Victoria's family did in the newspaper picture. She stopped tracing the pattern on Henry's bed quilt, and looked lovingly at her son, she was so nervous for him, he was still quite small for his age, although thankfully completely active again. The right leg was still thinner than his left, but yet it was improving all the time, and he could now bend his knee almost the same amount as on the other leg. He was also too young in her opinion to be away from his dear Mama. "Come here, Henry, embrace your Mama before you go, let us not part with any discord today of all days."

"Henry, Henry." Joseph was running up the driveway to catch Henry before his departure. He could see the Master and Mistress still on the steps of Bramble House, waving at the Landau. He mused how Henry had always scoffed at this vehicle, likening it to an oversized perambulator with horses where the handle should be. He would hardly now appreciate the irony of his father standing with one arm around his wife's shoulders acknowledging her undeniable distress as her 'baby' was perambulated away.

The Master had not allowed her to accompany Henry to school. He knew leaving him there would be more traumatic for her than this. Despite his resolute determination in this matter, he remembered all too vividly his own launch into the experience of boarding school. He had enjoyed his school days, but parting from his mother too, had been difficult for both of them.

"Thankyou for stopping, Pa, I tried to get away earlier but we were so busy I didn't see the time." Joseph walked past his father, perched as he was on the drivers box seat of the Landau. The horses looked magnificent with their plumes, and yet arrogant too, as if full of pride for their young passenger, off to school for the first time. He leant into the carriage and shook Henry's hand. "Enjoy your opportunity Henry, you'll have a wonderful time and make some great new friends, remember everything you learn so you can come back and tell me. I've made a little something for you." Joseph handed Henry a wooden box. It had a perfectly fitted sliding lid, and was polished so finely it looked almost like a looking glass, with Henry's blurring reflection staring back at him.

"It's for any writing implements or mathematical tools you may need for school." Joseph was puzzled as to why Henry hadn't said anything.

"I know what it is for, Joseph, I just can't believe you have made it for me. I am going to miss you, and Lizzibeth, I'll be counting the days until the holidays. I won't need to teach you anything, Joseph, you long since overtook me in being learned. Have fun with your wood, you are going to be a famous cabinet maker one day. And I shall buy all my furniture from you." Contemplating the games and lazy afternoons he would yearn for with his friends he lowered his voice so only Joseph could hear, and said. "I'll give Lizzibeth a time for the three of us to meet up again when I get back and can get away. She can get a message to you, shall we say the same place by the woods, or you could come and see me as soon as you know I am back to confirm arrangements?"

"Joseph, you've made an excellent job of turning those chair legs, you'll have no trouble completing your apprenticeship if you carry on like this. I 'ave to admit I was unsure about taking you on without any family in the trade, but I was wrong, you've a real talent with wood, I may have to look at remunerating you soon if we continue to be able to get more work through."

"Thank you, Mr Thackery, I've always enjoyed it, I'm glad I've pleased you. Will you show me how to do the claws when you come to do the bottom of the legs. I've looked at the books you have on furniture forms, I think Mr Sheraton's is the easiest to follow, but I would like to watch you when you do them."

But Mr Thackery was now looking straight past Joseph as his daughter Hannah came into the workshop.

"Oh. Er. Yes of course, Joseph, if we have the time. Now my Dear, what can I do for you at this hour of the day, Where's your Ma?"

Hannah had taken to coming into the workshop a lot recently, she adored her father and he her. He would always stop what he was doing when she arrived and would make her some little trinket to take away. Sometimes as simple as a clothes peg that she could dress up as a doll, or some wooden dice. Hannah was an only child, her Ma had nearly died when she was born and Mr Thackery had decided there would be no more children to endanger his wife and chance her being taken from him. He had also told Joseph that his wife's friend had died in childbirth. He felt that was too high a price to pay for the sins of the flesh. Joseph found this topic embarrassing when Jacob had confided, but he enjoyed seeing their close family, it reminded him of his own. Lizzibeth's parents weren't close of late, and her father was often to be seen staggering out of the Inn. Mrs Buxton was always complaining about him to his Ma. He was spending so little time working now or indeed with his family, but so much time drinking. That wasn't what he wanted to happen when he took a wife, he aspired to the marriages of his and Hannah's parents without any doubt.

Chapter 6

Dorset, June 1850

Lizzibeth sauntered along the winding path to the gates from Bramble House, day dreaming as she ambled. She intended to call at the Elliot's cottage to see Joseph on her way to her Ma's this Sunday. She would make him spend some time away from the cottage with her instead of just having to watch him work on pieces of furniture for his parents. They could arrange the next time for the three of them to meet together as Henry was coming home for the long glorious summer next week. And also, she wanted to confide in Joseph.

As she approached the cottage, she could see him sitting outside with his brother and sisters around him. She liked Louiza and had heard the staff at the house talking about how she was likely to get a job in service as an upstairs maid when she was twelve, on account of her being able to read, write and do simple arithmatic. Mrs Brookes thought she would be able to learn how to address and serve important visitors, along with other similar duties. If only she herself had been able to spend evenings with Joseph, he could have taught her as much, then maybe she could have earned better wages and be able to give more to her poor Ma.

As she got closer to the sibling huddle, she realised they were having a reading lesson from Joseph with one of the many books he had routinely inherited from Henry when he had finished with them. Joseph had even shown her some with

Latin words. Poor as her reading was, she recognised the foreign words and thought them indecipherable. Joseph found history and science the most interesting and devoured Henry's text books as quickly as he acquired them.

"Here's Lizzibeth everyone, do you want to take a break now, you can go back to playing with your whip and top Benjamin or even my old stilts, while I have a chat to her. Then it's your turn little Rose, I have some simple words for you to start with."

"Good morning, Joseph, how are you? No wood to be turned, bent or polished today, do you actually have time for me?" In turn, she tweaked Rose's nose, stuck her tongue out playfully at Benjamin and winked at Louiza as she spoke.

"Of course, Lizzibeth, I always have time for you, you know that. I just often have to practice something on the Sunday to make sure I get it right for Mr Thackery on the Monday. I usually can make use of what I have practised on though."

The two of them had started to walk along the road towards the town, Joseph knew that she would be on her way home to her Ma's house. It was a warm day, the blossom was falling from the trees along the path like a flurry of pink snow that fluttered round their footsteps.

"Joseph, I'm really worried about Ma, ever since Pa died last year she's had no interest in anything at all, or Bill, or me. She's not been to see your Ma since then either, she used to love to visit the little ones. They are so delightful. But now she stares at the walls and says she should have stopped Pa going to the Inn, she didn't realise he could die from drinking too much, so she blames 'erself. I've tried to tell her it was the business that finished him. It used to be the only one in town when his father had it before 'im, and it did so well. Pa just couldn't contend with the competition from Brown's, and then from Carter's of Poole too. I don't know how to help her, Joseph."

"I know Ma has been worried about her too Lizzibeth, and she has tried to call. Your Ma won't even let her into the house, so I presume that is on account of her not bothering with the housework either."

"Oh no she doesn't, Joseph, you're right. I know I'll be spending my afternoon doing that for her. My wages just seem to pay for the bills my Pa had. How did it come to this, we never used to be so penniless. Poor Bill can't keep going as he is with the forge."

"I don't know what can be done, Lizzibeth, it would be awful if your Ma ended up in the workhouse. Maybe the church can help. Is there anything we can do? I could try speaking to Pa?"

"Anything, Joseph, please, I don't know what to do." She began to tremble as she spoke. The mention of the workhouse had been too much. Suddenly there were tears coursing down her cheeks as if an unexpected downpour had swelled waterfalls behind her eyes. These were then accompanied by loud sobs that took many cumulative gasps to fuel each one. Joseph was alarmed, he didn't know how to handle a crying girl, much less a very distraught Lizzibeth. To his own surprise, he put an arm easily and comfortably around her shoulders and blocked their progression, letting her stand and weep into him. Many months of repressed distress emptied onto his shirt. He marvelled at how she had carried all this on her own for so long. With his right hand he stroked her thick black curls, muffled as sheep's wool to the hushed senses that time had taught him to accept. He muttered comforting soothing words, that were unmemorable but served his purpose. This was a terrible situation indeed, he would speak to his father.

"Excuse me, Sir."

Thomas had nervously entered Charles Ferguson's library. This was not a common occurrence, and more likely when summoned to the master, not requesting an audience. Thomas knew the master did not like to be interrupted when at his desk, but he had bowed to increasing pressure from both Mary and Joseph on hearing of poor Aggie Buxton's plight.

"Yes, Thomas, what can I do for you?"

"I don't really know, Sir, but I wondered if you were aware of what has become of Aggie Buxton."

"Aggie Buxton, the kitchen maid that married the farrier? Did I hear that he had died? Isn't she Lizzibeth's mother?"

"Yes to all of those Master, but her son is struggling with the forge and certain debts, and Mary says Aggie's in a bad way."

"Well I am certainly sorry to hear that, Thomas, but do you have a reason for bringing it to my attention?"

"I'm not sure, Sir, I just thought you would want to know, and I didn't know what else to do. Lizzibeth was very upset about it all on Sunday. She spends her afternoon off doing everything for her mother."

"Very commendable, but that is what a daughter should do. Is it not, Thomas?"

"Well yes, Sir, but she's only fourteen, it's very hard for her."

"I suspect, Thomas, that the problem started when Buxton put his prices up so high that everyone including me, started travelling farther afield for their work to be done. Before you know it, word gets around that there is trade to be done here, and opposition can be the ruin of many a good business." He tapped his quill on the desk and looked up again as though re-assessing the severity of the situation by reading Thomas' expression. He then continued in a more empathic tone, "However, that is no fault of his poor widow, I will instruct Cook to give Lizzibeth food parcels on a Sunday when she visits home, that may help a little. As for the son, he would be better off joining forces with one of his competitors, I can not solve every man's business problems for him."

"No, Sir, thank you, Sir."

"Lizzibeth, Lizzibeth, over here." Joseph was crouching at the edge of the woods that banked towards the east from Bramble house. He ducked further out of sight once he knew Lizzibeth had seen him. She came hurrying towards where he had appeared to her, with her heavy skirts lifted high to allow her to run without tripping.

"Oh, Joseph, I wish we didn't 'ave to do this, although I wonder if it would be so exciting if we didn't though." She giggled and flopped down onto the floor of the summer countryside still panting heavily. She kicked off her shoes, and rubbed her feet as she did so. "I must get some new shoes, Joseph, I've more holes in these than Cook's colander, my feet get soaked when it rains. The cobbler said there wasn't enough left to be able to repair them they are so bad. I tried to leave the house with my work shoes on but Mrs Brookes spotted me and made me change. Ma says she can't afford anything, even with my wages coming in. Bill tries his best, but as I told you the other day, 'e can't do the work of two. 'E keeps threatening to go off and find work in London, says 'e would earn more there, but Ma doesn't want him to, she says there's a lot of disease, people die of cholera all the time. What time is Henry coming?"

Joseph picked up one of Lizzibeth's shoes with horror and looked at her blistered feet wishing he could do something. He could maybe talk to his Ma, she might have some old ones that would be better than these. He realised Lizzibeth was waiting for an answer.

"Oh, he's riding here, he was leaving just a few minutes after I told the Master I was heading off home, he should be here very soon."

"Ooh who's he riding, I love the grey mare Snowdrop, I can ride up in front on her. I have been so excited about today, Joseph, haven't you?"

"Certainly, Lizzibeth, we do always have a lot of fun. It's more special since Henry has been at school 'cause we can't meet up as often. It's a worry to me though that we get through the day with you two still in one piece and with no broken bones. If anything happened we would be found out, and somehow as the oldest, I feel I would be held responsible by everyone, yet it is you two who are the reckless ones." Lizzibeth raised her eyes skywards in an exasperated, exaggerated gesture to indicate

Joseph worried too much. He playfully threw her shoe at her making her cower in mock defence as she laughed. "Anyway," Joseph continued, "you know we can't take the horse very far, it would be recognised, we'll leave it in the woods like we did before and collect it on the way back." Just then they heard the cracking of dry twigs under horses hooves coming from the north side of the woods.

"Here he is, Joseph, ooh and he is on Snowdrop, Henry, can I ride with you?"

"Of course, Lizzibeth, will you give her a hand up, Joseph, only to the other side of the wood though, then we can leave her while we go have some fun by the river. We can play the imagining game again. What would it be like, and what would we end up doing if we each took a different direction at the crossroads? You know, one go to Shaftsbury, one to Dorchester, and the other one to Poole or Salisbury. If you went to Poole, Lizzibeth, and I went to Dorchester, we could be martyrs and meet up between the two in Tolpuddle. What do you think?" He looked excitedly at his two friends who were so pleased to have him back for the summer, if only that it concentrated their own efforts to have some enjoyment and time together as well as Henry's company.

"No Henry, I want to go to Salisbury where the Cathedral is. Tolpuddle sounds a silly wet place. And what's a martyr anyway?" Joseph and Henry laughed together at her innocence. Joseph ceased with her evident discomfort, "That's just another piece of history I need to tell you about sometime, Lizzibeth, it's a long story."

"Oh, it is so wonderful to be back, school is just so boring, nothing exciting ever happens, it is just books, books and even more books."

"You should not bemoan your schooling, Henry, it's such a privilege." Joseph spoke sternly, but then smiled, not wanting to spoil their euphoric mood, but Henry realised how thoughtless his remark had been in this company.

"Sorry, Joseph, I forgot what a studious person you are. Have you brought me some clothes, I look very conspicuous like this, luckily I have changed a lot this term, don't you think so? I shouldn't be recognised anyway. Who's for swimming?"

Lizzibeth giggled as she was hoisted aloft to sit sideways in front of Henry,

"You have both changed so much since Christmas, you've got wispy hair on your faces and your voices are so funny. Joseph's is a'right now, but very deep, so your's will be soon, Henry." She cleverly mimicked the tone of each of them as she spoke, and tickled Henry's chin where hair was beginning to emerge. Henry looked a little hurt to be considered to be trailing Joseph, but they both laughed and remembered why they enjoyed her company so much. To them, she had undergone no transformation at all. Indeed they were blind to her emerging shape and subliminally flirtatious manner. Still scrutinising Henry, she exclaimed, "Did you know you have a bit missing out of your ear lobe, Henry? It's as if someone has nibbled the edge of it."

"Oh, I know, don't do that." He wriggled free from her inspection of this imperfection. "My Papa says his Mama's was exactly the same so I must have got it from him." Unimpressed with this explanation, Lizzibeth turned to stroke the horse's neck and her thoughts moved on to their adventure ahead.

"Will you teach me that new swimming stroke you've learnt, Henry? It's a lovely day for it and our clothes will dry quickly. I watched some boys in the river the other day on my walk home and they were jumping straight off the bridge into the river, I was so worried they weren't going to come back up again, but it looked great fun." She hardly paused for breath once she started speaking and was unaware of the boys amusement at this trait in her. She continued "Can I ask you both a question?" Still laughing Joseph interrupted, "It's not like you to ask permission, Lizzibeth, but go on anyway!" Joseph winked his reply at Henry, both of them wondering what her inquisitiveness had perplexed her with now.

"Well, why do girls have to ride this way on a horse? When I sat on their backs at the forge when I was little to brush their manes, I sat like you do. So why do girls ride like this, isn't it easy to fall off?"

Henry shrugged, "Don't know, but it just is not done for girls to sit astride, I think it is not deemed ladylike."

"I think it might be because of your different er, shape, Lizzibeth, you know, to protect you." Joseph as always looked for the more scientific explanation.

"Phoo. What nonsense, we're not made of glass you know!"

"Shall we see, Joseph. Ooh, now what do you think, Lizzibeth, are you sure you will not smash into a million pieces if you fall?" Henry leant her forwards over the mare's neck so she was in danger of falling, they all laughed but Lizzibeth squealed her laughter so loud that Joseph leading Snowdrop, halted their progress and admonished Henry and Lizzibeth to hush as they were approaching the edge of the wood. Henry and Lizzibeth continued to giggle softly as he pulled her back to safety.

As the trees parted, they could see the glorious sunshine awaiting them. Henry jumped down off his mount and went around behind her to change into the clothes Joseph handed him, telling Lizzibeth to look the other way as he did so. She wickedly countered by shifting her position on Snowdrop so that she was now sat shockingly astride the saddle and nudging her mount with her legs, she walked his shelter away from him, revealing his undergarments to the woodland populace.

"Lizzibeth Buxton, what do you think you are doing, you bring her back here now. You really are too shameless. Just wait 'till I get you in that water."

He dressed rapidly whilst trying to catch Snowdrops reins, then looping them round his arm, he pulled her down from the saddle tickling her mercilessly. Joseph was helpless with laughter at the image of Henry hopping around in his undergarments trying to catch hold of his horse. Lizzibeth fell to the ground kicking her legs wildly to keep Henry away from her. He stopped his torment suddenly, straightening himself back from her. "Where are your shoes, Lizzibeth? You can't walk to the river bank with no shoes on your feet."

"Oh, Joseph, I forgot didn't I. I must've left them where we met up in the woods, never mind, they're full of holes anyway, I might as well walk in my bare feet. Ma'll have to get me some if I don't go home with any."

Henry looked aghast, "Are you serious, Lizzibeth, your feet will get cut and raw?" Henry saw Joseph glance him a warning look and he shook his head. "No I'm sorry, Lizzibeth, you are not going to walk around with no shoes on your feet like a pauper." He fished in the pocket of the pile of clothes he had thrown on the back of Snowdrop, and pulled out a coin. "Here, get to the cobblers in town now, and buy any shoes he has in his window, and we will meet you at the river." He looked at Joseph who was stood anxiously awaiting Lizzibeth's reaction. Unbeknown to Henry, Joseph felt a mixture of concern for her pride, but shame for himself. He had more than enough put away now, he could easily have bought Lizzibeth some shoes, why did he let it come to this awkward situation, he felt his fist rush to tend the position of his eye within its socket. Henry identified that his friend thought she would see this gesture as totally shameful though Joseph had not enlightened him to her family's plight. He put out a hand tenderly as if to comfort her, then diverted the atmosphere of silence by altering his movement and playfully pulling her hair, adding cheekily "You can say it is a wage for making me laugh so much!"

Lizzibeth, initially stunned and bewildered by Henry's forthright instructions, stood looking at the shiny coin in her hand. Never had the differences between them seemed as vast as in this gaping moment. She turned to run her errand shouting back over her shoulder and laughing to hide her humiliation. "If that's what it's for, Henry Ferguson, you owe me a lot more than this!"

She had hardly bounded a few feet, when she bumped straight into Hannah Thackery, who in stark contradiction was floating elegantly towards them as though being delivered by a cumulus of the bluebells she trampled. "What are you doing here?" Lizzibeth curtly demanded.

"Joseph told me you were all going to the river and asked if I would like to join you. I know it's a secret, I won't tell anyone." Lizzibeth whipped round to look at Joseph, how dare he invite someone else into their private tryst? The day had just got even worse for her.

Joseph saw her expression and quickly interjected.

"I didn't think anyone would mind if there was another one to join us, do you mind, Henry, Hannah won't tell anyone?"

"It is fine by me, Joseph, there are four of us now for the crossroads game. It is very thoughtful of you to bring a friend for Lizzibeth, she must get sick of being the only girl. Don't you, Lizzibeth?"

"In truth, I actually like being the only girl!" She whipped her skirts around and continued on her way to the cobblers. Hannah, intuitively sensing a tension as taught as a cat's cradle strung densely between the branches, turned away from the boys and looking after Lizzibeth, shouted after her. "Hey, Lizzibeth, would you like me to come and help you?" Without turning, she continued on her way stomping her feet into the ground forcefully with every syllable,

"No thank you, Hannah Thackery. I'll never need any help from you, ever!"

Chapter 7

Dorset, Oct 1853

"Psst, Joseph, over here."

Henry was crouched behind the tree near the Elliot's cottage, Joseph had just come out of the privy, and thought he had heard something. He looked around him. Henry whispered again. "Joseph, here."

"Henry, what are you doing here, I didn't think you were supposed to be home at the moment? You don't need to hide, there's no-one here."

"Oh I just have a few days before my very last examinations ever, so I told the school my mother was ill and that I would be able to concentrate better if I was at home with her. They didn't even check with them, so here I am! Fancy a night at the Inn with me?"

"Well, you know my parents wouldn't approve of that Henry, not after what happened to Lizzibeth's father. Why don't you come in and have a drink of my father's whisky with me here, the rest of the family are visiting Sarah and David's latest addition to their family. I don't think he would notice if a couple of glasses worth are missing, it's really your father's anyway, he knows how much my Pa enjoys it, and so on various celebratory occasions, he's very generous and gives my Pa another bottle."

Henry followed Joseph reluctantly into the cottage,

"Take your coat off Henry, otherwise you won't feel the benefit of it when you go back out, - it's a little grand and swanky for this small town isn't it? You look like you're bound for the theatre dressed like that." Joseph made for the cupboard which held his fathers whisky. He carried it to the kitchen and returned with two glasses. Pouring a small amount of the fiery liquid into each glass, he handed one to Henry and took a sip from the other. Henry flung, then almost tenderly, smoothed his beige coat over the back of a fireside chair.

"I just bought it last week; it was a little extravagant from my allowance. It's made from cashmere, a new type of wool they have found on the underbelly of Himalayan goats if you please! You know how impatient I am to wear anything new, so I had to wear it tonight. Here, do you want to try it on?"

"Nah, fancy clothes have never interested me Henry, you know that. I hope the goat isn't left to freeze without its own wool! Come and sit down by the fire."

Henry had not often been inside the Elliot's cottage, and certainly not since he was old enough to really appreciate the social differences between them. He was humbled by the sheer size of their living area for six people. He knew there was also a parlour next door where Jack had been nursed, but he also knew that Joseph had said before that it was only ever used for visitors and Christmas. So this was the entire indoor world for six people. He considered how it would be to live like this. He also knew that the Elliot's were extremely comfortable compared to most workers, they had a separate area for cooking, and the bedrooms were upstairs with no-one having to sleep in the kitchen, which he knew to be the case in many of the cottages.

"Cheers Joseph, here's to the end of my school days. My examination results will decide my career for me, Papa wants me to go to University, but I want to go into the army. If I don't do well enough in the examinations, it is the army for me. So how do you think I will do Joseph?" He laughed to illustrate the fortuitous and controlling position he was in. Joseph was horrified.

"You mean you fully intend to do badly in the examinations, so that you won't have to go to University? I don't understand you Henry, I really don't. How I would have loved to have had your education."

"You have had my education Joseph, just second hand, that's all!" He laughed aloud, and Joseph smiled back. Henry was right, he had devoured every book he had been given. He was so much better at retaining knowledge than Henry that they both joked that he could do Henry's tests for him and most likely do better. Buoyed by his own good humour, he jumped to his feet and cajoled Joseph.

"Come on Joseph, lets go and have some fun in the town, I fancy making a whole evening of it, the walk to town itself will be pleasant, there is a full moon in the sky."

Joseph looked around uncomfortably, thought for a moment, but then justified to himself, he was now eighteen, and had very rarely gone out at all on an evening.

"A'right Henry, just give me a minute to write a note to Ma and Pa, I'll tell them you are home unexpectedly and we have gone for a walk, can you put the whisky back in the cupboard over there? You never change Henry, what will your folks say when they find you are back home?"

Ambling along the road towards the town, Henry had been entertaining Joseph by mooing to the cows in the field behind the hedge, they had laughed at the anonymous replies that came back to them through the darkness. "Henry, why are you so keen to go in the army, the stories in the newspapers about battlefields are just dire, you could be killed or maimed?"

Henry looked at Joseph, and thought how insular he had become compared to himself. They had been so alike as children, but Joseph's life experience did not go beyond the town in which he was born and brought up. His expectations in life, whilst ambitious in terms of career and education, did not extend beyond his own four safe walls. He on the other hand wanted adventure and excitement, and escape from his stifling if so much larger quarters. He considered what this said about their respective upbringings, that he felt so much more trapped in a large mansion than Joseph did in a small cottage. Yet to blame his parents would be wrong, indeed he felt his parents and Joseph's were very similar in the way they had been raised, with an abundance of love and direction, but little chastisement. He recollected the stories from other boys at school whereby regular beatings were considered good for children's development, discipline and character.

That left the only explanation to be their very different personalities, he himself had always been the adventurous one whilst Joseph, especially as they grew older, was always the voice of conscience and caution for them both.

"Ah, but Joseph, if I am maimed in battle, I know a very good friend who will support me throughout my long and painful road to recovery!" He smiled at Joseph, who realized there would be no serious reasoning with Henry once his mind was made up, so he played along with him.

"And pray tell me, what could possibly be in it for me this time, for I am already educated Master Henry!" They were both laughing again, when they heard a familiar voice coming towards them.

"Will you share your joke with me, or is it for boys only?"

"Lizzibeth, how lovely to see you." She looked sulky and hurt.

"What's wrong, we weren't laughing about you Lizzibeth."

"But you never told me Henry was home Joseph, did you want to keep it a secret and leave me out?"

"Don't be silly Lizzibeth, I didn't know he was home either, he is shirking school, naughty, wayward boy, so we were just going to be even more wayward, and have a drink in the Ferguson Arms in the town. Are you on your way back to the house?"

She relaxed, relieved that the boys were not excluding her. She always felt it would be inevitable one day soon, when their different genders and positions would get in the way of their secret interludes. But she was not ready for that, not yet.

"Do you have to go to that place, remember it killed Pa, and Bill already goes in there far too much. I don't like it."

"Lizzibeth, it's only if you drink too much that it is a problem. One night is not going to kill us, it's just fun. You really can't come with us though, it is only ladies with a certain reputation that go into Inns. Do you want us to walk you up to the house."

"No thank you Joseph, I walk in the dark loads of times, and tonight it's quite light anyway 'coz the moon's so bright."

"Wait a minute you two, we will have more fun if Lizzibeth is with us Joseph, why don't we go and sit by the bridge and tell ghostly stories in the dark. Then we can head to the fire monument and enjoy the atmosphere in the town, it is a light night, lots of people will be around. I have our own supply of the fiery liquor here!" He opened his beige cashmere frock coat to reveal Thomas Elliot's bottle of whisky.

"Henry, that's my father's whisky, I asked you to put it away in the cupboard. Now I'll really be in trouble!"

"Oh, Joseph, live a little, what's the worst that can happen. Anyway, didn't you say it was really my father's whisky?"

Lizzibeth had looked from one to the other, she had not expected any excitement tonight and her big dark eyes were glistening in anticipation and eagerness of Joseph's concurrence. She knew a way to sneak into the house late at night, there was a small window that never closed properly on the servants staircase, she had used it once before when she had been late waiting with her mother for her Pa to come home. No-one had known. And she wasn't on duty until the morning.

"Please say yes Joseph. Please." She tugged on his sleeve pleadingly, then snatched his cap off his head and made to run off with it. He grabbed her arm and pulled it up behind her back.

"Now Lizzibeth Buxton, put that cap back on my head right now or else." She giggled like a child and did as she was bid, gasping with the discomfort of her twisted arm.

"You are like an old married couple you two, do you know

that!" Henry had watched their banter closely as he took a swig from the whisky bottle.

"You're right, it will be worth it to have Lizzibeth's company, Henry, and we would have drunk too much ale in the Inn anyway. Whereas we need not drink very much of my Pa's whisky, and if we do, you are replacing it, Henry, I mean it. Is that clear."

"Goodnight, Joseph, remember, we know nothing, be quiet too, don't wake anyone."

"Don't worry Henry, all my family sleep like the dead, oo, sorry, not very funny tonight, but nothing wakens them, not even an earthquake remember!"

Joseph and Henry smiled guardedly at each other, and Henry took up the protective and warming position that Joseph had just deserted, of having one arm around Lizzibeth's shoulders. She had been quiet all the walk home, severely traumatised by the night's events.

The driveway to Bramble House had never before seemed so long, Henry had not spent such quiet moments in Lizzibeth's company. There was always noise wherever she went, it seemed to follow her around like an aura that halo'd her whole body. Tonight was understandably, yet so uncomfortably different.

Henry was aware that his intoxication was making him stagger rather than walk, especially on the gravel, which seemed as big as boulders tonight. Slurred shivering footsteps were difficult to hush, and the more he tried, the more he risked falling over.

Lizzibeth shook him off her shoulder just as they approached the house. "Henry if you are going to fall, don't take me with you." But her action caused Henry to wobble and before her sentence was finished, he had sprawled loudly across the small sharp stones. He shouted his expletive angrily at Lizzibeth.

"Don't be like that Lizzibeth, it hasn't been a great experience for any of us."

Futilely she whispered her own reply. "But my brother might hang Henry, how could my poor Ma contend with that?"

"I know Lizzibeth, but hopefully it will not come to that." His voice again had been a little too loud, wakening his father's new black labrador, Dickens, who spoke enthusiastically back to him from the kennel outside the house.

"Oh my God, the dog, I forgot, he hears everything, he loves visitors."

A lamp appeared in the doorway of the house, and Mrs Brookes and Mr Simms stood imposingly together on the front step, the moonlight accentuating their united redoubtable, formidable appearance. They were suddenly silhouetted by backlight as Charles Ferguson's study door opened behind them.

Their idyllic halcyon days, if blighted earlier tonight, had now ended.

Chapter 8

Dorset, June 1854

"Good morning, Joseph, come on up here, I am up in my room, I saw you from my window coming up the drive. What a splendid day for a birthday." Henry was leaning over the banister talking to Joseph as he climbed the stairs two at a time.

"Good morning, stranger, you haven't been home since Christmas, what has kept you away from us? Your parents have really missed you. They have been so thrilled about you coming home. Happy birthday though old man!" They shook hands as Joseph reached the top stair, and Henry then led him into his room, scattered with his unpacking as though a market stall had been commissioned.

"What's this I hear about a betrothal, Joseph Elliot, you are a sly old chap. Congratulations to you, and to Hannah of course, she's a lucky girl to have captured your heart. Mama said you were hoping to wed in a few weeks time. I hope I will still be here." He paused thoughtfully as if wondering whether his next sentence should be vocalised or left to hang unspoken in the breath between them. "You know I always thought you and Lizzibeth would get together in the end. Is there any news of her?" Joseph turned to the window to avoid his face being read.

"I hope you'll still be here for our marriage too, we are choosing a date in July or August, Hannah wanted to give her Ma time to make a special dress. But no, Henry, no news." He crossed to the bed in the middle of the room and fiddled with the ornate cord around the bedpost, and Henry busied himself with the sash on his shiny new soldier's uniform. Neither could grant the other eye contact. Joseph broke the silence. "Why don't we go for a walk, Henry, this might be the last birthday you spend here once you are a serving officer in the British Army, fighting the world's problems. So I want to tell you about my gift to you."

"That sounds interesting. But I thought, as it is my birthday, my choice, we could go for a ride."

"Oh, Henry, you know how horses and I don't really like each other."

"It will be good, Joseph, I have arranged for your Pa to saddle up the laziest most docile horse we have for you."

"A'right then, as it's your birthday, but a simple ride only, and not a gallop!"

Joseph and Henry were seated astride the bridge parapet over the Stour, their horses tied to the tree on its bank. Ducks played at the waters edge, coaxing their young into the river and flapping their wings causing ripples to span across its width. Mesmerised by their display, the young men had sat in silence for a few minutes. Nether knew how to begin their inevitable conversation.

"You said in your letter that she just took off without a word after her mother died in February. And you think she blamed herself for what happened that night. Does that also mean that she blamed herself for her mother's death? Because where was Bill in this, did he ever own up to his part?"

"Did we, Henry?"

"No." He prolonged his pronunciation as if unclear of Joseph's implication. "But we were not murderers, Joseph. What happened about the chap's body, Arthur Brown wasn't it? Why has he never been found, do they still just think he jilted his bride?"

"I think that's what was deduced, but who moved him, or where his body is, remains a mystery to those of us who know differently."

"Even at Christmas you know, when I was home, I kept wondering if the town constable would come knocking at our door. Anybody could have seen us there."

"I know Henry, I've had my moments of worry about it too, but if anybody had anything to say, I think it would have been said by now." He turned to look at Henry as he replied, but Henry was staring straight through the surface of the clear rippling water to its bed below as if straining to read the answers to his questions lurking there amongst the blurring pebbles.

"But Joseph, it doesn't make sense, if there was nothing to link Bill to any crime, why was Lizzibeth's mother so distressed?"

"I think it was the thought that her son was a murderer, Lizzibeth had told her everything, even though he wouldn't admit it. She just couldn't carry on with that knowledge. Besides that, she had to manage without Lizzibeth working for a living. You must feel accountable for that, making such a commotion on your way back into the house that night and wakening the dog and the household. Poor Lizzibeth was dismissed instantly. She came off worse than either of us, and yet we had drunk the most. We were only chastised for our drinking, and I was made to replace my Pa's bottle of whisky that we drank between us. But she lost her livelihood."

"I know, I did feel responsible, Joseph, of course I did, but I sent her some of my allowance regularly to make up for it."

"Henry, though that was undoubtedly thoughtful of you, there is more to dignity than having food on the table. Aggie Buxton was a very proud woman."

"So where do you think she went?"

"I don't know Henry. I kept thinking about the game we played, she always wanted to be the one going to Salisbury on account of Constable's painting of the Cathedral. She always admired it ever since it came here for an exhibition once. So

I wondered if she could have gone there. But Bill went off to London to find work after that night, and so that must be a possibility too. She made a big fuss of my birthday in January just before she left, so I did wonder if she may come back for yours, but I presume not as it's already past ten o'clock now." They both found themselves looking at the road to Salisbury, as if staring at it would produce the mirage of their choosing. Each had his own image of how she would look skipping down the road to surprise them both on her dear friend's birthday.

"We didn't realise what a bad decision we made to invite her to spend that evening with us, Joseph. She should have been back at the house and asleep in her bed. Then none of this would have happened. She would be here with us now threatening to push us off the bridge and into the river!" They both laughed at that thought, then Henry's face straightened taut as he remembered something else. "Do you think there was any truth in what Arthur said that night? I wouldn't like Mama or Papa to be in receipt of that particular rumour, where could it have originated from? If ever an enduring friendship was innocent, ours was. It was such an unjust remark."

"I know Henry, but people can find it difficult to understand friendships, they have to believe there must be some underlying decadence. We can sit here forever and it will not bring her back, but I do miss her, Henry, she's like a sister to me."

"I know, Joseph, me too. Let us try to think of something else. Tell me about this mystery gift you have for me."

"Oh, of course. Well, I have decided to make you a piece of furniture for your birthday. It is to be a very special piece, the one to firmly establish my proficiency as a Journeyman Cabinet Maker. It will be a Secretaire, Henry, I hope you approve." Henry's response of a delighted, sharp and yet prolonged intake of breath pleased Joseph.

"When will it be ready, Joseph, can I take it to my quarters, I will think of you often as I write to you on it."

"Oh, not for a long time yet. It must be perfectly finished. You may be a year older at least before you get it. All the joints must be faultless, and I have to learn the method of French Polishing to give it the perfect lasting finish. I will not give too much away, but I have to think of something unusual to make the piece my own, and I have decided to make a secret compartment for you. It will be with a hinge I have yet to design that will allow the leather inlay to lift slightly so you can store secret documents beneath it. How does that sound to you, Henry?"

"It sounds absolutely splendid, and so generous, Joseph, not like you at all!" He paused to field Joseph's playful punch. "Seriously, how can I thank you?"

"You have done so much for me, it is time I repaid you, Henry."

"Nonsense, Joseph, old chap, how boring would my life down here have been if it had not been for you and Lizzibeth, you will both always have a special place in my life, I just wish we had a clue as to where she is, then we could ride there and look for her." They gazed again towards the Salisbury road, legs swinging aimlessly over the water, words unnecessary, nostalgic for bygone summers and reverberating laughter. Adulthood so far had not disproved the theory that childhood claimed the best moments in life.

"Tell me about the Army then Henry, when do you start, I hope you have a long training period before you have to fight, then maybe this war in the Crimea will be over."

"I do not doubt that I will see some action there, Joseph, after what happened at Sinop, the Ottoman Fleet was annihilated. We have to respond to actions such as those, so it could be a long fight. I do have to train first though. I have been accepted as a Junior Officer at the Royal Engineer Establishment in Kent. I should be a Second Lieutenant as I leave to go into action. Mama is not happy about it all, as you can imagine, but it sounds a decent, noble and exciting challenge to me."

"Just don't go getting in the way of any musket fire will you, Henry, with Lizzibeth presently gone from our lives, you are the only friend I have left, I expect to see you at Christmas, if not before!"

"Oh, I do not intend to abandon my men half way through a battle, Joseph, I shall be there until the bitter end." He paused wondering himself how he would fare as a leader of men, then turning to Joseph, he asked,

"Tell me, when did you decide you wanted to wed Hannah?"

"I think it's been in my head for a while, Henry. We've always got on so well together. She's more serious than Lizzibeth, but very kind hearted, and she loves to read and learn too. She went to the town school you know, her father paid for her to go. She doesn't work, she's lucky that her parents don't need her to, but she helps out in lots of places in the town. She's been known to help with lambing season, vegetable picking, in the school and tending to the sick and aged. She has a kind heart there is no doubt. I'll be a very lucky man. Rose goes to the local school now you know. I'll do that too for any children of mine." He smiled wickedly at Henry and added. "Don't suppose I can ensure they'll save your children's lives and get it for free can I?" Unobserved by Joseph, Henry looked startled for an instant. Then he composed himself enough to supplement Joseph's absurdity, and prolong the enjoyment of their playful disposition on this day.

"The first thing I have to teach my children, Joseph, is how to ensure the safety of a tree before climbing it! Oh, and strictly no cats allowed! Failing that, make sure you or your children are passing by!" They both laughed long and loud for the first time today, reminiscent of carefree days just last year and for so many years before. Their hilarity was still causing them to rock precariously on the bridge wall, when Hannah came breathlessly and anxiously towards them, stilling their mirth.

"Joseph, Joseph, oh and Henry too, all the better, I thought you might be here. Lizzibeth's at our house, Bill has brought her, but she's in a bad way. She wants to see you both.

Joseph and Henry stood uncomfortably in the Thackery's

polished, perfect parlour. Mrs Thackery was facing them, her mouth was moving but they were both so much in shock from her first few words that the rest was not making any sense. She had explained that Bill had brought Lizzibeth to Hannah as her friend, to help her as her time approached. But she was in a weakened state. Bill had explained to her that they had been living in London, but Lizzibeth wanted to come back. He hadn't wanted to bring her until he had realised that she was with child. She had hidden it from him well, wanting to work as long as possible. He didn't want her with him in that state, any more than he wanted a child around, so he had agreed to bring her back. He wanted to return to London though, as soon as he knew she was recovered. "Truth be," she was impressing on them, "that the doctor says her ailment is actually the cholera, there is presently another outbreak in London, and in the area where they were living. She has been heaving her guts repeatedly, or else filling the pot, I doubt she will have the energy to bring the child. Her only hope is if she can beat the cholera first, and then rebuild some strength before her time comes."

Henry recovered first, "Was she married to a chap in London then Mrs Thackery?"

"Oh no, Master Henry, she's too far gone for it to have happened there, she didn't go 'til February." Joseph and Henry glanced at each other, to allow themselves time to absorb this information, Joseph then asked,

"Can we see her please?"

"She wants to see you both, I'll just go ahead and ensure it's appropriate."

Joseph and Henry walked uneasily and apprehensively into Lizzibeth's sick room, they tactfully tried not to react to the unspeakable unsanitary stench, as they turned to look at the small pale figure in the bed. In unison, despite themselves, they lilted cheerfully like seasoned thesbians, "Good-day Lizzibeth."

Her eyes unpeeled, then sparkled at the sight of them. "So good to see you both, you've no idea how I've missed you."

"You didn't need to miss us, if you'd only stayed here." Joseph interjected.

"But boys, this was the last straw for poor Ma," she indicated her swollen belly, "I had to take the shame away from the town and out of sight for the sake of her dear departed soul." She paused to draw more breath. "I had no work, had to find some. Didn't want this little mite to end up in the workhouse." Her sparkling eyes started to close with the effort of speech, her sentences were clipped and laboured, but she continued. "Where've you been spending your birthday Henry? I'd wanted to come to the bridge today, I thought you might both be there." She flashed them both a pitiable version of the familiar childish smile that had confidently crept unnoticed into womanhood, but was now plummeting perilously into death's dark vale of impending motherhood. Yet they were all children in this room. They were not prepared for such sadness and suffering amongst themselves. Henry replied enthusiastically as though reassurance could restore the day.

"That's exactly where we were Lizzibeth, we were waiting for you. Hoping you would come." He paused, realising how impossible that would have been. "But who has done this to you, why isn't he looking after you?" Henry's shocked expression had drained his pallor still further as he waited for his beloved chambermaid and friend to answer him. Joseph too was in deep shock, she shouldn't be suffering like this, how did Bill not notice before now? He should have brought her back sooner. He wondered where Bill was at this moment, in the Inn no doubt.

"I think we'd better let her sleep now gentlemen, you can come and see her later". Mrs Thackery had come back into the room, and was taking charge of her new responsibility, she liked Hannah having a friend in need to minister to. She was a slim smart lady of middle-age. A kind face nestled within a harsh hair-line which drew together tidily into a bun at the neat nape of her neck. Hannah had never gone out of her way to bring friends home before, but this one was indeed a challenge. As they all made to leave the room to appease this lady's bidding, Lizzibeth let out a cat-like wail, her body arching off the bed causing the simultaneous heaving of her wretched guts. "Oh no, her time's here, she doesn't have the strength, Hannah, go for the doctor, quickly. I'm sadly no stranger to these circumstances."

Joseph and Henry sat in total silence downstairs for what seemed like an eternity, but in truth only the afternoon had passed them by, and the sun was still visible through the small window. One of them would occasionally stand and pace around the room, on sitting back down, he was only to be replaced by his friend. There had been various comings and goings of a doctor that Henry insisted he would pay for, and a few local women experienced in the bringing of babies. Joseph broke the interminable silence first whilst rubbing his left eye unmercilessly. "Henry, I don't think I could put any wife of mine through this, it's unbearable. Poor Lizzibeth she's so young to bear this, she looked so sick."

"I just don't understand. Who could it have been Joseph, and how? We were with her most of the time, up until that night at least, I have no recollection of her mentioning a suitor. And please stop doing that to your eye, Joseph, it does not help. One of these days it will pop out of the back of your head." Joseph halted his fist, and looked up at Henry.

"Henry, can you remember what happened that night by the monument, I know it's only eight months ago, but I keep going over it, and I can't remember a thing. I just remember the incident, you know? Lizzibeth was obviously there, but whatever else may have happened, I certainly have no memory of. Do you?"

"No, Joseph, we had both drunk so much, Lizzibeth had too. I only remember what happened when Arthur came across the road. You are surely not suggesting either of us...."

"I don't know, Henry, I just don't know."

Their discourse continued, but was at length interrupted by the sound of a baby's cry. They both jumped up as Hannah came into the room. "The baby has survived, a girl, she's very small, but well. Lizzibeth though, is very weak, the doctor says only a miracle can save her. Cholera on its own is deadly enough without what she has just gone through too, but she's asking to see you both."

"No, no, Hannah, no. She can't die Hannah, she has only just come back to us." Joseph was rooted to the spot, his eyes pleading with Hannah as though the outcome was her decision. Henry put his arm around his shoulders, and lead him towards the stairs which would return them to the overpowering sick room.

Like two errant schoolboys, Joseph and Henry stood once more at the foot of Lizzibeth's bed. Kate Thackery stood on the far side of the bed, slowly shaking her head, as if recognising the imminence of sorrow. Henry's soft crowned brown hat was held respectfully in front of his chest, both hands rolling the brim unmercifully. Joseph as if in support, was screwing his cap cruelly into a roll. She was laid awkwardly on one side as though to minimise discomfort. Joseph thought how beautiful she looked despite her desperate predicament. The baby was by her side in the crook of her arm, wrapped in a familiar beige cashmere coat at her mother's insistence. Lizzibeth gazed lovingly at her daughter, cooing senseless noises to her as though there was no-one else in the room.

Thin tears trickled lazily down her sunken cheeks, reminding Joseph of that other occasion when her tears made him uncomfortable, now he wished for that day, it was nothing compared to this.

"Betsy Agatha," she whispered softly, "you're so perfect. You have everything you need, ten little fingers, ten little toes, the sweetest little mouth and nose. Your hair is so soft, and I just know you're going to be so clever and with such a fine disposition. All that and beauty too, you'll have a charmed life. The only thing you will be missing little one, is a mother to love you, care for you and teach you. For I'm not to be spared to see you grow to the bright young girl you will be." Her voice became thin and faint "But I want you to know that as I die, I willingly give you my life, for I wanted so desperately to give life to you. You're a celebration of my most deep affection for your dear Papa here." She paused to gather her next words economically together as little Betsy reached her newborn fist aimlessly to her mother's mouth assisting the words as they struggled to alight, and catching her tears as they dripped weakly onto her tiny fingers. "I love you dearly little one with all my heart. These people here will make sure you know that, won't you?" She paused to summon the effort to collect up her reddened dark eyes and engage her audience appealingly, whispering loudly now, "Hannah, you will won't you? Please? I implore you."

Hannah was busy distracting herself by gently stroking stray sweat soaked curls away from Lizzibeth's eyes. She looked around the room at the whole company. All unseeing glistening eyes were leaning towards Lizzibeth, ears reluctantly straining to hear her dying words yet wondering how this scene could humanly be borne. Hannah discretely wiped her eyes. But too late to prevent one bulbous energetic tear from splashing onto Betsy's forehead and rolling towards her nose as if beginning the baptismal cross; but veering at the bridge to run down its side poignantly, as though shed from the babe's own eye in sad response to her mother's moving oratory. "Hannah?"

"Yes Lizzibeth, of course I'll tell her, I'm sure she knows already, she can see and feel it now as you hold her." As if Lizzibeth's light was suddenly re-kindled, she tenderly kissed the baby's head and in a clear voice performed to her gallery for one last time, weakly attempting to proffer little Betsy to the crowd.

"From my nest of spices, here is our very own little Phoenix. Thank you for giving her to me, now I offer her back to you as the most precious gift of all. Take good care of her, I love you so much." The last words were barely audible as she slowly sank back lifelessly onto the bed, her eyes open but empty. Hannah jolted forwards instinctively to rescue the baby. Loud groans of distress exploded from Joseph and Henry simultaneously, both heads dropped into their hands as if the timing had been precisely rehearsed. The sorrow was too much for them to bear in their young and blessed lives. Lizzibeth had been no stranger to tragedy, but they had no template with which to draw from, they were distraught.

For each of her dearest friends, the presence of the other, in the end, prevented either from rushing forward and comforting her journey as she left them for another world.

"I can't believe what has just happened Henry, I just can't." Joseph was stood leaning against the tree trunk outside the Thackery's house, he was not ashamed of the tears rolling freely down his face. Henry was sat on the low wall to one side, his head bowed to veil his grief, ineffectual now for his emotion was evident in his wet words.

"What do you suppose she meant Joseph, who's the baby's father?"

"Well in my estimation, I think she was obviously referring to one of us, but as neither of us has any memory of that night Henry, who's to say? Are you sure you can't remember anything, about either of us?"

"Just that we were more affected by drink than we have ever been before."

Hannah stepped out of the front door holding the baby still wrapped in the elegant cashmere coat. "Well while my mother is busy starting to scrub the house clean to ensure none of us gets cholera, would you mind telling me which one of you is this little mite's father? Obviously and quite selfishly I hope it is you, Henry, not least on account of not wanting to begin married life with my husband deceiving me."

"That's what we've just been discussing Hannah," Joseph

replied, "it sounded that way, but although we know of one night when it's possible it may have happened, neither of us have any recollection of the events that took place on account of us all being so drunk. It's too awful to think about, whoever it was, has killed Lizzibeth."

"The cholera killed her Joseph, not the baby."

"If you ask me I think they both 'ad a go." They all turned to see the figure of a huge man step out of the alleyway, and recognised Bill immediately. Joseph and Henry made to remonstrate with him when Hannah stopped them.

"Explain yourself Bill, what do you mean?"

"Well, when I came out of the Inn, the night Lizzibeth was finished from the Big House. 'E was buttoning 'imself up, and 'e had 'is hands all over her, while she was making 'erself decent. I knew no good would come of that night."

Joseph digested this information, was that really what he had seen, he couldn't imagine that Bill would have a motive to lie about this?

Joseph moved towards Hannah, and lifting the coat slightly, he peeked tentatively in at the baby's face. As he did so, two small heavy bags fell out of the inside pocket. He picked them up.

"They're full of half crowns. Where did she get so much money from?"

"Let me see?" Henry jumped forwards. "That's what I sent her every week when she was first dismissed from the house. Joseph, why didn't she use it to take better care of herself?"

"I'll take that for me trouble!"

Bill had stepped forwards and snatched one of the bags from Joseph's dazed hand.

Calmly, but purposefully, Hannah leant towards Bill and retrieved the bag.

"Actually Bill, Lizzibeth mentioned she had saved money for the baby. I didn't know what she meant, but now…." She broke off to gaze into the sleeping infant's face. Joseph moved to her shoulder, aware of her emotion, and looked down at

Lizzibeth's legacy.

"Hannah's right, Bill, I think little Betsy Agatha here, will need this more than anyone."

Bill, unused to being challenged due largely to his over-bearing size, meekly accepted his chastisement from this mere slip of a girl.

Henry was beginning to feel nervous at the implications of tonight's events on his future. His own money as a trust fund for Lizzibeth's child unnerved him. "I don't know what you were hoping to gain peering at the child anyway Joseph, I don't think the answer lies in the face of a baby less than an hour old, don't they all look like Sir Robert Peel anyway!"

"Henry!" Joseph admonished. "I'm sure she'll be the image of Lizzibeth in time. But isn't this, your coat, Henry, it was new that very night we went out drinking?"

"I thought it was 'is," Bill spoke out. "I took it with me that night, and we 'ad it with us in London."

"Yes it is mine," replied Henry "I wondered what had happened to it, I remember we were all sat on it on the fire monument at one point that night."

Swapping her own shawl to cover the baby and removing the coat, Hannah pointed to one side of it. "Well it has been puked on, the smell still lingers. But there are other suspicious looking stains too. Were these there before you took it Bill?"

"Must 'ave been 'coz Lizzibeth would never let me use it in London, it's still as I took it away with me on that night."

"Perhaps then, if you two can remember which one of you threw up, then perhaps that is the same one of you responsible for the other stains. I don't believe your implications Bill. But one of you two has fathered a child and this poor little mite is already motherless, she should at least be claimed by her father." She threw the coat angrily down on the grass mound beside them and gazed questioningly at Betsy as though an intense study of her cherubic moonlit face might reveal the perpetrator.

In the silence following Hannah's revelations, a light sobbing became audible. "She's dead then?" Bill sat slumped on the ground with his head in his hands. In as many years, he had lost all three members of his family. Joseph tended to him saying they would help him in any way they could, he could go home with him tonight, his Ma wouldn't mind him sleeping on their fireside chair. Bill nodded, and as all three men silently tried to absorb the dark tribulations of this day, a horse and cart pulled up outside the house. "What is this?" Henry enquired.

"It'll be the men from the pauper's graveyard to take the body away," Hannah replied, "Ma sent the boy next door to get them, she wants to clean the bedroom thoroughly as soon as possible."

"Over my dead body." Henry screeched, then turning to the two men on the cart he added, "You will not go anywhere near her do you hear, fetch the undertaker from the town, and tell him Henry Ferguson sent you."

"But Henry, what will you tell your father, he won't pay the bill."

"He will not need to, Joseph, I can see to it myself now, I have means of my own as of today. Oh, Joseph, I forgot what time is it? I am supposed to be home for my birthday dinner at eight!"

"It's only seven Henry, you have time." Then as if prompted by the mention of Henry's birthday, Joseph added, "It's a coincidence that Lizzibeth's baby is born on your birthday Henry, isn't it? We'll sadly have a permanent reminder of this dreadful day."

Betsy Agatha began to cry, and Hannah sighed deeply giving the men an exasperated look, whilst cooing at the baby. "I'll have to go and sort this hungry little one out, but when I come back, I still want an answer from you two. There's a little girl's future at stake here." They watched with anguish as Hannah instead of Lizzibeth, rocked the swaddled infant in her arms.

Once she had taken her leave and was safely inside, Joseph composed himself and asked Bill the question they had both wondered about.

"Bill, what happened to Arthur's body?" Bill looked up at Joseph and Henry, bereavement had left him devoid of further aggravation for them.

"Didn't Lizzibeth tell you? I dragged him all the way home by the back of his jacket. No-one saw. When Ma saw him I told her I had found 'im like that, but that I didn't want any blame so I was gonna scarper. She hid 'is body 'til the next night. Then her and Lizzibeth, who'd been finished by then and was back home, dragged 'is body to the empty warehouse on Orchard Street and set it alight. They put the bottle in the fire too, so there was nothing to tell what happened. That's where Ma got 'er bad chest, from the smoke fumes, she never really recovered according to Lizzibeth, but t'was her own shameful news that finished 'er off in the end. They apparently thought the bones were a drunken vagrant sleeping rough that chose his bed unwisely, or else was careless with his warming fire, and that Arthur ran scared of marriage and fatherhood. No-one connected the two events. But I still 'ave to live with what I did, t'isn't easy, especially coming back here."

Joseph and Henry marvelled at the bravery of Lizzibeth and her Ma, all to protect Bill, and themselves too. Joseph wondered how much Lizzibeth had told her Ma, could she have known who had fathered little Betsy?

Henry agitated about the time, he didn't want his parents to ask too many questions.

"You go on back Henry, why don't you take my horse Bill, then Henry can take it back from our cottage. You can go in and tell Ma what has happened to Lizzibeth. That's all though, don't go saying things you don't know to be true. I need to talk to Hannah, she may want to break off our betrothal, who could blame her?"

"I'll go for now Joseph Elliot," he turned away to mount the steed being offered by Henry, but never leaving Joseph's gaze, he paused. "But I'll be back for the child soon, she is my kin with certainty, and you appear to have no idea whether or not she's yours!" As if to illustrate his menace, he returned to snatch the coat from the grass, in a defiant and threatening gesture. And then he was gone.

Joseph knocked on the door of their cottage. Hannah opened it. Her mother was sat on a chair feeding the baby some milk from a small wooden spoon, she looked very upset. "Your father won't like it Hannah, he'll be home soon, he did say he would be late with letting Joseph have a day off for Master Henry's birthday, what a day he's missed. Don't be long."

"I won't Ma, but Joseph and I have to talk."

"Hannah, I will understand if."

"Hush Joseph, I think I have the right to speak first. No matter how bad life ever gets, I will always remember tonight and count my blessings. No mother should ever have to go through the pain of bringing a child into the world, only to leave it themselves. It's too cruel and brutal for them. Too sad and heartbreaking to witness. Poor, poor Lizzibeth, her suffering now is over, God rest her soul, God bless her child."

They set off to walk along Dorset Road towards the town, and Hannah openly wept as she walked, the ordeal had taken its toll on her too. Joseph was too unsure of his position in her thoughts to risk comforting her and provoking rejection. He felt awkward, alone and inadequate, not for the first time tonight. A teardrop flowed unexpectedly from his left eye to rest momentarily on the mound of his cheek like a Pierrot clown and he quickly wiped it away, unnoticed.

Hannah composed herself after a few hundred yards and began.

"Joseph, from the facts as we know them limited though they are, it would seem that either you or Henry have fathered a child. The fact that neither of you can remember is worrying. I suspect, indeed I am sure, that the culprit knows only too well who he is. Ah, don't interrupt me please." She pulled some leafy foliage off a tree and began pruning it as she spoke. "Realistically, Henry could never admit such a deed, nor would he or his family accept such a child, and out of wedlock too, though he does not have a betrothal to lose. On the other hand you do, which would be your motive for any loss of memory. Ah, no interrupting, Joseph, please. However, Lizzibeth was our friend, her child needs a home and parents to love her. We're due to be wed very soon. I suggest that we see if the marriage can be brought forward, our cottage is empty now, we could move in next week if the Reverend is free for the service. The Banns have already been posted. Betsy Agatha need then know nothing of her tragedy until she's a grown woman and can be told the true sadness of her birth. I'll keep my promise to Lizzibeth one day, and tell Betsy how much her mother loved and wanted her."

Her bouquet was now reduced to a single twig, which she snapped and discarded in the hedgerow as if demonstrating the injustice of these events. "My mother's not happy, she saw Betsy as a chance for her to have another child, without the hazards of childbirth. But that's not what Lizzibeth would have wanted. Whichever of you she loved, she would know that Henry could not raise her and would want you to do it. I optimistically called Lizzibeth my friend, but I know she had no love for me, she knew I had your affection and hated me for it. Yet when she needed help, she came to me. I respect her for accepting my friendship in her hour of need, despite her knowledge of your feelings for me." They had reached the marketplace, and Joseph had listened in silence.

"Well, Joseph, what do you think?"

Joseph halted; he was incredulous at this astonishing girl beside him and spoke into the now dusky summer sky. "The problem may be if Bill decides to come for her, he threatened to take her as he was her only definite kin. We can hope that never happens, Lizzibeth would not choose for Bill to be Betsy's guardian. Your solution sounds all very orderly, Hannah, where's the disadvantage for me. It seems too good to be true; to be entrusted with Lizzibeth's child on the occasion of her death is an honour to our friendship, regardless of the identity of the baby's father. If this is a genuine proposal, then you're indeed a remarkable woman Hannah Thackery." He turned to face her, but paused in his intended kiss, as the inscription on the fire monument leapt out at him from the corner of his eye.

"Soon to be Hannah Elliot you mean." She giggled, then when the expected kiss did not reach its destination, she opened her eyes and enquired, "What is it Joseph." She followed his gaze to the inscribed words he was digesting.

"I think we can say that proves the theory that Betsy was conceived that night, and right here on this monument too, Hannah, do you remember her last words?"

"Now then Mrs Hannah Isabella Elliot, what do you think to married life so far?"

Hannah stood in front of the window in the small hotel room looking at her husband. With the sunlight behind her, she appeared ghostly and ethereal in her white wedding dress. Her tight and shapely corset was skirted elegantly in linen. Her mother had quickly finished it for her over the last week. Its long waist travelled symmetrically forwards over her flat belly pointing at the floor between her feet. Two long pointed starched lace lapels threaded with ribbons dripped from her neck and throat. Separate undersleeves trimmed with bows escaped from beneath simple wide pagoda sleeves. The skirt was held wide by a single hoop threaded into the lining.

Her Ma had promised to make her the full and newly fashionable crinoline frame for her wedding dress, but bringing the marriage date forwards had caused her to compromise on some aspects of her dream wedding. Her father had bought her mother a machine for sewing. It made sewing the seams much faster. But after a lifetime of hand-sewing her mother was distrustful of her new toy expecting the stitches to fall apart. And in her eyes, a garment as critical as a wedding dress, should not have been its maiden creation.

Her two bridesmaids Louiza and Rose had to make do with

wearing their Sunday best outfits as there had been no time to make dresses for them.

Hannah still held the posy of wild flowers in her hands that she had carried down the aisle of St Peter and St Paul's church this morning on her father's arm.

Her fair complexion was so creamy and delicate, with big sea blue eyes enhanced by the gilded outline of her long strawberry lashes and fine hair that framed her features so perfectly. It was decorated today with white roses arranged in a virginal wreath placed proudly atop the golden ringlets that danced loosely like soft shiny springs. Little beige dots sprinkled her nose to show the sun had seen her too.

Joseph loved her so much, but never before had he appreciated her exquisite beauty as much as in this moment, but synonymously in his own anxiety, she also looked a fragile, breakable vision to him. He was still incredulous at the forgiving nature of this woman over the last week. He turned away from her before she answered, as if afraid of the reply.

"Well Mr Elliot, I think it's just fine. Our parents gave us a wonderful send off, didn't they? They've all been so kind and understanding."

Henry's parents had given them a honeymoon night in a Hotel on the coast for a wedding present, and they had been driven to it in the Landau by Joseph's father. Hannah's parents were taking care of Betsy for the night. Her mother had come to terms with the position of Grandmother as opposed to mother. Jacob Thackery had been dumbfounded when he returned from work that night, but had adjusted slowly to the situation throughout the week. His beloved Hannah was happy, she had taken to motherhood so easily. What more could he want for her.

The Reverend had christened Betsy Agatha in the same service today and Henry had made his promises as Godfather. All wrongs had seemed righted on this happy occasion. Lizzibeth would live on in her child.

Betsy's possible paternity revelations were not shared with

anyone outside of the Thackery's front bedroom on the evening of her birth. Joseph and Hannah were hailed as true and kind hearted souls to take on the child of a friend as if their very own. Many who knew the friends, including their respective families had many and varied suspicions regarding the truth, but they were discrete, and wished them well. Lizzibeth and her family had been well liked in the town, and pitied for their misfortune.

Joseph wandered around the room, nervously picking up and replacing objects, then stopped at the window to look out to sea. The view was stunning, he thought how wonderful it would be to live by the sea.

He mused over the news this week that a water pump in Broad Street had been identified as the cause of the spread of cholera in the Soho area of London. Bill had said that was where they had been staying. Removal of the handle so water could not be drawn from that pump had stopped the outbreak. If only, if only. The Public Health Act sparked by these very problems, and passed only six years previously, had done nothing to help his Lizzibeth. He jolted out of his thoughts at the sound of his wife's soft voice.

"Husband of mine, you've just promised to love me and honour me, why are you avoiding attending me." She laid her bouquet on the table and sat down on the side of the bed, her eyes resting on her now empty hands fidgeting in her lap. Joseph turned to look at her.

"Hannah, I can't get the night of Betsy's birth out of my head, I never want to put you through that. My Pa warned me to be careful, and once wed, not to be so demanding of a wife that she's in the family way more often than is good for her. That's why I can't imagine that if I had erm, you know, with Lizzibeth, that I wouldn't remember. But I'm not sure I want to put you in the family way at all." Hannah looked up at him then, relieved that his problem was not so much actually attending her, but rather with the possible consequences. "That night was awful, Hannah, what if childbirth is as bad for you. We do have one child to bring up already."

"Yes Joseph we do, and she's adorable. I will never be able to say no to those big blue eyes of hers. I've changed my mind too since that night, I really hope she's yours, and not Henry's child. I feel that would make her more 'ours'. I'm sure she has your cheeky dimples too, I know she can't smile yet, but you can see they're there. Henry's more than relieved and happy to have the role of Godfather, which I know he'll take very seriously. I also know Lizzibeth adored you, but in the end she also trusted me, we need to make her proud and glad that she chose us to care for her beloved child. I believe she did that, Joseph, when she came to me. Don't you? I also pray that Bill has neither the intention nor any ability to look after her despite his idle threat."

She smiled at him then, and he at her. Then added, "I miss her already, Joseph, don't you? But I don't want to inflict a lonely childhood on her like I endured, simply on account of a fear akin to my father's. I can't pretend not to have my own trepidation about this part of our marriage, but I know you are a gentle man, Joseph."

Realising Joseph may take a little coaxing, she climbed onto the middle of the bed, hoisting her dress to allow the manoeuvre. She changed her tone and demeanour from one of quiet assertiveness, to the coquetry of an amateur seductress, and smiling at her husband softly purred, "Now, if you've a mind to love your wife at all, and consummate what will be a long and wonderfully happy marriage, then come over here now Mr Joseph Zachariah Elliot, and see that it is done!"

Chapter 9

Dorset, December 1856

Joseph stood at his bedroom window looking out over the hedgerows on Orchard Street towards the town square and the market place. In an hour or so it would be full of people and wares. The silence would be replaced with exuberant noise, a combination of indecipherable chatter both animal and human, and the rolling rumble of carts on the cobbles.

For now Joseph was glad it was quiet, Betsy was still asleep in her room, and Hannah was in blissful slumber with their baby's crib at her side. He crept back towards the crib, a masterpiece in light oak, over which Jacob and Joseph had lovingly toiled together. Looking up at him from such comfort was his new baby son Thomas Henry Elliot, only two hours into this world. Joseph smiled, he had not expected him to be awake and so peaceful. He offered him his finger to grasp in his palm, Thomas took it, and waved it as if formally greeting his father. Joseph looked at Hannah still sleeping serenely, and leant down to scoop his son into his arms. He took him to the window to show him his birthplace, but Thomas' eyes were fixed on his father. Baby blue eyes engaged the adult emerald ones with a promise to copy them exactly over the coming weeks. Dimples were already evident, there was no need to smile, and the dark curls escaping the warming bonnet were all Joseph's. Hannah had been so right, their son was an absolute miniature of his father.

Joseph felt a flood of emotion for this child he knew for sure he had created. He loved little Betsy so much, she was an absolute delight to them all. An enchanting and appealing little girl. So like Lizzibeth in her demeanor and with such natural charisma, yet so angelic in her appearance. He could not imagine loving any other child more. But the knowledge that he had without doubt fathered Thomas, and had watched him grow inside his wife's body over recent months, added wonderment and awe to this otherwise familiar emotion. That his beloved wife had survived the ordeal, and indeed had made light of it to him, added to the pleasure and contentment of this moment.

"What're you thinking, Joseph?" He looked round at Hannah, she was propping herself up on the bed, her struggle to do so defining her discomfort.

"Wait, Hannah, I'll help you, how are you feeling?"

"I'm fine, Joseph, what were you thinking about just then? You were miles away." Joseph had replaced Thomas in his crib and helped to prop his wife on her bolster. He sat down gently on the bed, and took her hand in his own.

"I was thinking that I'm the luckiest man alive Hannah Elliot, my wife is so clever to produce such a fine son for us, are you sure you're alright, he looks a big baby to me?"

"That's just because you remember Betsy, she was born a little early. Whereas, his lordship there was so comfortable in here," she paused to indicate and then marvel at her already shrunken belly, "that he decided to do a bit more growing before showing himself to us!" They both smiled and simultaneously looked into the crib. Thomas was still awake and gurgling with his fist in his mouth. Hannah continued, "He was worth waiting for don't you think husband? I told you two years ago we should've gone up to the chalk man at Cerne Abbas. But no. Load of nonsense you said, old wife's tale. How would visiting some chalk on a hill help us to make a child you said. Well?"

"And I still say the same good wife! It's nonsense! A pure coincidence that we happened to conceive him after a walk over that way." Hannah sat open mouthed at her husband's scepticism.

"Over that way, we walked all over him, it's a wonder there was any chalk left." She laughed at her husband. Lovingly accepting his tender, affectionate and playful embrace realizing she would never convince him that Thomas had been created by anything other than his exceptional virility. But for her, when she was ready for another child, she would without doubt be heading for the insurance of the Cerne Abbas Giant once again.

"How do you think Betsy will feel when she awakes and has some competition for our affections? It'll be hard for her, she's had complete attention from doting parents, grandparents, and godparents for two and a half years now, but I think she'll love the company too."

"I think, Hannah my dear, that when you are recovered from your ordeal, you should take Betsy to the market and buy something nice for you both, and let her choose something for this bruiser here too, that should make her feel less threatened by his arrival."

"Joseph are you quite well? Giving us money to be frivolous with, you must be sickening for something!" Hannah sneaked a wry smile at her husband, landing a playful punch on his arm.

"Well if that's the way you feel, perhaps it can stay hidden away, and you shall have nothing!" He feigned a stern voice, then placing a loving kiss on her forehead, bid her rest and sleep before their son demanded refreshment and attention. He left them alone and went to nap in Betsy's room for a couple of hours to distract her when she awoke, allowing mother and baby some precious time alone together.

Joseph was seated in the kitchen in front of the warm range. Betsy was on his knee dozing after waking early and wanting a drink. She had been a little confused to see her Pa in the room with her, but had been too sleepy to question him.

Joseph's cup runneth over this morning. He had his precious daughter curled up on his knee, and his beautiful wife and newborn son asleep in his bedroom. In addition he had completed his apprenticeship and was now sharing in the profits of his father-in-law's business. To add to all that, his dear friend Henry was due back from the medical base in Kent soon and may be considering coming out of the army altogether. He thought that his world was already perfect, but how wonderful it would be for Henry to take a wife, and have his children close by enough to play and frolic with his own. He had missed Henry's friendship since he had joined the army, but he did appreciate that it could be a very different Henry that returned to Dorset after his battlefield ordeals.

Joseph had followed the graphic reports of the war through the writings of the Times journalist William Russell. He had described horrible deaths through disease in inadequate hospitals despite all the efforts of Nurse Nightingale in trying to eliminate unsanitary conditions. He had spoken to the Master just yesterday up at the house when he delivered a new bookcase to them. Charles Ferguson had told Joseph that Henry had had a terrible time at the Siege of Sevastopol in the Ukraine, especially in this final and successful battle. He would not even talk about it, and although the whole war in the Crimean area was now over thanks to that very assault, he did not want to risk being sent back. Ever. His injuries had been less than most. Many of his men had died, if not in battle, then at the hospital at Scutari on the Bosphorus afterwards. Henry had been lucky, he had been spared, despite receiving a bullet wound in his right leg which had once again shattered his thigh bone. This time it had healed quickly, but his resulting limp would be enough for him to be medically discharged, rather than resigning his commission.

Joseph pondered on how proud he would be in showing off his new son to Henry, and wouldn't he be so astonished when he saw the change in his little goddaughter. She was so like Lizzibeth in everything she did, she questioned every instruction, barged through life at a phenomenal pace, and already showed all the signs of a wicked sense of humour.

Joseph could feel Betsy stirring on his knee, she would be as lively as a kitten in a few minutes. He hoped his mother-in-law would not be too long, he had asked the Doctor last night to call and tell her the news so she would come and help Hannah with the baby. He knew Jacob would manage without him for a couple of days so he could spend some time with Betsy to allow Hannah to recuperate fully. He could take his little angel out to look for a Christmas tree. They had not bothered with one before, Betsy was too young, and they had spent previous Christmas days between his parents and Hannah's so there had seemed little point.

"Pa, what's zis?" Betsy was holding up a little toy snowman.

"It's a snowman dear. Let's hang him from this branch here. Say snowman for me." Joseph had bought the small table top Christmas tree for their front parlour, and a few glittery toys to adorn it. He hoped Hannah would be pleased when she came downstairs tomorrow, she loved Christmas and would overlook its early arrival in their house. It was another week until Christmas Eve. She had been amazing in her recovery, and three day old baby Thomas was thriving. His big sister loved to cuddle him and help to gently wind him.

Betsy made her best attempt to pronounce the new word. "Well done, dearest. Now, where shall we put these last jingle bells?"

"Dair Pa." Betsy pointed to a branch near the very front of the tree, a prestigious position implying these were indeed a favourite.

"Time to get some lunch Betsy, how would you like some bread and jam, or there is some milk jelly left from yesterday? Then you can put your hat and coat on and play outside in the yard if you like, Pa will come out with you."

Joseph sat on the wall of their yard outside watching a muffled

Betsy load up her iron trolley with toy wooden bricks and animals. The air was cold, and Betsy's small lungs blew a cloud of dew into the air with every excited breath. A friend of Aggie and Frank Buxton's had rescued this old trolley for their own child from the Buxton's yard after Aggie had died, but had since brought it around for Lizzibeth's daughter to have. Joseph thought how sad and poignant that the most precious possession Betsy could possibly own in her life was this trolley, for it had been played with by her own mother a generation before and forged by the very hands of her own maternal grandfather. Yet how could he instill such a precious value upon a two year old child, to teach her to cherish it rather than bashing it around the yard as if it were to be discarded. He reconciled the robust nature of the metal and its consequent longevity despite battle-scars and smiled at her imaginative game. Lizzibeth would have approved her boisterous passion and fervor in all she did.

"How's my new Grandson then Joseph Elliot?" Jacob Thackery was approaching him purposefully, carrying a spray of winter flowers.

"He's just fine Pa Thackery. You've taken your time coming, he's four days old already, but don't you look delightful with your posy?"

"Yes, well, erm, I didn't pick them myself, I bought them from the market, nothing but the best for my Hannah. How is she? I wanted to wait until she was recovered a little before I came."

"She's well Pa, she's an extraordinary woman your daughter."

"Granpa, Granpa, look dair."

"What is it Betsy, have you got a truck of animals for your Grandpa?" Jacob squatted down next to Betsy and helped her to load and unload the bricks. He then began building a tower absentmindedly with her whilst discussing the current orders in the workshop with his son-in-law.

Joseph stood up from his recline on the wall of their yard and made for the door.

"Are you coming in to see baby Thomas then Pa Thackery, I'd

love to say he is the image of you, but sorry, he's a chip off this old block instead!"

Jacob slapped his back good naturedly and chuckled, "We'll see Joseph, we'll see, they change you know!"

Joseph turned to Betsy, "Come on inside Betsy, you can't stay out there on your own."

Betsy followed him inside taking the animals with her, she took them to play in front of the warm range. "Play here Pa".

"You stay there then dearest, while I go upstairs with your Grandpa. He wants to say 'good-day' to your new little brother. I'll be back down again in a moment."

Betsy sat down to play, pulling off her bonnet as she warmed. "Where doggy?" She asked herself, then remembering exactly how Grandpa had balanced him on the top of the tower, she went to the door. It was still slightly ajar, allowing her to slip back outside. Ma let her do that sometimes as long as she came straight back in again. She made straight for the wooden tower at the far side of the yard, but just as she approached, a hand reached over the low wall and snatched the toy dog.

"Peepo, Betsy." The little dog appeared again over the top of the wall, then disappeared. Betsy giggled and waited, watching intently for the encore.

"Peepo Betsy." Betsy giggled again, and wandered to the opening in the wall to look behind it. There was a big man holding out her toy dog.

"Here you are dear."

As Betsy stepped forwards to take her toy, the big man scooped her up in his arms and ran hastily from Orchard Road, heading away from the town, with a surprised and alarmed Betsy shouting for her Pa over his shoulder.

"Don't you think he's the very double of Joseph, Pa, even his eyes seem to have changed already to a greeny-blue now?"

"I'm afraid I do dearest daughter, I didn't want to, ugly brute that your husband is, but there's no denying it Hannah!"

"Think hard what that says of your Grandson Pa, he's beautiful."

"You know I'm teasing daughter, he's a beautiful child indeed, perfect, well done to both of you. I can't begin to explain my relief that you are safe Hannah, it's been such a worry to me. Are you going to call him by his full name, won't that be confusing with your father Joseph."

"Thank you Pa." Joseph took the congratulatory handshake offered by his father-in-law, then bent to kiss his wife. "I'd thought of that, what do you think to Thom, Hannah? With an 'h'. There will be no dropping of 'h's in our household!"

"That's fine by me Joseph, your friend will be proud of you, not to mention his mother!" They both laughed, Jacob did not share the joke, but did also not intrude on their obviously private mirth. Henry had previously shared the incident with his mother on the day of his departure to school. Since then, the subject of dropping 'h's, had been a source of great amusement to them all, with Henry mimicking his mother's revulsion, at every opportunity.

"I'd better get back to that daughter of ours and make sure she hasn't built a farm in our absence, are you coming Pa Thackery."

"Yes Joseph, I'll follow you down." He kissed his daughter's cheek and the two men descended the stairs, Joseph talking to Betsy as he did so. He walked to the range and picked up her bonnet, "come on scallywag, are you hiding from Pa?" Joseph was making a game of looking behind the obvious places as he had done so many times before, she loved to play 'peepo' with him. But Jacob had noticed the door ajar and was making for the yard. "Joseph, she must've come back out here, the dog has gone from the tower, I know I left it there when we came in."

"Oh my God Jacob, where is she?" Joseph was hyperventilating loudly, panic welling up so much that he felt he would choke.

"She can't have got far, you go that way and I'll go this, we'll find her, calm down Joseph, children wander off all the time, someone always brings them back." But for some reason Joseph had a sick feeling in the pit of his stomach.

Thomas Elliot was driving the Landau towards the market with the Mistress cocooned warmly inside.

"I won't be too long today Thomas, so if you will just wait at this end of the market, I will return as quickly as I possibly can, but I must have everything perfect this Christmas for Henry's arrival."

"Of course M'Lady, I shall wait in the usual place."

Thomas was used to passing walkers along this road as it was the main road into town, but this fellow looked familiar to him, his size was distinctive, it must be Bill Buxton, he didn't know he was back? As the Landau drew nearer, Thomas could see Bill was looking uncomfortable, and was carrying a large bundle. "Excuse me M'Lady, can I offer some help, this is Lizzibeth Buxton's brother Bill."

"If you must Thomas, but be quick about it, I have a lot to do." Thomas saw Bill having a tussle with his bundle, indeed almost admonishing it, it must be very heavy, or else a very awkward shape to carry.

"Hey Bill, how are you doing? When did you get back, is everything alright? Can we take your load anywhere for you?" Bill looked dazed, he answered yes and no monosyllabically, but refused any help.

"Meeting someone, need to get going. Good day to you Mr Elliot."

Thomas blinked thinking the cold was getting to him, he was sure the load on Bill's back, wrapped in a beige wool coat, had moved. He supposed he had poached something from the estate, but not been very good at the kill. He decided to get on his way before Bill was landed in trouble if M'Lady got suspicious.

"If you're sure then Bill, why don't you call in on Mary, she'd love to see you."

Bill had not expected to receive empathy and kindness in view of what he was doing. He nodded and gave a half smile before continuing quickly on his way, he needed to get a move on before Betsy was found to be missing.

Thomas pulled up the horses as he reached the edge of the marketplace and helped Henrietta to alight from her carriage. She assured him again whilst adjusting her coat and bonnet that she would not be long. Then she swished away in her enormous festooned and decorative crinoline to collect her vital supplies. He mused as he climbed back up to the drivers box that she would have difficulty in fitting through some of the doorways in that dress, he was sure she could hide two men beneath it! She reminded him of some of the Christmas trees shown in town squares lately, so ornate with ribbons and bows. But pleasing to the eye too. He had noticed his Mary too was wearing a hoop in her petticoat these days, and he liked it. She was still a very handsome woman if a little on the plump side, but what could he expect after bearing him four children.

His mind switched back to Bill, he was still feeling uneasy about him when Jacob Thackery came running over towards him.

"Thomas, Betsy's gone missing, Joseph's frantic, seems to think someone may have taken her, silly question really, but you haven't seen her have you?"

Thomas was off his drivers box in an instant, and began unhooking one of the pair from the harness. "Can you stay with the carriage Jacob, and explain to M'Lady when she comes back, I think I may well have just seen her." Thomas was astride the horse and leaving the marketplace before he had finished speaking. He left at such speed that his top hat flew across the carriage to land jauntily over one arrogant ear of the remaining carriage horse to the hilarity of the ignorant and oblivious marketplace.

* * *

Bill was walking very hastily past the entrance to Bramble House, conscious of not wanting Mary to see him from the coachman's cottage. He put his head down and was about to increase his speed past what he knew to be their kitchen window when he heard the sound of galloping horse's hooves coming from behind him. He quickly darted behind the hedge, staying below the level of the window and hidden from the road. He off-loaded Betsy and turned her away from him with his large hand chillingly over her mouth. She had not been able to make any sound since they had reached the marketplace, her shouting and sobbing had been such that she had no volume left at all. Now she felt the heaviness of this big man's threatening hand over her small face and tried to call for her Ma. She was puzzled as to why there was no sound. Looking around her she then realized she was in a familiar place, this was where Gramps and Granny lived. She struggled to be free, but the more she struggled the harder he held her, his voice puzzled her, he sounded nice and was trying to sooth her, yet his grip was rough and menacing. The sound of hooves stopping very close to them froze them both. Thomas Elliot's voice boomed beyond where they crouched and towards the back of the cottage.

"Rose, have you seen Bill Buxton go past here, it's imperative, I think he's got Betsy?"

"No Pa, he hasn't gone up towards the house, but he may have gone past on the road. He wouldn't hurt his niece would he? Is he just taking her for a walk?"

"I don't know Rose, but I don't want to wait and see, he did threaten to come back for her after Lizzibeth died." All through his dialogue, he was looking around the bushes behind the cottage. Bill took his chance. He crept round the front of the hedge with Betsy back up on his shoulders, parceled yet again in stylish and fashionable beige cashmere.

Rose, frustratingly seconds late in catching sight of his stealthy egress, wandered over to the carriage horse and stroked his velvet nose dreamily. She suddenly became aware of a voice from the roadside up ahead. She darted to the road shouting for her Pa, just in time to see the back of Bill disappearing down the road, but with Benjamin coming amiably towards him from the opposite direction and leading two carriage horses on his return from the farrier's in the next town.

"Good day to you Bill, I didn't know you were back. How are you?" Thomas was back on his horse and giving chase with Rose running as fast as she could behind them.

"Stop him Benjamin, stop him."

Bill started to run, his coat fell away from his load and Betsy could be seen crying as she jolted up and down on her kidnapper's shoulder. A puzzled Benjamin quickly put himself and the horses between Bill and his progress. He had responded not only to his Pa but also to the sight of Betsy slung callously over his shoulder. Thomas caught up from behind.

"Bill Buxton, you'd better have a very good explanation as to why you've snatched my granddaughter. Put her down this instant!"

"See what you've done now you stupid child, you were on your way to a new life with your Uncle." Thomas pulled the horse alongside him and menacingly coaxed Bill to put Betsy down.

"Bill you're frightening her, don't do this."

"You don't know she's your kin anymore than your drunken son does. But she's undeniably mine."

"No-one would dispute that Buxton, but how could you look after her, Joseph and Hannah love her, they are her parents now, they're all she knows. Stop frightening her, now. Good-day Betsy dear, are you having a piggy back ride?"

Betsy could not smile or speak, her silent terrified gulping sobs had paralysed any response, despite being relieved to see her Gramps. She tried to arch backwards to release Bill's hold on her.

"I have a woman now in London, she can take care of her." Bill struggled to restrain the wriggling child.

"But she doesn't know her, and Lizzibeth didn't know her, she wouldn't want a stranger to care for her child. Your sister would be more than happy with the present arrangements for Betsy, I know the last thing you want is to cause Lizzibeth's child any distress, but look at what you've done to her."

The mention of his sister in such tender tones had touched a nerve and Bill turned Betsy round to look at him. Her eyes were red with crying, but he could see they were not Lizzibeth's eyes, neither was her hair any mimic of Lizzibeth's. She would not remind him of Lizzibeth, this had been a bad idea, but yet had been an obsessive one for two and a half years until he had achieved a decent home to offer her. He now had, but he had not considered that she may not want to live with him. He put her down on the grass verge and knelt beside her still holding her tight. Thomas dismounted, ready.

"Betsy, do you want to live with me? I have a nice place in London, where the Queen lives, and a nice lady to look after you." He released his hold, and Betsy did not waste this opportunity, she ran straight into Thomas' waiting arms.

"I think you have your answer Buxton. I'd get back to London sharp if you don't want me to get the constables after you for this, kidnapping is a very serious crime!" He turned his attention to Betsy soothing her sobs, then added a parting postscript to Bill.

"I wish you well with your new life and lady, in the name of your dear Ma, God rest her soul. Do I have your word that you will not return Bill?"

But Bill had already retrieved his coat and turned petulantly away as Betsy had deserted him. Within minutes he had disappeared in the undergrowth and was gone. Rose tried to cheer Betsy by tickling and playing peepo. Thomas joined in whilst lifting her onto his horse, he hid his face behind the horses neck and then jumped out. Before long Betsy was smiling, he did not want to take her back to Hannah all red eyed, she was still in her convalescence. He hadn't seen his new grandson and namesake yet. Perhaps on Sunday the whole family could walk along and meet him. "Go and tell your Ma what's just happened Rose dear, we'll all have to be very vigilant from now on. Well done Benjamin. Now, back to work for all of us."

As Thomas rode into the marketplace with Betsy up in front of him, Jacob and Joseph were there to greet him. Henrietta, not realizing the full impact of what had just so nearly happened to this family, was impatiently awaiting being taken home.

"What's all this fuss about the child, Thomas? Joseph seems beside himself, did she wander off?"

"No M'Lady, she was taken off by Lizzibeth Buxton's brother, he'd threatened to come back for her, and so he just attempted to do so. All's well that ends well though, here she is." He handed Betsy down to Joseph who embraced her so tightly she started to wriggle with discomfort. She was still holding her wooden dog in her hand. As if suddenly remembering about it, she threw it hard onto the cobbles.

"Oh you have dropped your dog dear". Said Jacob as he picked it up and gave her it back. Betsy threw it back on to cobbles, much harder than before. "My not want it. Man had it."

The men silently conferred agreement to leave the wooden toy where it was, she didn't need it, and neither did they. Henrietta cleared her throat loudly to alert Thomas to his duties. Whilst now appreciating the severity of this situation, she was impatient to get home to direct the final preparations for Christmas.

"Come along Thomas, I must get home. Lots to do. She is a very sweet child, and obviously quite spirited. Joseph, you and Hannah are very noble to bring her up as your own. She is quite angelic looking. A little like Charlotte when she was a child. I hope she is not going to be as troublesome! I hear you now have a baby son too, congratulations, Joseph. I trust Hannah is quite well. I don't envy her that, I am relieved that part of my life is behind me. Most unpleasant. However the children we have as a result is worth it I suppose. Can we expect to see you at all over Christmas Joseph, if Henry arrives in time for the celebrations?"

Joseph stared blankly at an innocent and oblivious Henrietta. "Well, Joseph?" He glanced at both of Betsy's charlatan Grandfathers, they too, seemed unaware of her naïve revelation.

"Oh, erm, yes please M'Lady, I would like that. Thank you."

Chapter 10

Dorset, August 1857- April 1858

Since Christmas, Joseph had not been able to relax anywhere in the town. He had an unease that went beyond worrying about Bill and his possible return. He had discussed moving with Hannah many times. They were both reluctant to consider it, but Hannah was too frightened to allow Betsy out of her sight, and they realised they could not keep her this close as she grew; she would have to be out on her own at some time. Bill could just bide his time until then. Hannah's reluctance was because of her parents. She knew Joseph could start a business of his own now, and it could be better somewhere else. Lately it had not been as busy as usual. The special orders were still coming in, but the run-of-the-mill work which was their bread and butter, making basic furniture for the general populace, had taken a tumble along with the exodus to the cities for better work. She wondered whether her Pa would cope without Joseph, and if business was bad, how would both her parents manage? They had been used to a relatively easy life.

They had also had a frightening few episodes with little Thom struggling for air and wheezing. He had developed a rare lung problem that the doctor had referred to as a troublesome chest. The doctor had said that sea air could sometimes have a beneficial effect. Joseph was heartened to know that both Mr Disraeli and Charles Dickens had always suffered from the same affliction, and they seemed to be surviving well. He wondered if Dickens character Mr Omer in David Copperfield was a reflection of the author himself, as he too similarly suffered. Joseph was sure this problem had started after the smallpox vaccine, but the doctor said there was no known connection. Joseph remained suspicious about these new vaccines, but it had become compulsory for all children, and Betsy had had no ill effect from hers, and he certainly did not want his children to be sick with smallpox.

Joseph sat outside on the yard wall watching Betsy draw circles with a piece of slate on the flat stones. He suddenly felt his stomach lurch when he realised that the piece of slate was in her left hand. Yet somehow, he was not surprised, this was yet further proof of what he now supposed to be true. He was not sure of how it made him feel about Henry. He suspected Hannah was right, the culprit had surely known who he was. Disappointment in his friend was the clearest emotion; that he had not been able to admit his folly, and had in fact denied Lizzibeth in her dying moments. Indeed he had allowed his good friend Joseph, to consider the possibility of his own transgression and dishonourable behaviour. He didn't feel he could ever truly forgive him for that.

He watched Betsy again, there would be time enough to try to get her to change hands before she attended school. They were all in their Sunday best, as they had all just returned from church. Hannah liked to go most Sundays, but had become even more vigilant since Thom's birth. He smiled at the sight of Betsy's dress hoisted clear of her knees and displaying lacy bloomers to the world. So like her mother, yet when she turned to speak to him, it was without doubt another's face he saw. He couldn't believe it had taken an innocent remark of Henrietta Ferguson's to alert him to these, such obvious clues. He marvelled at how Hannah did not appear to notice, but then without that catalyst, would he? He resolved to keep it from Hannah, it would be better for all concerned, she wanted to believe he was Betsy's father, and so did he. It would ensure her rightful place in the only family it was possible for her to be a part of. She was their little girl, and always would be if he had anything to do with it.

His mind wandered to thinking about Lizzibeth. How she would have loved to be nurturing her own daughter. He thought about how she had suffered alone. Jacob had told his wife and family only recently that he had actually helped her on the night she was finished from the house. She had been exhausted and distraught on returning from the house in the early hours, and he had just been to the outside privy when he heard her distressing sobs as she passed by their cottage. He had comforted her and allowed her to stay in their kitchen chair to get warm and to compose herself before going home. In the morning she had already left and Jacob had never seen her again.

When Hannah had told Joseph of this, he had thought it very odd as Henry had told him at the time that Lizzibeth went to the stables of the house to sleep that night, and planned to walk home and face her mother the next day. She must have decided to get the ordeal over with, but then given in to Jacob's kindness.

Despite his misgivings about his friend, he had been so disappointed when Henry did not come home at Christmas. As a parent now himself he could not begin to imagine how Henry's family had felt. His poor mother had gone to so much trouble with all the preparations, and it had been so long since they had seen him. He had also been looking forward to handing over the long promised Secretaire to Henry. Joseph was so proud of it, and he had completed his apprenticeship in such style because of its original design. He thought now that it would be better to send it directly to Kent, as this was going to be Henry's long term base. He had decided to stay in the army when he had been offered the post of teaching the new officer recruits, with no likelihood of returning to the battlefield.

With these thoughts repeatedly cascading around in his head, Joseph made a decision. He spoke quietly to Betsy, "I'm just going inside Betsy, won't be a minute." He walked past Hannah busying herself with the Sunday roast, and into the Parlour. He opened a cupboard and took out the large box Hannah used for keepsakes, and rummaged until he found a little tin box. He opened it and paused gazing not just at its contents, but at how his lovely wife kept everything she cherished in such order. He took a lock of strawberry blond hair out of the tin. Hannah had trimmed it for the first time from Betsy just last week. He replaced the tin back in its niche. He then collected a piece of parchment paper from another cupboard, and carefully wrapped the hair inside it. Joseph picked up his quill from the top shelf, dipped it in his ink pot and wrote across the paper -'Betsy Agatha'.

Tucking the package into his top pocket he walked back towards the yard, patting Hannah on her bottom, he said, "Hannah dear, I won't be long but I just need to go to the workshop for something now while I remember about it. I'll take Betsy with me."

Joseph and Betsy set off down the road to the workshop at the other end of the road. Betsy was skipping along beside him singing a song her Pa had taught her. "Are you going to Scarborough Fair, Past me age, Rose very on time"

Joseph smiled at his little daughter and started to join in her singing, including the childish misinterpretations. He unlocked the door as they arrived at the workshop, and sitting Betsy on his knee, he sat down at the Secretaire. Henry at least should know.

Pulling out a sheet of parchment from one of its compartments and a quill and ink from another, Joseph began to write.

Dear Henry
I am so sorry it has taken so long to get this Secretaire to you. Please accept it now not just as a long overdue eighteenth birthday present, but also as a token of our enduring friendship.

I hope you have remembered about the special feature I told you about on the leather inlay, or you will never get to read this!

I missed not seeing you at Christmas, are you deliberately avoiding us? Your parents were so disappointed. I wanted to tell you about your new God-son Thomas Henry Elliot, born just before Christmastime. We call him Thom, firstly to avoid any confusion with my Pa, but the spelling is in recognition of our long-standing joke about dropped 'h's!, He is a delight to us, although he has also given us a disquieting time, as he suffers with a troublesome chest. It has made us seriously consider moving beside the sea as the air would be better for him there.

The other reason we are considering a move is that Bill tried to take Betsy away from us at Christmas, and when caught out, he threatened to come back for her one day. We are beside ourselves. I know you will share our concern, for Bill as a guardian would never have been Lizzibeth's choice.

There are other implications for us remaining in Dorset, Henry, concerning Betsy Agatha. I trust you have found the other secreted package. You should know that Betsy has shown early signs of being left handed. She has such fair colouring as you can see, that people who don't know our circumstances often mistake her for taking after Hannah in her looks. It is very fortuitous for our family that this is so, but we obviously know differently. At the time of Bill's attempted kidnap, your Mama saw Betsy for the first time and naively said she looked just like Charlotte as a little girl, but hoped she would not be as troublesome! I can tell you that she is not at all troublesome, but may well be in the years to come for she has her mother's character! Without a doubt she loves life, and literally bounces through every day.

I would not want her presence in the town as she grows, to cause your family any embarrassment or discomfort.

Hannah knows nothing of this.

Your parents said you are well and happy, enjoying your new role as tutor to new officer recruits. You made a good teacher as a child Henry, so I am sure you are an exceptional inspiration to your pupils.

We look forward to the day when you come home and settle down, although I now fear we may have moved away and will not be able to enjoy your company again, or enjoy the luxury of watching our children play together.

Affectionately your friend

Joseph

Joseph then carefully folded the letter, clicked the mechanism on the leather inlay of the desk, and when it responded by raising slightly, he tucked the letter and the lock of hair into it. He wrote a note and left it on the top of the desk which read simply:- For dispatch to Capt Henry Ferguson. Betsy had been sitting quietly all the time on Joseph's knee, watching his every move. Now as if granted permission to be herself again after the solemnity of an important task, she began skipping and chattering all the way home for their Sunday meal.

As they neared their cottage, a horse and gentleman pulled up alongside, shouting "Joseph Elliot, we have not seen you for a long time, how are you and that growing family of yours?"

"Oh, good-day Sir, we're well Sir, thank you for asking. And you?"

"Yes fine, Joseph, thank you. And who is this young lady, is it Lizzibeth Buxton's child? How time flies."

"Yes Sir, this is little Betsy, she's getting to be very grown-up now, aren't you, Betsy?" Betsy looked at the man on the horse and flashed him one of her most enchanting dimpled grins.

"I'm three now, I'm a big girl."

"You certainly are, you are such a young lady, and so adorable. Henrietta remarked that she had the same type of angelic looks that Charlotte had, but I think she is nothing like her at all, I just see the Buxton blood there Joseph, Buxton through and through, absolutely no doubt." Joseph looked quizzically at Charles Ferguson, what was he implying? His blatant attempt at vindicating his son from any wrong doing was obvious, but was he hinting at something more sinister? Henrietta's remark may have been innocent, but her husband certainly had understood its implications. Joseph guided Betsy through the opening into their yard, and instructed her to go inside and tell her Ma they were home and hungry.

"Well Sir you no doubt also heard about Lizzibeth's brother trying to snatch her and take her to London, it's been of much concern to us, she's our child now. We're considering moving away, also to be near the sea for Thom who has a troublesome chest."

"Oh dear I am sorry to hear that about your little boy Joseph. But moving is an excellent idea. The little girl certainly looks very happy and healthy with you as her parents. I have contacts you know, I am sure I could get a position for an excellent craftsman like you. Shall I make some enquiries?"

"It wouldn't harm to ask around I suppose Sir, I know Hannah is reluctant to leave her parents, and I'd miss my family too, but Lizzibeth wouldn't want Bill to succeed in his mission to take Betsy. And Thom may be much healthier living by the sea."

"Say no more Joseph, I shall see what I can do, I am even happy to help you financially to set up in your own business if necessary, you deserve such an opportunity."

"Well thank you Sir, that's very kind, but I'm sure I can manage with employment in a good workshop to start with."

"Good-day to you Joseph, my regards to your family."

"Thank you Sir, good-day to you too."

Joseph, replete after his meal, for Hannah was a good cook, sat by the range reading the paper. Hannah was beside him reading Betsy a story. Thom was asleep in his crib. "Hannah, listen to this. It says here there has been a terrible flood in the seaside town of Scarborough up in Yorkshire. 'Thursday August the 9th was an ordinary rainy day, but that night it increased rapidly until the drains were all over-charged. By the early hours it was like water pouring from vessels rather than rain. One terrace of houses looked like a lake and one wall of a hospital was carried completely away. Part of an ancient church has fallen with lots of the tombstones carried away.' It appears to have destroyed much of the town and they're in need of journeyman tradesmen of all types to help to rebuild it. Have you given any more thought to the prospect of moving, this could be a perfect opportunity for us. Although Yorkshire is such a very long way?"

"How far away, Joseph, would we be able to visit our parents?"

"I think it's almost as far as Scotland Hannah, a long way, visiting would only be possible very infrequently. Perhaps we shouldn't consider it."

"Joseph I've given it some thought recently, I know it would be better for lots of reasons, but my parents are such a help to us, and such a loss if we leave them here, so, what about if we ask them to come with us? Ma has her arthritis and sea air is also said to be very good for that too. I really don't think Pa could run his business now without you." Joseph considered her suggestion.

"But what about the business. It's still successful at the moment?"

"But for how much longer, Joseph, there's been a steady downturn in our money over the last year or more, I've assumed without asking too many questions, that it means there's not been as much business. He won't manage it alone and imagine how he'll feel if it can no longer be sustained. I don't want him to end his working days as a failure." She paused as if considering their whole lifestyle and all the possible implications of any changes. "We'd miss your parents too, but it's different for them, they've the other children to think of, and Benjamin is so good with the horses, he's going to make a wonderful Coachman just like your Pa. Their lives are here."

"Well, we can certainly think about it Hannah, let's sleep on it and see how we feel tomorrow. If we still feel the same, then perhaps I can see how your Pa would feel about it my dear, and you could talk to your Ma? I'll hold on to this article, it may be useful for work contacts in the future."

Joseph and Hannah concurred the following morning to leave the whole idea for the present time. It was too big a step to take for Hannah's parents at their time of life. Hannah had forced Joseph to contemplate his own concerns about the business though, the town's population was falling and that did not bode well for any trades people trying to make a living.

Joseph had an air of anxiety on his way to work this morning. He was charged with the task of delivering their happy news to Jacob. Hannah had told him last night once she was absolutely sure. They were both delighted. It was now the festive season again, Thom had just had his first birthday and Hannah thought the new baby would be with them by the summer solstice. He knew what a worry Hannah's first confinement had been to Jacob, and he felt sure any subsequent ones would be no easier for him. He would be sensitive in delivering the news, but it would be difficult not to show his own excitement and pleasure. Especially as this child had been so much quicker to conceive than Thom, and without walking on any chalk. What had he told her indeed!

He hadn't expected to find the workshop door open. He was usually the first to arrive these days, Jacob Thackery had taken to spending a little more time in bed on a morning as he aged.

As he strode further onto the sawdust carpet, the silence unnerved him. He shouted to Jacob but got no response. His heartbeat quickened as his imagination hurled scenarios into his conscious thoughts. Burglers, Bill Buxton, vagrants sleeping rough. Any of whom may attack him if they felt threatened. He calmly enquired, "Is there anyone there?" As no reply came, Joseph continued his progress into the workshop, the sight that he eventually encountered was worse than his imaginings had prepared him for. Jacob Thackery was prostrate across the table he had been planing, his precious Spiers plane was in his right hand, paused in its toil. His face was squashed as it had landed on his masterpiece, his nose pushed to lie parallel to his cheek and his mouth dusted with freshly planed sawdust as if caught furtively tasting its very quality. Joseph touched his cheek, he was still warm, but his eyes held no sparkle as though all moisture had already evaporated with his soul. He was overcome with sadness for this gentle man who had taught him all he knew in his occupation, and who had fathered for him the most wonderful wife. Hannah had told him recently that her Ma had caught him rubbing his chest and suspected he was suffering with his heart like his father before him, but Joseph had never noticed anything. Now, in the initial guilt that accompanies any bereavement, he felt he should have supported him more. How would he tell Hannah and her Ma, they would be distraught.

Ma Thackery was much younger than her husband, but she had depended on him for everything, she would be lost. And poor little Betsy, she loved her Grandpa so much, he always had so much time for her.

Joseph Elliot and his family stood on the station platform surrounded by well wishers for their new life in Scarborough. Thomas had his arm around Mary's shoulders. She bravely fought the tears she so wanted to shed for the loss of having her Joseph close to her. Thomas had reminded her that he too had left his family behind in Bristol to start a new life in Dorset, and at a much younger age, his family must have missed him too. He spoke to Joseph above the noise of the station.

"Joseph, I want you to have this old pocket watch for my namesake grandson. Make sure you tell him about his Dorset family, and how proud we are of you all."

"Thank you Pa, I'll make sure he treasures it always. "Joseph looked around for his son to avoid his father seeing the moisture in his eyes. Rose was carrying him, and bouncing him up and down on her hip to make him giggle, his white baby dress billowing outwards with each bounce.

Louiza was pointing out different parts of the engine and its carriages to Betsy having just returned from the ladies room with her. She was trying hard not to allow her to see her own sadness at their departure. Joseph had included his family in on the decision to move, and whilst they understood, there was the inevitable sadness that they would rarely see their son and brother, or indeed his family again.

The smoke from the engine was billowing black flecks like spring harvest flies onto everyone's clothing, and the noise and sporadic whistling of the enormous engine was too deafening for much to be said. Joseph knew they need not speak, it had all been said in the weeks leading up to these arrangements. They had felt the spring would be the best time to travel, without leaving it too late for Hannah to be settled before her confinement. The journey would take three days with many changes of trains and two overnight stops to reach their final destination by the sea.

Hannah and her mother were dressed formally in their Sunday clothes, it was only well-to-do people who travelled in this way, and they had an impression to give as they arrived for their new life. The family looked a picture of importance on this Dorset railway station platform in their fine bonnets and boots, with Joseph's new frock coat and felt hat making him look nothing less than a man of means.

The Station Master walked down the platform opening all the passenger doors, whilst shouting for travellers to board. The carriages were highly polished and looked to be quite new on the outside. Each one was reminiscent in design to three merged stage coaches. The central one was reserved for first class passengers looking quite the most lavish, and this was flanked by two basic third class models. Joseph helped Hannah up into their end carriage, as she left Dorset soil for the first and last time, then turned to relieve Rose of her bundle and pass little Thom up to his wife. He was just lifting Betsy up into the carriage when Charles Ferguson arrived breathless onto the platform. He shouted above the noise of the engine, "Joseph, I have finalised all those arrangements for you, you have accommodation in the station hotels of the two overnight stops and I have rented a pleasant house in Scarborough so you can move straight in when you arrive. Here is the address." He handed him a folded piece of parchment. "You are to report for work on the Monday morning at Wrigglesworth's workshop, Victoria Road. I hope this is all to your satisfaction. I bid you a good journey, and health and happiness in your new life." He turned to Thomas and added. "Hard day for a father eh, Thomas, I know the feeling well."

Both Thomas and Joseph in unison replied. "Thank you so much Sir." They laughed at their duet, and just as Joseph was about to speak further, Mrs Thackery sternly interrupted.

"It's the very least he could do. We would be better served in a first class compartment too!" Joseph, embarrassed, added swiftly, "You've been most kind Sir, thank you, it's very much appreciated."

"You are most welcome Joseph Elliot, we too shall miss your company. Mrs Thackery." Charles docked his felt hat towards Kate as she stepped up into the carriage, then continued to Joseph, "Oh, and Henry has written asking for your new address, so no doubt you will be hearing from him. There are barracks up north too, perhaps he will be sent to do some training and you can catch up with each other. Good-day Joseph." Turning empathically to Thomas, he added "Take your time Thomas, I do not require your services imminently, Louiza and Benjamin too, take your time."

Joseph deposited Betsy in the carriage, and turned to help his mother-in-law up the carriage steps, before stepping up himself with the large hamper of food and supplies for the journey, and left Dorset soil for the first time in his life.

The whistle blew long and loud, and the train started to lurch slowly away from the platform. Joseph was at the window, taking a last loving look at his family, he had no idea if or when he would ever make the journey back to see them again. The enormity of what they were embarking upon began to hit him, what if it was a mistake? Then he remembered the rationale behind their decision and settled back onto the seat next to his wife. Standing straight was not possible on account of the restricted height of the carriage, and he considered all the hours that would be spent sat on these hard wooden bench seats, this was little more than a wooden box, he turned to Hannah. "Will you be a'right here for three days dear? It's a long time in this confined uncomfortable space."

"We'll manage Joseph, we can stretch our legs at each station when we stop and use the lavatories, I'm just a little taken aback by how dark it is, I thought we'd be able to read, especially if the children drop off to sleep." Joseph looked around, there was only a small window on the upper half of the door, he had noticed the first class compartment had three windows. It was going to be difficult to read, they would need to think up some games to pass the time with Betsy especially. Thom had his favourite little toys with him and would hopefully sleep most of the way.

"Ma Thackery, you were very rude to the Master, he's helped us so much, we couldn't expect him to book first class travel for us too." Her reply was a sharp and inexplicable, "Huh." Followed by a 'tut' as she began to bounce Thom on her knee and sing to him signalling the matter was closed. Did she suspect the same as Joseph, or did she even know without doubt? She did spend most of Lizzibeth's last day with her, she could be keeping a deathbed promise. There could be no other explanation for her behaviour although widowhood had seen her become rather more outspoken on many issues.

The train was approaching Bristol station, the familiarized clickety clack sensations of their journey were slowing. Today's journey was not the longest, tomorrows would be the worst. Joseph looked at his wife with Thom curled on her knee for some warmth from the cold night air. Her pained expression, illuminated now as it was by the station gas lights, failed despite all efforts to disguise her undoubted discomfort. He was suffering himself, and he had heard many 'tut's and shuffles coming from the direction of his mother-in-law. He could not begin to imagine how Hannah was bearing this level of discomfort in her condition. His mind was made up.

"I should think so too Joseph Elliot." Ma Thackery remarked as they settled themselves the next morning into the first class compartment of the carriage which was to take them all the way today from Bristol to York. The hard wooden bench seats that had pained their behinds yesterday were gone, and they were now spoiled by the compliancy of padded leather. The three windows gave sufficient light to allow comfortable reading, as well as clearer communication between themselves. They had had a good night's sleep in the Station Hotel in Bristol and were refreshed and ready for this, the longest part of their journey.

"Don't get too used to it Ma, we're back in the basic coach again tomorrow, we can't afford to squander all the money we've brought just on getting there. But today is a long day, better that we're comfortable, and lucky they had room for us in this carriage today." He winked at Hannah, she knew he had done it for her comfort alone. It made little difference to the children, they could move freely around the compartment anyway, and when they were tired, they simply chose a suitable adult knee to sleep upon. Wickedly Hannah grinned at Joseph.

"Could you just see what you can do about the noise and the draughts now please Joseph!"

"Oh that's no problem my dear, I'll just ask the train driver to go even slower, maybe it'd be even better if we didn't move at all!" They laughed together as the now recognizable clickety clack began again; and Joseph settled himself with a newspaper he had bought from a stand at the station and smiled around at his family as they embarked further upon this new chapter of their lives together.

Part 2

Betsy

1858 - 1876

17 Years Later

Chapter 11

Scarborough, December 1875

The huge church doors opened as the carol service came to a reluctant end.

People spewed out around the two stately entrance pillars into the bitter cold evening on Falsgrave Walk like majestically be-hatted ants spreading around a discarded treat. The swarm continued to spill down the snow covered entrance steps of best quality Whitby stone towards the Railway Station opposite; only then to divide in formation to the left and right of this grand Wesleyan Methodist Chapel towards their individual abodes. It was the eve of Christmas, and there was much chattering amongst the adults, jollity amongst the bouncing excited children, and the issuing of good will and peace to their fellow church-goers as they dispersed.

Through the doors, the gold and white interior décor could be seen glinting in the candle light and the splendid organ was still playing the refrains of the outtro for 'Angels from the Realms of Glory'.

Never had this magnificent building more deserved its affectionate title of the 'Wedding Cake'. The snow fall of the last two days had completely encased its grand architecture, and had enhanced this analogous image. The two virginal bell towers looked longingly at one another as any loving bride and bridegroom should, perched so perfectly atop such confectionary.

Two lone young figures remained standing on the top of the steps between the pillars, half turned, reluctant to leave the music behind, reluctant to say their goodbyes. The last note hung on in the chilled night air as though the organist could not bear to leave his magnificent charge. Then suddenly it was gone, and silence fell in the emptying street. As if unexpectedly energized by the stillness, in one accord the two figures turned towards the steps and walked cautiously down onto the frozen wintry street below. As they fell in step with one another along the path, the young woman rubbed her hands together hard and blew hot breath into them. It didn't now seem such a good idea to lend her gloves to Mrs Swales on the pew behind, who had come out without her own. Finally satisfied they were as warm as she could make them, she tucked them inside her cloak and began her usual chatter.

"I wonder if I could ever be good enough to play the organ for a service like that? Although I love to be actually singing the Christmas Carols, it makes me feel so fluttery and happy inside. Does it do that to you?"

"I do enjoy it, that's true, but I wasn't keen on the new one that was handed out on the sheet tonight."

"Oh I loved it", she began to sing "Oh Little Town of Be-e-thle-e-hem, how still we-e see thee lie, ab…"

"Alright" he laughed and pushed her, "I said I didn't like it, no need to put me through it again!" He grabbed aimlessly for her hand to steady her footing on the icy pavement from his over zealous playfulness. He pulled an apologetic face. The physical connection between them shocked and stopped them both.

It was a dark winter's night but the crisp white snow was encrusted with multi-coloured diamonds as it reflected the full moon, and they could see clearly into the very depth of each other's familiar eyes. Their joined hands came up between them as though in greeting, but then as though precisely choreographed they released the firm grip. Slowly and compellingly it was exchanged for the soft touch of flat exposed palms that sinuously withdrew to leave their interlinking fingers lightly and sensuously caressing one another.

Thundering shudders passed like bolts of lightening between them as the hastening night slowed in their eyes. Her lips tingled, longing for him to make the expected move. He bent his head slowly and brushed them lightly with his own. As if scorched by them, he jumped away from her.

"Happy Christmas. Come on, we'll be late, your family went straight home, they'll wonder where we are." He had dropped her hand, and had begun walking away. Then as if rewound, he slowed, and began stepping backwards to where she was looking after him, a look of pure bewilderment on her face. He wasn't sure if it was perplexity at his kiss itself, or at its very brevity followed by his sudden abandonment. Equally confused, and without saying a word, he took her arm, and pulled her into the shelter of the nearest doorway. What did parental opinion matter, he knew this was what they both wanted. He began to kiss her palm, then cradling the sides of her head in his own large hands, he sprinkled kisses all over her face. His lips found hers and locked them in a passionate kiss, so powerful, that neither of them had the combination to unpick. Breathlessness eventually dampened their ardour and she looked excitedly up at her beau. He whispered urgently, "We might be seen here, lets go to my Grandmother's house, she's at our house tonight to be with us all for Christmas day."

He took her hand and pulled her along with him.

"We shouldn't, not yet, not until we're wed."

"Who knows when that could be, we can't wait that long. Can we? You look so beautiful tonight, so happy, and with the moonlight reflecting in your eyes." His lips fell onto hers again, "It's so cold out here, come on." His eyes appealed directly to her own as he tenderly stroked her face with his other hand.

"But what about my family, they will be wondering where we are?"

"Let's call in and tell them we're going to my house for something, they won't know we aren't really."

They fell excitedly in through the front door of his Grandmother's home. Standing in the living room, he turned to look at her as she unfastened the ribbon of her bonnet, "Oh, I do love you, you know. You're so beautiful tonight. I have thought about this day for so long. I'm so nervous that I'm shaking. Are you?"

She nodded her reply. Unsure as to whether her voice would do as instructed. She discarded her bonnet onto the table and threw her heavy cloak onto the nearest chair. But then as she shivered, her humour overcame her unease, and she added smiling,

"That's 'coz the fire has gone out and it's freezing in here you idiot." They both laughed nervously and he stepped towards her never leaving her gaze.

She watched him anxiously as his icy fingers fumbled with the buttons on her exquisitely made bodice with its intricate lace collar, and jumped when they made contact with her warm soft skin. He stepped back to marvel at the sight of her form as it was freed from its delicate restraint. She ran her hands across the narrow front of her matching skirt and, empowered by the gratifying effects on her entranced and impending lover, she untied its cords at the back where its fullness reached far behind her, and allowed it to fall to the floor. His eyes urgently devoured this curvaceous figure of womanhood at the peak of its youthfulness and took hold of her instantly. He fervently repeated the kiss that had first sealed this destiny tonight. This time the passion spilled from their lips to the rest of their beings. Frost clouds escaped from the leaky seal fashioned by their frenzied kissing in this arctic room. They fell gently backwards onto the settee behind them, nervously giggling as they broke briefly away to re-assess their comfort. Then clothes, limbs and souls became so entwined it was impossible to think that they could ever again become two separate entities.

17 Years Earlier

Chapter 12

Scarborough, May 1858

"Phoo Ma, what's that stink?"

"I'm not sure Betsy, it smells worse than the Dorset countryside after manure spreading on a hot day doesn't it?"

"Is it the smell of the Fair Pa? Can we go?"

"I'm afraid not Betsy, my dear, Scarborough Fair stopped in 1788, there hasn't been one since then."

The Elliot family emerged tentatively from the imposing railway station entrance, as if sneaking a look at their future before committing to it. Joseph broke away decisively, looking left and right for a carriage or cab, and spoke over his shoulder to his tired family.

"Don't be troubled by it, someone warned me that the night soil collection was stored close to the railway station, it'll be fine when we move away from here." He spotted the coaches and hansom cabs to the left of the arch doorway and moved back towards his family, herding them away from the entrance.

"Come on, over here, there are cabs for hire to take us and our luggage to the address Henry's father gave us."

The journey from York had only been three and a half hours, but they had travelled on wooden seats again, and three days of travel had tested the children's need to be entertained to its limits. Coping with them had become cumulatively more tedious and fatiguing for the adults. Journey's end now brought new and different challenges. What would their new life look like at first glance?

"This can't be the address Joseph. There must be a mistake." Hannah looked up at the new, sparkling whitewashed, three storey, double fronted corner property on James Street. It was on what looked to be a fashionable road not far from the centre of town. "But we can't afford to live here, we're not landed gentry!"

Kate Thackery muttered something in the front of the carriage. "What did you say Ma?"

"I said, - 'but maybe my grand-daughter is'!" Hannah looked away from her in disgust. "Don't be absurd Ma. And I beseech you to stop making such comments. Betsy's getting older, she'll wonder what you mean." She turned back to Joseph,

"Joseph, you must ask someone before we unpack anything at all here. There's maybe a mistake on the house number. Next door but one is a small cottage, look."

"I can see that Hannah dear, you all wait here, I'll be back soon."

Joseph returned to his waiting family. He leant over the carriage door towards Hannah.

"Hannah my dear, apparently this is all paid up for us for five years. The Master told the Landlord that he wanted to support us in settling into our new lives. He didn't want us to worry about finding a nice place to bring the children up in a strange town."

"But how can the landlord know all this?"

"It seems that the Master sent the Landlord a letter with a glowing reference for us. He said that by the time we needed to start paying rent, we may have saved up enough to either stay here, or at least know whereabouts in the town we want to settle. He told the Landlord that schooling for the children would be important to us by then." Hannah looked suspiciously at her husband.

"Don't look like that Hannah, I want to support my own

family too, but this is just such a kind gesture of the Master's, it would be ungrateful and also imprudent to turn this down."

He turned away, excitedly lifting some bundles down from the cab seat. "Come on Hannah, we're all tired, lets get inside and have a pot of tea. I'll go and see if I can find some milk for the children, the grocers are all open today, but it may be more difficult to get provisions later on, remember it's Sunday tomorrow." He helped her alight from the carriage carrying Thom, and then beckoned to his mother-in-law and Betsy to follow.

He continued his excited persuasions. "I'm surprised by the measure of his generosity, Hannah. It must be a reflection of how much regard he's always had for my father. I must write and thank him straight away."

Joseph's statement, stirred Kate Thackery to alight abruptly and stridently from the carriage, lifting Betsy down behind her. They both turned to look at her as she pushed ahead of them both, entering the large red door of the property, and preaching as she went.

"Well I for one, think it's nothing less than he owes us. God knows we've not had it easy these last months, think of the shame we've spared their family." She turned towards her daughter,

"Hannah your pride and honour'll be the death of you girl. Move along now, let's get the children settled. Betsy's so sleepy." Hannah and Joseph shared a look of bewilderment as she turned now to Joseph and continued,

"And as for you Joseph my boy, you must be the most naive person I've ever known, but your common sense and zeal must be applauded. Pay the carriage driver my lad, and let's get in and allocate rooms, I shall need one for my sewing too if I'm to make a living for my old age."

Hannah paused initially, then made to follow her in, smiling at her profundity. Then she stopped abruptly, and turned to Joseph as he was returning from settling the fare with the carriage driver.

"Joseph stop," she paused and took a deep breath, "I can smell the sea. It reminds me of our honeymoon night." Joseph walked back to her, and imitated her inhalation.

"You're right; you can smell it. Very apt for the start of something else new for us my dear, don't you think." He dropped a brief kiss on the end of her nose and put a steering arm around her shoulder as they continued indoors, firmly closing the big red door on all they had left behind.

"Pa, Pa, please can I ride a donkey, please?" Betsy was sitting on an old rug on the sand, watching everything happening around her on the beach, whilst idly digging a hole beside her with a make-shift spade fashioned cleverly from her father's oddments of wood. The excess sand was being tossed distractedly onto her discarded socks and shoes. Her cotton dress was covered in wet sand, and her protecting bonnet that her mother insisted she keep on, was twisted and centred over her right ear.

"We'll see Betsy, we'll see."

"That pretty lady in the very big hat has just taken her little girl off the black one. I like the black one Pa."

"Joseph, we're not so short of money that your child can't have the occasional treat you know, it was her birthday this week, and we do have a substantial roof over our heads for the time being at least!"

"I know that Ma T. but if we keep spending it on furnishings for this temporary house as we have over the last month, we'll have nothing left for when the five years is ended. We must be frugal for now. The salary for my work isn't going to make me a rich man."

"Phoo, I say let the child have the occasional treat, what harm can it do?"

They had spent the whole afternoon on the South Sands at Scarborough, enjoying the glorious sunshine that the month of June had brought.

"Do you realise Henry was twenty two this week, I wonder

how he celebrated?" Joseph spoke to no-one in particular, and was not surprised at the lack of response.

Kate Thackery was perched on a small stool behind Betsy. She was intent on her rural cross stitch of a milkmaid seated upon such a similar stool beside the most enormous rear end of a brown and white cow. She had said the picture reminded her of the countryside they had left behind. She had completed very few stitches this afternoon. Despite her puritanical disapproval of bathing suits, and regardless of the use of Brown's popular bathing huts for modesty, she had spent a considerable amount of time craning her neck to scrutinise exactly why it was she disapproved.

Hannah was reposed on a rug, keeping a protective shawl carefully over herself and little Thom asleep at her side. Joseph himself was sitting cross-legged on the sand, a newspaper across his legs. His trousers were still rolled up around his knees with his shoes and socks discarded near Betsy's hole. He had removed them to take Betsy paddling in the sea when they had first arrived at the beach.

"Pa, this looks like the sugar Ma put in my birthday cake." Joseph looked up in time to see Betsy about to taste the wet sand on her spade that she had excavated from the bottom of her hole.

"No Betsy dear, you mustn't eat it, it's just wet sand when you dig deep. You're right though, it does look like that brown sugar your Ma got from the Market Hall last week. That tasted really nice though, whilst this would be horrible." Betsy discarded the wet sand disenchantedly.

"Pa. Does 'we'll see' mean yes or no? You're always saying 'we'll see'."

He paused and looked at his daughter's disappointed face. "Oh. Come on then little one. 'We'll see' if we can find that black donkey!" She jumped up excitedly, took her father's hand and skipped awkwardly on the shifting sand towards the donkeys. Her bonnet managing to readjust to its rightful position on her head.

Hannah looked up at her own mother, "I knew he'd give in Ma, he's just like Pa was with me, he can't say no to her, she's the apple of his eye. It's so nice to see. Lizzibeth would be so pleased, don't you think Ma?"

"Yes I do Hannah dear. She's one very lucky little girl, you're a wonderful mother to her, not many could've been as selfless and understanding as you in this situation."

"But I'm her mother now Ma, the only one she knows for now anyway. I feel she's just like my own flesh and blood. Sometimes when people tell me how much she looks like me, I forget that she isn't mine." Kate Thackery looked back at her daughter from her gaze towards the bathing huts with yet another barely audible 'tut'. Hannah wasn't sure if it was because she had glimpsed something shocking, or indeed because she had missed an opportunity to be shocked!

"I've often imagined, Hannah dear, what could've become of her if Bill hadn't brought Lizzibeth back to Dorset when he did. We have him to thank for that. Maybe we'll thank him one day for this move too. I like it here Hannah. Look at these views." She gestured around the scenic picturesque bay. "It's a new start for me, not easy at my time of life, but I'm a lot younger than your father was, I've still some life to live, who knows I may find happiness again. I can't wait for that new Spa Hall to open, there's to be a Concert Hall and adjoining galleries to seat two thousand people. The musical entertainment is promised to be wonderful."

"Ma! What're you saying? You surely wouldn't think of marrying again so soon?"

"Don't be silly Hannah, of course not. I'm just saying that I could enjoy music and company at some time in the future. Life is for living Hannah, remember that whenever you can. Did I tell you my mother taught me a little of the piano? I must tell Joseph to get a move on with those seats they are building at his workshop for the Spa Hall!"

"Well, I hope it doesn't cost too much to get in Ma, you know what Joseph will be like about spending money frivolously, even if it's just once in a while." Both ladies chuckled. Then Hannah pensively added,

"Don't you have enough company at home with us Ma?"

But the question was skilfully out-manoeuvred by Kate's response to Betsy's excited shouts from 'Beauty' the black donkey's back.

"Hold on tight Betsy. Don't fall off dear." Beauty, as he was labelled across his nose-band, was trotting along with Betsy bouncing erratically up and down on the substantial side saddle, and Joseph absurdly running alongside trying to hold onto her.

Kate turned to her daughter, "that looks such fun Hannah. I do think this is a lovely place to live, especially for the children. But also my joints have never bothered me since we arrived. And Thom's chest has never been better."

"Yes Ma, I like it too. It's just such a relief to know Bill Buxton isn't around every corner. I don't think we need to worry about work here either, there are Hotels appearing everywhere, new buildings will always need new furniture."

"Imagine how much better still we'd be if we'd actually partaken of the Spa waters themselves. Did you know you're supposed to drink five to eight pints of it every day? I think I'll not bother myself with it."

"But if you think it'd be good for you, Ma, and Thom, perhaps we should do it?"

"Hannah my dear, I also have it on good authority that it tastes of acid and smells of ink! I don't think Thom would drink it, and why should he, he's fine already with the sea air. As for me, whilst I am not suffering with my joints, I will not suffer with distaste!" Hannah laughed, her mother was always quick witted and in the last weeks, she had enjoyed glimpsing the return of the amusement they had always shared at home. Kate Thackery picked up her cross stitch again, and peered at the weave of the material to determine where she should work the next stitch. Having secured the correct entrance for her needle, she looked up at Hannah,

"You know there's also quite a call for sewing here I believe. The lady next door but two up from the house, Mrs Hudson I think, says that she takes in sewing from the ladies living in what they're calling 'New Scarborough' up on the south cliff. I've heard some of those houses take money from guests you know." She looked for the shocked and scandalous reaction from her daughter as only a gossip can, and was not disappointed. "Anyway, they want their crinolines altering to the new style. There's so much material in them that they can be easily be altered. That would be simple work too. Better than starting from the beginning with a dress, and I have my machine, it could be done so much quicker than by those altering by hand."

"That sounds like a good idea Ma, you've plenty of room to do it too, in this house anyway. Is it this Mrs Hudson that gives you all the information about this town that you seem to be gathering Ma?"

"Well, her and that Flossie flat hat woman across the road on the corner of Oxford street, she knows everything about everyone. People next door to us, the Robinsons I think she said, are really stuck up and above themselves just on account of him working on the local paper. But you are surely not implying I am listening to local gossip Hannah?" As she replied, she followed her daughter's distracted gaze and saw the little figure running as if in slow motion on the uneven soft white sand across the Children's Corner section of the beach.

"Granma, Ma, did you see me on Beauty? The man let me stroke his nose, it felt all soft, but then it snorted and it's breath smelt bad."

"Yes you looked quite the young rider there Betsy, your Gramps would be proud of you." Hannah looked up at Joseph, struggling as he was, to fasten one shoe whilst standing on the other leg. She tried frequently to bring his family into the conversations, she knew how he missed them all already, but wanted to make sure the children remembered them as much as possible too. She could not imagine not having her own mother close by. She struggled to her feet and motioned for Joseph to pick up Thom for her. He helped her up first, then scooped up their sleeping infant and placed him gently in his wicker perambulator without waking him.

"I think it's time to go home now Betsy, I've our tea to get ready, and we all must bathe tonight."

"Come to Granma, Betsy, I'll put your shoes and socks on for you. Where are they?" Betsy turned around in two full circles, then back the other way, she lifted the rug she had been sitting on, and then her mother's. She looked up at everyone watching her and raised the backs of her hands to her shoulders in a comical flicking action.

"Gone." She said. "All gone!" Everyone laughed at her childish bewilderment at the disappearance of her shoes until the practicalities dawned on Hannah.

"They must be somewhere Joseph. How is she going to get back with no shoes? They're only the ones that are now a little small for her so they weren't worth repairing, but as I didn't want her to spoil the new pair in the sand I thought she could still wear them today, but she's very heavy to carry now." Joseph moved the top layer of sand all around them but the shoes were nowhere to be seen.

"It's no good Betsy, Pa's going to have to carry you all the way back home like a sack of coal! Coming to get you." Betsy started to giggle and run away from Joseph, hiding behind her mother's and grandmother's full skirts. Joseph made a game of failing to catch her until Hannah's laughter subsided indicating her fatigue, and she began to push Thom back towards the foreshore.

"Gotcha, gotcha, home we go. Good thing it doesn't actually mean new shoes young lady," he raised his voice deliberately to Hannah's earshot, "otherwise I might think your Ma had hidden them under the sand deliberately to go spending again!" He tickled a giggling squirming but captured Betsy. Hannah darted him a playful 'tut'. Joseph threw Betsy up onto his shoulder where he felt it would be easier to carry her for the long walk home. As soon as he had her balanced, he set off at a run to catch up with his wife and mother-in-law. He was arrested in his tracks when Betsy let out a piercing scream and her body became rigid on his shoulder. The family immediately grouped around a distraught and sobbing Betsy as she was deposited into her mother's arms. Between the sobs and her mother's soothing words she spluttered,

"Nasty man carrying me again."

Joseph shivered as he realised his error. But simultaneously he reluctantly acknowledged that by moving to Scarborough, they may have physically escaped Bill Buxton, but sadly they had not taken account of him being etched into Betsy's memory. She still needed their careful handling and reassurance. He must remember never to do that again.

Joseph was ahead of the ladies and pushing the perambulator, now also transporting Betsy, cuddled up to her sleeping brother.

He had raced up the steep slope of Bland's Cliff from the beach to the town, leaving Hannah and her Ma to come up at their own pace. He waited for them to catch him up at Newborough Bar. There, he chatted to a couple of acquaintances from work. They were gathered in the afternoon sunshine, drinking their beer from the Bar Hotel and enjoying their Sunday treat, a cigar from the 'Man's Cigar Store' at the base of this grand gothic gate. They praised his children, and endowed him with some of the Bar's history. Dark and imposing, it no longer housed the criminals of the town, from where it had gained its name of the 'arch of misery and repentance'. Its sinister imposing facade remained, mocked only by the poster strung between the commanding turrets, advertising 'Brown, Moon and Co's' - Yorkshire Relish tea!

He bid them good-day and began to slowly move off towards the Bar Church on the corner of Westborough and Aberdeen Walk when he reassuringly saw that his wife and mother-in-law had come into view and waved at him.

As he cut up Oxford Street towards their home he slowed further trying to make out the cart alongside the frontage of their house. Two men appeared to be struggling with something wrapped in a cloth at the back of the cart. They managed to free it, and setting it down on the pavement, they both straightened their backs before picking it up again between them. Joseph felt himself accelerate when he saw them set it down again at his own front door. He shouted over his shoulder. "You surely haven't ordered more furniture Hannah? I've told you in time I can make us everything we need!"

"Of course not Joseph, I wouldn't do anything without your agreement, despite all your teasing. Besides, who delivers on a Sunday?"

Joseph left the perambulator on the corner of the road for Hannah to collect, and dashed across to the men, who were patiently awaiting an answer to their knocking.

"Ee. You're 'ere. Mr Elliot, I presume. This arrived at the station for you just now. I'd finished me shift an' said I would deliver it to yer on me way 'ome Sir, t'was no trouble."

"Well, that was kind of you indeed, thank you for your trouble." Joseph fished in his jacket pocket and handed the man a coin, then added another for his lad.

"Thank you kindly Sir. Good day to you." The man and his lad jumped onto the front of his cart and with a flick of the reins, drove away.

Joseph sadly turned to face Hannah's bewildered look.

He knew without even looking under the cloth that Henry had returned the Secretaire.

Kate Thackery assisted Joseph in carrying the beautifully made writing desk into the front parlour. It wasn't too heavy, just an awkward shape. They set it down in front of the window, the obvious place to do any writing in this large, but poorly lit room.

"I can't understand it Ma T. I really can't. He knows I made it especially for him. It was a mark of our friendship, and a sign of my respect for him. Why would he do this. If anything, it's for me to be angry with him, not the other way around. I'm the one facing responsibilities, whether they be mine to face, or his."

"Don't fret so about it Joseph, if he's anything like that father of his, he won't see it from your perspective, the world exists for them and their pleasure alone, no-one else's. And anyway, we have gained the most beautiful piece of furniture that Jacob told me he had ever seen in all his working life."

Joseph watched bewildered as his mother-in-law left the room heading for the back of the house. He mused that she had become the authority on the subject of the Fergusons of late. Sometimes he wondered if she knew more than she was prepared to tell him. But he was distracted from those thoughts by the feeling of enormous pride at such a compliment from his beloved mentor.

He turned his attention back to the secretaire. Running his fingers over the exquisite marquetry pattern on its surface, he wondered what Henry had not liked about it. Especially knowing Jacob – such an expert, had loved it so much. His fingers moved to the handle to pull down the writing desk, as he did so he remembered the secret compartment and its concealed contents. Had Henry read his letter? Was that what he had found disturbing?

Anxiously he clicked the mechanism which lifted smoothly under his fingers. There, just where he had left them, were the two pieces of parchment. Disappointed, he inspected more closely, but there, next to his two pieces, was a third. He pulled it out anxiously, curious to know what had precipitated this most cruel and wounding of actions by his friend. Unfolding the large sheet of parchment revealed a very bureaucratic looking letter. The page was headed by the address of his official Army Headquarters, and the mode and style was formal and distant.

Dear Joseph

Thank you kindly for sending me this exquisite piece of furniture. Unfortunately I am unable to accept such a gift from you. Your letter, and hair sample, made it quite plain that you think I have deceived you.

I repeat, Joseph, that I most definitely am not little Betsy's father any more now than I was on the night of her birth. I feel more wounded than on the battlefield, that with everything that has passed between us over the years you are unable to accept my word on this matter.

Lizzibeth's child seems to be a delight to both you and Hannah, and I am happy for you both. Were I her father I am sure I would be very proud to say so.

I wish you and Hannah every happiness in your future together in your new life, but be assured you did not need to leave Dorset on either my, or my family's account.

My affections to my Godchildren, I will not renege on my responsibilities to them. I sincerely hope the sea air is having a good effect on little Thom.

Goodbye Joseph.
Your Childhood Friend

Henry Ferguson.

Joseph seated himself heavily on the chair at the side of the window. He stared blankly at the letter, no longer reading any words, but trying hard to see his friend as he had penned it. He had been undoubtedly angry and hurt. Joseph rubbed his eyes vigorously, pressing them hard into their sockets. He didn't notice Hannah entering the room but then sensed her presence beside him. She looked from him to the letter. Joseph passed it to her as she laid a comforting hand on his shoulder, she didn't need its contents to know her husband was in torment. She returned the letter to the writing desk and spoke softly,

"He must be angry Joseph, Betsy must be your child after all. I knew as much. Now we know for certain, for Henry wouldn't have returned such a gift if he was irresolute in this, then surely now Bill cannot lay any claim on her over her real father. She's ours now for sure."

Joseph took his wife's hand in his and placed his other hand gently over her ample belly soothing her worries as he said,

"You're right Hannah, she's most definitely ours now. We are blessed to have her. But Betsy is so blessed too. She has in you the most wonderful mother, and Lizzibeth would be so proud of you both."

He laid his head on her and spoke quietly to his unborn child as Hannah stroked his dark curls. "Come on out of there little one before you get any bigger, we need to look after your mother here, she's soon to be as precious to you as she is to the rest of us." Hannah playfully pulled the lock she was fondling, "Don't be foolish, you idiot, I'll be fine. I'll have my confinement in the morning and be black leading the fireplace in the afternoon!" They both laughed and Joseph pulled her onto his knee. "This is no good, husband, I have to feed you and your children as well as see to everyone's bathing tonight. Would you be so kind as to set up the tin bath in front of the fire for me?" She decisively left the room, saying tea-time would be very soon.

Joseph had made to go and do as his wife had bid him, then he turned and blankly stared at Henry's letter. If she wasn't Henry's child, then whose was she? She must be. She had Henry's colouring, but then that was not exclusively his, indeed, wasn't Hannah's very similar.

Joseph had known for sure since his wedding night, that drunk or not, he would not have forgotten having intercourse with anyone, let alone Lizzibeth. Why was Henry in such denial? There must be a reason, but it did not exonerate him in Joseph's eyes, more angered and yet bewildered him. One day they would be able to talk about this, but for now it was too raw for Henry at least.

Possible explanations continued to bounce around in his head as he returned the letter to its secret compartment, pleased that Hannah had not actually examined the caustic communiqué, and went in search of the family tin bath.

Chapter 13

Scarborough, Summer 1858

"Joseph, why don't you go for a walk down to the Spa celebrations tonight. Ma said this afternoon there was so much excitement there."

"Oh no, Hannah, we'll perhaps have plenty other opportunities to go there. As a special treat sometime. You're still very tired and weak."

Hannah was seated in the large fireside rocking chair with their new baby daughter at her breast. Betsy was playing with Thom on the rug by her feet, using his hands and toes to repeat the same nursery rhymes inherent in any mother and grandmother.

"I'm in good health, Joseph, just a little tired which will soon pass. Betsy and Thom'll be in bed soon, and I only have this little one to feed. Ma's just upstairs if I need help. You could meet up with some of the fellows from your work and have an ale, or two. You deserve to rest, you've helped me with the children these past weeks as much as you could. Many a husband would not be so thoughtful. I sometimes think that our childhood friendship adds a different quality to our marriage you know Joseph, you're so much more considerate to me than many a husband."

"Well of course dearest wife, you chose well!" They both shared a smile and Joseph winked at her. "I suppose the town is really excited about it all, and of course the famous musical acts that may come to perform here. It would be exciting to get a glimpse of all those seats being sat upon. Heaven knows, they were monotonous enough to make."

"You're wasted on mass factory productions, Joseph, you know that. You can make beautiful bespoke pieces of furniture. Go and enjoy yourself, Joseph, just make sure you remember everything so you can come back and tell me. Perhaps some time away from everything, to think about what you want to do about your work would be good for you too."

"I know dearest, but we now have three little mouths to feed as well as ourselves, I have to be sure of what I'm doing. We need a regular income, it takes time to set up a respected and successful business." He picked up his jacket from the back of the chair, "Are you sure you'll be alright, I'll not stay out late, and I'll try not to wake you when I come in." Joseph bent to kiss his wife, but paused patiently while she adjusted her clothing and settled baby Kathy Louiza onto her other breast. Having made his affectionate goodbyes to them all, he quietly left the house. Hannah was pleased that he had accepted her offer, she knew he wanted to join in with the festivities, but also knew he would need to be coaxed. The experience of Lizzibeth's death following childbirth had left him anxious around the whole process. And Kathy had been their most troublesome child in the two weeks since her difficult arrival. She would not sleep, and demanded her mother's constant attention both day and night.

Betsy had been fascinated with her at first, but soon tired of her noisy objection to life outside the womb, and turned her affections more than ever towards her little brother. Thom, at such a young age, was nonplussed at the new arrival, but relished the extra attention she appeared to have dealt him from his big sister.

The dusky summer sky was aglow with gas lights from the other side of the Spa bridge as Joseph hurried across. If devoid of the sense of sight, he could have been guided by the noise of human joyous expectancy and excitement. Such was the local thrill of this big day for the town.

Joseph wandered around the periphery of the crowds, taking in the splendour of the whole vicinity. The landscaped gardens were unlike any he had seen before. Lawns, plants, bushes and trees were precisely ordered as though themselves obligated to co-operate with the symmetry and neatness of the design, and in their efforts, had fragranced the affair.

The sea wall had been extended to encompass a promenade and carriage road thirty feet in width. This would now accommodate the vast numbers of coaches and cabs that would be depositing the expected fashionable and plenteous patrons. There was a colonnade of small stores and an open air bandstand expectantly ready and waiting to entertain this new breed of middleclass music loving holiday makers during the daytime hours.

Joseph could not get close to the new saloon itself because of the sheer size of the gaiety and fashion surrounding him. He could hear the strains of the orchestra reaching out to welcome its guests, and could see the lights shining from novel design sun burners within.

He wandered over towards the sea wall and inhaled deeply the salty fish aroma seasoned with seaweed, which so sensuously signified the seaside to him. The tide was high and the sea was still. He found it hard to imagine that sometimes the sea here could be extraordinarily destructive. A workmate had told him that twenty years ago, a previous saloon on this spot had been completely devastated by a storm and heavy seas. Joseph looked out now to the two arms that formed this bay, embracing the hundreds of vessels dotting the clear blue tranquil sea to its bosom. Their lights danced on the surface of the water like diamonds sprinkled from the heavens above, whilst the seagulls swooped and seemed to squawk cordially in time with the orchestrated symbols.

"Well good evening Mister, want some company?"

Joseph turned to see a lady coming up towards him. She was tall and dark with a very plain dark serge dress. The neckline was scooped very low and the hemline was caught high up on her thigh with a red ribbon, exposing black laced boots and more female leg than he had ever before seen in daylight. Joseph, not for the first time tonight, found himself facing a large ample bosom. His eyes quickly travelled up to her face to see if this was someone he should know or recognise. The stranger smiled back at him. The gaps, and the state of her teeth reluctantly designated her years. She put her hand on his shoulder and placed a provocative red kiss on his cheek. Joseph leapt away from her, rubbing at his face. Taken completely unawares he innocently realised he was being propositioned. This was what he expected to happen at night in certain hostelry's if you weren't careful, but not in the summer evening light, at a busy and stylish fashionable event. He moved away, and began to mingle with the crowd. It was struggling and straining in unison to see any famous dignitaries as they arrived for the opening ceremony.

A round of applause went up and a man came into view behind the carriage from which he had just alighted. He ascended the steps, waving to his audience, before turning to enter the building.

"Who is that?" A large well dressed burly man beside Joseph enquired to no-one in particular, but the intonation required an immediate answer.

"I think," replied Joseph, "that's Sir Joseph Paxton, he's the architect behind the design. He's famous for designing the Crystal Palace in London."

"Oh, is he indeed, not famous enough for me to know him eh?" his questioner responded, "Well done lad, I like someone who can answer my questions. How do you know him though?"

"I've worked on the seating for the galleries Sir, he came to inspect the quality and comfort of them a few weeks ago." The ruddy complexion and big dark eyes looked Joseph up and down. "I haven't seen you around before lad, and I have a tendency to remember faces, and consequently to know most families in the town. Who's your father? Where do you live?"

"I've just recently moved here Sir from Dorset, with my wife and family. We live on James Street. Joseph Elliot Sir." Joseph held out his hand in friendly gesture to the stranger.

"Well pleased to meet you Joseph Elliot, and welcome to our town. I should've realised your accent wasn't local. May you have a long and happy life here. John Hetherington. Doctor John Hetherington" He grasped Joseph's hand firmly shaking it.

"We hope so Sir, thank you. I do find the accent here difficult at times, it can be very hard to make out some meanings."

"Oh you'll get used to it, there's neither nowt nor summut to it!" He laughed heartily at his own mirth, and then continued, "We're witnessing history here tonight you know, they tell us this is to be the most popular Concert Hall venue outside of the capital, London town itself."

"Really?"

"So they say. Oh, and I hope that young wife of yours doesn't get to know you were chatting to old Millie over there, she's quite disreputable you know!"

"Oh I wasn't Sir, she just came up to me, I realised immediately and moved away." John Hetherington laughed aloud heartily, and Joseph realised he was being teased, just as another round of applause broke out from the crowd. "I can't help you there I'm afraid Sir, I've no idea who that is."

"No matter, my boy, I must find my son, he was here with a few school friends, but it's really past his bedtime now, I had better get him home." He moved away to look for his son.

Joseph looked back towards the sea wall in the fading light to reassure himself that the disreputable 'Millie' had gone. Instead he saw a line of five boys all precariously standing along the sea wall like targets for a catapult, giving them a paramount view of the occasion. He wondered if one of them was John Hetherington's son. He made to follow the man to point him in their direction, when another round of applause rippled through the crowd. Joseph turned back to look at who had stirred this reaction, but could not identify the flamboyantly dressed couple. They bowed their heads to their spectators before disappearing inside the Concert Hall. He looked around for the man, but he was no longer in his sight, his gaze returned to the boys on the wall, to his horror, the boys were clambering down from the wall, screaming and shouting as they did so. Joseph counted only four. He ran over to the wall, no-one else could hear them above the general noise of the crowd. One boy saw his approach and started to yell at him,

"Please Mister, Ed's gone over into the sea, he's in the water, quick look."

Joseph ran to the sea wall and looked over. In the fading light, he could make out frantic splashes from the water below. Hopefully that meant he was not hurt, but the water would be very cold. He threw his jacket on the wall and kicked off his shoes.

"Can he swim?"

"I don't think so Mister."

Joseph climbed onto the wall and jumped into the sea. He had to orientate himself for a few minutes on surfacing, the cold had shocked him and he had not realised how much his trousers would hold the water and pull him down. "Ed, is it, are you there?"

"Help me, help me please." A faint reply carried amidst the frantic splashes close to the sea wall. Joseph reached out for him.

"Hang onto me child, you'll be alright."

"Edward!" A shout came from above, Joseph, shivering severely, looked up to see his new acquaintance leaning over the wall. He managed a clear reply, "I've got him, but I'm not sure where we can get out from here."

"Come over to the left of you, there's a ramp at the end of the wall that leads out of the sea, I'll go round there." Joseph did as he was bid. Sure enough as the wall turned a corner,

Joseph felt substance under his feet. Once he could stand, he took a cradling hold of the child, and carried him out of the water to his waiting father, now surrounded by a growing group of onlookers. As he passed Edward into his father's arms a cheer went up for Joseph. Simultaneously a disenchanted disappointed dignitary walked unacknowledged into the Spa Concert Hall with his decadently dressed wife.

"Come on in, come on in, please." Doctor John Hetherington pushed through the door of his elegant house on the fashionable Crescent, carrying his nine year old son Edward, and motioning to Joseph as he went.

His wife appeared ethereally in the entrance hall, in a substantial white night gown ineffective in disguising her expectant state. She was significantly younger than her husband, her pretty face and delicate frame adding to her youthfulness. She began to flap her arms in blind panic. Her imagination, as is the prerogative of every mother began with the very worst scenario; gradually, evidence that her son was living and breathing allowed the prevalence of common sense and her pitch levelled with her angst. She began,

"Oh my Godfathers, John, whatever has happened? Oh, John, tell me please."

She anxiously hovered, waiting for her son to be alighted onto the chaise, and then enveloped him in a smothering embrace, retreating slightly only when her son's squirming reassured her of his wellbeing.

"Well, my dear, Edward here decided to see if the seawater had got any warmer since we took him paddling last week! Only this time he didn't just paddle, he went in literally over his head, off the Spa wall if you please. Fortunately, this young man here, Joseph Elliot, whom I'd just made acquaintance with a few moments before, saw what happened, and jumped in and pulled him out. So don't fret dearest, everything's fine." He gently put his arms around his wife coaxing her away from her son and onto her feet. "I'm going to examine them both, but I'm sure that, fortuitously, neither have suffered any ill effects from the experience."

Mary Hetherington was visibly shaking with shock as she turned her bewildered attention to Joseph,

"We are eternally grateful to you Mr Elliot, can I get you any refreshment?"

Joseph was standing awkwardly in the drawing room of this stylish terraced house, realising he was dripping sea water onto the polished wood floor. It was gathering around both feet like a thin resin rooting him to the spot.

"Er, no I'm alright thank you very much. It was no trouble, I'm just glad Ed is safe. Excuse me, I must get home. My wife will be concerned if I am too late, we have a new baby."

He stepped away from the puddle causing the water to flow like a suddenly un-dammed river towards the chaise as Mary interjected sternly.

"Edward, my son's name is Edward Mr Elliot, not Ed!" Doctor Hetherington stepped forwards dismissing his wife and her pedantic manner, "You can't walk home like this, you'll catch your death, at the very least a chill, it's very cold tonight, clear sky you know. You must dry off and take some clean clothes. Can you sort some from my wardrobe Mary. I'll just carry this little scamp upstairs, the same goes for him too, he needs thoroughly drying, then a warm dry night shirt. We'll talk about this tomorrow Edward, you could have been killed tonight, it was a very silly thing you were all doing."

John Hetherington bent to pick up his son just as his wife doubled in pain clutching her abdomen, and a pool of water appeared in an instant at her feet swelling the river of sea water. The doctor paused as though assessing the scene, then passed his son to Joseph, he instructed, "Top of the stairs, turn right, second door on the left. Towels and clean clothes in the cupboards or wardrobes. What would I have done without you tonight. Joseph Elliot, thank you so much."

"Joseph, where've you been, I was so worried when Kathy awoke in the middle of the night and you weren't beside me, then to not come home 'till this time?"

Joseph had set off for home as soon as Doctor Hetherington appeared downstairs in the drawing room this morning. He had safely delivered his wife of a second son. They were going to call him Henry Joseph. His wife's father's name was Henry, and the second name was apparently a unanimous choice between them both following the previous evening's events. Joseph had agreed to stay in the house in case the other children had awoken and needed anything whilst Doctor Hetherington was busy with his wife. Their hired help was not due to come in until the morning. Joseph's assistance though, had not actually been required, both Edward and his five year old sister Beatrice had slept all night.

"I'm sorry my dear, you won't believe everything that happened last night. I couldn't make this up if I tried." Hannah took in his clothes, obviously not his own, though very respectable, together with the exhausted look of her husband and grinned at him as he plonked himself into the fireside rocking chair. "What a way to start the day of rest!"

"What've you done now? Wait here and I'll make you a cup of tea."

Betsy and Thom threw themselves at Joseph's feet expecting some attention. They were to be disappointed when Joseph was heard snoring loudly within minutes, and Hannah knew the delivered cup of tea would grow cold at his side.

Kate Thackery came bustling into their kitchen having been out for her morning constitutional.

"Er, what time did Joseph come back last night Hannah dear?"

"He actually didn't come home last night, Ma, he's just arrived home this morning. You've just walked past him, he's asleep by the fire. Why do you ask?"

"I don't believe it. That Flossie Flat Hat woman must be right. I never would've believed it of Joseph, Hannah. Mind you it must be difficult for men when their wives are in the family way, but even so, he wouldn't have had to wait much longer would he? Now if it'd been your father, I'd never have been surprised, I suspected as much, but it was his choice not to risk another child, not mine, and I suppose if he did seek alternative comfort, he was discrete at least."

"Ma, what are you talking about? What did Mrs Jones say?"

"Whores, Hannah, you know, ladies of the night."

"What about whores Ma, I know what they are?"

"Joseph, last night, he was seen with 'Old Millie' she's the one we often see around the town. Bosoms and legs on show for the world, 'an half 'er teeth missing!"

"Don't be silly Ma, Joseph wouldn't go with a whore. Something happened last night, he's come home in someone else's clothes and is absolutely exhausted, he fell asleep in the chair as soon as he got home." Kate's horror was written in her wide eyes and open jaw.

"Well then, huh, what did I tell you. Whores Hannah, you mark my words."

Hannah was pacing the hallway with Kathy on her shoulder and was patting her tiny back as she went. She was grizzly again for no apparent reason, and Hannah was trying to keep her away from Joseph to allow him to sleep. She couldn't believe Mrs Jones's gossip. She was sure Joseph would not do something so hurtful to her. She had been as attentive to her husbands needs as her condition allowed. Her pacing became more frantic as Kathy's yells seemed to speed with her mother's anxious heart beat. Surely not. Even so, she wanted him awake to dispel the rumour before it spread further afield. It was just too humiliating.

Just then, there was a quiet knocking on the front door. Her mother pushed past her, I'll get it Hannah, you're busy, it may be for me anyway. She opened their large red front door, and to her surprise, Mrs Robinson from next door was posed in proferring a freshly baked cake, covered in icing and cherries. Mrs Robinson, her husband and three children tended to keep themselves very much to themselves and they had hardly exchanged a dozen words since they had arrived.

"I'm really sorry to trouble you Mrs Elliot", she was looking past Kate Thackery and speaking directly to Hannah, "but I just wanted to show my own gratitude to your husband for what he did last night. Our Peter was there with young Edward, my nephew Charlie and niece Lottie live in the Crescent, so they all play together. It could so easily have been Charlie last night. Your husband was very brave. I have to confess to being a little unfriendly to you as strangers in our midst when you first arrived, but I hope you'll accept this as a token of my apology. You're most welcome amongst us Mrs Elliot. And your family." She cast a smile at Kate. "Congratulations on your new baby too, oh she's adorable." Jane Robinson handed the cake to Kate, and was cooing over the bawling baby when Joseph appeared in the hallway. He rubbed his eyes hard into his head, then looking at Mrs Robinson, he said "Good day to you Mrs Robinson, if you will excuse me I'm very tired." He turned and walked back towards the back of the house where he could hear his children playing. Giggling coyly, like a flirtatious teenager, she replied,

"Oo certainly Mr Elliot, well done Mr Elliot, thank you kindly and enjoy the cake Mr Elliot." She turned on her heels and was gone. Hannah watched her go, then closing the front door, she turned to face her mother.

"Whores, Ma, Honestly!"

"Well Mrs Jones said….."

"Mrs Jones what?.... I'd rather believe my husband Ma, and the new found respect of some previously very suspicious and unfriendly neighbours!"

Kate Thackery had cooked their Sunday roast later than usual today due to Joseph's morning sleep. She was still helping

Hannah with the cooking as baby Kathy was feeding and crying so often. As she dished out the meal, she looked suspiciously at her son-in-law. "Are you going to tell us all what happened last night Joseph, or do we have to wrench it out of you?"

"Ma, leave Joseph alone, he'll tell us when he's ready, it sounds as though it was a rough night, I just hope you weren't in any danger my dear?"

"No. I'm sorry Hannah, I should've told you it all straight away, it's just that the night brought back so many memories, and they've been bothering me again ever since."

"Then don't go over it again Joseph, leave it for now. Let's just enjoy our meal with the children. We can talk about it later if you want." Hannah could barely contain her amusement as she felt her mother's eyes boring into her with every dollop of food she frustratedly dished up.

That night as they lay together, Joseph relived the whole night in illustrated detail to his wife, including his encounter with 'old Millie' and his late night swim with Edward Hetherington.

For the first time, Joseph also imparted his experience of the day Henry had nearly drowned. She had tears in her eyes as she listened to the emotional story that had previously only been alluded to, but now had a poignant sadness in view of Henry's recent behaviour and dissociation from them.

He mused to her that he had worried all his childhood and until now, that if it hadn't been for his father's encouragement that day on the lake with Henry, he would not have gone in the water. He had done it to please his father, not to save Henry's life.

"I can't tell you how embarrassed I felt by all the praises being sung to me at the time, Hannah. My father thought my pensiveness was due to guilt at briefly letting Henry go when he threw up in the water, added to a little self-indulgent pity. It was neither, just the knowledge that I was unworthy of not only all the heroic praise heaped upon me, but later, also all the benevolence and good fortune that followed it. The unfairness of fate seemed to grow with the years. Whilst I was waged for my good fortune, Lizzibeth and others, had no shoes."

He went on to describe also how, as Henry had became a pivotal part of his very being, he had tormented and chastised himself with this truth. He had felt increasingly weak and undeserving. For he knew without doubt, that had the positions been reversed, Henry would unquestionably have been the hero, and saved him.

Last night he had most definitely had a choice, and in the absence of his father and without giving a second thought, he had made the honourable decision for a stranger. This had become an important moment of exoneration for Joseph. Hannah listened sympathetically, saddened by his torment.

"You set high standards for yourself Joseph, I couldn't imagine many people doing what you did on either occasion".

"I know this, as soon as those sea water baths are completed on the foreshore next year, my dear, our children must be taught to swim. It's an unnecessary yet easy way to lose a life." Then, as if suddenly remembering something important, having counselled and settled his childhood plights; he continued,

"Well though, my dear Hannah, this isn't the end of it. I am once again to be embarrassed by a reward for my good deed. Can you believe that Dr John Hetherington has had early notification and therefore chance of tickets, to listen to Mr Dickens' himself no less, reading at the Assembly Rooms in town, on the 13th day of September!"

"But how is this 'your' reward, Joseph?"

"Well, his young wife Mary, is not at all interested. She was attending out of a sense of duty to her husband. But when he found me reading one of his Dickens' novels after little Henry Joseph was born this morning, and I told him how ardently and voraciously I read them all, he invited me to join him on his wife's half-a-crown ticket instead. Can you believe it Hannah? The great novelist himself is coming right here to this town."

Hannah smiled at her husband, this was good fortune

indeed.

"I feel this is one embarrassment, much like the other, that you will accept with good grace dearest husband."

"Hmm," Joseph wasn't sure if there had been a hint, if mischievous, of his parsimonious tendencies, and how he had profited from his previous 'reward'. "Unfortunately" he continued, "it is to be on a Monday, so I will only be able to attend the evening reading, and sadly not the afternoon one. Disappointing, as that will be Little Dombey, but the eight-o-clock evening reading is the Christmas Carol, what could be better?"

"You go and enjoy yourself Joseph Elliot, but I shall require a full account of the whole evening, including a full description of Mr Dickens himself, the rooms, who was there, and the story, oh and also the exact way that he read it."

"You don't want a report from me Hannah, you want a photographer!" He playfully patted her thigh as they snuggled together.

"You do know that there is talk of Mr Dicken's having left his wife, and has been seen in the company of a young woman? An actress no less, Nellie something I think, and the same age as his eldest daughter."

"Yes I have read something in the newspapers, but he is still a wonderful writer my dear, and has given such enjoyment to so many."

Joseph vividly described the style of Doctor Hetherington's house as they closed their eyes waiting for sleep to wash over them. He shared his own aspirations to provide for them like that one day. He told her of their family, and that Doctor Hetherington had suggested the two ladies had tea together one day to share the trials and tribulations of new motherhood. Hannah fell asleep in her husband's arms, while Joseph's mind would not permit his slumber.

Unbeknown to his wife, Joseph had also heard everything his mother-in-law had said to her in the kitchen earlier in the day. He had been pretending to be asleep to avoid the effort of entertaining Betsy and Thom in his fatigued state. He was amused by Mrs Jones' gossip. That had not worried him. But he was so shocked to think of his father–in-law being reduced to employing the services of such ladies of the night, he could not believe it of him. Not Jacob Thackery. Surely not. And why was he so troubled by this?

Chapter 14

Scarborough, November 1860 - April 1862

"Are you coming with me this afternoon Hannah? I know it's a cold day, but the children can be well wrapped up and we'll witness history being made. I'll certainly be giving my sewing machine a rest. A grand new Wesleyan Methodist Church for the town. We won't have to book seats in this church, there should be room enough for all God fearing people wanting to worship there. Doctor Hetherington and his wife'll be there, and the Robinsons are going."

Kate Thackery was putting the breakfast things away as her daughter was having a struggle trying to dress two year old Kathy in front of the fire. As usual Kathy Louiza it seemed, found great sport in making life difficult for everyone around her.

"Yes, Ma, I'd like to go, but it depends on whether Kathy's had her nap. Actually it'd probably be better if she hasn't, she may sleep in the perambulator then, and we can see and hear the foundation stone being laid in peace!"

Betsy ran into the kitchen with her hairbrush and shoes in her hands. She was dressed for school, and at six years old was now an uncommonly confident and capable little girl. She could be trusted to look after Thom when her mother was busy with Kathy, and was often a big help to both Hannah and her mother around the house. Recently she had begun to show an interest in sewing, and her Grandmother had been teaching her how to do a little hemming.

"Granma, please can you do my hair for me, I want to look nice coz it's my turn to stand at the front of the classroom and hand out the slates today. And to move the balls along the big abacus for the teacher when we do adding and take-aways. So will you do plaits please?" She jumped up and down excitedly. "Oh, and can I have ribbons in?"

"Of course, dear, sit down here for me." Hannah looked round at Betsy who could hardly contain her excitement, she had been so excited saying her prayers by her bedside last night.

"It's a very important job, Betsy, you will do your best for me won't you."

"Oh I will Ma, I don't want to do summut wrong like Johnny did last week coz everyone laughed at him."

"Something." Kate Thackery made everyone in the room jump with her booming correction of Betsy's colloquialism.

"Ma, you made me jump," turning to a startled Betsy Hannah quietly added, "Betsy dear, you know how your Pa doesn't like you talking like that, it's lazy." Betsy stared at the floor, appeasing her Grandmother by being as still as she could for her hair to be tamed into two tidy tails. Kate, humming as usual her favourite pieces of music, finished her task with the addition of a blue ribbon bow at the base of each plait. Turning Betsy enthusiastically round to face her, she nodded approval at the aesthetics of her grand-daughters hair. Then spoke to Hannah.

"I'll walk Betsy to school shall I?" Kate picked up her coat knowing that this arrangement would suit her busy daughter. "Then, as its Friday, on our way back from the church site, we could pick up one of those new fish suppers for us all for tea. That'd be a treat Hannah." Hannah was turning a fully dressed, yet squirming Kathy around to face her.

"Now young lady, that's you done, and me exhausted for the day. You should've learnt by now that you have to be dressed every day. Then you might just let your Ma get on with it." Then she responded to her mother. "Yes please Ma, if you don't mind. Be good, walking with your Granma, won't you Betsy. And yes, Ma, a fish supper tonight sounds lovely." Hannah straightened herself up from the fireside and turned her attention to Thom who, at nearly four years old, was seated quietly at the table drawing on his slate. By the time she looked down again at her younger daughter, she had removed one of her socks and was intent on removing the other one. Kate Thackery bent down towards her but Kathy quickly snatched the sock up before her Grandmother could retrieve it.

"My do it!" She shouted vehemently into the air. Her doting Grandmother was so taken aback by her impudence, she was about to chastise her, when Hannah, watching her daughter, caught her arm.

"Look Ma, she's doing it herself. This might be her problem, we keep doing everything for her and she wants to do it herself." She bent down to Kathy and quietly encouraged, "you're a clever girl, well done. Can you put your own clothes on for your Ma now?" She smiled at her and ruffled her hair. "Tonight when you get ready for bed, can Kathy do it herself?" Kathy beamed up at her mother, elated that at last someone understood her.

"My do it." She echoed with a decisive nod of her head and pointing a successfully 'socked' foot in the air at no-one in particular.

The crowd had gathered on the chilly, wet, north east corner of the clearing that was to become Scarborough's Grand Wesleyan place of worship to replace the now overcrowded Chapel in Queen Street. Opposite the shivering crowd, were the imposing archways of the railway station, hushed and abandoned at this inhospitable time of year on the north east coastline.

There was an excited chatter amongst the spectators, mainly regular church goers, but with a few curious passers-by. Few men, unless connected with the project were able to excuse themselves from their workplaces for such an event. But the dignitaries connected with the Wesleyan movement in Scarborough were there in full, dressed formally, to befit the austerity of the occasion.

Kate, Hannah and the children were in a prime position around the site, reserved early on in the proceedings by an officious Kate. The children were seated around the foundation corner stone markings with little Annie Robinson and Henry Hetherington. Their older brothers and sisters were at school. The Reverend Samuel Tindall was making a speech as he handed an inscribed silver trowel to Henry Fowler Esq. He was explaining that Mr Fowler had been chosen for this task by the unanimous voice of the trustees and members with whom he had lived in Christian fellowship for many years. He was indeed the same man who had carried out this task many years earlier for the Queen Street chapel, now too small for its growing congregation. Mr Fowler indicated to a group of workmen. They responded by carefully assisting him in setting the foundation stone into position amid an anticipated silence. As they straightened erect, signifying the completion of their task, he responded by confirming it had been duly laid in the name of The Father, The Son and The Holy Ghost. He continued with many and various gratitudes to individuals, not least The Heavenly Father Himself, before eventually announcing they should all sing the hymn on their sheets.

The whole gathering had been supplied with sheets on their arrival consisting of the words to this hymn, the Doxology and the National Anthem. The damp November afternoon stilled to enjoy the enthusiastic and harmonious singing. This choral congregation with one accord, was filled with hope for their prosperous future in this growing seaside town. More prayers were said by various church dignitaries, during which the skies eerily cleared, placing the site under a turquoise blue ceiling overarched by the most splendid of rainbows. Taken by the throng as clearly a colourful smile of approval from God Himself.

Finally, Mr George Ireland, a Trustee and Chapel Steward, stepped up to the dias. He was brandishing a sealed bottle containing current coins and a variety of documents which included a list of the principle subscribers and the Circuit Plan of the new church, a copy of the accounts, the local newspapers, and a copy of the hymn sheet. These would remain with the foundation corner stone, for the wonder and appreciation of future Scarborians who would unveil a magical piece of history many years from now.

After saying a few words, he dropped the bottle accurately and with a flourish onto the ground alongside the foundation stone. Hannah and Mary Hetherington looked startled. In their proximity, they had heard a shattering sound. Then catching each other's eye, could not contain their girlish giggles when they simultaneously realised the bottle designed for posterity had actually smashed. Kate Thackery and John Hetherington together cast disapproving looks in the young women's direction assuming a deliberately misunderstood phrase in a speech to be the cause of their embarrassing conduct.

The crowd applauded, a prayer was said with a blessing bestowed on all future worshippers, and finally the National Anthem was sung.

The gathering slowly dispersed, chattering about what the finished Chapel would look like, inside and out. Jane Robinson offered to collect both her boys and Betsy from school if Hannah would take Annie home with her. She hurried away. Mary's husband moved between Hannah and his wife.

"Would you two ladies like to explain your behaviour during that speech? You were worse than Kathy. Hannah, you need worry about her unruliness, what about you two!"

"I am so sorry John," his wife replied, "but didn't you hear the bottle smash? I doubt if there will be much left of those documents for posterity after a few years exposed to the elements, do you? The coins should survive though I suppose."

"You wicked pair, I wonder if we should tell someone?"

"Oh, John my dear, I don't think anyone will find out now, the workmen are filling in the area with cement as we speak, no-one here today will care anyway, this building will survive for centuries."

The two young women shared another stifled giggle, mocking their strife. "Are we staying for the tea-meeting, John dear, I know you purchased tickets for it, or do you still have patients to see today?" The hetheringtons moved away slightly from the others, discussing their arrangements as they did so. Mary turned to take their leave, "See you all some other time, good day Thom, Annie, good day Kathy." They all returned their goodbyes, the children waving to each other, and the Elliots set off to walk down Westborough and through the town towards home.

"Hannah I just want to stop in the Apothecary's here." The last part of Kate Thackery's sentence was spoken into the doorway unheard, and Hannah had no choice but to follow her in with the children. Boldly she approached the counter, and despite other people present in the shop, she stunned them into silence by asking the pharmacist loudly and clearly if he had 'curl papers' in stock. The portly gentleman, seemed to flush from his neck up to the tips of his ears, before clearing his throat, and checking that the other customers had all averted their eyes, he reached under the counter and produced a small bundle. Kate pulled some coins out of her black satin purse, pushed them towards the blushing pharmacist and picking up the seemingly offensive bundle, secured it into her purse.

"Thank you kindly Sir." She swept unflinchingly out of the shop leaving a stunned audience, whose eyes appeared magnetised to Kate's exit. She was followed by a bemused Hannah, a perambulator and mystified children.

"Ma, what was all that about? Do you have to embarrass me like that."

"Don't be silly Hannah, why should you be embarrassed by 'curl papers', I need to call in at the halting station on the way home, I'm quite desperate, and they never have any newspapers in there. I can't manage without, daughter. Do you have a penny I could borrow?"

Hannah felt in her pocket to oblige her mother, and smiled to herself. Her mother had become a much more confident, fun and independent person since their arrival in this new town and their new life. There was never a dull moment with her around, and Hannah enjoyed her company.

"Shall we get a fish supper then Hannah? We have to pass the shop on the way home, my treat."

"Yes, Ma, if you like, it may have to be your treat as I don't have very much money on me, but Joseph will be bringing some home tonight." She put her hand haltingly on Thom's head as he pulled repeatedly on her cloak, and then enquired, "Are these fish suppers expensive? Yes Thom, what is it?" She now looked down at her son.

"I got some money Ma." Hannah looked aghast at Thom's open palm filled with a shiny coin of each denomination. She took a sharp intake of breath simultaneously opening her mouth wide as she looked from him to her mother. Kate Thackery recovered first,

"Thom! Where did you get that from?"

"It all fell out of the broken bottle Granma. No-one else wanted it, so I picked it all up. Annie and I shared it."

"What do you think to it Hannah? Isn't it amazing? He is such a clever man, he talks with a very strange accent though. They say he's making a fortune, and his gallery in Sarony Square is a little gold mine. My mother thinks it is weird being able to look at us when we aren't there, she can't understand how it's done. Not that I do really."

Hannah and Jane Robinson were standing drinking their cups of tea on their doorsteps on James Street, whilst admiring the new and extraordinary family portrait of the Robinson's. The Photographic Gallery had been set up for four years now in the town, and was very popular with the well-to-do holidaymakers.

Hannah studied the photograph. A sepia William Robinson was seated upon a rather grand chair. The image had managed to turn the most kindly and mild mannered of men, if occasionally a little brusque, into a terrifying tyrant. Hiding behind no longer affable, but now formidable whiskers. He was dressed formally with his support elbow opening his jacket sufficiently enough to display an impressive pocket watch. His legs were crossed with one shiny black shoe cocooned on a thick sheepskin rug, whilst the other was supported in mid air obscuring the legs of his first born son Peter. His wife was standing beside him with Peter slightly in front of her. One hand was placed stiffly on the back of her husband's chair, the other on Peter's shoulder. The look on her face told of the impending doom looming towards her. She wore the new outfit that she had recently been using for Sunday best at chapel each week, including the ornate bonnet, which appeared a little over done and out of place for the parlour style photograph. Seven year old Johnny Robinson and his little sister Annie were seated on a little bench to their father's right. All three children, although dressed immaculately as for Sunday worship, were all holding the same tedious expression, with a lopsidedness which hinted at mischief. Indeed both boys had one hand behind their backs as though secreting a catapult to be used on the photographer the minute the image was complete. Annie though, whilst clothed in innocent white, and securing the many frills on her voluminous angelic dress fashioned by Kate Thackery forwards over her knees; somehow managed to look the most wayward. A large decorative firescreen completed the picture, showing a new phoenix bird in one corner arising triumphant from the ashes of its spicy nest, whilst the other corner displayed an arrogant peacock in full display, impressing a potential mate. The complete image was set into a brown folder bearing the stylish inscription of 'Oliver Sarony's Photographic Gallery'.

"You're taking a long time Hannah, don't you like it?"

"Of course I like it Jane. It is just so remarkable; I've never seen a photograph before of anyone I know. I know what your mother means. I want to study how close the likeness is."

"Of course it's a close likeness Hannah, it's a photograph, not a painting. I really don't understand how it works either. William has tried to explain it to me; they use it a lot at the newspaper. His job is to arrange any necessary photographs to go with each article that's printed. That's how we came to get it done for our wedding anniversary. But it does capture you exactly as you are. Even expressions. Isn't that just our Annie?" Hannah perused the photograph again,

"Well yes it is, although I don't think I've ever seen you, or William, looking quite so wretched." She giggled as she handed the image back to one of its models.

"Well you would look wretched if you'd just had to hold the same position for forever, while a man disappeared under a black cloth in front of you and kept saying 'hold still please, hold still now'." They both laughed as Jane imitated holding her pose for the photographer.

"Why are photographs always this brown colour, Jane, do you know?" Jane was still gazing at her proud acquisition,

"I really don't know Hannah, I did ask William that, but I didn't really get an answer, which more than likely means he doesn't know either!" They both shared a knowing smile just as Miss Briggs opened her door, and stepped outside her little cottage next door to the Robinson's house, and into the balmy stillness.

"I thought I heard voices out here, isn't it time you two went inside and attended to your husbands? They may require some refreshments before retiring. These summer evenings aren't for idle gossip you know. You young ones are all the same." Hannah inhibited her own wry smile and replied for them both,

"We were just going in Mrs Briggs, and you're right, Joseph will not be pleased if his bite of supper is not ready for him. I hope you're well today, and we didn't disturb you?"

"Well seeing as you're here, have you heard what happened to that lassie that used to help out at number eleven across the road? I heard they threw her out, such a shame, I used to teach her, she was such a bright girl."

"Well Miss Briggs, I believe she's in the workhouse now, along there on Dean Road." Jane Robinson replied, "she had twins you know, three weeks ago. They just couldn't keep her on with the twins, they've enough mouths of their own to feed. It's such a shame; she got on well with them too. I heard that her only company now in that place, is an eighty seven year old miller, a seventy seven year old labourer, and a plasterer and his wife in their sixties. All fallen on hard times, but not much comfort for a new mother of twenty two is it?"

"No indeed Mrs Robinson, no indeed. But, she made her bed when she did what she did, she made her bed. She must learn to live with the consequences if you ask me." She shook her head adding a 'tut tut' for good measure, and then continued to Hannah,

"Mrs Elliot, could you ask your mother if she'd like to take tea with me tomorrow. I enjoy her company. I shall expect her at four. Tell her the banging next door to me on the other side has started up again, she tells me it could be rats in the shared loft. Rats indeed, wait 'til she hears herself what I've to put up with."

"Hannah, have you heard the news?" Joseph came in from his day at the workshop looking quite shocked.

"Please close the door Joseph, it's bitterly cold whenever anyone goes in or out. Ma's just come

in from Miss Briggs' cottage and stood with the door open forever while saying their goodbyes. She goes in there quite regularly now you know; she says there really are some strange noises come from Mrs Hudson's house. Did you say something about news?"

"Prince Albert has died from typhoid fever." Hannah looked up from mashing a pan of potatoes,

"Oh Joseph that's terrible news, the poor Queen must be beside herself." She settled the pan back onto the heat and straightened herself up to look at her husband. "When did he die Joseph, was he at home?"

"I don't know, I've brought two newspapers home with me to read all about it." Joseph spoke as he returned from closing the door, and hung his coat on the back of the scullery door, then turned back to his wife. "I passed St Nicholas House today at lunchtime, Hannah. Mr Woodall, resplendent in a top hat to rival Mr Brunel's famous one, was having his photograph taken on the balcony, with all the Officers of the Rifle Volunteers standing on his lawn in front of him. Their uniforms are very smart, buttons badges and boots that you could see your face in."

"I don't like seeing all those guns Joseph, I just think of the damage they can do to human flesh."

"A necessary weapon though now, Hannah I'm afraid. How long before tea? Where are the children?"

"It'll be another twenty minutes, you have time to read the paper if that's what you mean. The children are all next door, it's Annie's birthday remember. They won't be home for tea, there's just the three of us."

"That'll be strange, I'll enjoy the brief peace and quiet." He settled himself smiling onto their settee in front of the fire, and picked up the first of his newspapers. "I really hope the Prince didn't suffer too much. He's done a lot of good for this country; he was an intelligent and honourable man."

It wasn't until later that evening when the children were back home and in bed that he got around to opening the Times. He had only got as far as the first page when a name leapt out at him from the emboldened print of those united in Matrimony.

Major Henry Charles Ferguson was married at Salisbury Cathedral to the Honourable Miss Amelia Harrington, followed by a most lavish wedding breakfast at the stately home of the bride's parents. They are to be based with the bridegroom's parents at Ferguson House, with married quarters also at Chatham Army base in Kent.

Joseph felt shivers running down his spine.

Henry had married without even telling him, let alone inviting him. Who was Miss Amelia Harrington, he had never even heard Henry mention her before. It must have been a whirlwind romance. He quietly handed the open paper to Hannah and indicated the entry. Hannah read it, and looked sadly up at her husband.

"Oh, Joseph, how has it come to this? This isn't what Lizzibeth would have wanted at all. Henry must also be so sad, Joseph."

"But it's of his doing, Hannah, not mine."

"Are you going to the new Church on Friday Hannah? You do know it's opening for worship, with the Rev John Rattenbury don't you? I believe the sound of the new organ is magnificent, two rows of keys, with thirty stops. Did you know too, that there is to be a presentation by Mr Cross the ex-mayor of a beautiful clock for the Gallery. It's very unusual, it can be wound from behind to save continually disturbing the front glass. I'm sure the whole event will far outweigh any reading Mr Dickens could give!"

Joseph fielded the look his wife shot him. He had teasingly never been forgiven for witnessing the renowned author reading his own works without having her with him. Joseph was lying in bed waiting for his wife to finish brushing her long fair titian hair and join him. She turned to face him as she replied, continuing with her task.

"Very amusing Joseph, I'm sure. Anyway, if the review in the paper was anything to go by, it said that the reader's own imagination would give a better picture of Mr Dicken's characters than the author himself!"

"Utter rubbish! And that was only one of them, Hannah.

Another reviewer reported Mr Dickens as making every character stand out boldly before us, as well as vividly bringing every location to life. Look at what a sell out the occasion was. The whole population of Scarborough can't be wrong now can they?" Hannah patted him playfully on his arm with her hairbrush.

"No need to revel yet again husband! He was only doing those readings to restore public adoration after his scandal, and also to travel the country with his mistress if you please! But as to the Chapel, yes, I'd like to go, Betsy and Thom will be at school so I'll only have Kathy with me. I'm sure Ma will want to go. I can't believe it's come round to that date for the opening already. The Fourth of April 1862 seemed such a long way off when they first proposed it as the finish date. Will you be there?"

Joseph had been mesmerised watching his wife, she looked so enchanting in the lamp light, and oh, so, desirable. He was struggling more and more to restrain himself. He adjusted himself in the bed to avoid such a view of her, and enable him to concentrate on his reply.

"Well, I was supposed to be there anyway, my dear, but as the job is now completed at the church, I'm due to go with Mr Wrigglesworth himself to look at the plans for the big hotel they are going to build near to St Nicholas House. Do you know where I mean?"

"I'm not sure, is it where the holiday places are? Woods Lodgings isn't it? You know, with the one Anne Bronte died in a few years ago while she was here convalescing?"

"That's right. Well it's said it'll be the biggest hotel in Europe. Did you ever manage to get hold of the book of hers that you wanted to read?"

"The Tenant of Wildfell Hall, yes, I found it in a book shop, but it was three volumes and so quite expensive. I thought I'd see if the library would get it. They have been reluctant when I've asked because a critic had said that it was 'utterly unfit to be put into the hands of girls'!" They both laughed as Hannah climbed onto the bed.

"Well, perhaps you shouldn't be reading it then my dear!"

"Nonsense husband, I might learn something. I lead a very sheltered life you know!" She provocatively purred the last words as she snuggled up to Joseph. He shifted his position, removing his arm from underneath her. She added pensively, "wasn't it sad that Anne Bronte died so young, she could have written so much more. I always think of her when Ma brings us cockles and whelks, apparently she was a regular visitor to those stalls while she was here."

"Hrrm, anyway, at this new hotel, the workshop may get all the fitting jobs. He wants me to help him with estimating the costs and quantities. There's also a new church to be built in the Ramshill area which may bring more work. And anyway, if the truth be told, I don't like being too mixed up with that lot at the Wesleyan Chapel Hannah, I cannot accept the necessity for complete temperance regarding the odd drink. And before you protest, Doctor Hetherington's with me on this opinion too."

"Well I agree to an extent Joseph, which is why I don't understand the need for temperance in other areas either." She paused and then turned to collect her husbands questioning gaze, then boldly continued. "Do you have another woman Joseph?"

"What! Hannah, of course not, whatever makes you think that, am I not a good husband to you?"

"You're a perfect husband in so many ways Joseph, but whereas many wives lament their husband's constant attendance upon them, I appear not to interest you at all."

"My dearest wife; it's not a lack of interest, far, far from it. It's torture for me lying night after night, feeling, seeing, smelling and sensing your closeness. It'd be such a relief to me to be able to show you just how interested I am. But, my beloved Hannah, it's the risk of another child that controls me. We're so lucky, we have three charming children, and for the price of two childbirths too, the latter of which was a little complicated if you remember. Wouldn't we be tempting fate to expect more joy than we already have. I need you Hannah, I couldn't imagine trying to raise these children alone. And Betsy's already lost one mother, I can't afford to lose a second one for her, not just for the sake of brief pleasures of the flesh."

Hannah snuggled up to her husband again.

"If that's your concern Joseph, don't be so fearful; believe me when I tell you, there'll be no more Elliot children for us. Really, I know, I promise you."

Joseph had absolutely no idea how his wife could possibly know this, but at his current echelon of inclination, he was blissfully willing to innocently accept his wife's assurance, and turned his body urgently to hers.

Chapter 15

Scarborough, August 1865

"Can you believe we have been here seven years already Hannah? It seems like only yesterday we had our first day out on this beach just before Kathy was born, do you remember?"

"I certainly do Joseph, it was the day Henry's secretaire was returned wasn't it?"

"Hmm." Joseph looked around the beach at the town that had become their home, feigning nonchalance at the mention of Henry.

"We've not heard of any children born to him Joseph have we? Do you think Louiza would tell us in her letters, or not?"

"I really don't know, Hannah." He thought of his sister's letters. "Her letters are so nice to receive aren't they? I do wish we could afford to take a break and visit home. I can't see Ma and Pa ever making this journey up here. But they'd so love to see the children. What a difference they'd see in Betsy and Thom. And they haven't even met Kathy or now little Albert Edgar of course."

"Could you get some time off Joseph, you could go by yourself, that wouldn't cost so much, and you'd get to meet your nieces and nephews."

"I know, Hannah, but I want Ma and Pa to meet our family too, not just me."

"Hm, and they only have Rose to marry off now, but Louiza said your baby sister is enjoying her role as a Governess in

Salisbury too much presently to even consider marriage. Your Ma must be kept very busy though with Louiza and Benjamin's children."

Joseph reclined back onto the rug they were both sitting upon, using his elbows as a prop. He was dressed in casual trousers and a jacket, with a neck tie and felt hat despite the heat of the summer's day. He closed his eyes and imagined his family in Dorset, and wondered if they missed him too. Life had been good to them up here, it'd been the right decision to move, but if only he could see his family every once in a while. See Henry too. They should sort out this uncomfortable situation, seven years is a long time for any quarrel. He'd write to him this week to inform him of Albert's arrival, but whilst ever hopeful, he would not expect a reply.

They had managed to stay living in the same house despite now paying their own rent. Joseph had begun to work a little in the back yard to make some extra money and was actually enjoying his work with wood again. He was getting a lot of requests for special items from the well-to-do residents of Crown Crescent on South Cliff.

Wrigglesworth's workshop was busily engaged on work for the building of the world's largest hotel on St Nicholas cliff, it was rumoured to be called 'The Grand Hotel'. And that it certainly would be. No, Joseph consoled his self indulgent homesickness, life was good, he could not complain. If there was a blemish in this utopia, it was that Thom's chest troubles had returned a little over the last few months, and they could not understand why.

And of course the mystery surrounding Albert's birth, he would get to the bottom of that in time. Their new little son was the image of his older brother, dark curly hair and the same piercing emerald eyes.

Still with his eyes closed, and his thoughts drifting towards his week ahead at work, Joseph questioned his wife.

"Hannah, have I told you about the theme Mr Broderick, you know, the architect, is using in the hotel?"

"No, you've told me lots of dull and dreary things, like how many millions of Hunmanby bricks are to be used, which incidentally, I agree with Miss Briggs, is a shame for the local Seamer Road brick works. But no, nothing as interesting as a theme, Joseph."

"Well, having fashioned it as a 'V' shape in deference to our queen; he's using 'time' as his theme. So it's to have four towers for each season, twelve floors for each month, fifty two chimneys for each week, and three hundred and sixty five bedrooms for each day!"

"That's clever, Joseph, how ingenious, and inspired. That's a lot of bedrooms though, will they ever fill them all? The town'll be very full if that many visitors come."

"I suppose they must think so, or they wouldn't have planned a hotel so big."

Hannah was sat awkwardly and restlessly on the rug next to Joseph. She was still a little uncomfortable after little Albert's arrival, and impatient for her clothes to feel more comfortable again too. Her mother had promised to buy her a new Sunday best outfit for her birthday from the Marshall and Snelgrove store on St Nicholas Street. They would have to wear their Sunday best outfits to even be allowed into the shop. The green liveried doorman was very particular who was permitted entrance, and imagine the embarrassment of being turned away! She couldn't wait for this very special of treats.

Hannah's day dreaming was not allowed the luxury her husband enjoyed of closed eyes. Despite her thoughts, she had her eyes trained expertly on the whereabouts of the children, and knew where they all were at any one time. They had Johnny and Annie Robinson with them as well as their own three children, not forgetting baby Albert who should be asleep in his perambulator most of the afternoon if she was lucky.

The beach was busy, it was a hot day, children were paddling at the waters edge, and the bathing huts littered the shallows like a chaotic carriage park.

Betsy and Johnny Robinson were building an enormous sand

castle with a metal pail and a wooden spade. They had been working on it for a while now, and Hannah smiled as she saw the tide slowly threatening to destroy their handiwork forever. Thom had some of his precious parchment and was drawing the scene with some charcoal. His pre-occupation with drawing pictures made him a quiet, easy child around the house, but he made little effort with his studies and was prone to day dreaming. This was often the source of some family amusement, but also concerned Joseph at times.

Kathy and Annie were running in and out of the water giggling, with their frills tucked into their pantaloons; occasionally fetching a requested bucket of water to assist with the architecture and construction of the castle.

Joseph, without moving a muscle or opening his eyes, opened the sensitive conversation once again.

"Are you ever going to tell me why you were so convinced we could have no more children, my dear. Not that I'm ungrateful for both Albert's safe appearance, and being spared the worry of his impending arrival. But I don't like being lied to Hannah, much less having secrets kept from me. You can't keep refusing to talk to me about it."

"I know Joseph, I'm so sorry, but I was so ashamed." Hannah's eyes watched without seeing her own fingers nervously fiddling with the ribbon at the straining waistline of her dress.

"Ashamed? Hannah, what did you do? I'll wait no longer, tell me now." Joseph sat forwards from his propped position, and lifted his wife's chin to look directly into her eyes augmenting his quiet but firm demand.

"Joseph! People are watching." She removed her face from the physical contact, so uncomfortably inappropriate and shameful in a public place. Then she realised, her choice of word had left her with no alternative but to tell her husband the truth, lest he should think even worse of her.

"I'm so afraid you'll either laugh at me and I'll feel such a fool, or you'll be angry at me for being so dim-witted. Either will be shameful for me." Joseph face was so puzzled, she continued quickly. "You remember the Cerne Abbas Giant?"

"Yes, and you thought we'd only had Thom because we walked all over it! Yet we had Kathy only a year and a half later without going back, so that proved as I said all along, what rubbish it all was."

"Well not quite, Joseph. You see, I did go back, I was worried when we first started talking about moving away, I thought we'd have no more children without him, so I went there one day with Thom as a baby. I was convinced that was the reason for my fertility, without him I was sure there would be no more. Little Albert has quite obviously proved me wrong. And of course, that you were right. I didn't want you to have the worry once I knew he was expected, so I had to try to keep it from you until it was all over. I'm so sorry Joseph, it was the hardest thing I've ever done, to keep pushing you away from me so that you wouldn't suspect."

"Did your Mother know?"

"Of course; mothers see any change in their child, I couldn't have fooled her."

"Well, I don't know what to say, you're certainly right about being dim," he allowed himself a relieved laugh, but continued when he saw Hannah's anguish, "but I suppose I must share the blame for believing what you told me without question. And we've another healthy son, with no detriment to you, how can I be angry about that. I must confess to being relieved by your explanation, Hannah. Very relieved." Wickedly, he then allowed a slightly lop-sided grin to hint at some amusement as he added, "Don't think though, that I am so unobservant. If you remember, more than once, I did try to delicately point out to you that you must be indulging too much as your girth was increasing!"

Hannah playfully punched her husband,

"You have no idea how much I had to bite my tongue on those occasions!"

Joseph allowed his face to soften, and then looked lovingly at his wife,

"I'm also sad that you bore all this alone for all those months, am I such a tyrant?" He smiled sympathetically, yet lovingly at his wife. Not expecting a reply, he continued, "I suppose we could say though that although that big chalk giant was not responsible for Thom or Kathy's arrivals, we can most definitely blame him, for little Albert!" Joseph tweaked his wife's nose fleetingly enough to remain publicly respectable, and they both smiled eloquently into each other's eyes. The gaze held tight, while Hannah, grateful for her husbands understanding, shamefully but discretely placed a light touch upon his thigh, diffusing her most intimate feelings into his receptive soul with that one light but sensual connection.

Hannah reluctantly broke the enchanted moment, and collected herself to check the children, a quick head count reassured her, and she turned to look at where Joseph was now indicating.

"Look who's coming towards us, it's Doctor Hetherington with his wife and family, a day like this brings everyone onto the beach on a Sunday. I feel a little uncomfortable with little Albert here, Hannah. John would love another child you know. He says Henry's like an only child being so much younger than Edward and Beatrice, and another girl would balance their family."

"Well, Mary tells me there's no way she'll have any more children, despite being a devoted mother, she doesn't like babies too much, or the process of getting them. So I don't think it's very likely."

"That's a shame for John. But he does have three healthy children, no need to be greedy eh?" Joseph rose to his feet in preparation for greeting.

"Ssh, they'll hear you Joseph. Good afternoon everyone, isn't it a lovely day?"

"It certainly is, well, let me get a look at this new surprise arrival then. Surely you knew he was expected Hannah, you're an old hand at motherhood?" John Hetherington spoke as he peered under the hood of the perambulator. "Fine healthy looking specimen though, Joseph, eh? Two boys now, and two girls. What I call a well balanced family."

Mary did not even acknowledge her husbands sentiments, or cast even a glance at Albert, but took a rug from a bag and arranged it near to Hannah and settled herself down on the sand to chatter with her friend.

Edward Hetherington seated himself a little distance away, and having surveyed the other children's seaside occupations, opened his book.

Beatrice took up her father's position of cooing over the perambulator, and Henry ran straight over to Betsy and Johnny's sand castle accidentally kicking an imposing turret as he arrived, to much admonishment from its creators. Betsy was the obvious leader in all their games and endeavours, and now she was busy giving Henry instructions as to his role in the task. The adults were all watching her with amusement. Joseph opened the conversation, unthinkingly.

"She's such a boyish little girl, so like her mother was at the same age. It's so comical to see." Mary's head snapped round to Hannah,

"Really, Hannah, somehow I don't see you as a boyish little girl at all, you're always so ladylike and feminine. I can't imagine you ever being like Betsy is."

Hannah shot Joseph a desperate look before replying,

"Oh, well, we can all change Mary. I was certainly a fun loving child, I'm not so sure about being 'boyish' though Joseph?"

"Where's Kate today, Hannah, she's not slaving away at her sewing machine on the day of rest is she?"

"Oh no John, she's gone for a walk with Mr Wilson from the photographer's, you know he works at the studio in the town, he took our family photograph for us last year. He's a widower you know."

"Oh, I know him, nice man, Hannah, nice man, hmm; Mr Wilson indeed."

Hannah and Mary smiled at each other; Kate had sworn them both to secrecy about Mr Wilson until this week, when she told them that they were going out for a walk and for tea. She supposed the secret tryst would become public anyway, as others may see them out and about. Kate had also enlightened Miss Briggs as to her admirer, when they were again contemplating the continuing strange noises from Mrs Hudson's at number twelve, so it was sure to be general gossip by now. Mary changed the subject.

"Have you seen any activity at the new Jail Hannah, it's rather close to you isn't it, just a little way along Dean Road?"

"Mary! Why are Joseph and Hannah likely to see any activity there? The rascals are locked away. I think it looks an impressive building actually, quite attractive. Too good for those in there, to be sure."

"I haven't noticed anything Mary, John's right." She was glad she was able to report no disasters since the jail opened close to them. Mary had been scaring everyone half to death about the murderers that would be in their midst. She continued, "Indeed it'll be good to be rid of the old building on Castle Road."

"Mother, Mother?"

"What is it Henry?"

"Can we go and get some boiled sweets from the little shop at the Spa?"

"Who's 'we' Henry, you certainly can't go on your own."

"Betsy wants to go too, and Johnny." Betsy and Johnny both looked up from their task and feigned a reluctancy with a nod that signified they were fine with that arrangement. John Hetherington stepped forwards from where he was chatting to Joseph.

"Go on with you, and get some for the others too, be careful and come straight back, you go too Beatrice and keep an eye on them all." He put some shiny coins into Betsy's palm, and they were gone, running barefoot in the sand, with Beatrice at thirteen and quite the young lady now, following demurely and reluctantly behind.

The ladies returned to their idle chatter whilst Joseph and John talked the politics of the day. Edward, a gentle natured but studious boy with a love of music, now at sixteen years old, could listen and watch all, whilst also absorbing his text.

"Palmerston is a little long in the tooth for the job of Prime Minister now John don't you think?"

"Well I do, but he won't give up without a fight, even if that fight could be the death of him." John replied.

"What do you think to Gladstone leading the country, he's ambitious enough to want the job?"

"Well, he has a strong commitment to Irish Home rule, and I suspect it's this fact that will either make him a success or a failure depending on how he presents himself and his argument. The queen doesn't favour him, she has a preference for Disraeli, but at her age, it may be the Prince of Wales he needs to befriend. The Prince is well liked now he has taken a wife and settled down. Alexandra will make a good Queen one day. Of course measurable success, Joseph, will also depend on the contents of any chosen cabinet!"

"Pa?"

"Yes Thom." Joseph looked a little startled. Everyone had forgotten Thom was still sat quietly drawing on the sand, as most of the children had gone off to the shop, Hannah had kept a close eye on Kathy and Annie." Everyone turned to look at Thom,

"Has Mr Palmerston had to choose another new cabinet?"

"Yes Thom, they have to. They do it every time there is a new government. Why do you ask?"

"Well, could you make a few cabinets for him, he would pay you lots of money for them I'm sure, then the prime minister won't need any more for a while."

The adult company all began to laugh out loud, John Hetherington was bent double with laughter, Joseph was the first to recover after a pleading look from Hannah indicating Thom's bewilderment.

"Silly boy Thom, 'Cabinet' is a word used to describe all the men the prime minister chooses to help him make his decisions. You must have been told that before, you'll have been too busy drawing a picture of something at the time! We'll have to start reading the newspapers together Thom, as I used to do with my father."

"Pa, Pa." The children came running back across the sand each carrying bags of sweets.

"Betsy, what's wrong dear, what's happened?"

"Pa, you know you always tell me not to drink out of the public water pumps, well Henry's just done it, I said I'd tell on him, but he carried on doing it, he said he was thirsty." John Hetherington was the first to his feet.

"Henry Joseph Hetherington, what on earth did you do that for, if you wanted a drink, you should have asked for one, those things are very dirty, you could get sick!"

Mary began to flap in a manner reminiscent of the night Edward had been carried home after his dip in the sea.

"Calm yourself Mary, he'll be fine, but we must go home, I'll try to make him sick just in case."

"But Father, I'm well, I don't need to be sick." The Hetherington's gathered their family and belongings all together and, anxiety making them curt, were leaving the beach in seconds having said their rapid goodbyes. Mary cast a glancing blow of blame in Betsy's direction, but an innocent Betsy let it roll straight over her un-noticed.

Joseph and Hannah sat in a stunned silence. No words were needed between them. They still lived in fear of this disease. Just yesterday, they had discussed the new sewer system that the papers reported would rid the capital of cholera, but it still lurked in all towns. The uncomfortable atmosphere the Hetheringtons left behind them, left many questions unanswered for the remaining children. They knew instinctively that this was a serious concern and not the time for children to enquire. They must be seen and not heard at this moment.

"Ma, where's Pa?"

195

"He's gone back down towards the beach with Thom. You know the old pocket watch that your Gramps gave Thom when we left Dorset?" Betsy nodded. "Well the silly boy took it with him to the beach, and has lost it, I don't have much hope that they'll find it, but it's worth a try. It was very special to your Gramps."

"Did you know Thom wants to be an artist when he grows up Ma?" Betsy was helping her mother prepare the roast meal.

"I can't say I'm surprised at his childish fancy, Betsy, but I feel he may have to find a trade to support him in his pastime. What do you want to do dear? it's not so long now before you'll leave school."

"I know Ma, I like reading Aunt Louiza's letters, and I like the sound of what Aunt Rose does, teaching children in a big house, so does Beatrice."

"Do you Betsy? I'm surprised at both of you, I doubt Mrs Hetherington will allow her daughter to go into service, and you've never had any patience with Kathy."

"But she can be so tiresome Ma, and she hates my singing, I love music so much, I suppose I get that from Granma?" Betsy looked at her mother for a response, and Hannah after an initial hesitation, nodded to appease her friend's daughter, "Henry and Annie are alright though, and so will little Albert be I'm sure." She smiled at her mother and continued. "Edward wants to be a doctor, so he'll have to stay on at school. Peter wants to be a printer, and work at the paper with his father, Johnny wants to work with wood like Pa, and Annie wants to work in Marshall and Snelgroves, she just loves fancy clothes."

"Well, I must say you all seem to have your lives planned out already Betsy, let's just see what comes along for everyone."

"Thom, when were you last aware of having your pocket watch?"

"Well I definitely had it when we sat down on the beach, coz I looked at what time we arrived there to see how long it would take me to draw the scene."

"Well, I think we'll have to give up. I'm very angry with you though Thom. That watch was special to your Gramps and he gave it to you when we left Dorset. It was for you to take great care of, as an heirloom, not just to play with."

"I know. I'm really sorry Pa." They were crossing back over the Cliff Bridge. Joseph paused to take in the view inland up Ramsdale Valley where the newly opened Valley Bridge, transported from the river Ouse at York after its collapse there, now spanned its width. This had opened up the town to the affluent south cliff, with Ramshill becoming the new social and shopping centre. The town, both as a resort and a settlement, was soaring in status, with the population increasing rapidly. Joseph felt immense pride in the part he was playing in its tasteful and successful growth. His lifted mood softened his austerity and disappointment in his absent minded son.

"Well, you've lost it now, don't go expecting a replacement though, but what's done is done. That policeman we saw was very nice, we might be surprised, he may find it for you. He has our address if he does. I can never tell your Gramps what you've done, he would just be so sad." He smiled down at his fretful son and tried to chivvy him. "Come on then son, we'll be late for tea, then we'll be in trouble for that, I wonder what time it is? I wasn't silly enough to take my pocket watch to the beach!" He tweaked the eight year old's ear, his accompanying teasing laughter faded into astonishment as he watched his son take out his watch from his pocket, tell his father the time, and calmly replace it.

"Thomas Henry Elliot, what did you just do?"

"What do you mean Pa?" Slowly, he realised his blunder. "Oh, my watch, it was in my pocket all along. But I'd thought it was in my bag with my drawing things. Sorry Pa, I'm really sorry, I forgot I'd put it back in my pocket!"

"Thom, your head is in the clouds most of the day, what are we going to do with you? You're so like your Aunt Louiza. I hope that policeman doesn't waste any of his day looking for it. Wait 'til I tell your Ma this one." He cuffed his ears playfully and pretended to chase him over the bridge and home, father and son laughing as they went.

Kate Thackery swept into the Elliot's kitchen in the early evening. She appeared to have grown in stature over the last few years, and at forty seven years old, was still a smart lady. She kept her family dressed extremely well with her sewing skills, including herself and very often Annie Robinson too. She had long since discarded her widow's weeds in favour of smartly conservative colours and lines. She made straight for her daughter to report on her assignation, and Hannah noticed how stylish she looked in her matching skirt and bodice. The skirt was fashionably flat at the front, but extended out at the back. There were stamped borders around the edge of the skirt to mimic patterned braid, and matching dark buttons fastened the bodice. The collar on the bodice co-ordinated with the braid and buttons, as did the trim on the bishop sleeves, and again on her bonnet. To complete the ensemble, Kate wore a smile that lit up her gently ageing complexion, compelling it to revisit its youth.

Hannah had no need of a detailed report, her mother's joy was transparent to the world.

"Hannah I've learnt so much today about the history of this town, I've been all over the very old parts, you know just underneath the castle walls, Church Stairs Street, where the old Chapel is. Did you know St Mary's church was built in 1485? He showed me which is Anne Bronte's grave, we've never been able to find it have we? And Quay Street is so old too. Did you know there's a market cross, the 'Butter' Cross, that dates back hundreds of years? No. I didn't think you did. Oh Hannah I have had a wonderful day, he is such an interesting and knowledgable man."

Joseph had been reading his paper, on hearing their exchange, though missing the nature of the conversation, he shouted to his wife, "Hannah, tell your Ma about Thom and my Pa's pocket watch, it's a story that beggars belief, but will put a cheery smile on anyone's face to take to their bed tonight."

* * *

Kathy came running out of school the next day looking for her mother. This was unusual. Hannah was used to having to find Kathy after school. She could often be found hatching some mischief or other with a similarly minded group of children at the back of the school, which always included Annie Robinson. Hannah and Jane Robinson often despaired of the two of them, but today was different.

"What is it Kathy, is something wrong?"

"Ma, Henry's really sick, Annie's cousin went to play with him yesterday after school, and he started to cry with pain and needed to stay in the privy. Do you think that water was really bad at the beach?"

"Oh Kathy I hope not, if it was the water, he'll be really sick, maybe he just ate some food that was too old. Oh poor Mary. We must walk over there and see if there's anything we can do. Are Betsy and Thom anywhere, we'll have to wait for them first."

Hannah and her children, taking it in turns to push the perambulator, arrived in The Crescent, and halted outside the Hetherington's house. Hannah instructed the children to wait at the bottom of the entrance steps, while she enquired about Henry first, in case he was still feeling ill.

She pulled the large doorbell, and their housemaid answered, she was just greeting Hannah, when a piercing scream emanating from the upstairs of the house, travelled down the stairs, out of the front door, and across the immense width of The Crescent. It must have reached the valley below and the Rotunda Museum. Hannah recoiled backwards, her children looked at her in terror. After collecting herself, yet aware of the horror that may greet her, she pushed past the housemaid and ran up the familiar staircase to what she knew to be Henry's room.

She recoiled as she reached the doorway, the familiar stench of cholera greeted her. Henry's wizened dehydrated and obviously now lifeless body was laid angelically in his large bed. Mary was continuing to scream, John was desperately trying to calm her. She shook her husband off, and fell onto her youngest child embracing him, sobbing, pleading with him not to leave her, but to come back. Hannah turned away, this was more than she could bear. There was a scenario worse than Lizzibeth's. To witness the loss of the mother of a newborn had been undoubtably heart-wrenching, but to witness this, a mother losing her child was somehow even worse and was ripping Hannah apart as she identified herself with this mother, another friend in the midst of tragedy. John suddenly noticed her presence and ushered her quickly towards the door.

"Not now, Hannah, thank you for coming, but not now eh." Mary heard his voice and looked round.

"How dare you show your face." Mary Hetherington boomed after her. "If it wasn't for your child wanting sweets, my Henry would still be here now. How dare you come here, get out, get out now." She flew at a bemused and shocked Hannah, only her husband's quick reaction in catching his wife, saved Hannah from being pushed to the ground.

"Go Hannah, go please, we'll talk later." Hannah hesitatingly backed herself down the stairs, still taking in John's words. Mary Hetherington was as a rag doll now, completely spent, bent in half over her husbands arms, no desire or ability to stand erect with her youngest child wrenched so cruelly out of her very core.

The Elliots walked sombrely home. Even Kathy behaved, walking slowly holding the side of the perambulator handle, not knowing how to react to her distraught mother. Betsy was quietly sobbing. They were nearly home, when Joseph caught up with them on his way home from the workshop.

"What is it, whatever's happened?"

"Henry Joseph died Pa." Thom spoke quietly as if the words

would cause further distress to his mother. Joseph stopped and turned to his family.

"Henry! No, no. Hannah, not cholera?"

Hannah nodded. Joseph's arm went to her shoulders, the contact and gentle movements he made offered comfort to them both. "No Hannah, it can't happen again, no. They are so close to eradicating it, oh no, no. Poor, poor little Henry. What can we do?" Hannah shook her head vehemently at Joseph for fear of him suggesting they visit. Bewilderedly, he gathered her meaning, and took over pushing the perambulator to speed their way. "Come on my dears, let's all get home."

Two days had passed, little Henry Joseph's internment was to be later that day. Joseph needed to know if Mary had stopped blaming them in her grief for what had happened. If so, they could pay their last respects without fear of upsetting Mary. Joseph decided to call at John's Clinic.

"Joseph, I can assure you Mary has no memory at all of Hannah being there on tuesday, and indeed it would be easier for their friendship, if she did not remember. Of course neither she nor I blame Betsy. It was Henry who wanted sweets, and Henry who had drunk the water despite Betsy's warnings. Beatrice was the elder of the group, she too should have known better and stopped him. But you must understand, that in grief, you look for someone to blame, Hannah walked in at just the wrong moment." Joseph shook his hand, holding it briefly between both of his own.

"We just didn't want to make things worse by showing up if we were not welcome John. I know I can't begin to imagine what you are both going through, but if I can do anything at all to help, you know that I will."

"Of course Joseph. But tell me, I have not told anyone it was cholera, just a fever, I did not want to cause alarm, I have had that water pump sealed already. How did you know?"

"Sorry John, it was Hannah. She's seen and smelt cholera at close quarters herself. That is why we are so fearful of water pumps." He paused, then impulsively made the decision to gain licence to share in John's grief by imparting his own. "Our very special childhood friend Lizzibeth Buxton died of cholera, less than an hour after giving birth to her daughter. Betsy." John's face showed his astonishment, then visibly softened towards Joseph.

"I'm so sorry Joseph, but so surprised too. Betsy is so like Hannah, at least in colouring. Well possibly it's just because she is so unlike you, one notices the likenesses elsewhere." The two men forced a smile at each other, then John conceded,

"This must be hard for you too, and poor Hannah, in addition to all else, she had to witness Mary's distress." Then as though remembering his wife, he added, "I won't enlighten Mary to your situation though Joseph, unwittingly in her present state, she may disclose this inappropriately."

"Thank you John, I appreciate it. Again, our heartfelt sympathies go out to you all."

Joseph descended the steps of the surgery where Betsy and Thom had been waiting outside for him. Amidst Joseph's relief at his reception inside, as he walked home with his own children, he considered sadly how John now had his balanced family. Losing a son he already had, was most certainly not how he would have wanted to accomplish this.

He made up his mind to write that letter to Henry tonight after the service, life was too short to allow this quarrel to continue. He would ask him to be Albert's Godfather too. How strangely poignant, if in the same week that little Henry Joseph lost his life, Henry and Joseph could begin a new chapter in their own.

Joseph looked down from his son to his daughter, "Come on you two, we need to prepare ourselves for the very sad day we have ahead."

Chapter 16

Scarborough, November 1867 - July 1868

Joseph had a very disturbed night. Not only on account of the wriggling two year old Albert in the middle of their marital bed. But his mind was in turmoil, exacerbated further by the very mystery of his anguish.

He had been elated by the receipt of Henry's long awaited letter yesterday which he had read and re-read many times. He feigned a share of the relief that Hannah expressed at what she took as proof that he himself must indeed be Betsy's father, when he had read aloud that section to Hannah.

Only he knew he was not. He picked it up again to read in the morning light, enjoying the flourish of Henry's signature indicating clearly the light mood in which it was penned. All could be well between them at last. But could it?

Dear Joseph,

I humbly apologise for taking so long to reply to your letter dated August 1865. It is very remiss of me not to have responded before now, but the army is a busy but fulfilling life and with threats looming in Africa, the training of British troops is a never-ending task.

I confess to feeling extremely angry with you at the time I returned the Secretaire. A gesture I have frequently regretted, as no other piece could compare to your work, Joseph. However you must understand how disappointed I was in you for not admitting your own recklessness with Lizzibeth, indeed trying to make me, your dearest friend, shoulder the responsibility. I knew for sure I had not fathered a child with her. Her deathbed words indicated it was certainly one of us, which left me to be extremely saddened on Lizzibeth's behalf, by your utter lack of gallantry.

The reason I did not engage vehemently with you at the time, was a selfish one. I confess now to harbouring a faint hope that regardless of our combined memory loss of that night prior to the incident with poor Arthur, there could also have been a mistake years earlier. That perhaps the doctor had been wrong after my accident and my injuries had not been severe enough in my lower abdomen to prevent me from fathering a child after all. However Joseph, I have to tell you that after six years of a fruitless marriage, I am assured as I'm sure you will agree, that there is no hope at all that Betsy is from my loins.

Thus fortunately, you can be reassured that you are providing for your own daughter, Joseph. I trust she and her siblings are all well. I count myself lucky to be Godfather to the children of my greatest childhood friend, whose action one day in October 1844 indubitably saved my life. I pride myself that my life was worth saving Joseph, and that your actions and injuries were not in vain. Many a soldier and his family have written that they are indebted to me for my various deeds and work.

My wife and I are very happy despite our lack of heirs. Amelia knew this was the case when we wed, and I was fortunate in that she was happy to have me on those terms. We will have to depend upon Charlotte's children to inherit and carry on the work of the estate in the years to come. Indeed my father remains hail and hearty at the present time, and is thankfully in no rush to hand over the reins.

By the by, I heard in the town that Bill Buxton has returned on many occasions looking for his niece. Your decision to move was fortuitous, no-one except our two families know of your whereabouts so you can rest assured Betsy is safe where she belongs.

I share your sentiments Joseph, about life being too short to prolong any disquiet, and we would be most happy to receive you and your family if you should journey to Dorset once again. My wife is indeed anxious to meet the friend she has heard so much about and I truly hope to introduce you and Hannah to her one day. I was pleased you had named your son after the dear Prince who did so much for our Queen and country Joseph. God rest his soul.

I trust you are making a good living and that both you and Hannah are well. Please give her and the children, my very best wishes.

Affectionately your friend

Henry

Replacing the letter on his chest of drawers, he continued to prepare for work. He found himself thinking again about that fateful evening with Henry and Lizzibeth. He shaved the front of his face leaving the fashionable side whiskers full to his jawline. Looking in the glass at his handiwork, he mulled over what he knew of the evening for sure. From their chance meeting with Lizzibeth, to her return home to her mother the next morning; he stared questioningly at the puzzled expression he saw reflecting back at him.

Suddenly, he focused on his blade. Gripping it perilously hard for his still diminished senses, blood dripped into the water bowl unnoticed, as an awakening left shivers running up and down his spine. He recalled the episode with Jacob as Lizzibeth had passed by the Thackery's cottage. Had he offered her more than just comfort? Joseph remembered Jacob telling him that there had been no more 'marital bed' for him and Kate since

Hannah's near fatal delivery. Jacob must have been a desperate man, but was he desperate enough to force himself on anyone. Was Hannah mothering her own sister? He shook himself. Surely not, more likely his mother-in-law had been correct in her assumptions, he would have sought willing comfort elsewhere, and paid the price. But then, could Lizzibeth have offered herself in her quest for comfort, or indeed some financial remuneration after losing her employment? Again surely not? Because then, what would she have meant about the phoenix and the nest of spices on her death bed? This was too much for him to contemplate, he felt disloyal to both his mentor and his friend for even thinking such a thing.

Hannah broke into his uneasy thoughts by shouting to him that his breakfast was ready. Joseph slowly descended the stairs and walked through to the table in the kitchen. There he stood looking at his wife, his mother-in-law, and finally at his elder daughter. All his previously scattered, troubled thoughts over recent months and years, orderly aligned themselves into a shocking but perfect sequence.

"What is it Joseph dearest? You look as though you have seen a ghost. Are you alright?" She looked from him to her mother as Kate quipped,

"He's probably felt another of those earthquakes after reading the account last night of that Grasmere one." Mother and daughter giggled, nothing could dampen their mood as they prepared for Kate's imminent nuptials.

"I think he was just wishing he had thought to sell a story of the one he felt years ago on the south coast, Ma; I bet Miss Martineau earned a pretty penny for yesterday's article. Is that it Joseph?" She looked for his expression to soften, then her eyes rested on where he was pressing hard on the palm of his right hand. "Oh no, Joseph, you're bleeding. What have you done?"

"Granma, can you show me again how to sew on these cuffs

for Thom's shirt. I really want to finish this for his birthday next week."

"Of course Betsy, do you want me to do them for you?"

"Not really thank you Granma, otherwise I'll never learn. And what if I wanted to make you a blouse?"

"Oh goodness child, imagine, someone making clothes for me! Come here then, I can't lift all this skirt I'm hemming off my knee to come to you." Betsy carefully detached her sewing from the machine and went over to where her Grandmother was sewing the hem of an evening gown in a blue-green silk taffeta.

"I'm so glad you still come here to do your sewing Granma, it wouldn't be the same if you weren't with us at all. Do you miss us too since you married Mr Wilson?"

"Of course I do Betsy, but it's also nice to have a little peace and quiet occasionally as I am getting older. Then I can enjoy the company of you all even more when I'm here. I need this room though to do my sewing, it's good of your father to let me keep it on, but Mr Wilson's house in Nelson Street is too small to have a separate sewing room." She put down her rustling shiny sea of silk, and looked up at her granddaughter, "Now let's have a look at these cuffs?" Betsy had been stood patiently listening; she eagerly bent down over her Grandmother proffering her sewing for inspection.

"See, I've sewn the first part on, but then I can never remember which way you stitch the seam allowance in so that it doesn't show."

"Oh you're nearly there, just catch it in this way with the interfacing, then when you turn it back to the right side, all the raw edges are hidden. See?"

"Aah, now I see, thank you Granma, it's like when I put that waistband on the skirt I made for Kathy, only a bit more fiddly. I'll get it right now."

"You certainly will, Betsy, your garments are just about selling standard already. I was much older than you before I could make any money at this. Is this what you want to spend your time doing now you've left school?"

Betsy, back at the machine, looked up at the ceiling in the back bedroom they used as a sewing room in the house, her fingers poised at her sewing keeping the material in position, her foot frozen on the treadle. She let her gaze travel purposefully down the wall diagonally to engage her Grandmothers eyes as she replied.

"I do like it, Granma, but I also like to learn things. I'd really like to do what Aunt Rose does, you know, teaching children in a big house. I think you'd never stop learning then. I'd also like to learn music Granma, I loved the lessons you gave me on the piano in Miss Briggs' house. But how wonderful it'd be to be able to play anything I like on the piano. I can still only play quite simple pieces."

"That's because I can only play simple pieces Betsy, I can't teach you what I don't know!"

"Oh I know Granma, and I'm really happy you have taught me so much, it's just that I'd love to do more."

"Hmm, I don't know how we can solve that little problem dear. Mrs Hudson along the road used to give Piano lessons before she took in sewing, but I don't think she still does. Anyway you know, we can't always have everything we wish for." They both continued their tasks in silence for a few minutes, then Betsy showed she had been considering this last remark with her contemplative reply.

"Well, perhaps someone should tell the banker man from St Nicholas House that, Granma. I heard Pa telling Ma, that Mr Woodall's determined to build this pier on the North Bay, even though no-one else wants it."

"Now, now, dear, I know we love the North Bay just as it is, totally unspoilt by anything man could add to it, but Mr Woodall's a good man, well respected in this town. He must have his reasons for thinking a pier is a good idea. Why else would he be investing more than £12,000 pounds of his own money?"

"Now, now indeed Ma T." Joseph had been passing the

upstairs sewing room having changed out of his work clothes for Sunday tea. He had been interested to eavesdrop on their conversation, especially to hear about Betsy's dream of piano lessons, he wondered if he could arrange anything with Mrs Hudson. "Betsy Agatha, this town is getting bigger, there's bound to be lots of building work all around us. We may not like it all, but it cannot be helped if the town is to continue flourishing. Mr Woodall will have his way. He has the money to get whatever he wants."

"Hmm, but I can't see why that side of the bay needs anything building on it at all Pa?"

"Now, now Betsy dear, have you seen how it's coming along? It really doesn't look too bad you know, do you want a walk along there with me before tea? I've heard it's one thousand feet in length up to the pier head. We'll at least get a good view out to sea when it's finished."

Betsy readily laid down her sewing. A stroll with her father was a luxury these days, he was usually working with his wood every spare minute he had. They had just started to descend the stairs, when Hannah's urgent voice bounded up to them. "Joseph, Joseph, come quickly. Thom can't breath."

When they reached the kitchen, Thom was on the fireside chair, with his mother smothering his distress. Every laboured breath was being dragged reluctantly and noisily into his chest as though having to be sucked through an invisible barrier. Thom was exhausted.

"When did this come on Hannah? He was with me sanding a wooden plate he had made for you a just few moments ago."

"He just staggered into here when I shouted you, Joseph."

"Betsy, please run for Doctor Hetherington. Quickly, we can go for that walk another day."

"Hannah, we've a big decision to consider, I wanted to leave it until today, Christmas Day, was over, and until we came to bed. Away from everyone else. Come here." Hannah turned to her husband, she could tell by the serious tone that something was troubling him; she seated herself on the bottom of their bed apprehensively facing him.

"What is it Joseph, You aren't going to tell me 'The Tenant of Wildfell Hall' is an unsuitable book for me having given me it as a Christmas gift are you?" Joseph smiled at her wit and shook his head,

"No nothing like that dearest."

"Come on then, you're worrying me?"

"Nothing to worry about my dear, I just have a proposition for you." No sooner was the word out of his mouth, than he smiled. He remembered his father explaining the meaning of a 'proposition' many years before. That was the one delivered by Charles Ferguson that had changed the course of his own life in so many ways.

"What are you smiling about?"

"That's another long story from years ago Hannah, it just came into my head."

He took hold of both of Hannah's hands, stroking the backs of her knuckles with his thumbs, he looked into the big blue eyes he loved so much, and began to share his plan.

"Since I was a child, Hannah, I've saved everything I've ever earned over and above what's been needed to live. For that, I know I've been the object of much cruel repartee. Oh don't deny it, my dear, for I hear all idle gossip!" He feigned being affronted, and continued, "I've always hoped that with hard work one day, I'd be able to purchase for us, a property of our very own, thus taking away all concerns of homelessness or workhouses in our old age. Of course I always hoped it'd be like John Hetherington's on the Crescent. But that was only a dream." He paused to indulge his vision for a second.

"Yesterday, I received an order for many bespoke pieces of furniture for a new dignitary who's secretly purchasing a large house up on the Esplanade. It was through another party, his identity is to be undisclosed. This could of course lead to many more. For me to accept, I'll need to continue working at the back of the house. The work at the Grand Hotel is now finished, so it could be timely to decide to set up in my own business instead of working for someone else. As you know, that gives us two problems. One is that we could not necessarily pay the rent if I had a lean month, and secondly, and most importantly, I can't be using the house we live in as a workshop if John is right in thinking it's the fine sawdust that triggers Thom's chest troubles, or asthma as he called it. Did you get any of those Halloway's Pills he suggested?"

"Yes of course, but it's too early to tell if they're helping at all. I see what you are saying, Joseph. At the very time you could take a chance on your own business, making the type of furniture you take pride in making; is the very time we find it could be detrimental to Thom's health. I can't believe we thought it was the sea air that had cured him, and all the time it was just not living with sawdust anymore."

"But there could be a solution, Hannah. I might not have saved enough to purchase a house in the Crescent, but I do have enough for one that has come up for sale in Belle Vue Street, you know just off Victoria Road?" He paused to enjoy the look of incredulity on his wife's face, "It's not quite as big as this one, but it still has three floors, we would not be cramped, then we would not have rent to pay. We would have no money for luxuries, at least for a while. But, I have spoken to Mr Wilson and your Ma. They are interested in taking over this house to rent. It's a little more than he can afford, but your Ma's happy to contribute from her sewing profits, and I'll contribute for the continued use of the workshop at the back. This way, your Ma has more living space, I still have my workshop, but Thom won't be living near any sawdust. There's obviously no question of him becoming a cabinet maker now. Such a shame, he was showing such creative promise in the designs.

Anyway, a new year, and a new era for us. What do you think, my dear?"

Hannah's wide eyed look of surprise had progressed to her

lower jaw hanging open in total disbelief. Joseph, smiling at her, let go of her left hand and with his right, he gently lifted her chin until her lips touched. She collected herself enough to whisper,

"Buy a house Joseph, I can't believe we could own a house. Your family'll be so proud of you. I'm so proud of you. Are you sure we can afford it?"

* * *

"Thank you so much Mrs Hudson, is the same time next week alright for you?"

"Of course, Betsy my dear, it's always a pleasure teaching you. You learn so quickly, you've a natural talent with music." Betsy was rolling her sheets of music and tying them with string when she heard the now familiar, yet unmentionable muffled shouts from upstairs. The gossip on the street from Mrs Jones on the corner, or Flossie Flat Hat as her Grandmother called her, was that Mr and Mrs Hudson used to have a son, but he was taken away to an asylum years ago. People had complained that he was depraved, inappropriately hugging and kissing everyone. Now, it was Miss Briggs' belief that they kept some sort of animal as a substitute in the bedroom upstairs. Definitely not permissible in these rented establishments. Betsy was always suspicious of this story, the noises she heard whilst having her weekly piano lesson with Mrs Hudson, were not like any animal she knew. She braved the unthinkable question.

"What's that noise Mrs Hudson?" She turned to look inquisitively at her tutor. Mrs Hudson tried to look nonchalant, hoisting her ample bosom upwards with her folded forearms. It always fascinated Betsy that this particular bosom, whilst always smartly clothed, appeared merged as one single very wide central contour.

"Oh I think I heard Mr Hudson come home from work early dear, he went upstairs, it'll be him, I'll go now and see what he wants." Betsy nodded as if that must be the explanation. She took her leave and walked along the pavement to the end of the road where she saw Mr Hudson returning from work and taking the short cut down the alley to the back entrance of the house.

"My Father says that now so many more men can vote following the Reform Act last year, Mr Gladstone will definitely get in with the Liberals at the next election."

"Who cares who gets to be Prime Minister Edward, it's all very boring."

"You girls don't understand what it's all about, that's why you think it's boring Beatrice, you just find yourself a nice husband to take care of you." He winked and nudged her elbow as he spoke.

"Peter! That's a terrible thing to say to Beatrice. Of course she understands it. One day women will be able to vote too, and then we'll show you we understand." Peter laughed as Johnny joined the debate,

"But Betsy, that would just be a waste, women'll just be guided by their husbands anyway, so it'll just give people more voting papers to count for no reason."

"Johnny Robinson, I'm shocked that you think women don't have minds of their own. Who's thought up most of the games we've played as children? Who got us into most of the mischief we've been in? What would you've done for fun without me?" Betsy flounced off sulkily, her skirts and petticoats rustling as she went. She was angry at the attitude of her friends, angry at Beatrice for being so passive in defense, and angry at herself for giving credibility to their comments by engaging with them.

At fourteen years old, Betsy was startlingly like Lizzibeth in all but colouring. Her blue eyes were large and compelling, just as her mother's had been, her fair curls thick and soft. Her exuberance and stubbornness was so reminiscent of Lizzibeth.

"Betsy wait, wait." She slowed and turned to see Edward running to catch her up. "Betsy, you know how Peter just repeats what he hears his Pa say, he's just trying to be clever and show off to Beatrice. She listens to his every word, and Johnny joined in just to antagonise you."

When he had neither elicited any response, nor slowed her pace, he added,

"Peter just thinks she's so pretty Betsy, honestly, he's just trying to impress her."

"But Edward, we've just been in God's house, he shouldn't be thinking of showing off to a pretty girl. He should think about what he's saying. We all know the way things are, and it may be fine that way. But it doesn't mean that we don't understand anything. I can learn things just as quickly as he can."

Edward quipped quietly but firmly.

"And he knows that Betsy. Don't be angry and spoil things. You're getting very snappy lately. Come on, let's go back to the chapel, they were going to serve lemonade as it's such a hot day." They began to walk together back towards the chapel hall.

"I'm sorry Edward. That was not a good welcome home for you. I'm sorry. I suppose I'm so bored at the moment. I'm just helping my Grandmother with her sewing, and I know I could be doing so much more. How's University? Is it really hard work? How many years is it before you become a doctor?"

Edward was just about to reply to her onslaught of questions, when a Hansome Cab pulled up alongside them at the top of Westborough.

"Excuse me, but would you happen to know where Belle Vue Street is?" A well dressed gentleman had leant out of the window to ask directions. "I hired this Cab from York Station, thinking it'd be quicker than the train from there, but we've been driving round the town for an age."

"Certainly Sir" replied Edward, "You're not far away, just turn first right here onto Belle Vue Parade, then it's left at the bottom and first or second right– Betsy?"

"First Sir."

"Thank you kindly. Lovely day. Good day to you."

* * *

"Ma! I'm home. Johnny's called home with me to pick up his Grandma's dish before he goes home. Oh, Sir." Betsy was walking straight past the parlour door, when something made her look in. She came face to face with their 'lost' gentleman from the Carriage earlier. She moved into the room, bobbing an almost imperceptible curtsey, closely followed by Johnny.

"Well good afternoon, Betsy I presume, as I've met the rest of the brood already. Charmed to make your acquaintance Betsy Agatha Elliot, Henry Ferguson, your Godfather no less. I trust you enjoyed your birthday last month, we share the same date you know." He stepped forwards to take Betsy's hand, raised it to his lips and brushed a kiss across her knuckles. Johnny Robinson could hardly contain his muffled giggles, and an embarrassed Betsy swiped her other hand back to stifle his behaviour.

"I had the pleasure of asking Betsy and a friend directions to your home Joseph, otherwise I fear I'd still have been driving aimlessly around this charming town."

"Oh so you've met already, Henry, you didn't say."

"Well it wasn't until she walked in here that I realised to whom I'd been talking. Where's the other friend you were with?"

"Oh Edward's gone home for his lunch. We all went to chapel together this morning. Edward's back for the summer now Pa."

Betsy took in the starched atmosphere in the room. Thom and Kathy were seated on the fireside chair, quite obviously on one of their father's 'be seen and not heard' promises. Albert at nearly three was missing as he usually was at this time, having a mid-day nap upstairs. Her mother looked on edge as though she was expecting some unpleasantness, but hoped her presence would ward it off. Her father looked anxious, worried even, yet simultaneously pleased with himself.

"Betsy your Godfather, Uncle Henry, has travelled up to see us with some disturbing news, your Granny down in Dorset is poorly and would like to see me, I've to travel back down with Henry here. I shan't be away too long."

"Can I go too Pa? Please, I might be able to help."

"Oh I don't think so Betsy, that wouldn't be a good idea." Hannah, Joseph and Henry all exchanged knowing anxious glances.

"Why not Pa? I was born there, it'd be nice to go back."

"Err, we'll think about it Betsy. Why don't you girls all go along now and see how long it'll be before lunch is ready, could you sort them Hannah please. You go too Thom, could you sharpen the carving knife for me?" Hannah realised this was her cue to leave the two men alone, and she ushered her children out into the kitchen, shouting goodbye to Johnny as he let himself out of the front door, completely forgetting the dish he had come for, but with news of a stranger to take home in its place. As they closed the parlour door, Kathy, angrily turned on her mother.

"How come she gets to go to Dorset with Pa? She gets everything. I get nowt."

Hannah continued into the kitchen, shocked by her daughter's reaction, but keen to move this altercation away from the men's earshot. "Don't be silly Kathy. Betsy's not going to Dorset. And what do you mean by her getting everything? And it's nothing, not nowt!"

"She gets piano lessons, just like Beatrice Hetherington. I bet they cost a pretty penny. What if Thom or I wanted any extra lessons? Bet we wouldn't get them. It's not fair."

"Kathy, what lessons would you like?"

"Didn't say I did. Just 'tisn't fair. She's always been the favourite daughter!"

Betsy had begun to set the kitchen table adding an extra place, assuming their guest was joining them. She had listened quietly to Kathy voicing at last her long pent up covetous feelings. Her own outburst earlier today amongst her friends, made her now take stock before speaking. But something she had learnt three years earlier whilst waiting for her father outside Doctor

Hetherington's surgery, now leapt to the fore and appeared to be the obvious retort to arrest Kathy in her explosion. Just as Joseph and Henry entered the kitchen doorway unseen, she turned to her younger sister, and calmly announced,

"Kathy, you have no competition, I can't possibly be anyone's favourite daughter, that position solely belongs to you. You're the only daughter. My mother was Lizzibeth Buxton, and she's dead."

* * *

"Henry, are you sure you want to go to your Hotel. You're more than welcome to a bed here." The two men were donning jackets in the hallway of Joseph's house.

"I know Joseph. Thank you, but no. Are you walking round there with me? I could get lost again otherwise and I don't have the comfort of a hired Hansome Cab now. We can discuss our travel arrangements to Dorset."

"Certainly Henry, it'll be a pleasure." Joseph shouted over his shoulder. "I won't be long Hannah."

"You know Joseph, I almost felt from your reply to my letter that you were considering moving back to Dorset, you know, that you were a little home sick. Missing your family, so a trip home will help you to decide. I suppose the threat to Betsy still remains though."

"Oh I don't think there's any chance of us moving back now Henry, I do miss my family so much, but I now have a big order for bespoke furniture which could be the making of a business here for me. The rest of the family is so settled too. Any thoughts of moving back south are now well and truly dispelled."

"Hmm. Well what do you think of Gladstone's chances at the end of the year, Joseph?"

"Oh I think he'll get in now, I hope his first job is to support his Mr Forster to get the education act he's talked about through parliament. Every child deserves the opportunity to be educated."

"I am so pleased to hear your passion for that has not waned Joseph, you are a man of principles and I am proud to be your friend. I would have availed myself of your generous hospitality Joseph, but I am anxious to try the bathing in this new and very Grand hotel. Is it true I will have a choice of four taps?"

"You certainly do, hot and cold freshwater, and hot and cold seawater, what more could you want!"

"It might do my rheumatic joints the world of good. That accident is catching up with me as they always said it would."

"It's said to be the grandest as well as biggest hotel in Europe. The opening Banquet was certainly an occasion, with many dignitaries present. The band actually played on the open terrace so the public could also enjoy their performance. I've been very lucky in witnessing some very grand events since we came here, Henry."

"It sounds a splendid place. Anyway, Joseph, I feel your family need some time alone to absorb Betsy's shock announcement today. What are you going to tell her about it all? Surely not those thoughts about Jacob that you have revealed to me today? It can't surely be true. Think of what Lizzibeth said before she died about the fire monument, you know the phoenix?"

"I've thought about that too Henry. How did Lizzibeth know about the nest of spices? That part isn't written on the fire monument. I didn't tell her."

"Oh I think I might have told her about the whole myth at some point, but maybe not. I don't know Joseph, really. Anyway, how was it possible that you did you not realise Betsy was eavesdropping on you, all those years ago?"

"We were all so distressed at little Henry's death, I was there the night he was born you know, in truth, that was the night I first got to know them. I must've just not heard her, I can't believe it either. Or that she's kept it to herself until now. Hannah's always wanted to tell her about Lizzibeth, and to say that I was betrothed to her before her death to make the story 'acceptable' for Betsy to live with. I think therefore, that now's the time to do just that. And that alone."

"I think so too Joseph, I think so too."

Chapter 17

Dorset / Scarborough, November 1870 - April 1871

"Oh Betsy, I'm going to miss you so much, what would we've all done without you this last year since Ma's relapse."
Rose Elliot was once again saying goodbye to Betsy on the Dorset station forecourt. They headed for the little tea shop. Time had left no mark on this edifice since they last parted here all those years before, whereas the same years had witnessed the scholar become a confident capable young woman and the little vivacious girl grow and poise herself at sixteen years old, on the brink of womanhood. They could've been sisters as they chatted easily together over their cups of tea. Both were smartly dressed, with their fashionable bonnets and black gloves giving an air of comfort, if not affluence.
"Well, I'm going to miss you all too, Aunt Rose, but now Granny's so much better, and you can get back to being in Salisbury all week, it seems the right time for me to go back to Scarborough. I miss my family too. I don't understand Granny and Gramps though, they seemed really keen for me to go back all of a sudden, I thought they liked having me here."
"I really wish you would forget the 'Aunt' part, Betsy, I'm only a few years older than you! And Ma and Pa have loved having you, make no mistake. It's just that they know your Pa will be cross if they keep you to themselves for a moment longer. Ma's

able to do simple jobs again around the house with her right hand at least, so between her and Pa they'll manage. Pa's letting David, the coachman, take over some of his duties now, so he can be at home a little more. Louiza will drop by as often as she can, although Ma finds the children tiring. The doctors have said that her type of brain apoplexy could happen again at any time, or may never give her any more trouble. She's just so glad to be alive now, and just wants to get on with things, the more we all help, the more useless she feels."

"I loved the days I spent doing some teaching for you in Salisbury, Rose, you know, when Granny just wanted you to help her, before she remembered who I was. I'd just love to have a job like yours. I suppose it could be awful if the children weren't nice though."

"Well it's the job of the Governess to make them nice isn't it? But you were very good at it too, you can be sure of that. Both the mistress and the children loved you, they're always telling me how good you were with them." Betsy beamed at her Aunt, and physically seemed to grow with pride at this report of her ability. Rose continued, "So what're you looking forward to most when you get back to the seaside Betsy?"

"Oh so many things, Rose. Pa, Ma, Thom, even Kathy, she can be so difficult but she's still my sister. Little Albert, he'll have grown so much, he's five now, he's breeched, and because of his trousers, now thinks he's very grown up. Pa said in his last letter that he's very cheeky too. Oh, and Mrs Hudson, I've so missed my piano lessons. Her letters say she now only takes in repair sewing jobs, she's happy that Granma tends to do all the fine dresses, saying she's too old to manage them as well as the piano lessons. Then there's my friends, Edward will nearly be a doctor himself by now, his sister Beatrice, although I'm not too sure she really likes me. Then there's all the Robinsons that live next door to Granma's house. Oh, so many things, I just can't wait to see them all."

"See, it's not so bad leaving us after all is it? I'd love to come up and see everyone too. Maybe if Governesses get longer holidays one day, then I could make the journey, what do you say?" Betsy eagerly nodded with her mouthful of tea. "I don't know why you've missed your piano lessons though, Betsy, you play so well now. Even Charlotte Ferguson told my Mistress that when Master Henry invited you for tea that day, you played like an angel."

"Well I don't think I'll be as good as Beatrice now, she'll have continued with her lessons while I've been away. We've always wanted to be better than each other."

"That's probably why she doesn't like you Betsy!" They both laughed heartily over their tea cups, giving away their guise as decorous, genteel young ladies.

"I'll miss everyone here though too. I've loved listening to Granny's stories about when her and my other Grandmother and namesake – Agatha Buxton, both worked at the House together. It must've been a very hard life back then, but they still seemed to have a lot of fun. I've only just got used to having a different mother, so hearing about another grandmother was strange, but nice too."

"Hmm, I can imagine. Well Betsy, you mustn't miss that train, I'll have Ma and Pa to answer to if you do. Come on, we'd better make our way to the platform now."

Rose was instructing Betsy as to the best papers to look for adverts for teaching positions as she hurried them towards the platform. Both had a subconscious awareness of a commotion near the station entrance, but were moving away from it, when Betsy suddenly picked up her own name being raucously shouted above the din of the engine.

"Betsy Agatha Buxton, stop, stop." She turned to see a rugged scrofulous vagrant running towards her, arms outstretched appealingly, causing his beige wool coat to open and display his unkempt clothes. She looked at Rose and took in the meaningful panic in her eyes.

"Quickly, Betsy, on the train. Now." She had taken hold of her elbow and was steering her towards the carriage.

"Who is it Rose, who is it, why does he want me, Buxton was

my mother's name wasn't it?" She hesitated in her tracks as she spoke, giving her pursuer the advantage.

"Come on Betsy, now, please!" Appealed Rose,

"No you don't Miss Elliot, you're not taking her away from me again. I've only just heard she's been staying with your family, and I nearly missed her." He slowed as he approached them, panting wildly, he spat out his speech, "Thankfully the coachman who informed me, had seen you alight at the station. I could have crossed your path Betsy, and never known."

Bill bent his body, supporting his hands on his knees to catch his breath. He looked up, gasping, and the anger melted from his frown as he took in the vision of his niece.

"Betsy, you're my blood, I'm your mother's brother. Bill." The three were now paused next to the open carriage door. Betsy looked from her Aunt to this man. He had a familiarity about him, but she could not think where from.

"Betsy please, listen to me. I'm your uncle, they've kept me from you all these years, I wanted to take care of you, but they wouldn't let me. I'm your only sure blood relative. Finding you has been my whole purpose since your mother passed. Don't deny me now I've found you again Betsy, please."

Betsy looked at Rose. "Is this true Rose? Is he my uncle?"

Rose looked briefly in her niece's growing anxious eyes, then averting them, spoke softly but urgently. "Yes Betsy, he's your Uncle, but you were being brought up and cared for by your father and his loving wife. This man tried to take you when you were very small, we didn't want to give him the chance to do that again. You were happy where you were, in the arms of my brother's loving family, and Bill had no fixed abode for you. We've all lived in fear of his finding you." She scowled at Bill, then turned back to Betsy, "We'd heard he was back in town and making quite a rumpus with a wild story involving your mother, Lizzibeth, and some friend of his who'd died. That's why Granny and Gramps wanted you to leave as soon as possible." Rose shot a warning glance at Bill, who had been pulling on Betsy's arm as she listened to her Aunt. Calmly

Betsy removed his hold on her arm and coldly spoke to her uncle.

"I remember you now, you carried me over your shoulder like a bag of coal, I was frightened. That hardly sounds like a loving uncle."

"I'm so sorry Betsy, but I had to get you away from them before I could explain to you, you were so young."

"Why weren't you pleased for me to be with my father? My mother loved him, she would've been happy to know I was with him."

"Huh, how do you know he's your father? I…" His voice trailed off as a commotion began at the other end of the platform. A tall and well built youth appeared, dressed as though a farm hand. He was brandishing a bottle, and ranting at Bill as he approached.

"Bill Buxton, Bill Buxton is it? Aggie Buxton's son? Arthur Brown's friend? Oh no, not friend, you don't go killin' friends do you? Remember October 1853? Of course you do, been bragging about it haven't you? Did you know what happened to his intended? Well I'll tell you, she 'ad her we'an, then died of a broken heart thinking her Arthur had deserted her for another. When all the time, as you've now told everyone in this town, you'd slaughtered 'im with a broken bottle. Then set 'im alight to destroy any indication of your deed!"

"Now wait, who are you…I .."

The youth, still moving menacingly towards Bill, his equal in size and stature, smashed the bottle on the side of the train, and swiped swiftly at Bill's neck.

"Where did you slash him? There, was it, or there!" He was flailing the bottle around Bill's head as Bill ducked repeatedly. "I'll tell you who I am Billy boy, Arthur junior. Brought up by my Grandmother to believe a sanitised story, only thanks to your loose tongue in the town, I now know my father was murdered, and you've my mother's blood on your hands too." He calmed himself momentarily, and puffed his chest out like an arrogant new phoenix, menacingly punctuating his words with the jagged bottle. As though proud of his achievements against such adversity he blurted, "and I will now have *your* blood on mine!"

His emphatic 'your' lost his composure for him again and he began to chase after the retreating Bill. The young Arthur Jones pulled at his coat to slow him, but Bill shed it like a skin as he ran down the platform for his life.

"Betsy, get on this train now, it's going any minute. He's no good, really, you can see that, go. Go." Rose hugged her niece and pushed her towards the carriage door and away from her uncle for the last time. Betsy reluctantly climbed aboard, imbibed words striving for order in her head as the whistle sounded.

"Write soon Betsy, promise." The train started to pull away. Rose looked away from Betsy's anguished face just in time to see Bill Buxton veer madly away from the moving train, only to trip forwards in his haste and propel himself uncontrollably forwards and onto the track flanking the other side of the platform; and the unstoppable path of an incoming train. In that instant, he had traded Arthur's swift painless blood letting end to life, for a much more brutal one. Rose saw the horror on the driver's face as he realised there was nothing he could do to stop the progress of this thirty ton steam engine as it brutally sent this pitiful man to his long awaited death.

Rose's shocked expression looked back for Betsy, she began frantically shouting for her. She need not return now, her adversary had gone for good, she could stay with them in Dorset forever if that was what she wanted now. She started to run alongside the train and reached up banging furiously on the moving window; but Betsy had already seated herself in the carriage and was obliviously talking to another passenger. She was bound once again for Scarborough and the North East Coast of England.

"So Ma, tell me what else I've missed in nearly a whole year?

I couldn't believe the difference in the town when I arrived. The new Pavilion Hotel is quite imposing as a first impression when you alight from the train, any other big changes?" Betsy was seated by the fireside jiggling five year old Albert on her knee and squeezing him periodically to reassure herself she was really home.

"Well the Pavilion is definitely the biggest new building. But, did you know that finally, education is now compulsory? And a new school is to be built to replace the one in Falsgrave village next year. I have always loved it along there, the little cottages are so pretty, and it's so quiet." Hannah had always shared her husband's passion regarding children's education, and continued. "The board men have been very strict in the town though, they're often around trying to catch children playing truant. I'll be glad when Kathy's left, she hasn't long to go now, but I'm sure she's more often on the beach with a crowd of friends, including Annie, than in school doing any learning. Your father would be furious. I worry about her, she has little interest in anything except enjoying herself and has a little too much vanity for our way of life. It's true she's a fine looking girl as anyone can see, and looks older than her years, but someone could take advantage of her." She paused as she allowed her thoughts to tie an uneasy knot in the pit of her stomach. Then continued,

"The Prince of Wales was here last year to watch the cricket with that Lord Londesborough, from Londesborough Lodge, you know, above the Spa, overlooking Valley Park Gardens. Well, I think she and Annie Robinson wandered around to wherever they thought he would be. They never did catch so much as a glimpse of him. They're always dressing up as the Queen and the princesses with Granma's oddments"

Betsy made a sound that compromised between concurrence with, and deference to, her mother's concerns, and yet amusement at her sister's fun loving antics. She made herself sound stern in her reply,

"Hmm, what work does she want to do, Ma?"

"Oh I've no idea, Betsy, she's not interested in sewing though. She would love to be a ladies maid she says – but I think she's a fancy for trying on all the gay clothes!" They laughed together then at this image of Kathy that so illustrated her traits.

Albert was beginning to get a little exasperated at being the object of Betsy's smothering affections, pleased as he was to have his big sister home again, he wanted her to talk to him. "Anything else changed, Ma?"

"Oh, let me see now. You know the North Bay Pier's opened don't you. We must have a walk up to the pier head together. One penny to get in, not bad really, you have an excellent view out to sea." Hannah was kneading some dough for their tea, she wiped the back of her hand across her forehead leaving a floury smudge which made Betsy smile.

"But Ma, you've the same view out to sea from the bay, the pier only takes you a few feet closer, which is nothing when you consider the vastness of the ocean." She pulled a face at her own perception of the ludicrous nature of Mr Woodall's 'progress' in her town, and cuddled up again to her little brother.

"You'll be the first woman on the council Betsy if I'm not mistaken." Hannah laughed at her elder daughter, the vivacious little girl that had been so like her birth mother in childhood, had allowed maturity to revolutionize this energy into an admirable sense of morality and citizenship. She mused that as this metamorphosis had occurred, Kathy had harnessed her sister's now redundant mischievousness alongside her own and was heading towards anarchic rebelliousness.

"What is it Albert?" He had been pulling on Betsy's collar since the mention of the pier.

"Betsy, have you got a tail like me, or has yours gone too?"

"Pardon me Albert, what do you mean?"

"Well, when we went to the pier with Pa, Annie had to go behind a bush, 'an I saw that her tail had completely dropped off, so I just wondered if yours has too, do they always drop off girls?" Hannah and Betsy exchanged glances before Hannah stifled the giggles of a much younger woman, lowered her head and beat the dough a little more thoroughly. Betsy, struggling to keep her composure, replied very seriously and secretly so as to dignify Albert's curiosity,

"Actually Albert, girls don't ever have one." To which Albert responded with an unbelievable and shocked intake of breath.

"Wait 'til I tell Thom that, he won't believe it." He jumped down from Betsy's knee and ran out of the kitchen, dragging the heirloom of Lizzibeth's now tired tattered tin trolley full of his favourite toys as he went. Mother and daughter indulged their stifled laughter for a few minutes, savouring the absolute innocence of childhood, then Betsy became suddenly serious.

"Ma?"

"Yes Betsy, what is it dear?"

"You know when I told you and Pa last night all about what happened at the station when I left Dorset?"

"Hmm," Hannah looked up from where she was braiding some of her bread loaves. She was so apprehensive about what Betsy was about to reveal, she did not hear her husband opening their back kitchen door. He was frozen in his tracks by Betsy's next words.

"Well, that Bill Buxton said Pa might not be my father, he said he himself was the only one with my blood for sure." Joseph, startled and motionless, listened in awe as his beloved wife responded with apposite empathy and compassion for their adversary, in befitting and respectful deference to his kinship to Lizzibeth, and of course, his niece.

"Take no notice of what Bill Buxton says Betsy dear, he's always said that. It's just to try and have guardianship of you. It's sad really, he'd never have done you any harm, Betsy, I just know it. It was just that he lost all three members of his family in as many years. He was devastated when his father died, but then to lose his mother and then Lizzibeth, so soon after. He just wanted someone to belong to. That's all, you can't blame him for trying can you, but he drank a lot my dear, we couldn't let you go to him. You do understand?"

"But Ma, what if he follows me, he might've known where I was going."

Hannah left her dough on the kitchen table and walked over to her daughter, she took her face in both of her hands and dropped a kiss on her forehead. Smiling at the comical pattern of fond floury fingers around Betsy's head, she hopefully added, "You've always been 'our' daughter, Betsy, let the station events put a final end to it, he can't possibly follow you up here now."

The tenderness of this moment was too much for Joseph, he rubbed his eyes hard, swallowed the huge lump gathering in his throat, and slipped noiselessly back out of the kitchen door. How poignant that Hannah thought he was the one whose blood bound this child to them, when he knew differently. What matter, she was a child to be so proud of, whatever her blood line, and he had chosen well in his wife, he was a lucky man. He took pride in knowing Lizzibeth would agree with him on all counts.

"Mrs Hudson, it's me, Betsy. I've just seen a man on one of those new machines. He was so far off the ground. I can see why they call it a penny farthing though, that's just what it looks like, as though a farthing was rolling after a penny." She was shouting as she let herself into the house. She hung up her coat as she was used to doing, every Wednesday teatime before she had left for Dorset. "Who was that man just leaving, he looked a real toff, Mrs Hu…"

Betsy stopped in her tracks, sat on the small sofa amidst a pile of her pending sewing jobs, and with a tear stained and sobbing Mrs Hudson, was a small squat young man with an unusual appearance.

Mrs Hudson looked up at Betsy with absolute terror in her eyes.

"Betsy, I ….I didn't know you were back, please don't say

anything, please Betsy, he's all I have now." The young man beamed a bluish smile at Betsy that lit up his whole face accentuating his curiousness, yet insisting an equivalent response.

"It's alright Mrs Hudson, calm yourself, I won't tell anybody anything, but I don't understand, who's this?"

Mrs Hudson, took hold of the man's hand, and turning to Betsy, she proudly announced,

"Betsy, this is Michael, he's our son." She turned to him and said. "Michael, this is Betsy, she comes here to play the piano." Betsy looked at Michael's smiling face, she had astutely perceived the tone of Mrs Hudson's voice to indicate that Michael may look like an adult, but the chronology of his mind was not equal.

"I'm very pleased to meet you Michael." Betsy reached out her hand to his. Michael held out his small cold hand in response, his other hand let go of his mother's and his short stubby fingers clasped his mouth to stifle a giggle, as he vigorously shook Betsy's arm as if it was a water pump. Betsy and Mrs Hudson smiled together at the enthusiasm of his greeting. Then suddenly without warning, Michael flung his arms around Betsy as though she were a long lost relative from faraway lands.

"I'm afraid it's a very long time since he's met anyone Betsy, and this is how he greets everyone he meets. He gets very bored and frustrated because he just loves to be with people. He hates it upstairs." Betsy extricated herself gently from Michael's embrace and seated herself on the sofa next to Mrs Hudson, she tentatively put a hand on her arm. Michael clapped his hands together, and flopped down cross legged on the floor next to them, thrilled at having a new person for company.

"But why are you so distraught Mrs Hudson? And why does nobody ever see Michael, why is he always upstairs? Is it him that makes all the banging noises?" Mrs Hudson looked directly into Betsy's eyes.

"Can I trust you Betsy? I mean can you really keep a secret?

They'd take Michael away if they knew we'd never actually taken him to an institution. I don't know what to do now without Alfred." Betsy looked puzzled.

"Of course you can trust me, but what do you mean without Alfred. Where's Mr Hudson?"

"That man that just left, he owns the company Alfred works for. Alfred's collapsed at work. They've taken him to the workhouse infirmary, but they don't think he'll live. I want to go to him, but I can't leave Michael on his own. I don't know what to do. I just don't know how I'd manage Michael without Alfred being around to help keep him hidden."

"Well the first thing you must do is go and see your husband Mrs Hudson, he needs you. I'll stay with Michael. Do I need to know anything?" She turned towards Michael. "Or will you be happy Michael if I read to you, or perhaps play a card game."

"Oh Betsy, would you, he loves to play snap, don't you Michael. You mustn't tell a soul Betsy, promise."

Joseph visibly bounded into the house, "Hannah, Hannah, where are you?"

"I'm in the kitchen Joseph, where I usually am on an afternoon, getting a meal ready for my hungry family. Would you mind putting the dolly tub away in the scullery for me, I didn't get it put away this morning? Whatever is it? You're red as a beetroot, have you been running?" He stopped in front of her to gather himself, then paused, looking around him,

"Where's Betsy?"

"She's having a piano lesson at Mrs Hudson's, why?"

"Bill Buxton's dead."

"Dead, how do you know?"

"There's an article in the paper all about it. It describes the altercation in the station with the youth who claimed Bill'd killed his father, just as Betsy and Rose had witnessed, but then it goes on to say that he fell in front of an incoming train.

I wonder if Rose saw what happened? But Betsy's safe with us always now. He can't touch her, or us anymore, my dear."

"Oh but that's dreadful, Joseph, what a horrible death."

"Forgive me Hannah, you're right, I'm not glad that a man has lost his life, he was Lizzibeth's brother after all. But he's caused us such distress, my dear, I confess I shan't weep for him. Apparently he was alive for a few minutes when they pulled him out too, enough to say a few dying words it says here, I hope he was praying for forgiveness."

"Poor Bill, his grief and his conscience wouldn't allow him a life after what he did, he can't have been all bad, he may as well have hung for the crime all those years ago. Did you know this friend of his? The one Betsy said he was accused of murdering? I do remember his disappearance. I knew his intended, she died not long after her child was born. Her mother took the baby in." Joseph picked up the dolly tub and headed into the scullery, muttering as he went,

"Arthur Brown did Betsy say? No Hannah, I didn't know him at all."

"Betsy play Snap with me again Ma?"

"No Michael, you must be quiet, Betsy has come for a piano lesson, not to play with you."

"Good afternoon Mrs Hudson, good afternoon Michael. Brr, its freezing out there, it feels more like January, not April. I'm a little late today because I went to listen to Pritchard's Band playing in the open air Band Stand at The Spa. They are such a mixture of men, Mrs Hudson, all different ages, and colours and styles of dress. Some have top hats, others bowlers, some tail coats, some frock coats some have modern ties, others older neckties, and they all look such fun characters, but you'd think they could all agree on what to wear! Still, they have their talent in common, they are magnificent musicians."
She hardly drew breath in her enthusiasm for the band as she busied herself with her music and settling herself at the stool.

"Oh Mrs Hudson, Mrs Jones is carrying something over to you, you may want to move Michael from view."

"Oh thank you Betsy, see that's the problem with allowing him downstairs, he's in danger of being seen all the time." Mrs Hudson ushered her son into the back kitchen and put her finger to her lips to indicate he must be quiet.

"I know that Mrs Hudson, but in much less danger of being heard. Now he isn't locked away upstairs all day, he's no need to shout and thump, has he?"

"I suppose not, but it's still such a worry." She opened the door in response to the expected knock, "Ahh Mrs Jones, what can I do for you?" Betsy had begun to play the piano, the dulcet tones of Mozart drifted into the street flowing around an unappreciative 'Flossie flat hat', as she was now known affectionately by everyone thanks to Kate.

"Oh nowt really, Mrs 'udson, I was merely wondering like, if you'd like some stew we 'ad left over today. I know well enough what it's like to lose an 'usband. Mine were much younger 'un yours of course, but Mrs Wilson says your Alfred went with the same thing that done for Mr Dickens, earlier this year. No Westminster Abbey or lines of mourners for the likes of us though eh? Anyway, you don't feel like cookin' for yersen for a while, so there you go." She handed the dish over to her neighbour and smiled, Mrs Hudson returned the gesture replying,

"Well that's just so kind of you Mrs Jones, so kind. What would I have done without the help of all my wonderful neighbours?" She exchanged a few more brief pleasantries, and closed the door, scurrying back inside. "My heart's in my mouth as they say, with him being down here Betsy. I'm so afraid he's seen, I couldn't bear to lose him too."

Betsy had stopped playing, and was looking from Michael's happy, innocent face to his mother's worried and anxious one.

"You know Mrs Hudson, from what you've said, it was only Michael's demonstrations of affection that posed a threat to him. I think I could teach him to just shake hands with people instead of embracing them, and that way, nobody could take him away. You could say he's been cured at the place you told everyone he'd gone to, and so has been allowed to return home. What do you think?"

"But Michael has always done it Betsy, it's part of his nature, I don't know how you could teach him otherwise. No harm in trying I suppose. You really are earning your piano lessons now my dear, you're such a dear and beloved friend to us."

Chapter 18

Scarborough, Summer 1871

"So if I was ill now, Edward, could you make me better? You said you'd be finished your studies this summer." Kathy was blatantly flirting albeit girlishly with Edward on their way home from Church.

"Kathy, stop it, you'll embarrass Edward."

"Why, Betsy? Doctors aren't supposed to get embarrassed are they Edward? You can talk to them about anything at all, can't you?"

"Hmm, I suppose so, but I have a lot still to learn I'm afraid."

"Well, would you rub some of that new antiseptic stuff on me if I fell over and hurt myself here?" She shamelessly lifted her skirts to show Edward her bare knee, "I've heard it stinks."

"Kathy!" Betsy exclaimed, Kathy dropped the hem of her skirt sulkily, while Edward, innocently assuming her to be interested in the subject, continued, having maintained his serious composure throughout her teasing.

"Antiseptic is an important new discovery, Kathy. Keeping wounds clean is vital to the healing process. It does have a strong odour, but it's not entirely unpleasant." Kathy, incredulous that Edward was taking her so seriously, then pronounced,

"Oh you're no fun at all Edward Hetherington, you're behaving like a grown up now. Come on Thom, Ma said lunch wasn't 'til one, so we could go down to the Spa and watch the carriages arrive for the afternoon concert." She turned back to where Johnny and Annie were dawdling behind, "Are you two coming too? We could go to the Fish Pier instead Johnny if you'd prefer to watch the fishermen. Do they still work on a Sunday? They are funny to watch, one threw a fish from the back of a cart at me one day, it was still wriggling too!" Annie giggled, and added,

"I remember that, but you deserved it, you were being cheeky about the big pipe in his mouth, Katie. I like their big baggy jumpers and funny hats." Johnny at seventeen, was not keen to be following his younger friends and sister, but had nothing better to do before lunch; and Kathy Elliot was so wayward, she was always amusing to spend time with anyway.

"Come on then, let's head for the beach, but just for an hour." Edward and Betsy were left as the young ones all disappeared from view.

"Where have Beatrice and Peter Robinson disappeared to Betsy, they were here a minute ago?" Betsy stopped and looked around her,

"I've no idea, Edward, they must've gone with our mothers for tea in the church hall. They get on really well together. I think Peter's a bit sweet on your Beatrice."

"I sincerely hope not Betsy, well not seriously anyway, Mother would never allow that."

"But why not Edward, they've been brought up so closely together?"

"Playing together as children is one thing, marriage is quite another Betsy."

Betsy shrugged her shoulders, she did not always pick up on the subtleties of Edward's comments. But she so loved to talk to him about medicine, it was such an interesting subject.

"Have you decided what type of medicine you want to work in Edward? Will you work with your father or do you have a mind to do hospital work?"

Edward stopped walking as a progression of three carriages trotted noisily past them, the horses snorting loudly in the heat of the day. He leant against the wall on Falsgrave Walk, forcing Betsy to stall with him.

"It's a big decision Betsy, my Mother would like me to come back here and work in that new cottage hospital on Springhill Road. The one that the widow of the Birmingham surgeon has opened, a Mrs Wright I believe. She so misses not having me around here. She has never really got over losing Henry, you know, I'm now her only son. So when I'm away, she feels she has lost me too. That's how Father sees it anyway. And she has become so irritable lately, poor Father and Beatrice have a lot to put up with when I am away. She's better when I am home. But the problem is that I'm really interested in studying more about diseases and conditions of the brain. There are so many things that have yet to be discovered. Do you know, on my last place of study, I ….I'm sorry, Betsy, am I boring you?"

"Not at all Edward, I could talk to you all day about medicine, I've become so interested since helping your father a little at the clinic with letters and things. It must be wonderful to be a doctor. Do go on."

"Well, in my last place of study, I spent some time with a physician called Doctor John Langdon Down, he's identified a condition whereby the children suffering from it, all have similar mental problems, and they all have the same facial features, their epicanthal folds, here," Edward indicated to his eyelid "are different, making them look like a race from the east called Mongolians. This is such a break-through, imagine working in an environment where discoveries are being made all the time. What a difference I could make to society Betsy. Betsy?" She had absorbed his every utterance, and a light had switched on behind her eyes which appeared to simultaneously cause her jaw to drop as she processed every word he fashioned.

"Are you listening to me Betsy, do I have something on my face?"

"Oh er, no Edward, I'm fascinated, that must be wonderful work. Hmm, these children, can anything be done to help them?"

"Not that we know of yet. But wouldn't it be wonderful if we could. There's no way of knowing at the moment what causes it to happen. Unfortunately they often die in infancy, childhood, or at the latest, early adulthood, heart problems seem to abound, circulation is poor, but mainly the children tend to live in institutions because of the lack of mental progression."

"Can they learn at all Edward?"

"Oh of course Betsy, just at a much slower rate, that's all. You are interested aren't you, anyone would think you knew a child like this!"

"Ma, you'll never know who we've just seen on North Marine Road."

Kathy, and Annie Robinson flopped breathlessly onto the kitchen chairs. At thirteen years old, they were now in the final stages of childhood, where their bodies and behaviours hinted at womanhood, but an air of innocence tantalisingly clung on, absurdly, further threatening that very virtue.

"No I probably wouldn't Kathy, who have you seen?"

"The Prince of Wales himself, if you please Ma'am." She stood erect, then bobbed an excited curtsey before flopping back down and continuing eagerly. "Large as life itself 'e was, strutting along from his carriage into the cricket ground!"

"H, he was, Kathy, not 'e was! Well I never did. Was the Princess with him?"

"No Ma, he takes his other lady out in the carriage, didn't you know that, but she didn't look like a Princess. She was a beautiful lady, but not grand like Princess Alexandra."

"Hmm." Hannah gave a knowing lop-sided smile. "Well Kathy, tell me what the Prince looked like?"

"Oh he was so handsome Ma, he'd a smart tail coat, with a shiny top hat, and a gold pocket watch that sparkled in the sun. He smiled at me too, Annie said it was at her, but I know it was me 'coz I'd just sneezed, and so he looked over at me and smiled!"

"I'm sure it was a royal smile for both of the subjects he saw before him Kathy. Did you curtsey to him?"

"Oh no, Ma, I forgot, oh no. He won't smile next time I see him now will he?"

Hannah was amazed at how a child with such rebellion in her nature, could be so captivated by the monarchy and the ruling system. She managed to placate her daughter that the Prince would see so many little girls everyday, that he would not recall who had remembered to curtsey, and who had not.

"Oh but I want him to remember me, Ma, I want to be his other lady when I grow up. You know Freddy in my class, well, his Ma, Mrs Crooks, said that the Prince has a wife to give him children and do all his duties for him, but others that he pays to have fun with. I want to be one of the 'other ladies', Ma, and get paid to have fun with the Prince of Wales."

Hannah spluttered, and her shock at her daughter's remark, however innocent, was still written on her face when Betsy came into the kitchen carrying a large parcel.

"What's wrong Ma? Have you seen a ghost?"

"Erm, no Betsy. But you know how we wondered what Kathy would like to do when she left school, well, she's just told me! I think we need to have a little chat later on young lady, with your father! And perhaps with Mrs Crooks. What've you got there, Betsy, has the post van just been round?" Kathy and Annie shrugged at each other, oblivious to what she had said that had caused her mother to scold her.

"Yes Ma, it looks like Aunt Rose's handwriting, I wonder what it is, I don't think I left anything down in Dorset, but it has my name on it." Betsy started to unwrap the parcel, and looked puzzled when she found it to be beige wool material. "It looks like a new coat Ma?" Kathy came around to Betsy's side, "Wow Betsy." Kathy had been much more affable to her sister since her outburst about 'fairness', and even more so since she had missed her so much when she had been away. She had done her best to ensure Betsy was still 'her sister'. "That feels really soft. But it looks like a man's coat. It would be too big for you to wear."

"I know that coat." The two girls looked up at their mother, she was fingering the cashmere wool and her mind was miles away.

"This coat could tell a few tales Betsy. It actually belonged to your Godfather, Uncle Henry. He gave it to your mother, and the night she died, Bill Buxton, her brother took it with him. It's been cleaned up though, there were a few marks on it that night, they're mostly gone."

"Oh look Ma, Aunt Rose has written a letter too." Kathy was so excited at this mystery gift.

Betsy was quietly contemplating why her Aunt would send her a coat that now belonged to Bill Buxton.

"Kathy, you go off now and read your book, there's a good girl, you could read it to Annie, you know how she prefers to be read to." Hannah steered her younger daughter and her friend away, she felt sure Betsy was about to find out about her uncle's death. "Come along, you can tell me what happens next in that wonderland of Alice's. Did I tell you Mr Carroll has published another book this year, it's something about Alice with a looking glass." They left Betsy to peruse her letter in the private stillness of the deserted kitchen.

My Dear Betsy

It has been with great deliberation that I am sending you this coat. I have taken the advice of many who know and love you before sending it. But in giving it to you I have the unenviable task of explaining how I came by it.

Remember the day in the station when your Uncle Bill accosted us? Then a young man came about, threatening him with a bottle because of something to do with his father? Well, according to what your uncle had told people in the Inn, it transpires that in October 1853, after an altercation with your mother,- his sister, a friend

240

of his was less than complimentary to her. In her defence, Bill was so angry, he went at him with a discarded bottle. Unfortunately for Bill, the bottle was broken, and when he hit him with it, it slashed his neck and he bled like a slaughtered pig. He was dead in seconds. Bill successfully disposed of the body, and has spent these last many years carrying the guilt for this. He blamed himself for his mother's death as she was distraught with worry, and then again for your mother's death because he had not protected her from cholera whilst she was living with him, nor had he realised she was with child until she was so ill.

To add to his tragedy, as he ran away from the young man on the platform Betsy, he fell in the path of an inbound engine. I hoped most sincerely that you had not witnessed that event dear niece, though I was not spared the ordeal. Sadly he was not killed instantly, and when I could hear him shouting your name, I wanted to run away, but my legs took me towards him. The train had rent his body into an unrecognisable form and I could see that he could not survive. I wanted to ease his mind in his passing so I knelt beside him and let him believe I was you. He made me promise that I would take the coat and treasure it always. It was the only thing he had of Lizzibeth's, he whispered between gasps that he knew how much she had treasured it when she had been with him in London, and how she had insisted that you, her newborn child was swaddled in it at your birth. It was all he had in the world to offer you. I assured him as I held onto the one hand still attached to his body, that you would treasure it always. I hope you approve my action on your behalf my dear Betsy; and indeed that he heard me too. As I had finished speaking, his eyes glazed over as though he could see straight through me, and I knew he had gone.

He led a sad life Betsy, he deserves both our pity and our compassion. My doubt as to whether I should do as he asked, and hence the delay my dear Betsy, is that I did not want to bring you such grave news. He was your mother's brother. Your Uncle.

But remember, he was also always a threat to your security as a member of the Elliot family that have loved and embraced you my dear, and now you know that he is gone forever. I hope God forgives him his sins, for I do not feel he was a wholly bad man Betsy, otherwise his conscience would not have killed him in the end.

I hope you feel I have done the right thing in passing his coat to you. It did belong to your mother once. I had it cleaned up for you in our laundry room at the house in Salisbury, you may remember how soiled it was when Bill last wore it.

My fondest regards to you Betsy, and the whole family. Affectionately Always

Rose

Betsy placed the letter on the table and picked up the coat. She held it against her face as though being close to it would somehow connect her to her mother. Suddenly she threw it down onto the table, something about the feel or smell of it had rekindled a memory. Slowly, the mist cleared, and she could see the houses and then the fields bobbing up and down through the shiny golden lining, her legs hurt from being held tightly, her tummy sore from bouncing on a shoulder, and panic welled up in her as she shouted again and again for her Pa.

Hannah ran anxiously back into the kitchen. Betsy was still shouting, but stamping wildly on the coat and pulling madly on the sleeves desperate to destroy this mantle of terror that for one day in her memory, had threatened everything she knew. Hannah took hold of her and turned her towards her, Betsy's wild thrashings calmed into violent sobs onto Hannah's shoulder. Hannah held her until the hysteria abated, then quietly she soothingly questioned her, stroking her hair as she cooed,

"What is it Betsy, what is it." Between dampening sobs and gasps, Betsy recounted,

"Oh Ma, I remembered, I was wrapped in this coat when he tried to take me away. I've had this memory for a long time now, meeting at the station made it real. But the feel and smell of this coat brings the terror of that day back so vividly. I was on his shoulder, he took me past Gramps and Granny's house didn't he?"

"Yes Betsy he did. Lucky he did though, because that's how Benjamin stopped him, and your Gramps got you back. He can't harm you any more, Betsy, he's gone for good now, there there, hush now."

Slowly Betsy composed herself, and sat down on a chair, folding the coat onto the kitchen table, she rummaged underneath it for the letter.

"How do you know he can't Ma? You haven't read Aunt Rose's letter."

Hannah sat down quietly next to her, as she brandished the parchment.

"Has Aunt Rose told you he's dead, and how he died?" Betsy nodded, staring again at her Aunt's misty words.

"My dear, there was an article in the newspaper, your father hid it from you, we thought the incident was best forgotten, you'd been upset enough."

"But Ma, I've been so worried that he could've followed me, you could've spared me that!"

"If we did wrong, my dear Betsy, then I'm so sorry. But I want to tell you something about that coat so you may shake off your own memory of it and replace it with your mother's, and treasure it as she did."

Hannah proceeded to describe their childhoods, their closeness, particularly that of Lizzibeth, Joseph and Henry. She talked of Henry's accident, Joseph's schooling, their secret meetings with Lizzibeth; the night the three of them had spent in the town where they had used the coat upon which to be seated at the monument. That somehow Lizzibeth had ended up with Henry's coat. She embellished the strength of the feelings between Joseph and Lizzibeth, as Hannah herself understood it. Betsy then interjected,

"But if my parents were so much in love Ma, why was my mother living in London with her brother anyway."

"You have to consider the shame of being with child, but out of wed-lock Betsy. Your father didn't know about you, Lizzibeth had left the town to protect him. But when she returned, and came to my parent's house, your Granma's, for her confinement, she was wrapped in this very woollen coat which she was reluctant to remove despite the clement weather, until she was delivered of you. Then she used it as your shelter and security. She knew it could do no more for her." Hannah, despite her own tears, went on to repeat as much of Lizzibeth's dying speech as she could remember, including her use of the phoenix myth, despite all the pain and sadness it awoke in her own soul.

Betsy held the sleeve of the coat and began stroking it tenderly,

"Are you sure Uncle Henry won't want it back Ma?" As she spoke she lifted her full ocean eyes appealingly up to a parallel pair. They responded in a full and knowing smile whose arms embraced her tightly, and then spoke,

"I know Uncle Henry would not dream of wanting it returned Betsy. It's yours to keep, and to think of how much your mother loved you, your father and in her own way too, your Uncle Henry." She kissed her forehead, and leaning forward, rocked her in a comforting embrace as though she were a distraught child who had scuffed her knees.

Tears streamed silently down Betsy's face and bounced momentarily onto the cashmere before being thirstily swallowed by it, as though desperate to bond some part of her, with those that had gone before. The auspicious yet so poignant incongruity of the only loving mother she had ever known, introducing her to the memories of a loving mother she could never know, was not lost on Betsy.

"Pa, Pa, I've seen the Prince of Wales this morning. He was at the cricket ground, he smiled at me!" Kathy had run to meet her father at the door as he returned from his workshop. They walked back to the kitchen table to join the family for their meal together.

"Did he indeed, Kathy, well I doubt he'll be back there for a while. According to Mr Robinson who's just got home from work, the Prince is very poorly tonight with suspected typhoid fever. Let's pray he's more resilient to the disease than his father was."

"Oh no!" The Elliot women replied in unison.

"Yes, apparently, there are some who are quick to blame the drains at Londesborough Lodge where he was staying, any excuse to cause trouble for the Earl. That man's done good work for raising the popularity of this town, but I suppose everyone must have their critics. The Grand Hotel is flourishing because of him, and the Prince coming here is good publicity as well as the prospect of this annual Cricket Festival he talks about starting."

"Is he going to travel back to London, or is he too poorly?" Kathy asked, full of concern for new royal acquaintance.

"Well, I'm not sure my dear, I think William knew a little more than I got out of him, but that wife of his never stopped butting in to the conversation, you know what she's like. Wittered on about people she's known with the typhoid fever, together with vivid descriptions of the various symptoms, and being a prophet of doom and gloom for the Prince's prospects of recovery!"

"Mrs Robinson's nice Pa, don't be mean."

"Mrs Robinson is very nice Kathy, but she can't help herself, she just loves to hear the sound of her own voice and compulsively interrupts. Would drive a man mad to live with wouldn't you think Thom?" He winked at his elder son. Thom grinned and replied,

"No wonder Kathy thinks she's nice, she's exactly the same!" The family laughed together, even Kathy could not stifle her mirth despite putting out her tongue at her brother.

"The Prince's visit has done well for Mrs Taylor's Royal Butterscotch and Simnel cakes, he apparently sampled them all and they are talking of imprinting his silhouette on the sides of their pies." The family all chuckled at this novel absurdity as they waited for their dinner to be served.

"How did you get on at the stonemason's today Thom? Are you enjoying your work? No chest problems?" Thom answered all his father's questions with a nod or shake of his head as he had a mouthful of the mutton stew they were all enjoying. He seriously wondered himself whether he'd be happy to spend his life chiselling stones into the required shapes. It didn't quite fulfil his artistic tendencies as he'd hoped it might. Sundays were his favourite days, when he could go out with his cherished easel, purchased with his first year's wages, and paint some of the beautiful scenery around them.

"Everyone else had a good day?" Joseph surveyed his family. Betsy and Hannah caught each other's eye.

"Well, yes dear, but we do need to talk tonight, Betsy has had some news today from your sister Rose. And I also need to share with you Kathy's plan for her future paid employment!"

Chapter 19

Scarborough, December 1873

"Edward, I'm so sorry. I don't know what else to say to you. I don't know how any of us are going to manage without him. He was just always there for all of us. I can't believe he's gone. How's your mother coping? She looks in a daze today, as if she doesn't know where she is."

They were all taking up their positions around the grave of Doctor John Hetherington, watching his coffin being laid to rest. The slow gentle and careful lowering into the ground was befitting for this most gentle and caring of men. The eerie silence surrounding this cold wintry graveyard was broken only by sporadic sobs from the women of the group and the monotone of the preacher. Only Mary was controlled. She gazed above the proceedings with unseeing cold eyes, awaiting permission from solitude, privacy and a clear mind, to grant her dignity in her grief.

Mary Hetherington was now forty one years old, a slight woman. She was shrouded in her widow's weeds, with a large black veiled bonnet, tied with the biggest bow Betsy had ever seen. Her features looked pale, old, shrivelled and shrew-like, with her cold expression adding a superior air of aged arrogance.

Beatrice was inconsolable, Betsy had seen Edward, Peter and her Pa all try to comfort her, but to no avail. She wondered if she dared try herself, but considered her chances of success very poor. She had always felt their friendship, though very amicable, a little superficial.

The final hymn at the graveside was baritone, only the men were composed enough to pay harmonious homage to this well respected man of the town. Mary Hetherington looked on as though critiquing the performance, then as the last note ran out of fuel and died, the mourners began to disperse, leaving her momentarily alone, to gaze down at the wooden box sprinkled with earth, that bore her soul-mate's earthly remains.

Betsy repeated her concerns to Edward, "How's your mother holding her composure Edward? She's doing better than the rest of us." Betsy hid her reddened eyes under the brim of her black bonnet that she had borrowed for the occasion from Mrs Hudson. She had hold of Albert's hand as she rejoined the path alongside Edward.

"I've given her something to keep her calm Betsy, but I just don't know how she will manage without him. My grandmother still lives near to us, but her and mother don't always see eye to eye. I shall have to move back to Scarborough of course, mother will not hear of me not continuing on with father's work here."

"But Edward, what about your work with this Doctor John Langdon Down in helping the children with this curious condition?"

"Betsy, what a good memory you have, you really are interested in my work aren't you? I'm afraid though, that was a luxury I can no longer afford. With my father gone, I will need an income to support us all." Betsy considered this, she did not imagine the Hetheringtons being short of money, but then supposed however much you had, it could not last forever without an income. Albert wandered away from this very serious of conversations, enjoying the crisp sounds his footsteps made on the frozen grass. Edward continued, "You will still work at the clinic won't you, Betsy, I'll need the same help that my father did, perhaps more until I become more experienced and organised. I'm actually going to spend some time at The Cottage Hospital, maybe I could at least get some surgical experience."

"Of course I'll help Edward, I much prefer working at the clinic to helping with Granma's sewing, and I'm offended that you needed to ask. Albert!" she scolded quietly, "don't stand on that grave, it's not respectful. Look, there's a little girl buried under there. Emmeline Foster aged three years and four months. Oh, that's so sad isn't it Edward?"

"I fear I will see a lot of sadness working at my father's clinic, so many children do die Betsy. Albert! Your sister told you to get down and show some respect!" Albert looked worryingly around his feet, then held a hand out to Betsy so he could dismount the grave with one large stride.

"Betsy, do you mean there was a dead body under my feet."

"Of course Albert, it's a grave."

"Well. Don't tell my Granma that, she'll be utterly horrified!" He scurried his childhood innocence away to protectively find his Grandmother in the dispersing throng; leaving Betsy and Edward unsure as to whether it was permitted to show amusement at such a solemn occasion.

"Joseph, is your arm bothering you, dear, you keep rubbing it?"

"No it's fine my dear, I just caught it and bruised it at work, but because I can't feel it properly, I have to rub it to see how it is coming along. I do get twinges from my chest though you know, where I broke my ribs, down here on this right side, but Henry's been told to expect arthritis in the area of his injuries, so I suspect it's just the same with me." Joseph inspected his arm where he had been chafing at it. Over the years, his lack of warning sensation had inflicted much damage, leaving blanched scarred areas covering its surface.

"We're going to miss John so much for all his advice, aren't we? It won't be the same talking to Edward, he's just a boy in my eyes."

"Well yes Hannah, but a very well educated one. I can't help but envy him that opportunity. I could've done that you know."

"I know Joseph, I know." Hannah looked sadly at her husband. He had done well for them, they had their own home, a business that was doing well, a lovely family, but she knew how Joseph had always ached for knowledge. He could easily have been a doctor, but it had never been possible from their background. She also knew Joseph would have loved to have paid for one of his children to achieve his ambitions for him, but Thom was never interested in his studies and Albert so loved to watch his father's woodwork, that it was looking like he may want to become a cabinet maker too. Joseph had already taken on Johnny Robinson as an apprentice cabinet maker, and he was doing well. Only Betsy showed the same thirst for learning as her father, but as a mere girl, that was not possible. Hannah returned to her ironing, picking up another flat iron from the hearth.

"Is it next month Henry's planning a visit up here Joseph?"

"No, not until April dear, about six weeks yet. There's apparently a training course he's involved with at a small camp in Richmond in the Dales, so he is going to have a few days here too. He did say that Amelia may come with him, and they'll be staying in a house on South Cliff that belongs to someone he knows, I've the address somewhere, but you know, I remember thinking at the time that the address was familiar, I wonder if I've made furniture for the owner at some time."

"Hmm, I'll be quite nervous meeting his wife for the first time Joseph."

"There's no need dearest, she's very nice, no airs and graces, I told you she was very friendly when I went down to see Ma, what four years ago now, she won't have changed you know."

"Oh, I know, it's just that if you want me to cook for them, I'll be a little nervous, that's all."

"If it bothers you that much, we'll eat out somewhere, or get a fish supper."

"Never, Joseph, that would be so rude. It'll be fine. Anyway, tell me what you've been reading in that paper tonight." Joseph looked up from the print.

"Well," he paused to select a piece of interest, "Disraeli, seems set to get back into the position of Prime Minister next year, he's having talks with people again about shortening the working day to eight hours. There's actually an 'eight hour' movement you know, calling for eight hours work, eight hours recreation, and eight hours rest! I ask you Hannah, what's anyone going to do with eight hours recreation every day?"

Kate Wilson scurried into her sewing room to where Betsy was helping her with a ball gown for a lady from the esplanade, and held out more ivory thread for her.

Betsy was seated on the chaise, bought specially for customers to use during fittings, with yards and yards of ivory organza silk all around her. She was hand-stitching the gathers for the numerous frills ready for them to be attached to the main body of the skirt which was hanging undressed on the tailors dummy to one side of her. The bare skirt was attached by pins to the low cut bodice with short, off the shoulder sleeves which Kate had adorned with beads and hand sewn rose buds.

"Betsy, Mrs Hudson has just stopped me on her way back from the butchers shop, she asked if you'd mind popping in to see Michael, she thinks he might not be very well. I thought he was a little quiet the other day, I didn't even get a handshake from him."

Betsy snapped instantly out of her daydream about wearing a dress such as the one before her.

"Really Granma, I've never known him **not** greet anyone. Do you think I should go for Edward?"

"Well I don't know what he can do Betsy, my understanding is that at twenty nine years old now, Michael's already out-lived Edward's expectations with this condition."

"I know, but I'd hate to think of him suffering, Granma, he won't understand, he's like a child in not understanding what hurts or why."

"Well, just help me pin this first frill onto the skirt Betsy, then you go along and see him and see what you think."

"Good afternoon Beatrice, is Edward home?"

"I'm not sure, I think so." She turned her neat figure contained within a tight fitting bodice, and swept her fashionable dark blue skirt with its trailing pleated and flounced bustle across the hallway, expecting Betsy to follow her.

She stopped outside the library and indicated for Betsy to go in saying, "Mother's in there, she should know." She then carried on walking towards the staircase, but threw the following words over her shoulder loud enough for her mother to hear, "I hope you're not wanting to walk out with Edward, Betsy. I shall have something to say if it is alright for you to walk out with Edward, but not alright for me to walk out with Peter."

She edged nervously forwards into the room, realising she had arrived at a difficult time.

"What can I do for you Betsy, it is not very convenient at the moment as you can see. Beatrice is becoming very tiresome. Edward is coming for his lunch any minute; I can give him a message for you."

"I'm so sorry to interrupt Mrs Hetherington, but Michael Hudson's not well, I thought Edward might come and see him."

"I'll tell him, but it will depend how busy he is with everyone else, after that, he needs to come and spend some time with his dear lonely widowed mother. I understood nothing could be done for that boy anyway. Good day to you Betsy."

"Oh, er, good day to you Mrs Hetherington. Ma says to remember her if she can do anything at all to help."

"Nobody can help me, but my daughter seems intent on making a bad situation even worse."

Betsy took her leave, and considered Beatrice's plight. She had already had a conversation with Peter Robinson about the way they felt about each other, but Mrs Hetherington was adamant, and was threatening to send Beatrice away to her Aunt's house in London where she could learn to teach music. Peter promised to follow her if that happened, and to get a position on Fleet Street. He had gone to work at the paper with his father at twelve years old, but was doing well now, as a journalist reporter, rather than a printer. Betsy could not understand why he was not suitable for Beatrice. She couldn't help herself wondering whether she would be good enough for Edward if he had been sweet on her, which she knew he wasn't.

She was hurrying along with her cloak up high to protect her from the biting February wind, wondering whether her mother had been right in thinking Mary Hetherington could be set on beating the Queen herself in her grieving. Her Ma had commented to her that whilst it was yet early days since John's unfortunate and untimely death from a kidney infection; Mary had previously defended the Queen whenever it was suggested that she had been in official mourning too long. She had condemned those disenchanted with the monarchy, and calling for an abdication over this excessive mourning period, saying it was quite befitting for a wife out of respect for an honourable deceased husband. She thought how difficult it must be at home for both Edward and Beatrice, when she suddenly walked headlong into Edward as he came around the corner.

"Betsy what are you doing here, it's your day off?"

"Oh I know Edward, but I went to see if you were home, to come and look at Michael for me, he's not well. He looks more blue than usual around his mouth, and he can't get out of bed today, or be bothered with anything, which isn't like him at all."

"It certainly isn't Betsy, let's go straight there."

"But your Mother said you had others to see first, including her."

"Mother has never been the most tolerant of the less fortunate in society whatever the cause of their adversity." The latter half of his sentence took on the haughty tones of his mother voice, and they both smiled. Betsy had noticed of late that Edward had been more relaxed in his mood, less dour and sombre. His company was becoming amusing as well as venerable, he continued, "She can make me stay here in the town, but she can't tell me how to run a medical clinic. Come on, let's go now."

After months of working with Michael, Betsy had taught him to greet her appropriately, when she was happy that this skill was reliable enough to be unleashed on others, she persuaded Mrs Hudson to let her bring Edward round to meet him. Edward had been very excited at having a patient of such an age with this rare condition and living within the local community he served.

His initial examination of Michael had lead him to express concern on two counts. Firstly, his poor general state of health. Secondly Michael's enjoyment of life, whether he continued to remain permanently cooped in a small house due public hostility; or indeed whether he did not, but became the object of that very antagonism rooted as it was in ignorance and fear. The first, much to Edward's chagrin, he could do nothing to alleviate.

He therefore considered the second. And just last month, he had persuaded Mrs Hudson to boldly tell everyone that her son was cured of his unacceptable behaviours, and was returning home. Unbeknown to her, he had also counselled the neighbours individually as to the nature of Michael's infirmity. Irrationally, pinning a medical label onto his condition, especially by Edward, appeared to give both credibility and acceptability to his very existence. Indeed even Jane Robinson, not known for her tolerance of any imperfection, had succumbed to utterances of a sympathetic nature regarding Michael Hudson. Thus when Mrs Hudson first ventured outside the house with her son, Betsy was by his side, and nobody was troubled by either his presence or indeed their affable but suitably restrained greetings from him. Almost mockingly, the boy who had spent the last few years living as a prisoner, was now in his last weeks at least, dying as a free man.

Mrs Hudson was seeing Edward back out of the front door, Betsy had stayed upstairs with Michael, holding his hand and pretending she was sleepy too. He had smiled feebly at her and closed his eyes.

"I'm so sorry Mrs Hudson, as I have explained to you before, heart problems are a part of Michael's condition, it's due to your exceptional care that he has done so very well and lived until now. There's nothing I can give you. But he's in no pain, he just doesn't understand why he's so tired, and that's confusing for him. Try to act as though it's perfectly normal for him to be sleepy, and he will just slip away."

Tears rolled down her rounded cheeks, she had felt such relief when Edward first talked to her about Michael's condition. To know she was not alone with this. That other people, often also late to parenthood, had suffered the same problems, was somehow comforting. Yet now there seemed little comfort or purpose in Michael's short life. The deeds of this all merciful God were not always easy to understand.

"Thank you Doctor Hetherington, you've been so kind, your father'd be very proud of you."

Edward, surprisingly emotional at her comment, stepped out into the chill afternoon, but then heard Betsy's quiet, and calm voice,

"Edward, Mrs Hudson."

They both ran up the stairs and into Michael's room and were met by a moving scene. The paradox of Betsy embracing Michael and rocking him in her arms after he had departed this life was too painful to witness. Standing up from the side of his bed, she turned to greet them, tears streaming down her face.

"He tried to say 'Good night Betsy', he mouthed it, but he just had no power in his voice. Oh, I'm so sorry Mrs Hudson."

"Henry, it's so lovely to see you." Henry beamed as he entered the Elliot's home once again.

"Hannah, my dear friend, I'd like to introduce you to my dear wife, Amelia."

"So pleased to meet you Amelia after all this time." The whole family including Kate hovered around exchanging greetings.

"Hannah, you are just as charming as Henry said. I am always commenting on his big blue eyes, having dull brown ones myself, and he told me yours were very similar, and so they are. You're a lucky pair, yours the colour of clear sapphires and Joseph's as dazzling emeralds." She took in Hannah's amazed look, the conversation was a little personal for an acquaintance of only a few moments, perhaps Hannah wasn't the only nervous one. Amelia justified her topic, "I have always noticed eyes my dear. Henry too, thinks me strange."

Amelia Ferguson, having taken Hannah's hand, released it and removed her gloves and then unfastened her bonnet which was fashionably smaller than the usual, and the high but narrow brim sat behind her tresses. She had the most elegant of hair styles, piled high on top of her head, with loose ringlets bouncing around her neck from where they were pinned. Her dress was smartly designed in two pieces, just as Kate had been making them recently, to allow for the fitting of a bustle beneath the skirt.

Hannah found herself asking inane questions about their journey, whilst taming stray hairs and positioning worn parts of her otherwise stylish dress behind her hands. She must get some new clothes, she hadn't had anything new since her mother's treat in Marshall and Snelgroves a few years ago.

"Joseph," Henry began, "this morning, having arrived at the house on the Esplanade, while Amelia powdered her nose, or whatever it is these women do, I had a wander down to the

Spa, that new bandstand over the pump room is rather elegant, I even ventured down the stone steps to sample the waters, foul tasting stuff you know! Hopefully water is less threatening to our constitutions now that Disreali has taken over public health, with a dedicated ministry for sewerage!" Henry paused to laugh at the absurd title of this new portfolio. "Anyway then I went up to the Grand Hotel. That proposed funicular will be most convenient if it is ever finished. But, you'll never believe it, there's a ball on there tonight, and I managed to pull a few strings, and got us four tickets, how's that for celebrating the first time the four of us have ever been together?"

Hannah's panic showed in her face as she looked at Joseph, who was himself taken aback. Joseph recovered first,

"But Henry, Hannah's been preparing a meal for us to eat here."

"Nonsense Joseph, the children can eat well tonight, but we shall eat as kings at the Grandest Hotel in Europe. We have a lot to celebrate, Amelia loves to hear stories about what we all got up to when we were young."

Kate was handing cups of tea around in the parlour, she smiled "Perhaps she wouldn't like to hear about everything you got up to eh, Henry." She hit her target, then quickly moved on so as not to allow any discomfort from her remark, "But I for one think it's a brilliant idea, Hannah, you haven't had a good night out for a long time." She turned to Amelia, "have you brought a ball gown with you Mrs Ferguson, or will you be hiring one?"

"Oh no, Mrs Wilson isn't it, I always travel prepared for anything."

"It's such a good job I've just finished that new one for you then Hannah isn't it? I know you did want it for the Summer Ball, but I can always run another one up for you by then."

"That's sorted then," announced Henry, "we will come for you in the carriage, 6.30pm sharp, what a night we will have, you'll have some competition though ladies, there are some handsome girls in this town, the sea air must give them a glow."

Joseph smiled at his wife, his mother-in-law had saved them from a sticky situation, he knew he could borrow a tails' suit from William Robinson. He had done so once before when the Grand was opened and he had to attend a minor function with his boss. What a night to remember this was going to be. He turned back to Henry,

"Did you know Henry, the funicular cliff lift works on the principle of two tanks gradually and alternately filling up with sea water to make the trams move up and down?"

"Really, that's fascinating Joseph, tell me…"

Hannah followed her mother back into the kitchen.

"Ma, what are you thinking, I haven't got a ball gown, summer ball indeed! What am I going to do?"

"Hannah, you'd better start hoping you're the same size as my customer, Mrs Harrington, but I've now got a busy afternoon ahead, she's likely to be at the same ball tonight, so it can't be recognised as hers. You'd better look after it too, no spillages or anything."

"Ma this is too risky, how can you make it unrecognisable, she came for a fitting recently didn't she?"

"She did, but so did Lady Carmichael for hers. They're very similar, but just different colours, with different coloured frills which are only pinned at this stage, if I swap them over, no-one will ever know." Hannah took a sharp intake of breath with one hand over her mouth, she had never felt so mischievous, ever.

Betsy came into the kitchen, looking behind her to ensure no-one else was listening, "Granma, what're you going to do?" Kate divulged the plan, Betsy offered to go with her and make a start.

"Ma, as soon as they leave, send Kathy for me, and I'll come and do your hair. I'll get Mrs Hudson to help us too, Granma. You'll be the belle of the ball Ma, just you wait and see." She followed Kate out of the back door, poking her head briefly back around to say, "especially with those sapphire eyes."

"Get away with you, Betsy Agatha." Laughing she returned to the parlour excusing Kate and Betsy to their guests.

"Ma you look like the Queen on her wedding day. You're so handsome; you really could be a princess. Granma will you make me a dress like this, please?" Kathy was enraptured at this vision of her mother. All four of her children were enjoying the finishing touches being added to their exquisitely dressed Ma on such a singularly exceptional occasion.

"Ooh, I bet you'd want to impress Johnny Robinson, Kathy, I've seen you making eyes at him, Kathy. And he's so sweet on you, he'd follow you off a cliff he would!"

"Phoo, I'm just practising on him, Thom. I intend to aim higher in a beau. Anyway, what about you and Annie? She's told me she's really sweet on you, our Thom!"

"I don't know, she was really funny with me this afternoon when she came round and saw our visitors, seemed like she wanted to talk to me, then couldn't leave quickly enough, I must've said something wrong, don't want a girl that's all grumpy!"

Hannah laughed at her children. She felt like a princess too. Betsy had done her hair in the fashionably high style with a few coils of sandy ringlets deliberately allowed to escape the glittering restraint on the right side, and so tantalisingly drape her milky neck. The excitement of the occasion had flushed Hannah's flawless complexion erasing years and accentuating the clarity of her sparkling ocean eyes with their long golden lashes. Her figure, although more rounded than a few years ago, was flattered by the cut of the fabric. She couldn't believe what her Ma and Betsy had done with this gown. It was made of all the finest materials, but whereas it was designed to be solid ivory in colour, Kate had swapped the very full skirt for Mrs Carmichael's pastel pink one, and had trimmed it with alternate ivory and pastel pink frills. The short off-the-shoulder sleeves, as one with the ivory bodice, had pink ribbon threaded through the lace. The same pink ribbon tied the larger frills into folds at the back of the dress. The end result was innovative and exquisite. Neighbours had rallied with a pair of short ivory silk gloves, the hair adornment, and Kate had made a pink velvet ribbon choker and attached Miss Briggs' inherited delicate pearl brooch. "I just feel a little exposed Ma, it's so low here, I've never shown this much of myself, ever."

"Rubbish my dear, that's the fashion for ball gowns, you've your husband at your side to ensure it's quite respectable."

"That's just it Ma, what's Joseph going to say."

"Well, let's see shall we, time to go. Come along Betsy dear, let's help your mother float this dress downstairs!"

"Don't forget to wave at Mrs Hudson Ma, she helped us so much today, and she needs to see nice things at the moment. Michael's left such a hole in her life, she's no-one left to care for."

"I know Betsy, but you're such a help to her, she doesn't know what she would've done without you." She gave each of her children in turn a hug, and promised to tell them every detail in the morning.

Hannah walked carefully down the stairs, her care of the dress allowed a natural air of decorum she would not normally have time to indulge. Joseph was preening himself in the hallway mirror as she approached; the whole family awaited his reaction. Initially, he could not even speak, his jaw hung open, his sparkling emerald eyes wide and youthful with appreciation of this vision before him.

"Don't look so shocked Joseph Elliot, I'm generally just too busy raising your family to spend this much time and money on myself!" Joseph closed his mouth and gulped. He resisted the temptation to tease and augment her humour, and instead offered his hand to hers, tenderly raising it to his lips.

"Your carriage awaits M'Lady. Smiling and allowing the clear glittering gems to focus on each other, he quietly added, "I'm the luckiest man alive Hannah Isabella Elliot, I have it all."

Mrs Hudson and the Robinson's had all come to wave them

off. Thom looked at Annie for signs that her mood was more affable, she smiled at him warmly. Henry alighted from the elegant Landau to assist Hannah into it. Next, he ushered in a very handsome and debonair Joseph, before waving benevolently to the gathered throng, and re-joining his wife and friends in the carriage. They were spirited away to the crisp clipped tones of the lively horses hooves on the cobbles.

The Elliot children waved at the carriage until it was long out of view, but Thom sidled over to where Annie had been stood, only to find as he looked round for her, that she had vanished. He shrugged his shoulders and sighed, perhaps she wasn't worth it, he knew one or two of the other girls liked him too. They all moved back inside the house and slowly closed the door, and knew they would always remember tonight as a very special moment in all their lives.

Joseph and Hannah were both excited as the carriage pulled up outside the Grand Hotel. There were excited muffled comments as each lady alighted from her carriage, but non more audible than the gasps as Hannah's dress came into view. Amelia too, was gracious in complimenting Hannah, "You look enchanting Hannah, I must get a dress made by your Mother, I shall order one before I leave. She's certainly very talented, and so artistic with her design."

Joseph was distracted as they made their way inside, "Joseph, what is it, are you alright?"

"Hannah, did you see that couple talking on the corner of the Spa Gardens? It was Beatrice Hetherington. That can't be a good idea for her reputation, I didn't catch who it was she was with. Hannah?"

Hannah had wandered ahead, her jaw ajar at the sumptuous extravagance she saw inside the hotel foyer. The magnificent, grand central staircase was festooned with ribbons and bows in a deep lavender contrasted with lemon to complement the lavish floral arrangements and décor around the room. She gazed upwards, taking in the splendour of the beckoning archways nudging the third floor, and the ornate marble columns perched atop the altar-like design of the first landing, its pretention equal to any opulent cathedral.

"Hannah, did you hear me?"

"Oh, I'm sorry, Joseph. I was enjoying the occasion. Yes I did hear you. Mary told me the other day when I called on her briefly to enquire as to her well-being, that Beatrice was becoming very difficult over this thing with Peter Robinson. Do you think we should tell her?"

"No absolutely not Hannah, if we hadn't been coming here tonight we would never have seen them, we can't interfere with their lives. And why should we? They make such a lovely couple. Come on, my enchanting wife, let's go to the ball!"

Chapter 20

Scarborough, September 1876

She was standing on the cliff path between the Esplanade and The Spa holding her wicker basket, waiting for the next pain to grip her, and hoping for a lull in the arrivals at the Bazaar, before descending further. It looked like rain, but it was a balmy evening and the sun not yet set, was still finding its way through the clouds bathing the bay in a strangely mysterious, yet beautiful light.

She marveled at this picturesque scene. The clouds appeared like dull whipped meringue being spread southwards across the fading light of the sapphire evening sky. The castle sat imposingly atop its own hill, its silhouette supported to the west for many centuries, by the bell tower of St Mary's Parish Church. Under their watchful eyes sat the old town of Scarborough, where the fishing community lived and worked, and where now thousands of holidaymakers spent their summer days. The yawning sweep of golden sand stretched deserted on this eighth evening of September, yet come the new dawn, weather permitting, it would again be heaving with children playing, bathers, huts and donkeys. The clouds moved in on the sun leaving only a porthole for it to peer through. It resisted their cover, fighting to keep admiring its own reflection shimmering on the mirrored, peaceful dusky ocean.

She watched, reassured by the key in her pocket as people

drifted into The Spa, and wondered how long before this would all be over. She was suddenly again bent double with a pain which seemed to rip through her. Yet how befitting, that a beautiful event should take place on such a beautiful night. She stifled her groan by biting hard into her shawl and secreted herself behind some bushes when she heard the new funicular rumble past, easing its South Cliff visitors into their festive evening down at the Saloon.

Having waited for them all to enter, quickly, seeing no-one now on the promenade, she made a dash past The Spa Saloon and down the ramp at the steps of the sea wall and onto the beach; immediately turning to follow the wall so she was concealed from view. She heard other guests arriving at The Spa, and puffed out a slow deep breath of relief that she had not been seen. Only the seagulls could watch her now, and they would keep her council at this time of night. She spread out her sheet from her basket, and seated herself upon it with the sea wall as a backrest, and waited for the advent of her labours.

Exhausted, yet relieved by the speed and ease of her safe deliverance, she laid the baby girl gently onto the sheet. She indulged herself for a few moments looking for features to tell tales, but in the wrinkly new born face, she saw none. Removing her skirt, and scooping up her little bundle, she stealthily crept down to the water's edge in her petticoat. There, tucking her frills clear of the water, she meticulously cleaned them both. Returning to the sea wall, she dressed herself, then opening her bodice, instinctively allowed the baby to suckle at her breast, she could not bear for her to be hungry overnight. Picking up her shawl, and shaking it free of any sand, she was swaddling the baby tightly, when the first drops of rain fell on her daughter's face, as God himself baptized and welcomed her into his world, promising to care for her.

She cowered at the top of the steps hearing voices outside the building, one of them sounded familiar, but she couldn't be sure, and did not want to risk her own exposure in getting too close to identify them. As the voices moved around the back of the building, she took her chance and ran to the front. Fumbling in the pocket of her skirt, she produced a key, and let herself into the ticket office. There, she hugged and kissed her watchful baby and carefully laid her in the basket she had bought just this afternoon.

"I'm so sorry I have to leave you little one. You'll be safe in the morning. I hope one day you'll understand. Living with your mother and father at least presently, is not possible, please forgive me. I'll never forget you, I'll think of you every day. I wish you a long and happy life. God bless you always."

She allowed a tear to course its way slowly down her cheek, then abruptly wiped it away with her hand. She left the office, carefully locking it behind her.

Cowering at the front of the building until she was sure no-one was around, under the distraught sobbing heavens, she made her dash for the trees behind the building once again. She could still hear voices below, surely the Bazaar had finished by now, she must have been on the beach a few hours, but maybe there had been a lot to clear away. Feeling a little over-come, she paused a while to compose herself before slowly ascending the hill. It would have been quicker to go over the toll bridge, but she did not want to risk being seen. With no shawl tonight too, she would surely get wet.

"Bea where've you been? You're soaking."

"I've been looking for you, Peter, I thought you said to meet you at The Spa?"

"Oh, Bea, I said the Bar, - Newborough Bar, I've been out of my mind with worry, I never know if your mother has sent you away when you don't meet me." Both anxious, they had collided on the corner of The Crescent.

"I'm sorry Peter, what are we going to do? You'd think she would be better now the Queen herself is out of mourning. She keeps holding dinner parties to introduce me to 'nice, respectable' young men. I don't know who she thinks I am, you'd think it was me that had been made Empress of India this year, not the Queen! Couldn't we just run away, Peter?"

"Just tell me when, Bea, and I'll arrange it, we've really waited long enough. I actually thought you were going off me recently, I've seen so little of you of late, especially with you going to your cousin's when she had her baby."

"Well I'm back now Peter. Let's just wait until Edward is back from his surgical examinations in London, then maybe we can make a stand. I couldn't leave her now while she is on her own. I hope Edward returns in the same good humour he left in, his mood so affects Mother's own. He can be so melancholy, but before he left, he was actually quite jovial, and mother was so much improved for it."

"Whatever you say then Beatrice, let's walk down the town, there are lots of people about, there's been a big Bazaar at The Spa tonight."

"Oh, is that what was going on there?" They wandered further down Westborough, and reached the corner of Aberdeen Walk.

"Look, there's your Annie."

"Oh yes, she's with Kathy Elliot too, wonder where the lads are. They usually manage to sneak out when the rest of the family is in bed as well as the girls!" They crossed the road towards the Bar Church to greet them.

"Peter, Peter, have you seen Thom or Johnny? I was supposed to meet Thom at The Spa gardens tonight, but I couldn't find him," Annie was in a panic.

"Kathy had given Thom a key for the ticket office so we could go courting in there, but when I got to the gardens he was nowhere to be seen and when I tried the door to the ticket office, it was locked. I ran up through the gardens and bumped into Kathy here."

"Calm down both of you. I do know that Johnny was hoping to meet you from work tonight Kathy, he obviously missed you. We're all getting soaked just standing here, let's get under the church doorway here." He helped the girls to straddle the low wall to gain access to the doorway. "Funny how it doesn't matter so much when it's warm. Anyway, I think it's stopping now so we should all dry off before going home."

Kathy uncharacteristically agitated, was looking frantically up and down Westborough,

"I'm worried about the key to the ticket office, if our Thom's lost it, I'll be in real trouble tomorrow at work, there must always be two keys on the board."

"Kathy, Kathy, I've been looking for you everywhere, where've you been?" Johnny Robinson was running up Westborough towards their huddle in the impressive porch entrance to the Bar Church. "Those chaps outside the Bar Hotel say the Spa Saloon's on fire."

"Oh no, what if Thom was locked inside the ticket office, he could have fallen asleep." Annie had already straddled the wall, and had started to run down Westborough towards St Nicholas Street and the cliff bridge. Kathy was on her heels shouting that she kept a lot of her own belongings in the ticket office, she hoped the fire wouldn't spread from the Saloon itself. Beatrice followed, yelling over her shoulder to Peter and Johnny that they must save Thom. The Robinson brothers looked at each other, shrugged their shoulders, and ran to join the rescue party.

Despite the dampness, as they crossed the cliff bridge, flames were shooting high into the night sky. Men were running around throwing buckets of water at the edges of the fire which seemed to make the fire spit and sizzle, mocking their futile efforts. The volunteer firemen, newly at the scene, were providing some sort of order, but the building was so well ablaze, that all onlookers could see unequivocally that The Spa Saloon in its recent form, was doomed.

Annie, Kathy and Beatrice all ran around the front of the building, Johnny shouted after Kathy,

"Why worry now Kathy, no-one will need a key to get in there in the morning!"

"But what if Thom was asleep in there as Annie says?" Suddenly, their party froze as they saw Thom running towards them carrying something. Beatrice swooned, caught readily in Peter's arms, "Oh Peter, what a relief, he's alright, I feel quite faint with worry."

"How silly you are Beatrice, yes he's fine, but what's he got?" Kathy and Annie had thrown themselves at Thom, shouting above the commotion that they were worried about him being locked inside, Thom had not stopped moving despite this greeting, he was putting as much distance between himself and the smoke as possible.

"I wasn't locked inside, but this little bundle was." He paused as they reached the sea wall and he handed the baby over to Kathy so he could bend over and catch his breath. The smoke was making him wheeze and struggle to suck enough air to sustain him, he spluttered between breaths. "I never had the key you left for me Kathy, I couldn't find it. I thought you might've given it straight to Annie, so I came down here to see. The place was already ablaze, I was worried you might be inside, Annie, so I went to see. Good thing I did. When I got close, I could hear a baby crying. I broke down the door to get it out. It would've been lost for sure, nothing's going to stop this fire now 'til it runs out of fuel and is down to the bare stonework." Kathy and Annie were standing mesmerized as they looked at the babe in her arms. Johnny was the first to break the ensuing silence,

"Well Kathy, I hope that wasn't what you meant by 'your own belongings' you keep in the ticket office?" She looked up startled,

"I'm sure it isn't Johnny! What would I be doing with one of these." She off-loaded the bundle into Annie's arms as though it was scalding her.

"Well don't give it to me, I don't know what to do with it." She gazed down anxiously into the infant's face.

"Don't be like that Annie, it's a baby, there're all lovely."

"Well I don't see you taking a turn with it, Beatrice." Her face softened as she cooed at the tiny bundle, "Wasn't it there when you left work Kathy?"

"Annie, don't be daft, would we have left the ticket office tonight with a baby in there?" She 'tutted' at her friend and looked heavenwards as if she despaired of her remark. Peter had left the group to talk to a policeman closer to the fire, he returned.

"Are you alright to move on Thom, the policeman says you were very brave to go in for the baby, but all he can tell us is to take it to the workhouse infirmary tonight, they haven't time to do anything right now."

"The workhouse infirmary? The poor thing." He replied, "Surely someone we know would take it in?"

"Well I must be getting home now Peter, if mother was to rouse and find me gone." Beatrice turned to walk away, looking sadly at the Spa Saloon that would surely be a shell in the morning. Peter turned to the others,

"Will you all be alright going to the workhouse with it, it's a moral duty now Thom has saved it. But I must see Beatrice home safely." Beatrice had started to walk away, but she added to his parting remark,

"Well of course they must Peter, you can't leave a child to die! "Come on though, it's getting very hot around here."

"It's fine, Peter, you go and tuck Bea up in bed, we'll deal with the unpleasant things." Johnny waited until they were out of earshot before having a further snipe at his older brother. "I wouldn't mind, but how long are they going to carry on like this, her mother must think she's the Princess Beatrice, daughter to the Queen. When in fact, she's quite ordinary, no different to us. Are you alright now Thom? I'm not sure I'd have smashed doors down and dashed into a fire to save a strange bawling baby, well done pal."

"I hope you would Johnny Robinson, what a horrible thing to say, I'm ashamed you're my brother. Poor thing didn't ask to be left in a burning building." Annie jiggled the infant in her arms as she walked.

"You're a natural Annie." Kathy quipped, and winked at Thom.

They were just approaching the turn into Dean Road when Betsy came running towards them with Hannah closely following.

"Thom, Kathy are you alright? We heard The Spa was on fire and Ma was worried you were all down there, she knows you sneak out to be unchaperoned in your courting on a Friday night." She slowed as she took in their bundle.

"What've you got there Annie?"

"It's a baby Betsy, Thom rescued it from the fire, wasn't he brave? We're taking it to the workhouse infirmary." Hannah was immediately beside them, she took the child without a word and cooed at the chubby newborn face.

"Now who could possibly abandon you little one?" She unwrapped the shawl slightly grimacing at the state of the soiling as she did so.

"This little girl needs cleaning up, she's newborn, tonight I would say, I doubt if we'll wake anyone at the infirmary now. We can take her in the morning. Johnny and Annie, your mother is as aware of your escapades as I am, hopefully she's asleep presently, and so blissfully unaware of the fire. As would we be, if the volunteer fireman next door had not been knocked up so loudly. You can sneak home now, but tomorrow, I want to talk to you all about what has transpired tonight."

The Elliot household was quietly contrite in hungrily consuming their broth and home made bread. Joseph and Thom had returned from their Saturday half day, and Kathy had returned from viewing her former workplace, reporting it to be no more than a skeleton of stonework, just as Thom had predicted. There had been a somber atmosphere around the site. The town's people devastated at the loss of their jewel in the crown, their cultural magnet for holidaymakers and their subsequent prosperity. The directors of the Cliff Bridge Company though, had been a large presence, promising to rebuild, bigger and better than before, but today, that was of little comfort to a town gutted by yet another disaster at the fated site of Mrs Farrow's historic healing spaw waters.

Joseph looked around the table at his family, then began,

"You know, I'm really proud of what you did last night Thom, but something doesn't quite add up. Why would you go close enough to a burning building, Thom, to hear the muffled cries of a new-born infant? Why were you all down there? You could have all died, it's remarkable that no-one did, and your Ma and I didn't know you were there."

Kathy and Thom looked at each other, then down at their bowls.

"Sorry, Pa." They said in unison.

Betsy had been sitting quietly eating her broth, she needed to get back to the clinic for an hour again after lunch, she added her own concerns.

"I find it difficult to believe that if all six of you were there individually at some point last night, yet none of you seemed to see either a baby being abandoned, or the fire start?"

The conversation was interrupted by the hungry cries of their lodger. "I'll get her Ma." Kathy volunteered. Thom spoke aloud one thought he had during the night.

"Pa, do you think the owners could have done it deliberately for an insurance claim, they said last year they wanted to make the Spa buildings bigger to have more room for all the extra visitors it gets now. Did you know, nearly three times as many cross the toll cliff bridge now, than when it opened in 1858?"

"Yes, I'd heard that Thom, they've taken £9,000 this year, a big increase since the £3,500 they took in 1858. Your theory is possible I suppose, but it was the council not the Company, that favoured a re-build, saying it would be more economical and aesthetic despite the disappointment of dismantling a substantial building. The directors of the Cliff Bridge Company wanted to extend by pushing the sea wall out further. The council didn't want that to go ahead any more than the town's people did. Why spoil the coastline any more than we already have." He dipped more bread in his bowl as Kathy returned to the table carrying the baby, she interjected,

"I think that would have been criminal Pa, the sea wall's just fine as it is, Johnny and me have said that. How dare this company think they can mess around with God's work? Let them re-build their Concert Hall instead now, perhaps bigger and better than before, but leave the coastline alone."

"Hmm, I'm surprised you care so much Kathy, but I applaud your sentiments. You appear to have picked up Betsy's banner regarding moral decisions in this town. She's far too busy fighting disease with young Edward now to bother with such issues. However Kathy, its 'Johnny and I' – not 'Johnny and me'!"

Kathy's smug smile from her father's praise inverted quickly to a dejected frown at his pedantic correction of her grammer. Joseph, oblivious to his effect, continued. "Why's the baby still here Hannah did you say. Hmm, I hope you haven't been keeping secrets from me again have you dear?" He flashed a wicked and mischievous grin at his wife.

"Don't be absurd Joseph, though wouldn't that be an easy solution Joseph, she's adorable. They asked if we could keep her for the weekend as they don't have enough nurses to cover night feeding. It isn't a problem is it Joseph, I'll do it, they've given us the milk we need and some napkins for her."

"Of course it isn't a problem, you just wonder what'll happen to the little mite. What's her story? Where's she come from?" He continued as he leant over the table to get a better look at her as Kathy sat back down rocking her to sooth her cries.

"You know Hannah, she's like a Phoenix from the ashes of the Spa, the ticket office was her nest of spices!"

"Strange you should say that Pa, she was actually laid in a basket of herbs and things!"

Joseph and Hannah exchanged glances.

"You know Hannah that particular Greek Myth is following

us around!"

Johnny and Annie Elliot arrived at Belle Vue Street a little after three-o-clock in the afternoon.

"We've told our Ma what happened Mrs Elliot. As you said she knew we were meeting on Friday nights, but she's scolded us now on not tellin' someone where we're going."

"I should think so too Johnny, you may be twenty two, but you're expecting to meet up with our Kathy who's still just eighteen."

"Ma, you were married at my age!"

"Indeed I was Kathy, and as a married lady, if I'd chosen to walk the streets at night with my husband," she paused to accentuate the last word, "then that would've been fine. Do you get my meaning?"

"Yes Ma."

"Anyway, the other issue is exactly what has made your father suspicious. Did any of you know there was a baby left in that room?"

"No Ma, of course not." Kathy replied, shocked at her mother's question. Hannah moved around the room.

"Annie? Johnny? Thom, especially Thom? Well what about Peter or Beatrice, I believe they were just as involved?" She was met with a shake of all heads. As a mother, she was adamant that she knew when her children were lying. But she knew herself only too well how things can be concealed from those around you, and she had an uneasy feeling about this.

"Honestly, Ma, we were all shocked. It was my fault we were there. Annie and I were going to borrow the key to the ticket office to use it for some privacy, only we never actually got it."

"Oh, how thoughtful Thom. So this baby is nothing to do with you, but if you had carried out your plans, the one that came along in nine months time would have everything to do with you!"

"Sorry Ma." All the young adults in the room with Hannah

peered uncomfortably at the pattern worked in the rug in the centre of the parlour. Joseph listened quietly with interest from the fireside chair.

"The key's a mystery Ma, I left it in Thom's room, on the table, he says it wasn't there. It's a good thing no-one will miss it now." Kathy had lifted her eyes to her mother, then when she received no empathic sign, she eased them back down to the rug with the others.

"Well, like your father, I'm a little suspicious about the whole night's events, but I doubt we'll get to the bottom of it if you are all resolute in your story."

"Anyone know who's this is?" shouted Betsy from the hallway, "there's a key on the front doormat."

Joseph and Hannah were drinking a cup of tea before retiring.

"Joseph, I'm not happy about this situation. I know only too well how this condition may be hidden. What if it is one of the children? We could be handing our flesh and blood over to the workhouse."

"Hannah, do you seriously think they would not be able to tell us if that was the case. We would not be thrilled with a child out of wedlock, but they surely don't think us tyrants?"

"I don't know, I just feel uneasy Joseph." She sipped her tea, daydreaming into the kitchen range. Joseph watched her pensively for a moment.

"Hannah, can we, or you, in all honesty, cope with another child, really? You have brought up four already and Albert is now eleven. Do you really want to start again? And most likely with the child of a total stranger."

"But what if it isn't Joseph? If it had been a few years earlier, I think Mrs Hudson would have taken her, or even Ma, but not now, they're too old to start all over again with a new born." Joseph sighed hard. This wouldn't be his solution, another child's education to pay for, sleepless nights, the list was endless, much as he had enjoyed his own family. Hannah smiled a promise at her husband, she was nearly there in guiding him to her decision, she had one final tool to give her leverage.

"Will you let us keep the child Joseph, if I promise not to say anything about Arthur Brown?" Joseph's eyes startled as he froze mid swallow.

"W.. what do you mean Hannah?"

"Albert innocently showed me what you had taught him about secret compartments in writing desks such as secretaries, a few weeks ago." She paused to allow this piece of information to sink in before qualifying it, "I've read Henry's last letter Joseph." She looked skywards in recalling the quote precisely, "'*that regardless of our combined memory loss of that night prior to the incident with poor Arthur*'!" She waited to savour his amazement, then continued, "then what was it you told me, erm, let me see, *'Arthur Brown did Betsy say? No Hannah, I didn't know him at all'!* Well, exactly what else do I not know about Joseph?"

Joseph looked appealingly at his wife. "You know everything my dearest wife. Henry Lizzibeth and I were unfortunate enough to witness Bill lose his temper that night, and poor Arthur was dead in seconds, it really was a kind of accident. Bill just instinctively struck out at a derogatory comment Arthur made about Lizzibeth and us. He was defending her honour. It was the worst night of my life Hannah, I can still see that part as if it were yesterday, but mostly, I block it out. I wonder if that's why I can't remember the rest of the night."

"I'm sure that it's blocked by the whisky more than anything else, though Joseph. Why did you keep it from me?"

"It gave me nightmares Hannah, what would it've done to a sweet natured person such as you, - who wants to give a home to every foundling baby!" He smiled the last words at her, then added. "As we're raising old issues tonight my dear, would it be facetious to point out that you once told me when you yourself had concealed being with child; and I enquired as to whether your mother had known, I think I quote your reply correctly, 'mothers see any change in their child, I couldn't have fooled her'."

"Ah, Joseph, but you assume the mother to be our daughter, - what if it's father is our son?"

She smiled back, walking seductively towards him, "so can we offer this poor child a home then, husband dear, or should I say, he who is an accessory to murder?" Joseph patted her bottom affectionately, and responded,

"So dear wife, you will stoop to blackmail now, what creature have I married?" Turning towards the bassinet, he spoke softly and gently to the new infant. "Welcome to the Elliot family little girl." Then putting down his cup, he pulled Hannah onto his knee, "You know Hannah, in the back of my mind, I knew she was never going to leave us when you brought her home last night." He planted a tender, gentle kiss on his wife's lips, the added impudently, "So Hannah, exactly who is your first suspect as 'mother'," he teased, "perhaps they should choose her name!"

Part 3

Eliza

1878-1900

23 Years Later

Chapter 21

Scarborough, December 1899

"Come on Eliza, there's a good girl, you're nearly there, just one more push and we'll have this baby born this century!"

Eliza's unfocused exhausted eyes, settled appealingly on her sister's face. Betsy stroked her forehead empathically recognising her fatigue. She quietly whispered to her, ignoring the bullying tones of the ageing midwife.

"Come on, you can do this Eliza, come on, try a little harder as the nurse says, and it'll soon be over." She looked around this stark corner of the workhouse infirmary to give herself a break from this agonising experience. It was torture indeed to helplessly watch a dearly beloved, wracked with pain, fear and exhaustion in the bringing of a new life to this new dawn of the twentieth century.

Betsy continued her gentle encouragement throughout the nurse's increasingly stern instructions which seemed to make her many sombre chins wobble with each syllable. The baby continued its slow, sluggish struggle for deliverance from womb to world, as the old century ticked its last moments.

"At last. Well done. In the end, you would have thought you were an old hand at this." She reluctantly conceded, "And you have a daughter, born together with the new century, I'm sure that means she'll be blessed her whole life through."

Eliza managed a weak smile at Betsy, before her head fell back on the pillow, only to jerk suddenly forward as she was startled by a clang of tin plates, bells, whistles and general human merriment as it passed by the window facing Dean Road. It filled and marked this memorable moment in history, and unknowingly welcomed a new life into their midst.

"Let me read it again, Betsy, where is it? Please, I know I've read it over and over, but I like to see his words again and again." The nurse did not turn from her task of swaddling the new infant as she interrupted,

"I think you need to be cleaned up and then sleep, Eliza, time for reading later."

Betsy startled at her sister, and watched as she struggled from her repose, replying quietly yet somehow aggressively,

"I need to read my husband's letter before I could possibly sleep, it'll only take a moment." The nurse looked shocked at her sheer audacity for a moment, before laying the swaddled baby next to her mother on the bed, and replying as though she were presenting the most extravagant of gifts,

"Five minutes only, then your sister must leave. I'll be back in a moment." Using both forearms to raise her drooping bosom temporarily back to its younger location,she strutted huffily to the other side of the ward.

Betsy took her favourite oversized cashmere coat from the back of her chair, and laid it across the bed to add extra warmth to both Eliza and the baby. Then she laid a bunch of hand tied spices across the infant. She noted Eliza's puzzled expression and shrugged her shoulders.

"Just seemed the right thing to do Eliza, my mother apparently spoke about the phoenix arising from a nest of spices when I was born, so I have always associated spices with new a life." Betsy didn't wait for a response, but turned and pulled the crumpled re-read page out of Eliza's bag, and watched as her sister absorbed the words yet again. She would not pry, but she had to admit to being curious as to its contents, and why Eliza guarded it so vehemently.

To My Dearest Wife Eliza

It was without doubt, the hardest thing I have ever done in leaving you. But you know my dear, we must have an income, and I am resolute in not following my father in a lifetime on the fishing boats, despite his displeasure over this. Your frailty since Charlie's birth, has meant that I need to provide more substantially for you so we can keep this little one with us, and make a home for him or her. I know my sister is taking good care of him, but when your strength returns we must make a home for him too. It breaks my heart to see the look on your face when he runs to her as his mother.

This life so far is not bad. I did much marching up and down at the Barracks before we left Aldershot. Then we had to march to the Railway Station as the whole Battalion left at 8am for Southampton. Flags hung in gardens and people cheered us all the way there, and then again from the quayside, whilst a band played all our favourite tunes, which made us all melancholy at the thought of leaving our loved ones. It did make us all feel very important though, but fearful at the same time wondering what lay ahead. No-one is quite sure what to expect from the Boers or the Country itself.

The photo enclosed is of the ship we are on, The Doune Castle. We have physical drill twice a week and have had a concert on board.

We will soon arrive at Cape Town where I hope to post this to you saying we have disembarked safely.

Anyway my dear Eliza, please keep safe, I know Betsy will take good care of you, and I will be home soon, no-one thinks this war will last long, but I will earn enough to give us a better start for our family.

I'm so sorry for this action that I am aware has added to your distress, and I pray every day for a safe confinement for you.

Until I return my dear, my love is yours always. Give my little five year old son a secret hug from his father.

Micky
1st Battalion The Princess of Wales' Own 19th (Yorkshire Regiment)

Betsy watched Eliza as she had finished reading, and followed her smiling gaze to the little bundle that had caused so much angst to her mother tonight.

Eliza gazed lovingly at her new daughter, searching the tiny face for any traces of the features she knew and loved so well. Tears trickled down her cheeks as she pictured his face before he left. Eyes deep as chocolate almost hidden under his domed pale helmet; muscles set with tension in his painful valediction, changing the normal contour and softness of his face. His body felt taut in his unyielding prickly uniform beneath her frenzied embrace. She thought of how his retreating image had diminished with the increasing distance between them, and her last focus was on the perpetually moving shiny knee length boots taking him further away from her with each reciprocal step.

Betsy broke into her thoughts.

"What are you going to call her Eliza? Did you discuss it with Micky before he left?"

Eliza lifted her gaze towards the ceiling, as though forcing her brain to remember.

"We only talked about boy's names, we'd settled on either Richard or Edward, but we'd never mentioned girl's names." She looked dreamily down at her new born daughter and smiled, "No-one but me is going to look after you, my dearest daughter, no-one but me." She landed a gentle kiss on the baby's forehead. "What name do you think suits her Betsy?"

"What about Elizabeth, I wanted Ma to name you Elizabeth, but Pa wasn't keen. If I'd ever had a daughter of my own, I was going to call her Elizabeth after my real mother. Not that she was ever called Elizabeth, everyone refers to her as just Lizzibeth, but my Granny in Dorset assured me she was baptized Elizabeth."

Eliza looked away from Betsy, and practiced greeting her daughter with her new name.

"I like it Betsy, and I'd love to name her after your real mother, she always sounded a lovely fun person from all the stories about her, but it's quite a mouthful. We could shorten it to 'Beth'?" They both smiled, happy with their consensus, just as the baby decided to test her lungs and make her presence felt. "I'd like to put Ma's name in the middle too, Betsy. Elizabeth Hannah. otherwise known as Beth. How do you do young lady? Are you hungry? Is that what all this noise is about?" The nurse was returning to their corner of the room carrying a cup. Betsy noticed she had tidied her plaits since Beth's delivery, they had threatened to unwind, but now they were firmly back in place wrapped tightly around each ear looking like two thin grey cartwheels supporting the sides of her severe face. Her break appeared to have softened her mood and she spoke warmly to Eliza.

"Get that down you love, you'll feel better in the morning." Betsy smiled, she could leave now, Eliza was in good hands, "That's your first cup of tea this century Eliza. The twentieth century, eh." She gazed upwards rehearsing the sound, then looked down at her new niece. "At least we'll never forget your birthday little Beth. The twentieth century, now doesn't that sound strange, no doubt we'll get used to it in time."

21 Years Earlier

Chapter 22

Scarborough, September 1878

"Kathy, Kathy, wake up, wake up."

Kathy shook her sister away, "Leave me Betsy, it's not time to get up yet." Betsy shook her frantically again,

"Kathy come on, we'll be burned alive, the house is on fire, we need to get out now." As she spoke, she swiped the knick knacks and Victoriana off the small windowsill, and struggled with the catch on the window. Kathy wiped her eyes as they adjusted to the darkness, and realised her sister was grave in her distress.

"Betsy, you're dreaming again, come on, there's no fire, come back to bed."

"Kathy, this is no dream, can't you see and hear the flames flickering, feel the heat, we must get out and raise the alarm, help me here." Betsy found extra strength in her panic as the window suddenly came free, allowing instant access to the chilling and sobering night air. "Come on Kathy, before it's too late." She had raised herself onto the window ledge and had swung one leg awkwardly over the sill, the length of her nightgown inhibiting her escape. She hovered above the yard below.

"Betsy! No! You'll be killed, there's no fire, look." She made to open the bedroom door, but paused as Betsy, straddling the window ledge, screamed at her,

"You'll let the flames in Kathy, we'll die for sure, no, please, no!" Kathy calmly continued putting her hand on the door handle and quickly jerked open the door as Betsy screamed.

A few seconds silence ensued, Kathy and Betsy looked at each other, then Betsy, embarrassed, accused Kathy,

"You could've killed us both, you must never open a door when there's fire on the other side!"

"Betsy, there was no fire, I had to stop you killing yourself, which you would've done for sure if you'd gone out of the window. Ever since the Spa burned down, you've had an agitation about fire, and you weren't even there!"

"I'm sorry Kathy, I think I must envision what could have happened to little Eliza if Thom hadn't rescued her."

The quiet of the early morning light was shattered as a cry signaled the inevitable wakening of little Eliza, following Betsy's scream. Joseph appeared out of his bedroom, dressed just as Kathy had always imagined Scrooge had looked when he encountered Marley's ghost. Bleary eyed he turned his own ghostly gowned figure to his daughters,

"Now look what you've done, Eliza's awake and your Ma'll never get her back to sleep now. What's the commotion about anyway girls, who's being murdered?"

Betsy looked sheepishly down at the floor, hoping to hide the disarray in their room. As she slowly lifted her eyes to reply, Kathy stepped forward.

"It's fine now Pa, I'd a dream that Annie didn't turn up at the altar next week to wed our Thom and I woke up shouting at her!"

"Goodness me Kathy, if that's the most you have to worry about, at least find something that's believable to a sober soul. That girl idolises Thom!" He turned and walked back to his bedroom, still half asleep, they knew the new dawn would wipe all memory of this encounter from his head, Betsy had escaped humiliation. She smiled her gratitude at her long time troublesome sister and wondered as she closed the window before climbing back into the large bed they had always shared; when exactly Kathy had metamorphosed into this selfless considerate young woman whose company she now cherished. She re-drew the curtain across the window, but it did little now to shut out the early morning light that was replacing the star littered darkness, and both young women stared into the muted shapes, knowing sleep would now be difficult.

"Betsy?"

"Hmm." Betsy turned to face her sister in the bed, wondering what question she may pose tonight.

"Do you miss Beatrice?" Betsy considered carefully before answering.

"Well of course I miss her Kathy, why do you ask?"

"It's just that I heard Johnny's Ma telling our Ma that she never really had any friends here and she won't be missed. It seemed a very unkind thing to say, especially as you and her seemed to be very close before they left. You were, weren't you?"

"It is a very unkind thing to say, Kathy, of course she had friends, including me, who will miss her, and Peter too. But this job Peter was offered in Leeds, had too many prospects for him to turn it down, his next move could be on Fleet Street in the capital!" She turned towards Kathy and continued, "And let's be honest, they had waited patiently enough and yet hopelessly enough for Mrs Hetherington's approval. It was time for them to make a stand, nobody blames them. It's just left Edward to shoulder the responsibility for her alone now, she's getting more and more dependant on him. He'll never be able to have a life of his own."

"It's a good thing you don't have any hopes of marrying Edward then isn't it?" She laughed at the absurdity of her suggestion. "He's such a serious man, no fun at all, although before he went off to do his surgical exams, he'd lightened up a lot don't you think?"

"You're right Kathy, he did. Then after Michael died, he said he'd learnt from a simple but amazing human being, how to laugh and be grateful for each and every day. However his work's so important to him, that since qualifying in some surgical techniques, he's back to being very serious about life again, and his work is paramount. His mother allows him that, in deference to his father of course. It's a shame in many ways. He should have a life too."

"Is it true Betsy, that Mrs Hetherington has completely cut Beatrice out of her will since she heard they'd married?"

"I believe so Kathy, very cruel and hurtful, but Beatrice has Peter now, that's always been her only concern."

"It's so romantic Betsy. Do you think you'll ever feel like that about anyone one day? I can't imagine I will. Not really!"

"I'm sure we all will Kathy if we wait long enough! What about Johnny, aren't you as sweet on him as he so obviously is on you?" An endless few minutes of silence ensued, and Betsy was beginning to assume sleep had overtaken her sister, when she quietly confessed her feelings aloud.

"I want to be Betsy, but there just isn't the rush of feeling and swooning I imagined, you know, going weak at the knees, like for Mr Darcy in Jane Austen's book."

"That's a shame Kathy, you could do worse you know, Pa says Johnny has a good career ahead of him as a cabinet maker, especially if he buckles down and stops getting into scrapes, usually trying to impress you! 'A bird in the hand is worth two in the bush you know!'"

"I intend to do better than 'could do worse' Betsy. Maybe I need more than a 'bird' in my hand!"

"Annie, you look so beautiful. Granma, you're so clever, I hope you have plans for my wedding dress too. If it's possible, I want it to be even more special than Annie's!"

Kathy nervously giggled with Annie. Herself and Betsy had pretty peach coloured dresses as Annie's maids, with peach roses for their hair. Kathy was dressed and ready, but Betsy's dress was still hung on the door. She was still at the clinic with Edward and would have to rush to change as soon as she could get away. Kate was attaching the last minute detail to Annie's dress. The mother of the bride, Jane Robinson had just disappeared into her bedroom to get her own wedding necklace for Annie to 'borrow'.

"You'd better get a move on then Kathy, I'm getting a little old for this now at sixty. You do most of the work for me now anyway, with a little help from Betsy when she has time." Annie's eyes drifted from her reflection, happy that she looked her absolute best, and chipped to Kathy.

"Johnny wouldn't care if you walked down the aisle in tatters Kathy, he'd marry you tomorrow. Why won't you marry him?"

"I just don't feel ready, Annie, or maybe Johnny just isn't quite right for me, I don't know." Jane Robinson was framed in the doorway, the beaming smile she had worn all morning had slipped completely from her face.

"Well perhaps you should try to find out what you don't know Kathy Elliot, and cut our Johnny free to find someone who is right for him, instead of leading him on and wasting his time while you don't feel 'ready'!" The air stilled in the awkwardness of the room. Kate had turned from her task, and sensing the atmosphere, she quickly attempted to limit the damage her grand-daughter's words had wreaked.

"That she may very well need to do, Jane dear, but not today, come on, let's all enjoy Annie and Thom's very special day." Kathy pulled a contrite face behind Jane's back towards Annie, she certainly did not want to spoil today for anyone and was grateful to her grandmother for saving the discomfiture. To ensure the moment was passed, she turned to Jane,

"Would you like me to fix you hair around your hat for you Mrs Robinson? We need to be leaving for the church soon. Oh, and here's Betsy, that's good, I can do her hair too and fix her roses for her."

* * *

"Kathy, Granma told me about the awkward moment when Mrs Robinson had overheard you saying you didn't think Johnny was the one for you." Kathy looked downwards, she didn't know what to say. Betsy nodded a greeting to another guest, and continued,

"She's right though you know. You really shouldn't keep leading him on if you have no intention of marrying him."

"Betsy, I've tried to end it, but he just won't listen, he gets very upset and says I will marry him eventually. I've tried, honestly."

"You'll have to be more insistent. Then you may meet someone who makes you go 'weak at the knees' Jane Austen style." She laughed at her own humour to lighten the impact of her words, and remembering Kathy's romantic notions, but Kathy did not join her. She continued to look anxiously at her sister.

"What is it Kathy, why so serious, I was only saying,"

"I know you were only trying to help, Betsy, but you don't understand, Johnny threatens me with things if I end it, we used to get up to all sorts, he could cause trouble." Betsy was incredulous,

"What sort of things Kathy? He can't own you forever because of some childhood pranks, what sort of things?"

"Nothing Betsy, forget it really, perhaps I should just marry him, it's going to be so awkward anyway being back next door to him."

"No Kathy, you mustn't do that whatever you do. You'll be so unhappy, promise me you won't do that?" But Kathy had already moved out of earshot and was heading for her brother and new sister-in-law.

Annie and Thom's wedding had caused a big shake up in the Elliot household. They needed a house to live in, and whilst both sets of parents were happy for them to start their married life sharing with them, it would not have been ideal. The solution was suggested by Kate after being suddenly widowed earlier this year. Mr Wilson had collapsed and died whilst alighting from a cab near to their house. Kate had mused sadly, that neither of her husbands had needed her to nurse them, they both made swift departures from this life, as though sparing her any bother.

The house in James' Street was too big for only one person. It still housed the workshop area at the back which now employed not only Joseph and Johnny Robinson, but since the summer, also young Albert. He was showing the same natural talent displayed by his father at this early age. The large sewing room upstairs was still a hive of regular activity, mainly thanks to Kathy but with a little help from both Kate and Betsy at hectic times.

Betsy was now spending more and more of her time helping at the surgery and even doing some nursing tasks now, as well as organizing Edward's workload for him. The world of medicine fascinated her. She was enjoying learning new nursing skills and borrowing Edward's books, absorbing information at every opportunity. Betsy had become very popular with all the women and children who attended the clinic, but appeared to have no interest in finding a suitor for marriage and children of her own. She had even started to take some courses and lectures, and had traveled to Leeds to sit some oral and written examinations. Hannah took Betsy's studiousness as further proof she had inherited Joseph's, and not Henry's genes.

Kate had offered Thom and Annie her house if they could take over the rent, and she would look for something smaller. Joseph and Hannah considered all options, and decided that James Street was no place for Thom, it could flare his asthma up again, and her Mother should not be looking for new places at her age. They came upon the perfect solution. The whole family would move back to James Street, and share it with Kate. This would ease the work and the rent cost for her as she grew older, and give her some company too. Thom and Annie could live in their house on Belle Vue Street, paying rent to Joseph. This also gave Thom somewhere to paint in his spare time without Eliza's little fingers around to spill and spoil his work. Despite still working many hours at the stonemason's, he had recently sold one of his paintings at a bazaar in Whitby, and the whole family were very excited for him.

Everyone had been more than happy with the arrangement except Kathy. She, like Albert and Joseph, had acknowledged the convenience of being very close to their workplaces, but she had reservations about moving back next door to Johnny Robinson.

* * *

"Have you thought of any names yet then Annie?"

"Not yet Ma, it's a little early isn't it. Ma told me it was unlucky, she'd lost two babies before she had our Peter."

Annie had come to talk to Kathy, but finding her up to her eyes in a ball gown for a regular client, she had left her to it, but accepted her mother-in-law's offer of a cup of tea before returning home.

"I never knew that, Annie, your mother has never mentioned it."

"I suppose that was before you moved here." She took a sip of the hot tea, "How did you decide on names, we're all named after grand-parents, isn't that what you're supposed to do?"

"Only if you like them Annie, you don't have to do that, we did for some, but not for all of our children."

"What about Eliza?"

"Now that's an interesting one. Betsy, Kathy and I took her for a walk in the perambulator down to the Spa ruins after the fire, when she was about a week old. Tied up against the Spa wall was a small fishing boat, we had never seen it there before, or since, but along its side, in clear red letters, it said 'Eliza'. It just seemed appropriate that she should have the same name as another brief visitor to the Spa. It also appeased Betsy who had wanted to name her after her mother Elizabeth, but Joseph was not keen, so 'Eliza' seemed a happy compromise. Henrietta, her middle name, came from Thom, as you know Henry's his middle name, and he was the one who found her."

"That's a lovely story Ma." then guiltily watching Hannah do her ironing, she added, "Well Ma, if you won't let me help, I'll go home and get the tea started before Thom gets home."

* * *

"Mary, how are you? Betsy told me you've not been too well. So I've come to see if you'd like to come with me to see the new foreshore road now it is completed all the way from the Harbour to the Spa Bridge. I have Eliza with me, do you feel like a walk with us? We could even go along and have a look at the new Spa Grand Hall, I believe it's already open to the public. Although the official opening of the whole complex, isn't until next summer some time."

Hannah was standing at the top of the steps outside Mary Hetherington's house, she indicated to the perambulator down on the pavement. She had rarely visited this home since Henry's death. Indeed she had seen Mary at church many times since then, and Mary had reluctantly attended Thom's wedding with Edward, but their friendship had never been the same since that fateful day. Moreover, John Hetherington's untimely demise had undoubtably increased Mary's reclusive tendancies. She heaped all of her attention onto poor Edward. The maid who had answered the door, was obviously instructed not to allow visitors admission into the house, consequently Hannah found herself being addressed now on the doorstep. Mary looked waxen, pale and thin. She had never been a big woman, but now appeared frail and on a different scale to the rest of humankind. Her clothes were out of character for Mary, immaculate, yet old fashioned, they still had the fullness of the earlier half of the decade. Years ago, this would have been considered such a faux pas for the younger Mary.

"Hannah, how lovely to see you." The flat monotone of the delivery created a paradox with the words. "How kind of you to think of me, but I'm afraid I am very busy today, Edward will be home soon too. I trust your family and that sweet little foundling scrap you took in, are all well? Very noble of you indeed. Good day to you Hannah." Mary closed the large heavy door purposefully and Hannah was left standing on the doorstep feeling that she had indubitably been dismissed.

* * *

"Is it a boy, Ma? Or a girl?"

"It's a little girl, Eliza. She's called Alice Jane."

"Oh, can I play with her."

"Not yet Eliza dear, she's a little small yet, but in a little while you'll be able to."

Hannah was conducting this conversation with Eliza from outside the midden at the back of the house. Eliza had taken to wanting privacy like the rest of the family, when visiting the midden, but she still required some help, so Hannah hovered nearby.

"But that's not fair Ma, you said the new baby would play with me!" To emphasise her disapproval, she slammed the midden door shut.

"No Eliza, don't shut the door, it gets stu..!" But Hannah was too late, the door had jammed. Hannah felt the panic rising within her, this had happened once before with Albert, but he had been able to reach the inside catch as well as the handle and could get out with Joseph pushing from the outside. Hannah ran inside for a stool, she climbed up and peered over the top of the door. Eliza was still sitting on the midden, and was singing her favourite repetitive nursery rhyme. Hannah looked around her, Joseph and Albert had gone to buy wood today, Johnny was not around, he'd probably gone home for his lunch, Betsy was at the clinic. She ran inside shouting up the stairs to her mother and Kathy. She heard them making their way downstairs, and returned to Eliza. Looking over the door again, Eliza was ineffectively shaking the door,

"Ma, Ma, I stuck!"

"I know dear, It's fine, we'll get you out, don't worry."

"What is it Ma, what's happened?" Kathy took a swift intake of breath as she realized the implications of Hannah's position on a stool at the side of the midden. "Is she alright, how are we going to get her out?"

"I don't know Kathy, Albert really struggled a little while ago when the door had slammed, there is no possibility of her managing that lock." Kate arrived at the scene, smiling, "You've got to see the funny side Hannah, I nearly did it yesterday, it's getting quite difficult. What a place to be locked in. I'll go and see if William Robinson's in next door, he might be able to do something." Chuckling, she scurried away.

Kathy and Hannah exchanged places, Hannah pacing the yard and rattling the door, and Kathy on the stool, trying to placate Eliza over the top of the midden door.

Just then, Johnny bounded in from next door,

"Have you heard Kathy?" Johnny lowered his voice. "John Woodall the banker has died, and his son is donating St Nicholas house to the council. They're saying that building is to become the new Town Hall, won't that be grand? I'm determined to make it onto the council one day Kathy, no point moaning about our lives if you're not prepared to do anything to change it."

"I had heard, and it's without doubt a good gesture, but we've a more pressing problem currently in our household Johnny." She shot him an impatient look that both signified the inappropriateness of his remark in view of their dilemma, as well as indicating the nature of it.

"Oh dear, Mr Elliot told me this door was starting to catch a lot, I know there's a knack to opening it, but I doubt if Eliza'll be able to reach, let alone fiddle with it. Erm, what about if I climb up and lean over the top of the wall, Kathy can you hold onto my legs, and I'll reach down and get hold of Eliza."

"Are you sure Johnny, what if I drop you?"

"Well, I'll probably end up cracking my head open at Eliza's feet! What choice do we have Kathy!"

"Where's Granma?"

"She's nattering to my Ma now. Why, do you want her to do the climbing, or the bit holding onto my legs?"

"Stop bickering you two, and let's get Eliza out as quickly as possible."

"Yes of course Mrs Elliot." Johnny climbed onto the stool,

then heaved his body up onto the high wall of the midden. Both Kathy and Hannah held onto a leg each as he trustingly leant himself right down into the midden and held his arms outstretched towards Eliza. He lifted her up, and shouted out behind him, "pull me down, but slowly!"

Kathy and Hannah pulled Johnny's legs gently downwards, by the time Johnny's upper body became visible, they realized it was going to be tricky for him to hand Eliza down without falling himself. They paused giving them all time to consider the safest way to proceed. Johnny moved first, he rotated his body slightly,

"Hold me steady a minute," he coaxed Eliza gently, and slowly managed to position her sitting precariously on the top of the wall, keeping one restraining arm over her knees, he managed to pull one leg around until he was straddling the wall. From there, he easily handed Eliza down to Kathy stood again on the stool. From there, Hannah snatched a relieved Eliza and scurried inside to ensure no detriment had occurred.

"Can you get down yourself Johnny?"

"Just hold out your arms for me Kathy, I've already fallen for you, marry me?"

"Thank you so much Johnny, what would we have done without you, you were so brave, if we'd let go, you could've been killed."

"You know how you can repay me Kathy, marry me?" He puckered his lips for a kiss. Kathy, softened by his deed, reached a small peck onto his cheek.

"Perhaps I will, Johnny Robinson. Go and finish your lunch and I'll go and see if Eliza and Ma are alright."

"Did you just say yes Kathy Elliot, did I hear you right?"

"You heard Johnny Robinson, you heard!"

Chapter 23

Scarborough, August 1880

"Well done Betsy. You now have certificates for, let me think, the theory of anatomy, the theory of physiology, hygiene and practical nursing." Edward was counting the accolades emphatically yet non-patronisingly on the fingers of his left hand with his right index finger. "That's very good in such a short time. You'll be a hospital Lady Superintendant before long!"

"Oh, no Edward, I don't think so. But I have loved the studying, and I love my work, you know that."

Edward and Betsy were perusing her latest acquisition, the certificate of practical nursing, in the reception area of The Cottage Hospital on Springhill Road.

"I do know Betsy. But you are working as many hours as I do these days, and I know you also still help with the sewing at home sometimes. You should take a break, why are you here today? It's a Sunday."

"Oh, nonsense Edward, I'm fine." Edward rarely stopped his work for idle chatter of late, he had become a dedicated and respected local medical expert. He uncharacteristically took hold of Betsy's hand, smiling he looked directly into her eyes, "Betsy, I was invited, with Mother, to the Opening Banquet at The Spa tomorrow night, August the second. It will be a very grand affair, not really my thing, but we deserve a break. Mother says she has one of her heads that will go on for days, so we can't go. But why don't we go together? The tickets are much sought after. Have you anything suitable to wear?"

"Oh Edward, that would be a treat. I'm sure Granma and Kathy could sort something out for me."

"That's sorted then, I'll pick you up at 6.30pm sharp. Prepare for a very special evening."

Betsy was standing in the middle of the sewing room at home on James Street. Kathy and Kate were fussing around her tasteful but hastily created gown. In dark fuchsia, it featured the fashionable flat sweep of folds of fabric from the front and sides of the skirt, around to a posterior bustle. Kate had begun with a bodice from an old dress, brightened it with braid, ribbon and sequins, and attached the taffeta skirt. Betsy's figure had gently rounded over recent years, despite her boundless energy. Indeed Joseph often remarked that it was a rare day when Betsy stayed long enough in one place to warm a seat. Tonight she was radiant, with her piercing blue eyes, strawberry blond colouring, but thick shiny Buxton curls and an enchanting and captivating smile.

"You look wonderful Betsy, you couldn't look more glowing if it was your wedding day itself."

"Now steady, Kathy, this is just a night out, not the romance of the year, don't get any of your 'Jane Austen' style ideas now! I'm more excited about witnessing this particular occasion. I followed the selection of the architects when the Cliff Bridge Company turned the new design into a competition to be won. I always thought that the designs by Verity & Hunt of London would win. They were definitely the best, and the most in keeping with the original feel of the Spa area. Don't you agree?"

"Well, I'm just so glad they didn't get to move the sea wall Betsy. That would have been criminal in my opinion."

"Well I'm sure we all agree, Kathy. Though perhaps not quite as criminal as if the fire was actually started deliberately? I doubt if anyone will ever get to the bottom of what happened that night."

"Well I don't much care, Betsy. It served a purpose whatever happened."

The two sister's eyes locked for a split second, when Kate interrupted,

"Do you two ever stop talking, keep still Betsy if you want this finished for tomorrow night!"

"Oh, it'll just be so exciting to actually be there for the official opening Betsy, and with the Lord Mayor of London there too! Ma and I watched them arrive at the station yesterday evening. The station looked so fine, decorated with lots of flowers, everyone cheered and the procession leading to their state carriages was so colourful. Their robes were so magnificent Betsy, and you'll get to see them close up. The Lady Mayoress was very serious though, maybe she'll be more fun at a banquet." Kate looked up from her task,

"Well, I actually saw them all arrive at St Mary's church for the divine service this morning, and very smart and fine, and 'fun' they all looked too." Her grand-daughters both looked aghast at her,

"Granma, you never said, who did you see? Oh, I wonder how close our table will be to them tomorrow night."

* * *

It was a beautiful evening as Joseph stood on his doorstep awaiting Edward's carriage. He was allowing himself a rare smoke of his pipe as he watched the children in the street playing marbles and hopscotch. There was the cringing scrape of metal on metal as two small children tried unsuccessfully to run with their hoops. An older girl was skipping while her friend counted the turns of the rope by chanting a rhyme about the knees of old Mother Brown.

He straightened on hearing the approach of a carriage, and shouted humorously inside to Betsy. "Your carriage awaits M'Lady." He turned back just in time to see a young boy with a whip and top veer quickly out of the horse's path.

Betsy appeared, framed in the doorway, just as Edward's carriage drew level with the house. She knew instantly by the look on Edward's face as he alighted from the carriage, that all was not well.

"Evening Mr Elliot." Edward rushed past Joseph to greet Betsy. "Betsy, I'm so sorry, but Mother has made a remarkable recovery, and is now well enough to attend the Banquet herself. Unfortunately, I only have the two tickets, so I have to disappoint you Betsy, I'm so sorry." Joseph looked from Edward's, to his daughter's face, hers desperately displaying a valiant attempt to disguise her devastating disappointment. He had never seen her look so trodden and crushed. Leaving Edward to console Betsy, while she herself feigned and dismissed any inconvenience, Joseph moved to the side of the carriage, and leant into the open door.

"Evening Mary. So good to hear you have recovered." She angled her beautifully coiffed and delicate head at Joseph in acknowledgement of his greeting. He lowered his voice,

"However, I do feel you could have allowed Edward to keep his promise to Betsy. She has so looked forward to this evening."

"Joseph, how absurd! The ticket was addressed to me. You don't seriously think I'm going to let my only son, a respected doctor in this town, be seen with an illegitimate woman, whose family have also taken in another such child. You have harmed your family's reputation no end with your good deeds Joseph Elliot. Good evening to you."

She looked straight ahead in an obvious dismissal of her adversary.

Joseph was astonished, but he now fully empathised with Hannah's indignation at her own dismissal on Mary's doorstep recently. He felt disappointment in his friend John's betrayal of his promise of discretion regarding Betsy's birth, and yet was shaken at Mary's unequivocal prejudice on this issue. Edward returned to the carriage, noticeably penitent in his avoidance of eye contact with Joseph, as he stepped up and settled himself beside his mother.

"Good evening Mr Elliot, I'm so sorry for any inconvenience."

Joseph's heart ached as he watched Betsy move back into the house, flattened and dejected.

"Betsy, wait here a moment." She looked up at her father, unable to altercate with him, she did as she was bid, watching after him as he ran up the stairs.

She was propped on the open doorway, watching the children playing in the street when Joseph returned.

"Now then young lady, your mother has given me permission to go out for the evening with my very beautiful daughter. She gave me her best bonnet for you to wear, here." He dumped it unceremoniously over the top of her hair decoration. "The occasion is a very special one indeed. We may not have tickets for the Banquet, but that doesn't mean we can't enjoy the rest of the ambience, my dear. Will I do?" He proudly indicated to his change of clothes as he picked up his bowler hat from the Hall stand, offered her his arm, and awaited the expected compliment from Betsy as she tied the bow on her bonnet.

"I'll be delighted to accompany you Pa, let's go and watch history take place."

The Spa bridge and Promenade were teeming with people when Joseph and Betsy made their way along to get a view of the proceedings. Many dignitaries were already inside, and carriages were cluttering the complex despite the many organisers ushering the coachmen to move away as soon as they unloaded. Joseph and Betsy were just about to leave the bridge to descend the hill, when they heard some cheers go up from behind them, and realised the state carriages were slowly beginning to cross the bridge behind them. They moved to the side to watch them pass. The tardy progression of the carriages appeared to be due to the Lady Mayoress insisting on stopping periodically to speak to the spectators. Betsy was fascinated by the coachmen. She was used to seeing her Gramps in Dorset in all his finery, perched on the box seat of the carriages, but these coachmen were quite different. They wore splendid fur-trimmed scarlet cloaks with a matching triangular fur-trimmed hat. You didn't need to see the occupants of these carriages to know they were much esteemed and important people. She was still marvelling at the spectacle, when the carriage pulled alongside them and the Lady Mayoress spoke,

"Good Evening. Lovely evening isn't it? What a beautiful view from here. Are you attending the Banquet? You are surely too elegantly attired for promenading." Joseph smiled at his daughter as he watched her swallow hard in surprise.

"Oh no, Ma'am, I'm just out with my father enjoying this lovely occasion."

"It is a splendid occasion isn't it? I hope you enjoy your evening." To their surprise, she beamed a lovely smile at Betsy stretching one pearly white glove out towards her. Without thinking Betsy returned the gesture, and the two ladies shook politely. Joseph lifted his hat to the carriage, and they were gone.

"Pa, did that really just happen?"

"It certainly did Betsy, I doubt if you would have met them at such close quarters in the banquet itself. Glad you came out with your Pa tonight?"

She took his arm again affectionately, "Of course I am Pa, lets just enjoy this view here a minute, we don't need to do down to the Spa Promenade, we've seen who we came to see."

They both turned to lean on the railings and take in the view across to the castle hill on this balmy summer's evening.

"It is beautiful you know Pa, we take it for granted when we see it every day. We're so lucky to live in such a charming place."

Joseph surveyed the whole panorama.

"You're right Betsy, in all directions, everywhere you look. That Mr Anderson Smith has an enviable view from his new house on the very edge of Holbeck over there. Can you see it, Holbeck Hall he's called it. They say he's been warned about the soil creep in that area, but he's ignored it. At his peril if you ask me, I'll wager it'll be in the sea before too long."

"Well, as long as it's a few years away, it won't worry him Pa will it? And for the present, what a view he has." They laughed together as they watched the gas lighter make his way along the bridge in the fading summer evening light, when unexpectedly Betsy noticed some lights appear simultaneously around the Grand Hall. She pointed them out to Joseph,

"How did that happen Pa, those lights down there all went on together just now."

"Hmm, that's quite impressive isn't it. It must be the electric lights they've talked about. You just have to turn on a switch. It doesn't need a spark, as it isn't actually a flame. William next door says this electricity is going to replace gas eventually as it's cleaner easier and safer. This poor man could find himself out of work before long." They watched in silence for a few moments, then Joseph broached the delicate subject that had danced awkwardly above their heads like an unwilling aura. "Betsy, do you have expectations with young Edward my dear?" He stilled Betsy's protestations, and continued, "I do know you have much in common, and you would undoubtedly make a lovely couple, but I fear it can never happen whilst Mary has breath in her body." He stopped his oratory to look for a reaction, Betsy was fiddling with the ribbon on her bodice, she would let him have his say. "That woman has had an unwholesome need to keep Edward selfishly to herself since John's death, no, maybe even since little Henry's death. I doubt Edward even realises, on account of him being so busy, and he's not strong enough to fight her, Betsy my dear. Don't wait for him, find yourself a nice young fellow to share your life with."

"You're right in everything you say Pa, and there was a time when I had expectations, but no more. Perhaps I will meet someone else, but the hospital is my life at the moment, and I love my life."

"I know dearest daughter, I know, and you are such a credit to your Ma and me." He smiled proudly and offered her his arm,

"Shall we make our way back now dear?"

"Hmm, thank you Pa, I've had a lovely evening. It couldn't have been better. They say every cloud has a silver lining."

Joseph grinned,

"You and your sayings, Betsy, you seem to collect them, you have one for every occasion."

"Betsy, you didn't miss much dear, have you read the newspaper report of the whole occasion?"

"Granma, I didn't miss anything! I had a personal conversation with the Lady Mayoress!"

"You what? How? Your Ma told me Mary went instead of you. How have you not told us this?"

"I have worked such long hours this week, I thought Ma or Pa would have told you." Hannah walked through the kitchen where the family were gathered for Saturday breakfast.

"We thought we would leave you to tell your own story Betsy, especially in view of Edward telling you they were seated near the reporters, and not even close enough to see the Mayor or Mayoress in the Grand Hall!"

Betsy explained the events as they had transpired on monday night with an avid audience of her Granma, Kathy and Albert. Eliza was totally unimpressed and continued loading her toys into the ageing tin trolley to push out into the yard. Kate was the first to speak, she was still reading the article in the Scarborough Mercury.

"Well, you deserve to wallow in some divine retribution for that bitter woman's actions, Betsy. But also it says in the paper that the reporters could not comment on any of the speeches as they were unable to hear from their unfortunate position!"

Kathy and Albert stifled a giggle knowing that Betsy would not wish for them all to revel in Edward's misfortune that evening. But justice had been done in their eyes.

"I can't believe it's Christmas Eve again already Betsy. Thom and Annie's baby will be here in the spring, and I can't believe Alice is one and a half already. She's so funny with things, she keeps leading me all over by my finger to get her whatever she wants. Poor Eliza gets very cross with her. She's had to share any attention I suppose."

"It'll be lovely tomorrow with the children around though, Pa has made them both new toys, and Ma has knitted for their dolls. It's about time you settled on a date for your wedding Kathy and had some children of your own. Johnny has been very patient since you agreed to a betrothal with him."

Kathy twiddled with the decorations they were fixing to the little table top tree that Joseph had brought home yesterday. Since Prince Albert had died, national mourning had caused a fall from popularity of the Christmas trees he himself had introduced from Germany. The Queen's emergence from her grief had allowed a resurgence of its previous popularity, and this year the shops had been full of trees of varying sizes.

"I know Betsy, Johnny will make a good husband, he behaves himself now, something just holds me back, I know it isn't fair, perhaps in the new year."

"Can I ask you something Kathy? Did Johnny have something to do with the Spa fire?" Kathy looked up sharply at Betsy, ready to refute her suggestion vehemently. Then she reconsidered.

"To be honest Betsy, I really don't know. I suggested one day, in jest, that it would be a good idea because of the proposed alterations to the sea wall." She saw Betsy's look of horror,

"I was only joking Betsy, but lots of times I would joke about doing something and he would actually do it to impress me, then he would say, 'but you told me to Kathy'. That's really my reservation about spending the rest of my life with him. I would always have to watch whatever I said, for fear that he took me seriously and actually did it. I have truly never mentioned the fire, I'm too frightened of what his answer might be, and whether he may implicate me for suggesting it." She paused to reflect on what she had said, then added, "What made you suspect him Betsy?"

"Oh, hmm, nothing really, just a hunch."

William Thomas Elliot was born at Belle Vue Street in March, his arrival was met with great approval from his big sister, Alice, who attended him constantly.

The family's joy was short lived, as news of his safe arrival one day, was followed the next day with the sad news of the death of Joseph's mother, Mary Elliot.

Rose had written after Christmas preparing them that her health was not good, but Joseph was saddened that he had not been able to visit more often since her initial illness. Betsy too was sad; she had grown close to her Granny during her stay and was concerned for her Gramps in his loss.

A week after Rose's letter, Joseph received one whose hand was instantly recognisable. Henry. He had written to reassure Joseph that his father was coping well. Rose and Louisa visited regularly, and Cook ensured he had a substantial lunch every day. He was not to worry. Nevertheless, Joseph resigned to travel south at the earliest opportunity.

Joseph waited until the whole family had gathered after baby William's baptism. The Elliots and the Robinsons had congregated in the parlour at the James Street house, and Joseph had already thanked Albert for his toast as godfather and was about to tackle the suggestion of a visit to Dorset, when there was a knock at the front door. Hannah excused herself to answer it. She returned with their visitor behind her.

"I'm so sorry to intrude on such a private family occasion, but I have a matter of great urgency I would like to discuss with Miss Betsy Buxton, my name is Arthur Jones."

"Mrs Robinson was so disappointed to be sent home, Betsy,

she wanted to find out all the gossip, I believe for once she might not have interrupted. She's lovely really, but Pa's right, she could win a prize for interrupting. You're so lucky it's you he wants to talk to. Now he- is- de-fin-ite-ly- a- Mr- Dar-cy!" She punctuated and drew out each word to reinforce her swoon.

"Kathy, you're betrothed! Anyway, Pa is obviously not going to let me talk to him. He's been with him for ages, I wonder what he wants. I remember him being very angry with my Uncle Bill at the station in Dorset, I think he accused him of murdering his father. I don't know what he could want with me."

Just then, they heard the parlour door open, and Joseph and Arthur emerged.

"Kathy, do you think you could make Mr Jones a cup of tea? Betsy can you come and talk to your Mother and I please. Forgive me Mr Jones, but I think this story is better told by us."

Betsy settled herself in the parlour in front of her mother. Hannah smiled at her, she could not help thinking, how much past family trauma was this daughter of hers to take?

Joseph closed the door behind him, and began Arthur's story.

"Betsy. Arthur's Grandmother, Mrs Jones has just died recently, she had a long illness, and had time to tell Arthur something he should have known a long time ago. His mother Molly had been very close to both Arthur Brown and your Uncle Bill Buxton as they grew up. One night she had been a little tipsy with too much wine, and got a little too close to your uncle, Bill Buxton. Her mother caught them, and encouraged her daughter to immediately go after Arthur Brown instead, just in case there were repercussions from her transgression. Your Uncle Bill was already known to be a heavy drinker, and in view of his father's early demise through drink, Mrs Jones wanted better for her daughter. Arthur was a hard working fellow. Molly succeeded in seducing and procuring a betrothal to Arthur. The rest you know.

Mrs Jones always knew that Arthur must really be Bill's son. And she's right, the likeness to your grandfather, Bill and Lizzibeth's father, is remarkable. In essence Betsy, this young man, Arthur Jones, is your blood cousin. Having found that he had a living relative, he understandably wanted to meet you." Joseph, took a deep breath and then reached for his pipe.

Betsy sat in silence as she took in the story. What had the Buxton's done to deserve such tragedy. She and Arthur at least seemed to have survived the curse, and must put all this behind them. If she could help him to do that, she would.

There was such irony in his confrontation with his father that day at the station. Bill had spent his life trying to find Betsy, thinking her to be his only living relative. Tragically, it was his son, living and working under his very nose in Dorset, who in his own ignorance of the whole truth, on confronting his father, unquestionably sent him to his death.

"I'd like to go and talk to him now Pa." Hannah and Joseph nodded to her, proud of the empathic young woman they had raised as their own.

As Betsy walked quietly into the scullery, she was immediately aware of the Jane Austen scene so palpably playing out in front of her. 'Mr Darcy' was unmistakably captivated, and Kathy was indubitably 'weak at the knees'!

Chapter 24

Scarborough, July 1883 - September 1885

"Ma, I'm going to miss you so much. Promise you'll come down and see us soon. The train journey is so much better now than how you remember it."

"I'm afraid Kathy, that if I make it back down to Dorset, I may not want to leave again. Especially now you'll be down there. You promise me that you'll come back often to see us though, and bring any new grandchildren for me to meet!" Hannah's voice began to wobble as she finished her sentence. To endeavour to hide this, she uncharacteristically embraced her daughter. When she released the startled Kathy, she had recovered her composure. She turned to her new son-in-law standing behind them with Joseph on the station forecourt. "You be sure and look after her now Arthur won't you, she's never been away from us for long."

"I've just vowed before God to do just that Ma Elliot, and I intend to, that I can promise you, ''til death do us part'." He spoke as he smiled at his new wife, putting an adoring arm tenderly around her shoulders. She returned his loving smile, their story had a happy ending at last. But the path to their true love had not run smoothly. Johnny Robinson had not taken kindly to Kathy breaking her betrothal of marriage to him. She had done her best to let him down gently after she returned from her stay with her Gramps for a few weeks. She had wanted to be sure her and Arthur really had a future together. Kathy had been concerned that their feelings for one another had been influenced by the romance of Arthur finding that he had a cousin living in Yorkshire, and the subsequent reunion after his lonely childhood.

"You know Arthur; your grandmother Agatha Buxton always wanted her daughter Lizzibeth, Betsy's mother, to marry the son of her best friend, Mary Elliot. That's Joseph here of course." Hannah indicated towards Joseph. "She knew before she died that could not be. It's perhaps a happenstance she would well approve, that the Elliots and the Buxtons are united at last by her own and Mary's grandchildren."

Arthur beamed at hearing about his family, he had incessantly questioned the Elliots about all the Buxtons. He regretted not having his father's name, but in view of living in the same town where Bill's name was synonymous with tragedy, Kathy and him had decided that Jones was just fine as a name for them. Arthur thought of another question to ask Hannah about his paternal grandparents, so Kathy turned to Betsy and they took hold of each other's hands to say their goodbyes.

"Kathy, did you ever ask Johnny the question we talked about?"

Kathy looked at the ground between her feet and shook her head.

"Don't spoil today by talking of him Betsy." She looked up into her sister's knowing eyes, and knew Betsy would be persistent. Kathy decided to appease her as far as she could. "I did ask him, he evaded the question and said that it would be my punishment, to spend my life wondering about whether I'd been the spark!" She looked up at Betsy then continued, "But I won't Betsy, I've nothing to feel guilty about, I imagine it was surely just a gas lamp that got out of control. He's out of my life now for good, and I've a new start with my dear Arthur. I do feel guilty that he's gone off to find work in Leeds with Peter though, poor Pa and Albert are left with all the orders to do."

"Don't worry about that one bit Kathy, Pa said they were really pushed to have enough work for three once Albert finishes his apprenticeship this year anyway."

"Well, it's been awkward for Thom and Annie though, not to mention for Ma and Pa. You can't blame the Robinson's for being aggrieved with me. I did break a promise. There was no need for the comments to Ma about us 'getting above our stations' just because we have friends who are land-owners though, especially when she implied everyone around us thinks the same. Ma so hates people gossiping." She paused as Betsy smiled empathically at her. "You'll come and see me Betsy won't you, I'll miss you all so much."

"Of course dear sister, and you give my love to Gramps, Louiza, Benjamin, Rose and all the family." Kathy nodded, her voice hoarse from shouting above the level of the engine noise. Slowly she looked around, surveying this scene beside the train. Time slowed as she committed her family to memory exactly as they looked to her now, dressed in all the finery they had worn for her wedding. None so fine as she herself had looked today. Between her and her grandmother, they had created a wedding gown that had left gasps behind her as her proud father paraded her down the isle.

That dear father was frowning now in slow motion, sharing something grim with his childhood friend Henry who had moved to his side after talking with Albert's young lady, Lottie. Arthur had been a gardener at Bramble house since he was fourteen years old, and Henry had stood as his witness at the wedding. He had kindly prepared a cottage for them on their return; indeed, now retired from his army duties, he was spending most of his time running the family estate at Bramble House.

Albert was standing sombrely with their brother Thom, no doubt considering how much less lively the house would now be without their sister around. Next to them hovered her sister-in-law Annie, unsuccessfully hiding the tell tale signs of her imminent arrival under the full folds of her dress, and jiggling her toddler William on her hip. She was deep in concerned and anxious conversation with her cousin Lottie who lived with her family in a small house near the Crescent. Albert had only begun courting Lottie recently, after taking months to find the courage to ask her to walk out with him.

Kate, beginning to take on the mantle of an elderly lady, chatted with little Alice as she kept a tight hold of her hand, mindful of the dangers of these powerful engines. Kathy watched her grandmother, she owed her so much, she had been her mentor in teaching her all she knew regarding the art of dressmaking and had produced for her the most beautiful wedding dress anyone had ever seen. Having surveyed a full circle, she came finally to rest her eyes once again on her mother and sister Betsy, and took the final snapshot. The two women she would miss the most. Then she noticed the little figure behind the folds of her mother's skirt.

"Eliza, come and have one last hug with me, the whistle has just gone and I have to go now." The furrow in Hannah's skirt grew deeper, as the seven year old disappeared completely. "Eliza, come here, come now, don't take on so, I'll be back to see you before you know it." Kathy prised Eliza away from Hannah and a lump rose in her throat when she saw the silent gulping sobs and tears cascading down her little sister's cheeks.

"Why were you so serious on the platform today Joseph, what was Henry telling you about? Your Pa's not sick is he?"

"No my dear, but Henry's Pa is. Charles Ferguson is failing quite rapidly it seems. Henry was saying how difficult it is to see a man everyone revered and respected so much, become unable to remember day to day things, and need help with very basic tasks. It's sad for his mother too."

"When does he travel back, I'm surprised he has stayed away so long then? It's been nice to see so much of him, but I'm amazed that Amelia didn't come with him when he was coming here for so long. It was such a special night when we all went out to eat on his and Betsy's birthdays, he's very generous to us."

Hannah paused in brushing out her hair from it's elaborate 'mother of the bride' style in front of the bedroom mirror. Speaking to Joseph's reflection, she continued, "It occurred to me today you know, that it was the first time since her birth, twenty nine years ago, that we had all been together on that date."

"Yes Hannah, I'd thought about that too." He climbed onto their high bed, "He's only just got word of his father's condition deteriorating though, I'm sure that will make him return soon. Apparently though, Amelia has been spending some time with her family, her sister has a big family and she likes to visit them. Henry says there's nothing to do there, and he so much loves the house he rents from a friend on South Cliff, I wonder that he has never invited us there, but I do think he could end up spending longer and longer up here." Hannah gestured an astonished countenance as she digested the implications of Joseph's thinking. Having prepared for bed, she carefully hung her outfit onto a hanger before placing it into one of the large pair of matching oak wardrobes Joseph had made for her last year.

"Well if that comes to pass Joseph, you'd better be buying me some fine gowns, that man likes fine living, and quite obviously enjoys our company with it!"

"Albert, have you decided upon the piece you'll create to finish your apprenticeship and become a journeyman cabinet maker, just like your old Pa?"

Joseph smiled, he and his younger son were working together on a banqueting table for a large country house on the outskirts of Scarborough, near Cloughton. Joseph loved his son's company as they worked, it reminded him of those early days learning his trade with Jacob; before those memories had become tarnished with the revelation that his father-in-law may not have been the man he had thought him to be.

"I've thought about it a lot Pa. I really think I'd like to follow in your footsteps, and make a secretaire." Joseph stopped in his toil and looked up at Albert as his son endeavoured to validate his choice. "Apart from being a very useful piece of furniture, we have all availed ourselves of your desk over the years Pa, and it can be such an interesting piece. I've already drawn plans for the secret compartment and it's completely different to yours. I want to design a mechanism that involves a lever folding flat the letter compartments. As they lower, the upper wooden strut also lowers, revealing a previously hidden, narrow shelf." Joseph beamed with pride, his son was going to be just as enthusiastic, inventive and conscientious a cabinet maker as himself. Qualities that had never been evident in Johnny Robinson. He looked forward to building up an even more successful business. Albert would without doubt take this legacy forwards into the twentieth century.

"Lottie, what were you discussing with Annie yesterday at the station? You both looked very uneasy about something." Albert and Lottie were walking out together along Queen's Parade on Sunday afternoon. Lottie looked aghast at Albert.

"Did you hear anything we said Albert?"

"Of course not, Lottie, otherwise I wouldn't be asking you would I?" His question had been light-hearted, but Lottie's anxious reply wiped his smile and its mirth. "What is it Lottie, what's troubling you."

"I don't know if should say. Annie has never said anything."

"What do you mean, what are you talking about, Lottie?" He stepped round in front of her, blocking her progress, and tilted her chin up to bring her eyes in line with his own. "Tell me Lottie?" Lottie turned away from him, and moved to the railings on the edge of the cliff. He joined her and looked across the north bay towards castle hill. The horizon beyond was obliterated by the abundant straight tall dark sails of the herring fleet.

He lowered his gaze and re-focused beneath them where the

tide was out and many groups of children were playing on the sands ridged and patterned by the wheels of scattered bathing huts. One cluster of girls was building a sand castle. Their competence and delight was not only hindered by the many yards of material in their pristine, calf length, smock pinafore dresses; but also by the incessant fussing of their minder. In her attempt to shield the complexions of all, she fluttered and hovered with her small inadequate parasol, with the obvious annoyance of a stinging insect.

Albert cast a glance at Lottie to see if she was ready to speak, he wondered which words to use next as a prompt, for his curiosity now was roused. He focused his gaze just beneath where they stood, where many couples and families were gathered in Clarence Gardens. A familiar figure limped the path below them with his now crucial cane, docking his cap to two passing gentlewomen with elaborate hats and parasols, and then paused to chat to them. "Look there's Uncle Henry, he must be enjoying the sea air too, he's found someone he knows, look." Lottie physically stiffened at the mention of Albert's adopted uncle.

"He's most likely being very improper with them!"

"Don't be ridiculous Lottie, why would he do that?"

"Because he's done it to Annie and me, that's why Albert. I know he's your Godfather, and I shouldn't have said anything, but he just isn't as much of a gentleman as you all think."

"Tell me Lottie, tell me exactly what's happened, I'm sure you have both misunderstood. I demand that you tell me, now, this instant."

Lottie turned to face Albert. She lifted her chocolate lashes, and her matching eyes met Albert's concerned and perplexed gaze.

"Albert, yesterday at the station, your Uncle Henry asked me to meet him at his house later, he said he would make it worth my while. I don't think he realises we're courting, I've always been regarded just as Annie's cousin." She paused to ensure Albert's expression showed the appropriate distaste. "I talked to Annie straight away because I was so shocked. She told me that one day a few years ago, when she was working at Marshall and Snelgroves, she'd been asked to fetch something for the supervisor from the Grand Hotel. In her haste, she stumbled into your Uncle Henry at the top of McBean steps, you know at the side of the Grand Hotel?" Albert nodded that he knew where she meant. "Well he was less than courteous with her, and wasn't about to wait for her to meet at his house, he tried to take liberties with her there and then, it was late afternoon, overcast, and only early spring, so still quite dark. Annie was terrified, but she didn't meet him with your family until later that same evening when he collected your parents in a carriage to take them to a ball at the Grand Hotel." Albert raised his head and inhaled deeply remembering the evening well. Lottie continued, "She had never told anyone until yesterday, when he tried the same with me."

Albert could hardly take in what was unfolding about their close family friend. His gaze had drifted out to the smudged horizon with the many sails passing gracefully by where the brilliance of the turquoise summer sea and sky blended as one.

"What happened with Annie?"

"Luckily Albert, a young Gentleman and his wife were climbing the steps, and came into view despite the fading light. Your Uncle Henry made his escape. He has never shown any recognition of Annie, but she has never had any doubt it was him. She said apart from anything else, his voice and accent is so distinctive around here. My experience yesterday confirmed it to her." As she finished, Albert had rested his forearms on the railings, and had dropped his head into his hands.

"Does Thom know?"

"Annie told him, but he just said she must have been mistaken, his Godfather would never do that, after all he said, 'he has a wife and is happily married'." She paused herself to reflect upon his motive. "Annie let it be, she didn't want to upset the family."

Lottie comfortingly, and yet so daring in such a public place, put her hand on Albert's back, "I'm so sorry Albert, I didn't want to tell you, you insisted remember."

"Lottie, I want to punch him on the nose, but I can't destroy the friendship Pa has had with him all these years. You're never to be alone with him ever again, do you hear?"

"Don't worry, I don't intend to. If you notice, Thom may say he doesn't believe it, but he sticks to Annie like glue whenever he's around, his eyes never leave her. There's one more thing Albert, I'm sure your Grandmother knew exactly what he was saying to me. I'd vow she gestured to disregard him, as though she knew well what he had suggested."

Hannah excitedly opened the letter which had just arrived in the morning post in Kathy's familiar hand. The year had progressed to its winter months, and Hannah shivered as she moved from room to room, her numbed fingers struggled to undo her daughters news. She sat down at the kitchen table with the chilling remnants of her morning tea to digest the neat and even words in front of her.

When Joseph came into the scullery for his mid-morning snack, he found Hannah looking distressed, and playing with her handkerchief in front of her.

"What is it Hannah, what are you fretting about?" She looked up at her husband, as he took in the familiar handwriting in front of her.

"It's nothing really Joseph, I just miss her so much, I should be with her, she's not been well after losing their first unborn child, and she's now in the family way again. Oh, Joseph, she needs her Ma."

"Hannah, you may visit whenever you wish, you know that."

"I know Joseph, but what about Eliza, she's still at school, she still needs me too. You read it. Tell me what you think." Joseph read the letter, smiling at various descriptions of people and places he knew so well.

"Hannah my dear, have you not read the very last page? She says how much better she is, and how they are planning to come up here next summer after the baby is born, Henry has agreed for Arthur to take the time off."

Hannah snatched the post script on the back of the letter from Joseph, reading the words for herself, her shoulders visibly dropped and she sighed her relief back down into her seat.

"Now Hannah, while you make your hard working husband and son a cuppa, I'll read what has happened in the town," he settled himself close to the fireside, and reached into the shelf at the side for the newspaper. "I didn't even get to the Gazette this weekend. I want to see if they have any pictures of the North Bay Pier disaster. I haven't had time yet to go along and see for myself. I bet Betsy is pleased, she never wanted it to be built in the first place." Joseph distractedly began to read the front page, but continued his chatter as he read. "It was bad enough when it was hit and damaged by the trawler 'Star', and then the steamer 'Hardwick' only three weeks later, but then for some of it to be washed away by a storm, you have to question how well it was built." He started to flick through the pages, "Here it is, oh dear, Hannah, the storm has completely washed the bandstand clean off the pier head, what a mess."

"Albert." Hannah shouted out into the workshop at the back of the house. "Teas out for you." The muffled sounds from the other side of the door could be heard as Albert shouted back, "Won't be a minute Ma."

"Hannah, there's an article here about the volcano that erupted in the far east in the summer, not long after Kathy's wedding. Krakatoa, do you remember? They say more than thirty six thousand people died, its unimaginable isn't it." Hannah had begun to start preparing the lunch, having eased her worries regarding Kathy, her mood was lighter and her humour surfaced,

"With your reputation for feeling earthquakes Joseph, it's a wonder you didn't hear that Volcano blowing, wasn't it supposed to be the loudest noise ever heard before in history?"

"Phuh, get back to your cooking, woman, you're not a good wife poking fun at me!" Their eyes met and they were both laughing as Albert came into the scullery. He took in the sight and sound of his parents teasing banter, and smiled inside as he seated himself with his mug of tea, putting his feet up onto the fireside shelf.

"Pa is there anything in there about the railway being finished between Whitby and Middlesbrough? There was such a delay with the viaduct at Staithes ten years ago. Poor Thom is so eager to get up the coast to do some scenic paintings."

"Can't see anything Albert. Wasn't the delay for safety reasons though? I seem to remember it required some strengthening measures after the Tay bridge collapsed."

"Yes, but the viaduct was finished two years ago, it's the rest of the line that needs to be completed now."

"Oh, here it is Albert, it's due to open this week, see, December the third. Thom'll be happy then."

"Well it's a start, but it still needs the Scarborough to Whitby line to open before he can get to the fishing villages beyond Whitby."

＊ ＊ ＊

"Pa, Pa, I've just seen a man rolling along the street on wheels, he was moving so fast. Can I have one, please, please Pa?" Eliza stopped short of careering into the kitchen table and the familiar sight of Joseph reading the newspaper and drinking his tea. He straightened up from the print and his steamy mug, his shirt sleeves black from where they lay on the paper, as Joseph's failing reading eyes positioned themselves close enough to make sense of the fuzzy words.

"A man rolling on wheels Eliza, whatever next!"

Albert was nervously polishing his shoes, ready to go for his tea with Lottie's family. Previously distracted by his thoughts, he realised her confusion and started to laugh.

"Pa, the baker on Dean Road has just bought one of these

new safety bicycles, I was talking to him yesterday, he said he never liked the idea of the penny farthing, but this one is ideal for getting his bread delivered quickly. It's easy to get on and off, and is much safer, hence its name. So that's what it is Eliza, a bicycle." Eliza looked impatiently at her brother Albert, ungrateful for his interruption.

"So please can I have one Pa, can I have a bicycle? Please."

"I'm afraid Eliza, that you will be much too small for one just yet, maybe by the time you're big enough, we'll be able to afford one, and maybe too by then, we'll be riding in one of these horseless carriages too." He indicated to a photograph in the newspaper with a carriage that was propelled by an engine instead of being pulled by a horse. What do you think Albert?"

"Well I do hope so Pa, they look very fine indeed. We could all go out into the country." Eliza jumped up and down excitedly.

"Oh, Pa, Pa, I nearly forgot, please, please can I go on a train to the seaside with Alice, William and little Joe?"

"The seaside Eliza, you live at the seaside!"

"No, the other seaside Pa, Thom says the railway now goes further than Whitby, and he wants to go to a little fishing place on Sunday to paint the fish."

"I doubt very much that he is going to paint the fish Eliza," he glanced at Albert and Hannah who had turned from her cooking to listen, "but he has actually said for a while that one Sunday he would like to go up the coast for a quaint setting for the painting he wants to enter into an exhibition." Joseph paused as he took in the painting on their wall of the herring girls gutting fish on St Vincent's pier. Thom had painted it many years before. Then bringing his thoughts back to the trip, "Staithes I believe is the place he's interested in. Since the railway opened up the coast beyond Whitby more than a year ago now, he's been desperate for the Scarborough to Whitby line to be finished. Perhaps we should go sometime Hannah too, it would be a grand day out. I think it was only completed a few weeks ago, sixteenth of July if my memory serves me correctly. I remembered the date because it was exactly one year since Kathy, Arthur and little Emily came up to stay and I booked the table at that new Grind Waterside Eating House for their famous fish and chips." Joseph paused to savour the memory of his whole family being together again. It had provoked feelings of guilt that he had left his parents and travelled miles away to live his life totally separate from them; and yet simultaneous gratitude that improvements in travel would facilitate more frequent visitations from his own daughter. He looked again at the expectant Eliza, "You know Eliza, I'm sure it was just such an eating house that Dickens refers to in Oliver Twist, do you remember?" He caught her exasperated expression on the long awaited answer to her request, and with difficulty, inhibited a wry smile, "The train journey along the coast will be a nice day out for the children though won't it?" He smiled and winked at Hannah, "What do you think Ma, shall we let this little scallywag go too?" Hannah augmented his teasing,

"Oh Joseph, I'm not sure if I can spare Eliza, it's baking day tomorrow, Eliza always puts the jam in the tarts for me." Eliza ran to her mother's side,

"Please, Ma please, I promise I'll help more next week." Joseph and Hannah laughed, Eliza wasn't sure whether that meant yes or no, she looked appealingly around the family. Betsy had just finished setting the table, and came across to her, shooting scolding eyes at both her parents.

"They're teasing you dearest, they're so cruel, of course they'll let you go," she held out her hand to her, "you come with me Eliza, I'll get you the really big biscuit we made and had saved for Pa, and you can eat it in front of him!" A big grin spread across Eliza's face as she skipped towards the pantry laughing with her sister. Betsy smiled at her Pa, "you should know better Pa, 'he who laughs last, laughs longest!'" Joseph feigned distress while the rest of the family laughed heartily. Eliza had forgotten all about the safety bicycle.

The Elliots were gathered in the parlour of the James street house. Joseph had opened a bottle of sherry to celebrate Albert and Lottie's news.

"Welcome to the family Lottie, I feel you're already a part of it anyway. Have you thought about where you're going to live?" Albert and Lottie looked at each other, then Lottie averted her eyes lest their request should be denied.

"Pa, we rather hoped we could live here for a while at least. We're quite young to manage a rent on our own, and this is such a big house, and so convenient for my work obviously."

"I promise I'll help around the house Mrs Elliot, and I'll carry on working a little to help out with the money too." Lottie added enthusiastically. Joseph and Hannah smiled in the unison they had perfected over the last thirty one years.

"Absolutely no need for your wife to work my boy, there's plenty of work around this home, and there'll be more too with an extra one. At least we get to keep your remarkable secretaire in this house as well as mine, for the time being at least. Perhaps if you want to do something, Lottie, you could help Albert's Grandmother with the sewing repairs she still takes in." Everyone turned their gaze to Kate, she smiled politely and raised her glass.

"Are you alright Ma?" Hannah's concern showed as her Ma seated herself, grabbing at the chair as she lowered.

"I'm fine Hannah, just don't let that son-in-law of mine give me sherry on an empty stomach again, he forgets I'm pushing towards the end of my seventh decade!" Everyone laughed and raised their glasses,

"To Albert and Lottie."

"To Albert and Lottie." chorused back harmoniously from all the Elliots, plus Edward Hetherington, who happened to have called on them this day.

Later that night, Kate crept downstairs in her night gown. She took out some parchment from Joseph's secretaire, and began to write.

To my dear son-in-law Joseph,

I think before either of us departs this life, one of us should tell you the truth about many things. By 'us' I refer to myself and my half brother, Charles Ferguson…………..

As she finished her story, she added her signature with a flourish. She folded the parchment well and carefully pushed the button which lifted the leather inlay displaying the secret compartment. Kate had long ago watched Joseph using the covert mechanism, so was no stranger to its secrets. She pushed the letter inside, and replaced the inlay. Tidying the pen and ink, she closed the secretaire purposefully yet silently, and returned to her bed.

Chapter 25

Scarborough, September 1887

"One potato, two potato, three potato, four, five potato, six potato, seven potato, more. You're 'it' again Eliza, count to ten before you come looking for us."

"Oh no she isn't young Micky, she has to come inside now before it gets dark, and you'd better be getting home now too, and the rest of you."

Eliza and her friends groaned in unison making futile appeals to Betsy. Reluctantly waving goodbye to her friends, Eliza followed Betsy back into the house, offering shelter from the whisper of an autumnal bite on this dusky September evening.

"It's not fair that all my friends live so far away that they can't come in and play Betsy, why are there no children my age in our street, Micky and the others come all the way up from Sandside?" Betsy laughed as she jiggled her sleepy nephew on her shoulder.

"Don't let Granma know you're mixing with those ragamuffin's from down street. Anyway, it won't be long now before you'll be able to play with little Bertie here. It isn't anyone's fault that a few years went by with no children being born on this street." Betsy thought for a moment, "Actually, Eliza, there were twin girls born just along the road the month before you were born, but they both tragically passed with diphtheria. So you must be thankful for your own health, and not be melancholy about a lack of playmates."

Betsy indicated the stairs to Eliza, "Come on missy, time for bed. Ma and Pa are getting ready in their room for our night out, but you can go and say goodnight before you say your prayers."

Eliza led the way up the staircase, her desolate demeanour depicting her despondency. At the top of the stairs, Eliza, sensing a delaying opportunity, turned to Betsy,

"What's a foundling Betsy?" Betsy stopped on the stairway, "Whatever made you ask that Eliza?"

"Micky's sister said I was one. What is it?" Betsy continued up the stairs behind Eliza. Why had they not all prepared an answer to this inevitable question?

"Well Eliza, a foundling baby is one who has no idea where they have come from, or who their parents are."

"I'm definitely not then, I know well who my parents are, and my sister's and brothers. I think I'm more a surprise baby, Betsy. I bet Ma and Pa were not expecting another baby after such a big gap!"

"They certainly weren't Eliza, you were definitely a surprise, that's a fact."

"Shall I look after Bertie while you get ready Betsy? Where are Albert and Lottie? I could go and talk to Granma with him."

"You're very shrewd young lady, but thank you kindly for your impudence. I'm already ready to go out! Bertie's now fast asleep anyway, and I shall take him up to his basinet. His Ma and Pa have taken a stroll in the evening air, but will return presently. Now off you go to say goodnight to Ma and Pa, and I'll expect you up on the next floor and in bed in your room in two minutes!" Betsy made to chase her little sister sternly across the landing towards her parents bedroom, but inhibited her action lest she woke her infant charge. Eliza giggled and ran into her Ma and Pa's room to escape her sister's mock wrath.

Betsy came down from the top floor of the house, Eliza had eventually settled into her bed, and ten month old Albert

John, referred to within the family as 'little Bertie', was quiet for once in the nursery next door to Albert and Lottie's room. His parents had returned from their constitutional walk along the north bay, having given a graphic report of the doomed north pier, further damaged recently by the yacht Escalpa crashing straight through it. They were to have the house to themselves tonight.

Joseph, Hannah, Kate and Betsy had all been invited to dine with Henry at the new Spa Grand Hall Restaurant which had opened with much ceremony the year before. They were all curious as to the occasion, but suspected Henry needed to talk to his friends for support since the death of his father Charles in June this year. Betsy turned into her own bedroom doorway to collect her velvet purse, then knocked on her Grandmother's door and entered after the invited response. The room was dark, the lamp had not yet been lit, Betsy eyes adjusted around the spacious, tasteful but simple room.

"Granma, what are you doing in bed, you should be ready by now, Henry's sending the carriage for us at seven thirty."

"Betsy, I'm not going my dear, I don't feel well, I think I may be going down with a fever. I certainly couldn't contemplate having a late night, or indeed eating. And I cannot imagine that Henry has anything of interest to say to me, or me to him."

Kate spat the last words as was her tendency where the Ferguson's were concerned. Betsy had always been curious. Her growth in maturity and status now entitled her inquisitiveness.

"Granma, why don't you like him? What is it you have against the Ferguson's? What've they done?"

Kate paused, she fumbled with the cotton handkerchief in her hands.

"I'm sorry Betsy, it's not my place to make such comments. Forgive me. The Ferguson's have been good friends to your father's family over the years. They're good people in countless ways. A good many in their position would not have faced up to their obligations in the same way as they have. I'm genuinely sad that Henry's father has left this life Betsy, but I want nothing from him."

"But I don't understand Granma, why would we get anything from him anyway?"

"Oh, such details are of no consequence my dear. But I do want you to promise me two things. Will you?" Betsy was peering into her Grandmother's increasingly indecipherable expression in the diminishing light. In the absence of any evidence at all, she was attempting to solve this mystery by her grandmother's countenance alone .

"Of course, Granma, anything you say."

"Do you know, Betsy, that I brought you into this world?" Kate did not wait for a reply, she felt sure this had been mentioned when the revelation of Lizzibeth's existence had first come to light. "I don't mention this for your approval or gratitude Betsy, but more for you to understand that I spent your mother's last hours with her. She wanted you so much, and wanted a happy, healthy and settled life for you. I know she would have been so proud of you, my dear, you've grown into such a fine young woman. My daughter has counted herself very lucky to have been able to call you her very own." Kate lightly blew her nose on her handkerchief, and dabbed at her nostrils delicately. Betsy mused at how her Grandmother, despite her working class roots, had always been such a lady. Kate re-poised herself, "I know you love your vocation, Betsy, but I also know you love Edward. He's so wrapped up in his work, and his mother, that he doesn't see beyond those two things. I want you to promise me that you'll make him see what's under his nose. You deserve some happiness. You've both given your youth to the health of this town. Spend the remainder of your lives together in happiness, and make your mother, Lizzibeth Buxton sing in her grave."

She had taken hold of Betsy's hands and whilst her voice and touch pleaded her request, the darkness relieved Betsy of her grandmother's sad, beseeching eyes, permitting her some privacy in her sorrow.

"You're assuming I want to be noticed Granma, and that Edward will like what I make him see." Betsy gave a little laugh, hoping to relieve the moment. Kate did not laugh, she continued.

"The second thing, Betsy, you must promise me, that when I die, you'll tell your father that I've left him a letter. It must not be opened until I've gone, becoming infirm is no permission. I must be gone completely from this life. Do you hear? Promise me. He'll know where it is. You can tell him I've always known his secret place. Jacob, your grandfather told me, he thought it was so ingenious." She smiled to herself, and shook Betsy's hands comfortingly. "Promise me, Betsy."

✳ ✳ ✳

"Joseph. Hannah. Betsy. How lovely to see you all. But where is your mother Hannah? I was expecting her company too." Betsy answered first, she could see her mother was too busy absorbing the atmosphere of the restaurant.

"I'm so sorry Uncle Henry, she's indisposed quite suddenly tonight. She sends her sincere apologies."

"Oh, no matter, my dear, we shall continue in her absence. We should have an enjoyable meal. Martin Lutz's Band is playing all evening for us whilst we eat, I have heard such wonderful things about them." He gestured in the direction of the music, across the other side of the sea of elegantly dressed tables, with their shiny silverware, crisp linen, coiffed napkins and classic candle lights. Hannah thought how much nicer any food would taste when presented with such stylish sophistication. She smiled inwardly, she was already captivated, and yet she hadn't even begun to soak up the clientelle yet, or indeed, their fancy attire.

"Henry we're all so sorry about your father. Err, aren't we Hannah? How are your dear mother and sister?" Hannah was rudely awoken from her busy observations, and she concurred eagerly with her husbands questioning.

"Oh, they are coping well, Joseph my friend. The months

leading up to Papa's death were quite distressing. His passing was almost a relief to us all. My only regret was that I was away in London when he died. He did not know any of us at that stage, but I should have been there for Mama and Charlotte."

"What were you doing in London, Uncle Henry?"

"Well that was the irony of it, Betsy, I was having the best night of my life. It was my birthday as it happened, indeed 'our' birthday. I had been invited to the Golden Jubilee Celebrations, in honour of my service to Queen and Country. The national celebrations were such a success, it's hard to believe that a few short years ago, our dear Queen was falling from grace with her excessive mourning, and now we are once again a country of devout royalists. God save the Queen." Henry paused to raise his glass, and the Elliots echoed his toast. Henry continued. "There were fifty European Kings and Princes at the most lavish banquet. The even bigger irony is that Papa would have loved to tell everyone that his son was there. I like to think that wherever he was after his passing that night, he was watching his son, and I hope, feeling proud." His audience gestured their recognition of such an impressive, auspicious occasion.

Hannah then out of curiosity and politeness, enquired as to the whereabouts of Henry's lovely wife.

"Amelia, hasn't accompanied you again. She can't be as taken with the north east coast as you are Henry?"

"I regret that you are right, my dearest Hannah, she finds the cold does not agree with her constitution. She takes the opportunity to visit her family when I travel north."

"Well, Henry, I declare that has to be the best meal I've ever tasted. You're so kind to us all."

"Nonsense, Joseph, it is your company that pleases me, and that of your family of course. Now, I have arranged to have a small sitting room at our disposal for our coffee and brandy, I have something to discuss with you in private." Henry nodded to a waiter in the corner of the room, who immediately gestured to a doorman. Joseph, Hannah and Betsy shared inquisitorial eye contact, but made to follow Henry and the waiter. All had no idea what was about to unfold.

Henry waited until the waiter had served their coffee and brandy and taken his leave, before seating himself opposite this family that he considered so much his own.

"What I have to tell you all is very confusing for me, and I assume will also be to you. Although in many ways I also hope you can shed some light on this matter, despite the implications if this is the case." Henry shuffled in his chair, swapped his crossed legs, and cleared his throat, exemplifying his discomfort in this confrontation with his friends.

"My father's last will and testament is curious to say the least. Despite sensing, without doubt, his disapproval of my constant and continued association with you all over these past years, you have benefited from my father's estate. Now whilst I can rationalise that it must be to do with his incredibly high regard for your father, Joseph; and incidentally, when I arranged for the engraving over the family vault after Pa's internment, the stonemason had already been asked by him to carve one for your father. Hail and hearty though he presently is!" Henry chuckled at his own humour as he paused to absorb the stunned expressions on his friend's faces. He quickly carried on lest they become too expectant regarding the echelon of this benevolence.

"However, what I don't appreciate, is that, if this is all because of your father, Joseph, then why has he left an annuity to your mother, Hannah? Which incidentally on her death, transfers directly to you." Henry resisted the urge to smile at Hannah's dropped jaw. Whatever his father's reason, he was sure Hannah too was ignorant to it. "Furthermore, Joseph, my father has left the coachman's cottage for the sole use of the Elliot family for as long as they require it, in other words, after your father passes, it will be at you or your family's disposal indefinitely. Since Pa bought his horse-less carriage, the motor car, he has little use of a coachman, let alone the position of head coachman, so the cottage has become surplus to requirements." Joseph's frown furrows deepened, and he rubbed his eyes hard, straining them to re-focus on this childhood friend.

"But Henry, this is too, too generous."

"Wait Joseph, there is yet one more disturbing revelation. The house I always rent on the Esplanade, appears to have belonged to my father, I always rented it through a third party so I was never aware of the identity of the owner. However, a condition of my stay was that I never took any 'Elliots' there. Strange admittedly, but I never questioned it. It became my retreat, so stipulations did not matter. Well, I can rent it no longer my friends, for in my father's last will and testament, he has bequeathed it to Betsy here!" Three simultaneous sharp gasps made Henry pause and study the astonished expressions facing him. "Joseph, I have tried to contact the Doctor who supervised my recovery, to see exactly what was told to my father regarding my, err damage. He passed away a few years ago, but I can only think that my father must have considered that was a chance I was Betsy's father, despite what he had personally assured me."

Hannah, shocked, turned quickly and anxiously to look at Betsy. This was too awful for her to take in. Never over the years, had she been given reason to question who had fathered her. To Betsy, Joseph had always been her father. This was too cruel, despite the generous gift that had accompanied the revelation. Hannah had left her seat and had pulled up a stool next to Betsy. She took hold of her hand, and let futile soothing words escape her mouth. Betsy stared blankly ahead of her. Joseph, having recovered from his shock, rounded on Henry,

"Couldn't you have talked to me about this first Henry! No amount of benevolence makes up for having your parentage questioned in such a vulgar manner. You are no father Henry, or you could not have just disregarded your daughter's feelings in such a way." Henry looked at his three friends, sensitivity had never been one of his virtues, but he had certainly not intended this destruction either.

"Joseph, Hannah, Betsy, I am so sorry, I am such an ass, I never thought. I only considered it as fortunate news for you all. Please forgive me, if anyone has taught me over the years about values, it is you Joseph. I am so ashamed, what undeniable thoughtlessness. Betsy please forgive me, I am so sorry. In the unlikely event of my being your father, then you have benefited so much more from Joseph's direction than you ever could have done from me. Your upbringing has been exemplary, indeed an example to families everywhere." Henry had raised himself onto his feet, grabbing for his cane as he did so. "I'll go now, I am travelling back south tomorrow, please receive me again my friend, we lost too many years once before. Despite my thoughtless foolishness, let us not do that again. Good evening to you all, my dears. My carriage is at your disposal, I shall use the funicular lift up to the house for the last time."

Chapter 26

Scarborough, September 1887 - April 1888

The next morning was Saturday. Albert was in the workshop at the back of the house. Joseph and Hannah were taking a long time over their porridge, they had been up most of the night talking after Betsy had gone to bed. Joseph was unsure as to how to discuss any of these revelations with Betsy though he knew he must when she returned from the hospital at lunchtime. He had reinforced to Hannah his own certainty that he could not be her father, but he also tried to minimise the significance of such. After all he pointed out, Betsy has been fathered. The job is done. Is any of this of any relevance now? He was also sure it would be of no usefulness at all for him to suggest his own suspicions regarding his father-in-law. Hannah had been of the opinion that Charles Ferguson was buying his passage into heaven. Had there been any doubt that the Doctor had been wrong, and Betsy could be Henry's, then as a final act of contrition, he wanted to put things right.

"Leaving the cottage for use solely by the Elliot family is kind Joseph, but what I don't understand is why Ma gets money from him."

"It's a mystery alright Hannah. But that one we should surely get to the bottom of when your Ma arises this morning. I wonder what she got up to when she was young. Perhaps she had a thing with him when they were both youngsters."

Hannah feigned a shocked expression, for she too had

considered this possibility. Joseph headed for the back door.

"Anyway, I must go and help Albert my dear. Where's Eliza?"

"Oh, she's out playing with the children from down street. We won't see her until lunchtime now. I'll take Ma a cup of tea up, Betsy said she felt feverish last night."

Joseph picked up the denatured alcohol from the shelf, and some shellac natural wax flakes. He began to mix the two. Lately, Joseph had taken to dealing mostly with the French polishing side of the business, whilst Albert created the cabinets. Without discussion, or any verbalisation, they both knew that Joseph's arm was struggling with heavy work now. The French polishing could be executed with one strong arm to do the work, and one as a prop, so a silent system of managing the workload had perceptively evolved between them, and Joseph's ego was delicately spared.

"You and Ma are quiet this morning Pa, did you have a good ni......" Albert's initiation of their conversation was cut short by a piercing scream emanating from inside the house, somehow unmuffled by the doors between them. They dropped everything and ran into the house and up the stairs. On the first landing they caught up with Lottie and little Bertie, and followed them into Kate's bedroom. Hannah was sitting on Kate's bed, staring into space, the drooping teacup, now relieved of its contents, hung by its handle from her index finger. Lottie handed a bemused little Bertie to Albert, and was immediately at Hannah's feet trying to roll Kate over to face her.

"It's no good Lottie dear, she's gone. Looks like she fell trying to get the pot from under the bed. Something looks broken, see her leg is twisted, and she's so cold. Oh, poor Ma, poor Ma." She looked round at her husband, "Joseph we should have looked in on her last night, we knew she wasn't well, we were so wrapped up in Henry's news. Oh, poor Ma." Hannah's chin fell onto her chest and silent tears rained into the cup and onto the stranded tea leaves.

Joseph stepped forwards, "Albert, go and get Edward, please."

He tenderly rubbed Hannah's back. He felt for his wife's grief for her mother, but he too felt wretched. This woman had also been as much a mother to him since they came to this northern seaside town she had loved so much.

"Hannah my dear, why don't you go for a lie down. It's been a difficult few days for you. Betsy, Annie and Lottie will go and relieve Mrs Hudson and Jane upstairs with the children. They've both been very good to us all in our sadness." He shared a knowing look with Betsy and turned into the parlour. He sat down at his secretaire. Betsy had told him about Kate's letter the evening after she had died, but Joseph felt he could not read it until she was gone from their house. There seemed something disrespectful about reading her last words in the same room as her body. He would have felt she was watching him from her casket in the centre of the parlour. Now he looked at his name, sloppily scrawled uncharacteristically by her hand across the folded piece of paper. He felt an overwhelming sadness, and wondered when she had begun to struggle, why had she got old so subtly under their very noses, undetected by them all. He unfolded the paper and began to read.

To my dear son-in-law Joseph,

I think before either of us departs this life, one of us should tell you the truth about many things. By 'us' I refer to myself and my half brother, Charles Ferguson.

I know this will come as a shock to you, it's not something that I have ever divulged to anyone. I have three revelations to make to you regarding the dishonour of the Ferguson men. The first sadly, involves my mother. She was only sixteen years old when she was taken advantage of as a kitchen maid at Bramble House by Charles' father, William Ferguson. In return however, my mother was well looked after, and as a child I wanted for nothing.

Secondly, Charles had a similar reputation as a young man. Indeed one of his conquests was a childhood friend of mine, Emily. He put her in the family way, and sadly both she and the baby died in childbirth. Thus began my own Jacob's fear of procreation and its possible consequences.

Henry and Hannah my dear Joseph, are cousins, albeit sharing only one grandparent.

Charles has always been courteous to me over the years, and undeniably was generous on many occassions, in recognition of our connection.

This all changed for me however, the night Lizzibeth died, and this final truth must now be passed to you, Joseph, to deal with as you choose.

Lizzibeth was absolutely sure that Betsy was Henry's child. She confided that she had been in love with Henry, and not you as everyone suspected, for years. She knew she could not have him, but she snatched some memories from him one night on the fire monument before he was gone from her life for good as she knew one day he surely would. She knew also, she may have to suffer the consequences of that love, but even that, she embraced. She was ignorant, as were we all at that time, to Henry's affliction. She was also not to know how cholera would play its part in her fate.

That night, Joseph, when you all returned from the town, and Henry and Lizzibeth were exposed, she intended to sleep in the stables and sneak away at first light. Her dismissal by Mrs Brookes and Mr Simms had been observed by Charles. I'm so sad to say that he followed her to the stables that night, and took advantage of her position and vulnerability. In a distressed state, she decided to return home immediately. This was when Jacob heard her sobbing as she passed our yard and he comforted her regarding her dismissal, gave her a drink, and offered her the fireside chair for the night. As you know, she had gone by the morning.

In the light of Henry's affliction Joseph, it can only be Charles who is Betsy's father. Not Henry, not you, as you knew only too well, and certainly not Jacob, as I know you suspected.

Betsy and Henry are therefore half brother and sister. Hannah has admirably, as I'm sure you'll agree, mothered her young cousin.

Little wonder Joseph, that Charles wanted Betsy out of the way of suspicious minds and loose tongues. Especially when his own wife commented on her similarity to their daughter Charlotte. His generosity in supporting our move from Dorset was founded in totally selfish motives. As was his purchase of the South Cliff house and the order for endless furniture to keep you busy up here after your mother's illness. He could not risk you returning when he knew Betsy had the Ferguson appearance. Little wonder too, that she also resembled your wife, my daughter.

Sadly Joseph, Henry too has this dishonourable streak. Ask your sons if you don't believe that. He tried to compromise both of their young wives prior to their connection to the family. It would be very naïve to imagine they are the only ones. The silver lining here (as Betsy would say) is that this father to son trait now dies with Henry. God, in his perceptibly cruel but infinite wisdom, has ensured he cannot pass it on.

These facts my dear Joseph have both angered and yet strangely consoled and sustained me over the years. Rightly or wrongly I have kept them secret, but I have no desire to take them to my grave. Do with them as you will Joseph, the secret is now yours to keep.In all other regards, Joseph, the Ferguson's are good people, you must hold on to that, for all your family have their blood coursing through their veins.

Thank you for being everything Jacob and I could have wished for in a son-in-law, Joseph. Jacob as you know was a true gentleman,

I thought he was alone in this, but your father has instilled the same respect for womankind in you, and I witness you in turn bestowing this on your sons. You are a credit to your parents Joseph Elliot, and to me.
As you will only be reading this if I am gone, please continue to look after our beloved daughter Hannah for both of us.
God Bless You

Kate

Joseph sat at his desk for many hours, the light of the day had faded on the page. His eyes were sore from his constant attention. Who would benefit from this? He sent skywards an apology to Jacob, how could he have doubted him. He would be repentant for his guilt over his thoughts for the rest of his days. He had even confided that suspicion to Henry. He shivered at the thought.

Hannah, Betsy, Henry, what should they be told, if anything? His thoughts juggled the consequences of each knowing any part of this truth. One thing was for sure, none should know all there was to know, therefore the letter must not be shared. He replaced it in his secretaire. Hannah knew the secret compartment, but she did not know of the letter's existence, so she would never look. He knew both Hannah and Betsy would prefer himself to be Betsy's father, so where was the harm in that. He could now justify ensuring this belief was encouraged and sustained.

Henry would require an explanation for him to atone his father's will in his own mind, so he would need to offer him something. The thought of Henry now angered him, yet somehow there was no surprise, he had long suspected Henry had become quite experienced with the ladies during his time in the army. Joseph had long suspected that Henry did not have the loving marriage he and Hannah had so enjoyed over these many years. Amelia had appeared increasingly cold, and excessively vain. He had suspected that Henry's circumstances had suited her well in preserving her youthful figure. Surely now though, Henry's increasing infirmity must have curtailed any such dishonourable activities.

He considered the implications of Kate's first two revelations being exposed, and decided the only victims of such an action would be Charles Ferguson and his father William. Neither of whom could suffer any consequence now.

It should give Henry enough information to appease his curiosity.

Yes he would disclose only the first part of Kate's letter to Hannah and Betsy, and he would write to Henry explaining the same. Now he could justify considering himself Betsy's father, and convincing Betsy once and for all of the very same.

The actual truth was too awful to contemplate, not only for himself and Betsy, but, with a physical shudder, also for his poor dear Lizzibeth.

"Eliza, come in here this minute." Eliza lowered to the floor the fishing rope she was twirling with another girl as a third skipped. She shrugged her shoulders at her friends and followed Betsy into the house.

"What is it Betsy?"

"Where are your shoes?" Eliza looked down at her feet, black from the street.

"Oh, that. Betsy, none of my friends have shoes, or if they do they have to save them for school and aren't allowed to play in them. If I keep mine on then it looks like I'm showing off."

"Then perhaps you need to change your friends young lady, Granma would be turning in her grave, playing in bare feet indeed!"

"But the weather's warm now outside, it isn't as if it's wet. My shoes are just there in Bertie's tin trolley look, I haven't lost them. I won't get cold." Eliza looked appealingly at her older sister, but saw no softening of her demeanour. She decided to change the subject. "Anyway I'm glad Granma died when she did."

"Eliza, what a thing to say, why in heaven's name are you glad."

"Well for one thing, she got to have her Christmas dinner with Jesus didn't she? And another thing, Miss Briggs is older than Granma was, and she's going funny now, I wouldn't have wanted that to happen to Granma."

"Yes I'm sure Granma enjoyed her Christmas Goose with Jesus this year Eliza. But what do you mean about Miss Briggs going funny dear?"

"Well Micky overheard in the butcher's shop, that Mrs Robinson had told the butcher that Miss Briggs had shouted at Mr Robinson in the street. She had screamed at him that she wasn't letting him have his way with her anymore, and he would have to find someone else. That sounds funny to me, Betsy, even though Mrs Robinson never stops talking, I can't imagine that Mr Robinson would turn to Miss Briggs for favours!"

"Eliza! That's enough." Betsy then spoke softly, "Oh dear me Eliza, that does sound like she's a little confused, she's getting on for ninety though now I think, that's a grand old age to reach. I must go and see if she needs any help. But it doesn't happen to everyone as they get older, Eliza. Granma would have been fine if she hadn't got sick and then fallen. Now, come on upstairs, you can help Ma and me turn the sheets, after all, 'many hands make light work'. Then, if you want to go back out to play after that, put your shoes on young lady!"

Chapter 27

Scarborough, April 1889 - August 1890

Edward twiddled nervously with his pocket watch and looked anxiously behind him. Peter Robinson was seated beside him in the front right hand pew of St Mary's Parish Church. Edward shuffled uncomfortably on the stark wooden seat.

The austerity of these basic wooden pews, cold stone floor and pillars, and the simple white alabaster walls in the church, were crucial in insisting the eyes of the congregation rested solely on the splendour and majesty of the stained glass windows. In raising the eyes to absorb these magnificent works of art, it was difficult not also to be awestruck by the grandeur and intricacies of the ornate ceiling.

Today, the church was bathed in spring sunshine, and the chill of the stone was visually warmed by the matrices of light glittering through the glowing coloured glass, illuminating and uplifting the otherwise solemn interior.

Such gravity was subversively created by the necessity to tread on, and be seated amongst, the numerous vaults of mortal remains from many previous generations of eminently notable Scarborians.

"You'll be fine Edward, really, there's nothing to it. The first ten years are the worst!" Peter whispered blithely as he slapped him good naturedly between his shoulder blades. Edward forced a smile in thankful, but distracted return. In equally hushed tones he then replied,

"I'm not worried about marrying Betsy, Peter, I just rather hoped Mother would have the courtesy to make an appearance." Peter nodded empathically.

"I do understand Edward, but you know in your heart she won't come. It's not only the desertion she perceives in your taking a wife, let alone one as 'lowly' as Betsy; but also your disloyalty in associating with us. I feel so much for Beatrice. She has sadly lost hope that one day her mother will reconcile with us enough, to at least entertain her grandchildren." Edward looked up at his brother-in law.

"You mustn't blame yourself Peter. You and Beatrice were made for each other. She had no right to try to come between you. It's her loss that she has no relationship with her only grandchildren." Then smiling, remembering yesterday's repartee, Edward continued, "They are an absolute delight Peter. We must make an effort to see more of you all, I should like them to get to know their Uncle Edward, and Aunt Betsy now of course too. It's funny that so many people have thought that little Abigail is so like Eliza. In fact Peter, both are very similar in stature and looks to mother don't you think? You sure you didn't sow any wild oats with whomever Eliza's mother may be, before you and Beatrice got together?" They stifled a quiet chortle in recognition of such absurdity, then paused their murmured conversation and allowed the organ music to pervade their own thoughts. The church gradually filled with many townspeople wishing to add their support and congratulations, to two of their most respected fellow citizens on this, their happy day. Edward then rekindled a previous topic, "You know Peter, why doesn't she think Betsy's good enough for me? I wouldn't even be here today if her father hadn't saved me from the sea when I was nine years old!"

"Ooh, I remember that night, we all got lectured about the dangers of the sea too. But I don't know why she feels like that. The same reason I wasn't good enough for Beatrice I suspect. Still aren't in fact, despite being a fine upstanding husband and laudable father for over thirteen years!" He chuckled quietly at his mock self acclaim and commendation.

Edward continued without acknowledging Peter's humour, "I also feel angry with myself that I have delayed my actions in this regard. Betsy wanting to sell her house on South Cliff brought me to my senses, not that I couldn't have bought something similar myself, but it gave us an easy solution in terms of leaving Mother. Once and for all."

"No matter. The catalyst is unimportant Edward. Sadly for your Mother, no-one would ever have been good enough for you, or Beatrice. It's her loss." He turned in his seat and winked at his three year old son seated behind him on his own delighted mother's knee. Jane Robinson was thrilled to have her elder son and his family back in the town, if only for a few days. Beatrice was helping Betsy back at the James Street house together with Kathy and Hannah. Abigail was with her as she and Eliza were to be Betsy's bridesmaids. Kathy's two young children Emily and Billy were already in church with Arthur, and seated with Thom and Albert's families. As though inspired by the sight of his own son, Peter continued, "Your father would have made her see sense you know, he would have loved Betsy, and me, joining your family. He had a lot of time for Joseph, and my father too. Beatrice takes comfort from that, she always felt closer to him, especially after little Henry died." He twiddled with his shirt cuffs, and shrugged them clear of his jacket sleeves. "You know Edward, I always felt something in your mother died with him and I fear it left her quite disturbed, indeed even lacking in some very human qualities."

At the mention of his father, Edward had lifted his head, and his gaze fixed on the crucifix on the altar. Peter was right, his father would have celebrated this day, and that was exactly what he himself intended to do. He had wasted enough time with Betsy, luckily she had waited patiently, and he had not lost her. The rest of their lives lay ahead of them, and he resolved to let his mother interfere no more. She would miss sharing in their happiness more than they would notice her absence today.

Edward's change in demeanour was simultaneously signalled by the changing tempo of the organ, heralding the arrival of his beloved bride.

"Betsy, what a shame Miss Briggs didn't live to see this day. So sad Betsy, but she's gone to a better place, without doubt, she'll have raised a glass to you both today. Together with Michael and my Alfred of course. You've looked absolutely radiant all day. Your dress is stunning, but somehow you've had such an inner glow, you would've looked wonderful in rags!"

"Thank you kindly Mrs Hudson, but I'm afraid my sister Kathy here must take much of the credit, she's made such a creation in a very short time. The silk is so beautiful though. I got it from the retail silk merchants in Newborough, you know George Dale Smith's." Jane Robinson was feeling the quality of the material,

"Oh I know where you mean, Betsy, it often has some things out on the pavement to try to tempt you in." She broke off to guern an impressed expression, "very high class indeed. When it's dark you know, the shop window is lit with those new electroliers."

The group of ladies surrounding Betsy all exchanged meaningful enthralled glances between themselves. They had excitedly crowded around her as she was about to go and change into something from her trousseau. They had enjoyed a small luncheon party at the St Nicholas Hotel following their wedding ceremony, with Beatrice accompanying a lot of the proceedings on a splendid grand piano forte. For one piece, that had been familiar to them both as children, she had happily played a complicated and impressive duet with the bride, to much rapturous applause from their audience. The sisters-in-law finally at piece with each other's proficiency.

Kathy stepped forwards,

"Come on Betsy, Edward is watching the time, your train is due to leave in less than an hour, and you still have to change!

The treasures of the ancient city of York await you." Betsy warmly hugged Mrs Hudson thanking her for everything, "I'll come and see you when we get back."

"If I'm spared, Betsy dear, if I'm spared." The others locked eye contact in amused acknowledgement of Mrs Hudson's somehow, cheery yet predictably, persistent pessimism.

Betsy excitedly picked up her swathes of ivory silk and swished towards the staircase and her future life with Edward as Dr and Mrs Hetherington, residents of the exclusive Prince of Wales Terrace, South Cliff.

"Look, Eliza, there he is, that's Prince Albert Victor, the Duke of Clarence, there, just alighting from the carriage now." Hannah was leaning in towards her daughter to enable her to follow the line of her arm pointing to the Queen's grandson. He was visiting the town to open the new Royal Albert Drive, sweeping the coastal line of the north bay. They were standing high on Queen's Parade with a good view overlooking the proceedings.

"Can't we go down there Ma, we would be able to see him better."

"Oh, Eliza you can run down if you like, but I'll just sit down on that seat over by the Albion Hotel. It's the walking back up the hill that would finish me off. I used to be able to do it pushing your perambulator, but not now, your Ma's getting old you know." Hannah tweaked her daughter's pigtail in response to her look of concern. Eliza at fourteen was a delicate, pretty child, of slight, even precarious build, different to Betsy's rounded figure, and Kathy's solid, if slender frame. "Go on with you, if you're anything like your sister Kathy, you'll probably get him to smile at you! If you don't come straight back up, I'll see you back home in time for tea."

Hannah ambled to the wooden seat outside the Hotel, and settled herself. The afternoon sun was hot and she could feel the heat through her bonnet. She wished she had brought a parasol with her. When she was younger, she had hated the freckles the sun deposited on her fair skin as well as the fading of her brows and lashes. These days she didn't worry too much about any damage to her appearance. Hair, skin and figure were seasoned well with time, but she saw no point in courting discomfort. Age needed no assistance there. Hannah was beginning to suffer with rheumatics, and she needed to rest her weary limbs often throughout the day.

Looking across the bay, she couldn't control the smile lifting the edges of her full mouth, for the view was indeed breathtaking.

Multicoloured gems bounced on the sea where the gentle breeze disturbed and ruffled its surface in the sunshine. The horizon was a clear straight line as though drawn with a rule between the two differing shades of bright heavenly cerulean. The beach appeared from this distance as a large sweep of golden cinder toffee, deserted as though newly created. The activity on the new roadway, although the cause of the virginal sand, was not visible from her position. A juncture in the proceedings had hushed the babble of the gathering, and Hannah felt that life could not appear more idyllic than it was at this moment.

She considered the changes they had witnessed in the years since their arrival in this town. Only this year had Falsgrave Village finally become joined with Scarborough town itself. There had been much publicity about the advantages of the town's growth, permanent residents had now tipped the count of eighteen thousand. Hannah had reminisced with Joseph over the many Sundays when they had walked through the countryside to the Village. Then it had consisted only of quaint cottages, and they used to treat the children to strawberries from the gardens on Mount Park Road. Yes, thirty three years had seen many changes here, but it had also retained its appeal and beauty, today's view assured her of that.

She, like many others though, vehemently disagreed with the impending demolition of Newborough Bar. She agreed with Joseph that it contributed to the charm of the old town, the last of the town's defences. Built to keep out unwelcome invaders. It now seemed ironic to demolish it on account of it being hazardous to the increasing traffic from seasonal invaders, welcome or otherwise.

Hannah brought herself back to the present, and realised that Eliza was obviously not returning imminently. She straightened her creaking body, and moved off in the direction of home. She considered the company Eliza was keeping and felt a tinge of sadness, but she would not allow herself to interfere, Micky was a good lad. Who was she to say he wasn't good enough for Eliza? Indeed, who was Eliza? She certainly did not want to risk any rift in the way Mary Hetherington had done by thinking along those lines.

As she approached Castle Road, she spotted a horse drawn omnibus, manoeuvring for its return journey to the Esplanade. She thought of Betsy at home on her own awaiting her confinement, no doubt passing the time on her magnificent piano Edward had bought for her as a wedding gift. She decided to visit her. She opened her purse to ensure she had enough coins, and forced her aching hips to speed towards the omnibus.

As Hannah walked slowly along the Esplanade, she passed two ladies with parasols exercising in the sea air. She pulled her shawl around her, smiling to acknowledge their presence. She was a smart lady herself, but had not dressed up especially this morning, nor had she changed when agreeing to accompany Eliza to the opening ceremony of the Royal Albert Drive this afternoon. She knew she did not look her best. Dismissing any feelings of self consciousness, after all she was of the Dorset Ferguson stock, she lifted her chin with a demure smile, and continued on her way. She considered how proud Lizzibeth would be of her daughter, an admired nurse in her own right, married to a revered local doctor, and living in a splendid, respectable residence in an exclusive area of town.

Hannah paused at the railings and took in the view. It was

quieter than usual on this south side of the promontory; presumably most of the townsfolk were on the north side for the celebrations this afternoon. A few gentlemen were chatting and smoking pipes on the rooftop of Sir Joseph Paxton's observation tower on the Spa complex. Directly beneath her, there were a few parasols moving slowly and aimlessly as though the exclusive puppetry of the sun. Looking across the south bay, Hannah focused on the old town. The harsh contrast was never more evident to her than from this vantage point. Her near view displayed the elegance and affluence of the Spa and its wealthy visitors; her distance vision, sharp as ever despite her advancing age, proffered the humble dwellings snuggled beneath the castle. Here lived the fishing families, eking out meagre livings in the towns oldest, most unpredictable and sometimes tragic industry. With a touch of sadness over the unfairness within humanity, Hannah turned down into Prince of Wales Terrace towards its elegant residences.

She watched as a very elegant cab pulled up sharply outside Betsy's house, the horse was immaculately groomed, the brass-work and lanterns shone in the glint of the sun. The top-hatted coachman carried an excessively long whip, and appeared very grand in his responsibility. Even before the cab had halted, a man leapt out and ran up the entrance steps to Betsy's house. Hannah realised it was Edward. Perhaps she should not disturb them. If Edward had taken some time away from work to be with her, they certainly would not welcome her presence. Abruptly, Hannah registered the urgency of Edward's entrance to the house, and panic welled up inside her. Betsy. Was something wrong? She noticed a small boy running back up the road. The coachman flipped him a coin. Hannah painlessly ran towards the cab, "Mrs Hetherington? Is she alright?" The cab driver doffed his hat at Hannah, "Not sure Missus, just had to get the doctor back here quick as possible, message from this little lad 'ere." She did not wait for his full reply, but was up the steps and rapping on the front door as though time had rewound, and inexplicably rejuvenated her body.

* * *

When Hannah eventually walked back into their James Street house that night, Joseph was immediately there to greet her. She had sent a messenger ahead earlier to explain to the family what had happened.

"She's going to be fine Joseph. The ordeal was awful for her; she was so much further on this time. To go through that, with no baby at the end was heart breaking, Joseph. The baby didn't have a chance; it was already blue when it was born. And so small. I had dared to hope, I remember the Duke of Clarence himself had been born two months early too, and he had no problems." She faltered in her narration to allow Joseph to dab her lone tear from her right cheek with his handkerchief. She sniffed and then continued, "Betsy could not have had better care than Edward gave her if she had been the Queen herself. But it was not to be. Poor Betsy, I could not help but think back to the night of her own birth Joseph, and how much poorer our lives would have been if she herself had not survived that night. And poor Edward, how helpless he felt. Life is so unfair Joseph." Joseph held his wife's hands, soothing them with his thumbs.

"You're right Hannah, just as life improves. Diphtheria can now be prevented by vaccine; unacceptable sanitation is no longer a threat to life; education for all children is not only free now, but also compulsory; our poor daughter is not able to bring a child into this safer, more acceptable world. Unfair indeed. Does Edward have any idea why this has happened twice now Hannah? It isn't usual is it?"

"No it isn't usual, Joseph. He doesn't understand it either." She shook her head in puzzled dismay. "Poor Albert and Lottie don't seem to be having any luck with increasing their family either. Lottie was telling me yesterday that nothing seems to be happening for them, and they would love a brother or sister for little Bertie. It's my suspicion that when Lottie was so poorly with a fever immediately after his arrival, she may have had some damage, they may never have any more you know Joseph." She busied herself tidying the scullery shelves to distract her traumatized thoughts. "But we'll see, if it's God's will, they may yet be blessed further. It seems to me that most of our grandchildren may be in Dorset. Kathy's twins this year have equaled the Scarborough total of Thom's three plus Bertie." They smiled at each other and Joseph kissed his wife's forehead.

"We've still done our fair share of swelling the population quite significantly you know, Hannah. Counting Betsy, and Eliza, the Elliot marriage with a little help from our daughters and sons in law, has produced, so far, a total of thirteen extra citizens!"

Chapter 28

Scarborough, January 1892 - October 1894

The mood was sombre as the Westborough Methodist Church poured out its congregation this January Sunday morning. The townspeople had come together on mass, swelling the usual Sunday worshippers to pray for the soul of the recently departed Duke of Clarence, and to share in the grief of both the Queen and her country. The town had felt it had a special alliance with this member of the Royal family on account of his recent visit, but the influenza epidemic had robbed the country of this popular heir apparent.

As Hannah emerged with Eliza around one of the imposing pillars, she found herself face to face with Mary Hetherington.

"Mary, how lovely to see you out and about. How are you?"

"I'm fine thank you Hannah, and you?" Hannah had continued to attend the Methodist Chapel despite her older children preferring the Parish Church of St Mary's. The men in particular agreed with Joseph regarding the unnecessary abstinence of liqueur in the Wesleyan movement.

"Very well, thank you, getting old you know and creaking and groaning a little, but generally well. You never seem to look any older Mary. You look really well."

"Good breeding Hannah is the key, my mother also retained her youthfulness until the day she died." They moved to one side to allow their fellow worshippers to pass to one side of them. "Is this the foundling baby? Quite the young woman now isn't she. I hope she is not going to bring any shame on your household, you really have no idea of her breeding you know!"

Shocked, Hannah glanced round at Eliza, taking in her daughter's stunned expression, she rounded on Mary,

"Mary, how could you be so thoughtless and insensitive." For the second time in her motherhood, she found herself jumping to the defence of the children of others. She turned back to Eliza, for once her younger daughter had remained speechless. Her wide eyes and open mouth illustrated her total astonishment.

"Eliza, a foundling just mea...."

"Ma, I'm well aware of what a foundling is, I asked Betsy years ago!" She glowered at Mary Hetherington, then turned and ran down the church steps, straight to Sandside and the arms of a certain fisherman's son, Hannah suspected.

"Oh dear, Hannah, looks like someone has not been honest with the little thing!"

"Mary, before you say anything else, I feel I should point a few facts out to you about breeding. It has obviously escaped your notice, but that could be partly because you will not entertain your only daughter and her family, but your Grand-daughter Abigail is the image of Eliza. Indeed both girls have the countenance of yourself as a younger woman don't you think? Eliza was found one night when all of our children were out and about, and all could easily know more about her than we do. The possibility of her being a grandchild of ours was my motive for giving her a home. Ask yourself Mary, what's your motive for your cruel maliciousness? For as the years have gone by, I'm convinced, that whether or not she's bred from our stock, shame or not, she's most certainly from yours!"

Leaving a startled and shocked Mary on the steps of the first tier of this magnificent edifice, Hannah swept away with her nose in the air as though she had the joints of a twenty year old.

Eliza paused at the top of Blands Cliff having run down Westborough and Newborough without stopping. She caught her breath at the street lamp, and considered how different everything looked in the winter months. Even Naomi the palmist and character reader's premises were shuttered; and the street itself, normally buzzing with buxom women gossiping whilst sweeping their shop-front doorsteps, was deserted. Recovering her composure, she continued down the steep hill towards the sea.

Emerging onto the seafront, she scanned the sands for her soul mate. The dreary day made her task more difficult. All colours were muted and merged. The dark grey sky blended into monotone with the angry sea, the golden summer sand had turned to beige and the boats and people appeared as smudges on this dull canvas.

"Micky, Micky." Eliza ran across Foreshore road and onto the beach where she could see a group of young men propped around an upturned boat and cowering into their coats against the bitter cold from the chilling north sea. They were repairing their fishing nets. Young Micky Walker looked up in surprise, he laid down his nets and hurried across the hard cold sand to meet her.

"What is it Eliza, I thought you were going to church this morning coz of the Prince?" He realised Eliza was not going to stop running, so he opened his arms to halt her. She fell into his muscular shoulder, sobbing. "Eliza, don't take on so, what is it. Tell me what's happened, surely this is not all for the Prince?"

As Eliza calmed herself, she spluttered her encounter with her mother's friend.

"But Eliza, we did try to tell you about this a few years ago, but you wouldn't believe it. Most people knew, you can't suddenly appear with a baby without people knowing there has to be a story."

"But I never felt any different, I should have sensed that I didn't belong and I didn't Micky, I didn't! Where do I belong?"

"There there. What does it matter now? It just goes to show what a good job the Elliots have made of bringing you up Eliza that you never knew. You don't take a child into your home if you are not going to treat them the same as your own. You're their's now. I bet they've even forgotten that you're not!" He chuckled at this, trying to alleviate Eliza's distress. "Come on love, let's go back to mine and you can warm up, you're freezing." He turned and waved at his fellow workers, and putting a loving arm daringly around her shoulder, he guided her hurriedly back across Foreshore road towards the old town.

Just before they reached his family's house, Eliza stopped and turned to him. "Do you really think they think of me as their own? Who do you think I do belong to? I know sometimes when Kathy was being quite awkward, Joseph used to joke about her being too wayward to be his and said he blamed the milkman. He always winked at Ma when he said it so that everyone knew it was in jest, but do you think it's me that belongs to the milkman?"

Micky threw back his head and laughed aloud. Her face showed bewilderment and he realised this was no laughing matter to Eliza. He turned to her and lifted her chin to look at him, then pulling her face to his, he seriously and tenderly added,

"You are most definitely not the milkman's Eliza. I think you most likely belonged to a very well brought up young lady who transgressed with an unsuitable gentleman, and could not own up to her family. You can tell by your breeding." He smiled as he breathed the words gently into the fine cold curls skimming her ear and tamed by her bonnet. Eliza turned her face to meet his, and their lips brushed as they had many times before. This time Eliza did not tease him and bolt away, but held their connection, sanctioning this attention. The seconds stretched to minutes, their passion awoke and rose between them, Micky backed her up to lean on the wall of his house and they explored the pleasure of intimate kissing that had been so chaste until now. Suddenly they heard laughter coming from the inside of the house. Micky's parents had been to the local hostelry and were merry with their infusions. Their voices carried through the draughty window frame.

"Where's our Micky, Aggie?"

"I think he said he was repairing ropes Ma." Eliza and Micky stifled a chuckle as his sister replied.

"That's good," his Pa's voice could be heard, "as long as he's not with that foundling girl again, he's spending far too much time with her, she'll not be any good in this family, too frail to gut fish or be any good to us."

"You're right Freddy, have you seen her hands, never done a days work she hasn't. Airs above her station too, and yet, *she* could be from anywhere!"

"Ma, do you mind if I go out on Christmas day this year? I know you like us all to be at home, and I know Betsy wants to cook the Christmas dinner this year. I'll still be here for that, but you know how we went to the memorial for the men from the Evelyn and Maud disaster last week at St Mary's?" Hannah looked up from her darning and nodded in Eliza's direction to acknowledge her understanding, but was unable to reply as three pins projected from her clenched lips. "Well," Eliza continued. "There's going to be a fund-raising football match and tug of war on the beach on Christmas day between the fishermen and the firemen to raise money for their families. Micky and I knew the second and third hands really well, they were ages with Micky's two brothers. They both had families too." Hannah paused in her work and removed the pins from her mouth.

"I think that's a really nice idea, Eliza, perhaps we should all have a walk down and support them." Eliza looked surprised.

"Really Ma, would you do that? It should be fun too, they are all going to dress up to make it very festive despite the sad occasion. They say it may even become an annual event."

"Eliza, you appear to be very fond of Micky. It is commendable that you want to support him in his father's profession. We are your family, therefore we will support you."

"Thanks Ma." They had moved on a lot in the last year and a half since Eliza had discovered the truth surrounding her mysterious birth. She had been told as much as anyone else knew, and found it hard to blame her family in any way. They had already admitted they should have told her earlier, after that, there was not much else to be said. Eliza became open about her circumstances to anyone who asked, almost goading them to criticise her. She often jested that she could have regal connections. After all, the Prince of Wales himself had been a frequent visitor to the town, and this was her armour in defense of her shadowy beginnings.

Buoyed by her mother's encouragement today, Eliza continued. "You know Ma, did it matter that Thom didn't want to be a cabinet maker like Pa?"

Hannah looked up at her in surprise at the sudden change in topic.

"No more than it mattered to your Gramps that your Pa didn't want to be a coachman." Eliza looked shocked,

"I never thought about that Ma, why didn't Pa become a coachman?"

"Well, really, it was because he never got on too well with horses, and he loved working with wood. Why are you asking Eliza?"

"Micky hates fish Ma, he really doesn't want to spend his life catching them for other people to eat!" They laughed together at the absurdity of a fisherman not liking fish.

"Are you serious Eliza, what does his father think. Does he know what he would like to do instead?"

"It doesn't really matter what he would like to do, his father won't hear of him doing anything else. He's so unhappy though Ma."

"Then you just have to offer him all the support he needs to decide what he would like to do, and help him find the courage to act upon it."

"Thom is so lucky Ma isn't he. He's now starting to make a living doing what he loves, and it all started for him when he sold that first painting."

"Well he can't quite give up his stone masonry just yet, but he does seem to be getting quite a reputation for his work. Apparently there are quite a few painters coming north to see the picturesque fishing villages of this coast since Thom's painting of Staithes was exhibited in London. It does look a pretty place, and Thom says the people are so friendly and love to be painted. They'll stand posing for hours for a few coins."

"Eliza, I want to ask you something?"

She was walking along Foreshore Road with Micky Walker. She had just met him from on his return from a three day fishing trip, and he had escaped from his father and the rest of the crew for a few minutes. The season was well underway, the sun was high and hot, and the beach and pavements were alive and littered with street musicians, organ grinders, photographers, apple girls, and hurdy gurdy players. A rich tapestry of seaside sights, sounds and smells to stimulate the senses.

"Anything Micky, what do you want to know?"

"Will you marry me? Not now, I know we're too young, and none of our parents would consent. But if we wait until we are twenty one, then will you marry me?"

"Oh yes, Micky, of course I'll marry you." She jumped up and kissed him on his cheek. "But why won't our parents consent? I think mine would, I'm nearly eighteen." She hooked her arm through his, making him swap his jumper to hang over the other arm, then he lifted her hand to his lips.

"I don't think mine would Eliza, we'll just have to wait. You know my Pa thinks you aren't sturdy enough to make a good fisherman's wife, and I can't tell him yet that I'm not going to take over his boat."

They both had a lilt in their step as they ambled aimlessly

along the seafront content in their mutual devotion. They laughed together as Mr Bland shouting 'cockles alive alive 'o'! ', competed with Mrs Hick's 'any fish today!'

Without warning, a seagull swooped down and cheekily stole a fish from Mrs Hicks stall, she remonstrated with it as though it may reconsider its action.

Instead, it swooped again, this time to make a deposit instead of a collection, and the unfortunate target was Mickey's shirt. Eliza laughed so hard, she had tears rolling down her face.

"Oh, Micky." She spluttered, " Swap it for your jumper, and I'll take it home to wash for you. Isn't this just the best and most fun place ever to live? "

"Joseph, I can't believe you're mending that window today. Betsy spent many winters asking you to see to it when she was freezing with the draught. Then when Eliza moved into her room, she too has begged you to get rid of the cold air whistling through the gaps. Talk about the cobbler's children! Now you wait until a hot sunny day when there is no snow, wind or hail, to mend it. Indeed how will we know if it is mended?" Joseph was fixing a ladder up against the back wall of the house to enable him to reach the first floor rickety window. Hannah was taking in some washing from the line as she good naturedly chastised Joseph for his tardiness in house repairs.

"Hannah, if you had to go up a ladder outdoors, would you do it on a cold windy winters day, or on a nice sunny afternoon. Be sensible my good woman." He affectionately patted her bottom as she passed him with an arm load of washing, and she retorted,

"Be careful Joseph, we don't want to have to replace a whole window!"

Joseph made his way up the ladder to assess the tools he would need. He had already guessed from what he saw from the inside many months ago, that the outside beading needed replacing to give a better seal between the frame and the bricks.

At the top of the ladder, he peered at the structural defect, nodding to himself that he had guessed correctly, and he would need to cut and shape some new beading. He was about to descend, when his attention was caught by a fisherman's shirt on Eliza's bed. He leant further sideways to get a better view. Using his left hand against both the window and his face to shield the glare of the sun, he relied on his right hand to steady his position.

Shocked he had identified the garment quite correctly, he resolved to confront this matter later and turned to address his descent. He stared in total terror at the blood ferociously pumping out of his right forearm. He saw the broken glass fixed into the previous putty on the window sill. He had not felt the shard pierce his skin as he had leant onto it in his curiosity. Joseph recognised he had already lost a lot of blood, he was no stranger to this type of mistake, he knew he must get down the ladder quickly. He tried to hold the ladder to descend, but his fingers would not close around the rung, he let his right hand drop and tried to manage with his left hand, but the bricks and the window started to circle around him and he lost his hold. As blood loss deprived his consciousness, his feet slipped through the rung of the ladder and he somersaulted backwards to be caught abruptly upside down, his back abnormally arched and jammed by his legs brutally rammed between two rungs.

Hannah fidgeted nervously at his bedside, stroking Joseph's left hand with her own. Striped screens were pulled around the bed.

"Hannah. Where am I?" Hannah turned swiftly to look at her husband. Were those weak soft unsteady words really his?

"Oh Joseph, you're alright." She rose with difficulty from her low stool, "I must get the doctor, he wanted to know when you woke up." She disappeared from his view for a moment to tell the nurse on the ward that her husband was awake. On her return, she realised she had not answered his question, and added, "You're in the workhouse infirmary, it was the nearest place to bring you when you fell, do you remember falling?"

"I, I think so." Then as if everything was coming into focus in his head, "My arm, it had been pressing onto some glass, I hadn't felt it."

"No Joseph, that's what we assumed had happened. But then you had passed out with the loss of blood, and fell through the ladder. Albert and I managed to lower the ladder with you on it. We then got you here with the help of the horse drawn delivery van and boy from Stewart and Leeks bakers, you know, on Westborough next door to Eccles chemists." Joseph weakly nodded his acknowledgement of his Samaritans.

"What damage have I done, Hannah? Tell me." He paused as he waited for Hannah to think through the order of her answer. "Oh, I'm so sleepy."

"Of course you feel sleepy, Joseph. Most of your blood is all over the yard floor, you can't have much left in your body!" Hannah tried to smile her humorous reply to lessen her husband's angst. She sighed as Joseph slipped back into his slumber, grateful she had not been pushed further to enlighten him as to the extent of his injuries. She crept silently out from the screens. She must talk to Betsy and Edward now, about moving Joseph to their town hospital.

Sixteen years earlier it had been much extended from Mrs Wright's original building, and Edward had overseen much of the designs and alterations. During the last few years, it had taken more of a convalescent role within the town, and that would be a more appropriate place for Joseph to be, until he could come home at least.

"Ma, you really couldn't cope yet with Pa at home. Let him stay here a little longer."

"Betsy dear, he's getting very distressed, he needs to be back in his own surroundings. He knows his limits, really. And

Lottie and Eliza are there to help." Betsy looked anxiously at Edward.

"Do you think he should go home Edward? I'm worried that it'd be difficult to care for him properly without moving that leg. You know very well, he'll not allow Lottie or Eliza to help you, Ma. Besides you don't see much of Eliza these days, she is trying so hard to fit in with Micky's family. I admire her devotion to him, and I do believe she is becoming more sturdy with all the work she's doing with them, she looked almost buxom when she came to see Pa yesterday."

"Oh I know Betsy, but did you see her fingernails? She looks like a pauper."

"Rubbish Ma, she is still well dressed and well spoken, she will be a good influence on them all. She seems to get on very well with Mickey's sister doesn't she?"

"Yes, she does, Edith I think, that's who she stays over with when they've worked late, her brood is increasing at a rate of knots, I don't know how there's room for Eliza to sleep." Edward stepped forwards,

"Hmm, can we get back to the matter in hand, fond as I am of Eliza, it's your father who presently needs our attention. Now, he does need to be kept completely still until the leg is healed, otherwise the hip may never take his weight again." Hannah sighed deeply, how could she keep everyone happy?

"I understand Edward, really, but you know how your father-in-law is, he'll be happier at home, and the man in the next bed to him has a terrible cough, he's concerned he may have that added to his afflictions!"

"Well, your Ma is right about that Betsy dear, he may at least escape the germs of others on the ward if he were to go home, and we can go and help your Ma with him whenever we can." He had added to Hannah's defense, and in doing so, had voided Betsy's.

She knew now that she was defeated in this matter. Generous with her exasperated demeanour, she flounced out of the ward office.

Betsy had persuaded Edward to allow her to return to work. They had begun to accept they may never have children of their own following a further two, albeit much earlier miscarriages, and Betsy was bored and frustrated at home all day, knowing there was work to be done at the hospital. The final decision was made after Mrs Hudson's sudden passing last year, Edward conceded it would be good for Betsy to get out of the house and keep busy.

"Fine, I'll organise for a carriage and some porters with a trolley to carry Pa safely into the house. Ma, you go and get Albert to arrange a bed in the parlour!" Edward winked at his mother-in-law, and they followed her off the ward.

Joseph had in fact sustained a severe fracture of his left hip as he had been flicked backwards on the ladder. A jarring of his spine had left him with a degree of discomfort both in his back and down the length of his good leg. What worried him most was the injury to his right forearm. The wound was healing well. Edward had dressed it with lint soaked carbolic acid, and had used the new catgut to stitch the large gash rent by both the sharpness of the glass and the neglect of Joseph's deadened senses to warn of the advancing damage. What Edward had been unable to repair, was the severed nerves and tendons which had rendered Joseph's right hand entirely useless. Joseph had mused miserably, that the damage in Bramble lake over fifty years ago had finally caught up with him, and won.

He knew he would never be able to mould or stain wood again with only one working hand, let alone any unsteadiness on his feet. He had a lot of time in the hospital to consider what to do with the rest of his life.

Joseph was reading the newspaper propped in his bed in the parlour, when Hannah appeared with the post.

"How's Eliza this morning dear, any better?"

"She'll recover Joseph, she's eaten something this morning. She says she's had this ailment for some time and has not had time to rest or eat properly. Some motherly love and attention with some good home cooking and a break from fish will see to that!" This was not the time to share her worries with Joseph, he needed to concentrate on his own health, she could worry enough for the both of them. For indeed, Eliza's state of health was of grave concern to her, despite Edward's reassurances that in time, she would recover fully.

"That's good to hear, she certainly looked rough when she came home a couple of days ago. Micky looked quite frightened so she must've been very poorly."

"I think on top of everything, it was her monthly time, so her body just couldn't cope with everything."

"Hm, tell her to come and talk to me when she feels up to it, to cheer her old Pa."

"Of course Joseph." Hannah held out a letter to him, "A letter from Henry today, my dear. I did write and tell him about your accident, I knew he would want to know. We've not heard much from him since you told him about his father and grandfather. I still can't believe Ma told you all that, Joseph, and made you keep it to yourself, but it must've been quite difficult for Henry to accept, and come to terms with such news about his loved ones. I wonder if he's shared any of it with his sister. I'm sure he'll spare his mother any discredit of her husband."

"I'm sure you're right, Hannah dear. Is that a letter from Kathy too, what does she say?"

"Oh, you can read it, she just wishes she was up here to help take care of you."

"Rubbish, I'll be up and about in no time, just you wait and see. In fact, I keep thinking about old Jack, do you remember he had the shaking palsy, and my Ma nursed him in their parlour until he died. I need to get up soon, otherwise I shall die in this bed!" They both laughed, but both also knew it would entail enduring a few more weeks yet.

"Let's see what Henry has to say then." He began opening the letter, then paused as his thoughts continued, "Do you remember Hannah, I told you it was Jack's relative that came from a seaside town in Yorkshire. That was the first time I had ever heard of this place that became our happy destiny." Joseph let out a long sigh in his reminiscing, "I wonder if there's a time in your life my dear, when it's right to return to your roots?"

Chapter 29

Scarborough, May 1896 - September 1896

"Hannah, please tell me you will at least one day consider us moving back to Dorset? It's so difficult for me to be virtually a tea boy for Albert. He's doing all the work now, yet still feels I have to be on the books. We don't need the money, what with your Ma's annuity more than paying the rent, and we have our savings. I could be out of his way and he could take on an apprentice to actually be worth his wages."

Joseph and Hannah were walking back along Valley bridge from visiting Edward and Betsy. It was a cold yet sunny spring day, Hannah's favourite time of the year in this town. The weather was clement, the town had opened up its doors to the summer atmosphere and ambience, yet the season was not yet fully underway, enabling pleasant easy movement around the town. The days were longer and bedtimes could be later with more light to enjoy reading. A few more weeks, and holiday makers without a care in the world would abound, ambling around the town impeding residents in their daily chores.

The very hot weather could also bring as much discomfort from Hannah's rheumatics as the very cold, so she enjoyed the temporary relief brought by spring and autumn.

Joseph now empathised with her suffering, for his broken leg had left him with comparable problems around his own left hip. He walked well considering his injury, but needed a cane to support him if going any distance such as today. He had been warned that he could need to use a bath chair in time. He had joked that his broken hip could outlive him, for other than injury, fate had been kind in terms of general health, and he was an otherwise fit man for sixty one. Hannah had quipped, that a bath chair could be a good investment for them to share in the future.

Reaching the town side of the bridge, they headed for Westborough, Hannah had started to limp, and lean heavily on Joseph's arm. She indicated to the wooden seat.

"Can we sit down a while if you must talk Joseph." They ambled towards the wooden seat and eased themselves down, giving the obligatory expulsion of air as they lowered, so indicative of their age.

"There are many reasons Joseph why I cannot consider what you request. I know Charles Ferguson made it a very easy option for you, especially now your Pa has sadly passed away. You cannot alter that you weren't there with him Joseph, by returning now."

"Oh I know that Hannah, and it wouldn't have made any difference, Kathy said he had just passed in his sleep one night, only a few hours after she had visited him. That's the best way to leave this life, sleep away." Joseph laughed as though considering his own mortality. "He had a good life though, he loved his work as a coachman, and he lived to see all his children and grandchildren educated. That was his own personal regret, not to be properly educated to him was a human humiliation. I'm proud that he passed that value on to me, Hannah, our children too are all educated and wise." They both stared straight ahead, whilst in their own ways, they contemplated each of their children's successes with well deserved self indulgence of their reflected glory.

Joseph broke into their thoughts, "tell me then Hannah, what exactly are your reasons? You've said so often that you would love to go back. Especially with Kathy and Arthur having so many children now, baby Hannah makes five. Our spirited little Kathy appears to love motherhood."

Hannah smiled, "I know. Who would have thought it. Her whole world and demeanor changed when she met Arthur. He was the best thing for her. She would never have been happy with Johnny Robinson." She paused to recall some information, gossip amongst other things now took an effort to recount with any accuracy. She had blamed it on the change of life, but also wondered if the new pills she had been taking for her rheumatism could sometimes cloud her thoughts. "I believe he's settled in Leeds now you know. Jane was telling me. He has a lovely wife and things are going well for him with a big building company making the mass produced things you hate so much, Joseph."

"Ah well, all's well that ends well, as Betsy would say! But you still haven't answered my question!"

Hannah sighed deeply, she too would love them to end their days where they had begun, but how could they?

"Joseph, there's nothing I would like more. However, we have children to consider. They may be grown, but we're still parents, do we ever relinquish responsibility for them, or indeed should we?"

"Not if they need us, I agree. But do they still need us Hannah, really?"

Hannah looked at her husband, she knew she could never agree. But could she make him see that without worrying him too much.

"Joseph, let's see." She held out her left hand and pointed with her right index finger to her thumb, "Betsy, I do not have any concerns for her, she's well cared for now, and despite her childlessness which is undoubtedly sad, she has a good and fulfilling life." She paused as though punctuating Betsy before moving on to her index finger, and Thom. Before she could continue, Joseph pensively added,

"You're right about it being sad, Hannah, I can't imagine how empty our lives would have been without children. Edward once told me that he had requested investigations after the second and worst miscarriage. You know, when you were with her; and the problem the baby had was something called," he paused to ensure his pronunciation was correct, "erm, erythro-blas-tosis. I think that's right. It's to do with the blood, there's no explanation though, well not yet anyway, maybe one day. Edward did say they had been unlucky though, because when he has seen similar cases before, there is often a healthy first child. Even one would have been such a blessing for them both."

"No point dwelling on what might have been though Joseph." She continued her reasoning, "Now, Thom is also independent. He'll know when the time is right to give up his stone masonry to be a fulltime artist. Annie and he are solid in their family life, she works hard, and their three children are doing well." Her index finger moved along to Kathy's middle finger.

"Kathy, is obviously not in question as we would then be close to her, and her children, but she may not welcome it, she's been away from us now for so long." She paused on Albert's ring finger, running her forefinger up and down its length and circling her wedding band to gather her thoughts.

"Albert's a good carpenter Joseph, like his father. I have no worries about his ability to earn a good living for himself and his family, small though it is, and Bertie is a delight to them. However, I worry that they'd struggle to keep up the house on their own, and if they could not, then what about the workshop at the back of the house?"

"Do you think I wouldn't have thought of that? Actually I've discussed it with Albert. He understands that it's Kathy's turn to have us around, and also our 'pull' to Dorset. We've looked at the price of some yards to rent close by, and we could sustain that for him from the minimal rent money we take from Thom and Annie for the house in Belle Vue Street. They would then be able to rent a smaller house, indeed if it were to be just the three of them, they would prefer that. There would then be no need of the house in James Street at all." Hannah had studied her husband as he had described the perfect plan. As he finished, she very pointedly moved to hook her right index finger completely over Eliza, embracing it firmly.

"And what about Eliza, Joseph, have you completely forgotten her in your plans?"

A silence fell between them, Joseph knew Eliza was the problem for whom he had no solution. He would like to take her with them. He had not accepted her fraternizing with the fisher folk in the same way that Hannah had. But he felt that would not be a popular suggestion. He decided to make it anyway.

"Couldn't she come with us, it would be a new start for her."

"Joseph, you know she'll never leave Micky, that's unfair to expect her to consider it. She's also still very weak after her illness, Joseph. It seemed to take a lot out of her, I would worry so." A silence fell between them whilst each considered the options.

"So, Hannah, should Eliza recoup her strength and be settled in her personal life, we could consider moving?"

"I assume so Joseph, but that could be a long wait I fear. Come on, let's get ourselves back home, my bones are aching everywhere." Joseph rose to his feet relatively easily using a firm push from the arm of the wooden seat with his good arm. He straightened himself erect, with the same prolonged groaning sound he had made when lowering. Then he turned to offer assistance to Hannah. She found it increasingly difficult to get up from a chair, and often chose to rest in the dining chairs at home for ease of rising. They continued on their way, and turned down into Westborough.

"Look at Stewart and Leek's baker's Hannah, they're all outside having a photograph taken. What a picture, they all look very smart with their pristine white aprons and baker's hats. They've even got the delivery vans in the picture. I wonder what the occasion is?"

As Joseph and Hannah drew level with the shop on the opposite side of Westborough, they stopped behind the photographer to take in the scene. Thirteen staff were posed outside the shop, some in the doorway, some in the upstairs windows, with one even standing on the ridge above the bow window.

The delivery boys proudly stood beside their vans, boasting 'English and Foreign Confectioners', one hand on hip, one possessively on the van, as though it were the most important responsibility in the world.

Hannah suddenly gave a sharp intake of breath, Joseph looked round at her, "What is it Hannah?"

"Look up there, that's little Bertie with his friend from school being lifted out onto the ledge." Joseph peered against the spring sun,

"Well so it is, how did he get in on the act?" He looked at Hannah's anxious face and laughed, "Hannah, there are six men all around them, he's nine years old now, and having fun. Its only for a photograph, his friend must belong to the firm. I was doing all sorts at his age Hannah, don't take on so."

"Yes Joseph Elliot, at nine years old, you were under the water in a lake getting your ribs and nerves damaged!"

Laughing, Joseph replied,

"See what I mean, and I'm still here."

"Only just, Joseph Elliot, only just!"

Eliza was secreted nervously in the eerie duskiness of Quay Street. She had walked down Longwestgate and Tuthill, then cut down Custom House Steps hoping to meet Micky on her way, but she could not be sure he was coming directly from his home. Even in the early evening, there was little light between the high austere walls of these steps. She could feel her heart quicken anxiously until she reached the openness of Sandside, before making her way to Quay Street. She had been down this end of town earlier today when Hannah had sent her to Dumple Street for some of Mrs Robert's famous hot cakes and bacon, and a bladder of lard. That was when one of the young fisher lads gave her a message from Micky. He asked her to meet him there on the corner by the old timber house at eight o clock, as he had some news for her. She cowered between the front doorstep and the large bow window that reached almost to the ground, she wondered why anybody would want a window with thirty five panes in it. She had never seen who lived in this house, but in her childish fantasies she imagined Tiny Tim and Bob Cratchet ate their Christmas goose each year behind these candlelit panes. It was quiet despite the warm September, and easier to meet covertly. Since Eliza's illness, Micky's father was even more opposed to their union, judging her to be totally unsuitable for fisher work. They used to meet by the Butter Cross, in Princes Square, as did many other courting couples, but Mr Walker drank regularly close by, so that was no longer easy for them. She wasn't so sure about this as a new meeting place, it felt sinister in this light.

An unexpected rumbling took her by surprise, until she rationalized the approach of a coach and horses, she pressed herself hard against the wall of the house when she assessed the speed and proximity of its approach to be surely out of control. The clatter of its arrival peaked, then fell away as though it had passed safely and uneventfully by, missing her nose by a whisker. Eliza slowly let out her breath in relief that she had chosen to stand between the steps and the window thus protecting herself; that relief was followed swiftly by absolute bewilderment. She was visibly shaking when Micky appeared around the corner. She fell into his arms,

"Oh Micky, I was so scared, I thought I was going to be crushed." She sobbed into his shoulder.

"What by, my dear, what by?"

"A coach and horses was coming at me and went by so fast, Micky." She gasped for breath, "Only thing was, I saw no coach, or any horses. I just heard and felt it." Micky started to laugh, he looked around him as though he may still see some evidence.

"You must've seen the Quay street ghost, Eliza. Not many people have witnessed it, you're honoured." He held her away from him to look at her as he spoke. "I'm sorry Eliza, we won't meet here again. But neither will we have to. That coachman saves his appearances for very special occasions Eliza, and this is definitely a special day. I wanted to tell you that I have booked the register office for the week after your twenty first birthday this month. Then our families can say nothing about it. We'll both be twenty one."

"Joseph, where are we going? And what was so urgent that it couldn't have waited until I had finished black leading the fire. I'll have to start on the tea when we get back, and then I'll be working on it this evening and you know how you disapprove of me doing housework on an evening."

"For goodness sake, my good woman, will you please stop mithering away. Wait 'til you see what we are doing on Sunday afternoon. Come on keep up, my dear."

Joseph was striding out ahead of Hannah, and had turned onto Castle road, they crossed the junction with Dean Road, and pulled up the incline towards Victoria Road. Joseph slowed to allow Hannah to catch up and take his arm as they crossed Victoria Street and approached Vine Street. He led them over to the corner of Foxton Mews where there was a large advertisement.

'Horse drawn Charabanc rides to the Country, return fare 2 shillings per person.' Hannah paused as Joseph walked ahead and spoke to one of the men from the livery stables. She took in the lively atmosphere of the Mews, and wondered curiously if the visit to the coaches and horses was a part of Joseph's grieving for his father. She thought fondly of her father-in-law, not as Kathy had last described him, but as she herself remembered. A large muscular man. Dependable, much respected, and so at home in just such an environment as this.

A coachman walked across the yard, resplendent in his uniform. Smart black velvet collar to his red frock coat fastened with polished gilt buttons, a shiny top hat, black leather boots and white gloves. Many stable hands were busy buffing the coaches and horse brasses. The smell of horses pervaded with a pungent yet earthy aroma.

"There that's settled then Hannah. You and I are having a trip into the country on Sunday afternoon on one of these charabanc things. It's time we explored a little of this area. Before we leave it, eh? Who says I'm a skinflint now?" He playfully nudged Hannah, ever hopeful for his retirement dreams, yet knowing they were certainly no nearer being able to leave Eliza than ever.

"Well that'll certainly be a treat Joseph. I shall look forward to it, but I fear we will have a long time yet to enjoy this area." She paused as they set off back down Victoria Road. "I do understand Joseph, and all the more since Amelia's terrible riding accident in the new year. Poor Henry, he must be devastated at his loss, and I know it would help him if we were there, but our children must come first Joseph, you do understand?" Joseph squeezed her upper arm affectionately, and crumpled his face into the aged version of his dimpled smile, that had crept up on him in recent years, yet encompassed his emerald eyes in the same charm and appeal that Hannah had always found so endearing.

"Of course I do, my dear Hannah, of course I do. Now forget I mentioned it again, and let's enjoy our Sunday jaunt to Cloughton."

Chapter 30

Scarborough, June 1897 - September 1899

"Anyway Betsy, to cut short a very long story, he began to talk to us when we had a little stroll around the outside of the grounds of this big Hall at Ravenscar." Hannah and Betsy were walking down Eastborough towards the beach. "The Charabanc, stopped for quite a while for us to have a stroll in the sunshine. Oh, and did I mention the view of Scarborough from the road near Cloughton? It is spectacular Betsy, you can even see the castle." Hannah enjoyed the amazed look on Betsy's face at her narration of the world beyond their town. She continued, "Anyway, Joseph had recognized the name of the Hall as being the very same that he and Albert had made a very grand table for, many years earlier." Hannah glanced at Betsy to reassure her attention. Well, the gardener was clipping the outside of the hedge, Joseph was telling him all about his father being in service in a big house, and how our son-in-law is now a gardener at the same one in Dorset. The conversation went on to the inscription on his father's headstone showing how well respected he had been, and your Pa mentioned the actual name of the house." She paused to ensure Joseph and Eliza were still close behind them as they progressed towards the beach. "Did you ever read Kathy's letter that told us what was written on his headstone?"

As Betsy shook her head in bewilderment, Hannah continued, "Oh dear Betsy, it must've slipped this old mind of mine to tell you, it read, 'In beloved memory of Thomas Elliot, for thirty seven years a True and Faithful Servant and Loyal Head Coachman to Charles Ferguson of Bramble House'."

She turned her head to Betsy to punctuate the end of her quote with an impressed countenance, and to receive Betsy's own in response. "Well, that was when the gardener realized that he knew of the same house. It turned out that his Great Uncle was Jack, you know the head coachman before Gramps. Your Pa always talks about him because his Ma nursed him in their cottage until he died, of the Shaking Palsy, if I remember rightly."

"I remember Granny telling me about him when I was down in Dorset, Gramps must've thought a lot about him. But that's such a co-incidence. " Betsy looked at Hannah's tiring gait, "Are you struggling a bit Ma, here link my arm, that should help a bit. It's a shame they can't just make you two new hip joints isn't it? You'd be as right as ninepence in no time." Hannah laughed, "If only it were that simple Betsy!"

She paused for a moment, then remembered the reason she had begun her story. "Hmm, anyway Betsy, the gardener, he was amazed to hear of Charles Ferguson's generosity to you as Lizzibeth's daughter. His Grandmother – Jack's sister, stayed in touch with Mrs Brookes after she had left Dorset, you know, the housekeeper at Bramble House? Well she'd received a letter from Mrs Brookes, saying how angry Charles had been with Lizzibeth the night she had come back to the house with a very drunken Henry! He'd stormed after her, and when she'd been missing in London for those few months, Mrs Brookes' imagination had concluded that he had 'done for her'!" Hannah's eyes were wide as she awaited an astonished response from Betsy. She was not disappointed.

"Well, Ma, it does make his legacy totally inexplicable. Perhaps Lizzibeth totally charmed him, and convinced him the drunken behaviour had all been of Henry's doing!" They giggled acceptingly at this so obvious explanation, then tamed and melted their laughter into a warm greeting as Joseph and

Eliza arm in arm, caught them up at the junction with the seafront. Eliza tripped slightly on the board propped outside the souvenir shop welcoming the Admiral, Officers and Men of the Channel Fleet. They were due to stop by the town as they often did, sometimes with as many as twenty worships anchored in the bay.

They had been laughing about the fortune teller trying to coax Eliza into her parlour, she said she had something to tell her, 'her gentleman friend would soon 'pop' the question to her, and she wasn't to concern herself with the age difference!' Joseph and Eliza had burst into peals of laughter, and left the bewildered fortune teller 'tutting' on her doorstep.

"Well maybe you really are going to get a proposal soon Eliza, you never know." Betsy winked at her sister. Eliza was speechless and suitably coy.

"Come along now, let's get along Sandside to where the foundation stone is to be laid. Thom and Annie were going to come too, and Lottie with young Bertie." Hannah paused to remember another foundation stone many years before. "I just hope there are no keepsakes being buried at this ceremony, Thom has a habit of collecting them. I live in fear of the Westborough Chapel falling down and the discovery of the missing coins. Goodness knows where they are now."

"Still got them Ma." Thom and Annie appeared from behind them. They had begun to see a little more of them again since the children were older. Alice had a position in a local bakers shop, and William, or Billy as he was now often called, had recently begun an apprenticeship with Albert.

"Thom, lovely to see you. How are you all? Do you really still have them?"

"Yes, all of them, one of each denomination! Don't we Annie? My wife was guilty too remember Ma! We're all well thank you, and you?"

"Well, I never! Yes we're muddling through alright, Betsy was just saying I could do with new hips, but other than that!"

"Nothing wrong with your hips Ma, is there Pa?" He gave her

a playful pat on her rounded behind and winked at his father. "We have some news about little Joe though Pa, he's won the prize for Art for the whole school, and the prize is a complete new set of paints and brushes. As you can imagine, he's really thrilled. Of course he's been coming to Staithes painting with me for some time now, so he has quite a selection of paintings."

Thom and Annie basked in the plethora of expressions of congratulations that followed this announcement, with the swollen aplomb exclusive to many a proud parent.

"Oh look, here's Bertie with his Ma." Betsy held out her arms to greet her nephew and on his reluctant receipt of this embrace, she planted an enthusiastic kiss on his mortified forehead.

"Bertie, have you been climbing trees again, you've pulled a thread in your trousers. Can you see it Lottie, there, a stitch in time saves nine remember!"

Betsy looked around her as she saw her whole family stifling their amusement. "What's so funny?"

Hannah was the first to recover her composure, "don't tell me you don't realize when you are throwing all these sayings at us Betsy dear, it's much appreciated of course," she allowed herself then to smile, "but it's also very funny." Thom threw an arm around his sister's shoulder, "come on sis, we don't want to be late for this, 'the early bird catches the worm'!"

The Elliot's arrived at the huge gathering on the seafront just as the speeches were starting. Many townsfolk had come to watch the foundation stone being laid today. Partly on account of understanding its significance in linking the two bays of the town; but also because it had been heralded as a momentous enough occasion to be the chief feature that would mark Scarborough's own celebration of the Queen's remarkable Diamond Jubilee this month.

The ceremony itself whipped up enthusiasm for the very concept of the linking of the two bays by a Marine Drive, and the National Anthem concluded the proceedings, leaving the entire gathering with a buoyant sense of pride in both Queen and town.

"Eliza, wasn't that lovely? Did you see the actual stone? It was huge. Are you my sister-in-law now then?" Everyone turned to see an ungainly, tall, buxom, yet pretty girl coming towards them with an overloaded perambulator, two children hanging onto it's side, and another child on her hip.

Eliza covered her embarrassment by immediately making a fuss of the child being carried.

"Edith, how lovely to see you, and you too Charlie. Come and see Eliza." Micky's sister handed her charge gladly to Eliza, giving a groan of relief as she off-loaded him from her hip. Charlie gladly accepted this new attention.

"Eliza, look what I just found in my nose!" He proffered a slimy trail of nasal mucous dangling from his finger as though it was the most treasured and cherished of offerings for his favourite aunt. Eliza recoiled, not quite knowing how to politely refuse such a special gift.

Edith admonished Charlie, surreptitiously slapping his hand away from his face and wiping his finger with her shawl as she did so. She then entreated her other children to hush as she waited to be introduced to Eliza's family. Hannah tweaked the cheeks of the children whilst the other Elliots made their excuses about needing to be somewhere else, and moved away. She made an attempt to remember the children's names as she was introduced one by one. "You've been busy Edith, how have you managed to fit in having this many children? You must be exhausted!"

"Well these two 'ere are twins," she indicated the two young children on each side of the perambulator, "and the two little 'uns are twins too." Hannah looked at the babies in the perambulator, one girl and one boy, not yet sitting up, but seated between them was a toddler of perhaps one and a half to two years. The little boy in Eliza's arms looked not much older. Goodness, Hannah thought, perhaps she had been blessed in not readily conceiving children, this number of blessings was ridiculously sublime.

"And who's this little one Eliza?" Eliza had been singing and swaying Charlie, secure in her mother's distraction by Edith's many children.

"Oh this is Charles Ma, or Charlie as he's known. He's two years younger than the big twins." Eliza smiled at the two older children.

"Well I must say Edith, you have a lovely family. And they're all so well behaved, you must be very proud." As she spoke, Hannah stroked the soft skin on the left side of Charlie's face which made him shrug his left shoulder in reflex to its tickly sensation. She repeated it, laughing, and this time his reflex made him giggle as he shyly took refuge in Eliza's shoulder.

"Oh I am Mrs Elliot, I am, they're all very good." Hannah nodded, acknowledging Edith's answer as her hand, shaken off Charlie's face by his coyness, found itself tickling his ear. She stopped suddenly as she registered the feel of his lobe. A significant, and familiar indentation in the outer rim of its cartilage sent shivers through her spine. She had only known one other person with this defect. Henry Ferguson. Eliza's affection for this particular child was obvious. She smiled at her youngest daughter and her gaze swung from Eliza's azure eyes to the child's. She rummaged abstractedly in her purse.

"Well Eliza, you don't appear to have answered Edith's question. Are you her sister-in-law yet?" Eliza looked down at her feet, Edith pulled back the corners of her mouth horizontally, realizing she had made a complete faux pas.

"I'll take that as meaning yes then, Eliza. You stay here with Edith if you like, I'll start my slow walk home. Here, get the children some rock, they're all enchanting Edith, catch me up when you're ready Eliza." Eliza gazed at the generous confectionary money her mother had bestowed on them, and pulled an enthusiastic, excited expression to the children.

"Alright Ma, if you're sure."

"Joseph, Joseph, do you still want to move to Dorset?" Hannah had floated up Eastborough and along St Thomas Street towards home, quicker than she had moved in a long time.

"Well, yes I do Hannah, but I understand why we must wait. There's no rush, really." Hannah had removed and hung up her hat and was filling the pan purposefully with water as she spoke.

"We're not needed here Joseph. We can go with an easy mind. Eliza has been ill, but she'll get stronger I'm sure of it. She'll definitely marry Micky. She lacks confidence in herself, and is vulnerable on account of only seeing the best in everyone, but she'll be cared for. I'm now absolutely sure of that. I know who her parents are. You may make plans whenever you like. Dorset, and retirement are ours. We must write to Henry, and Kathy of course, I can't wait Joseph. We're going home."

Hannah had struggled up the front steps to Mary Hetherington's house in The Crescent. She looked around her at the semi circular sweep of imposing houses. Domestic servants abounded, scrubbing the doorsteps with yellow-stone lest the mark of an autumn footprint may blemish the whole magnificence. A coachman on his carriage patiently awaited his passenger, whilst the horse whinnied and nodded its head up and down as though chivvying the fare. A young boy scurried along the crescent to shovel the waste from a previous carriage into a barrow, no doubt to sell to local gardeners. She blinked hard, committing this view to memory. For before little Henry Hetherington's death, she had spent many a happy hour here with Mary. It had been so much a part of life in her early years in this town.

Pulling herself up to her diminishing full height, she rang the doorbell. The door opened slightly.

"I should like to speak with Mrs Mary Hetherington please."

"Wait here." Came the reply, Hannah pushed the door open.

"No I'm sorry I can't wait, Mrs Hetherington will want to see me, I know where to go."

Hannah pushed past the stunned housekeeper. She swept into

the drawing room where she could see over the back of an elegant antique chair, a silver pleat, immaculately pinned into position on the back of Mary's dainty head.

"Who is it Ruby?"

Hannah paused before speaking, silenced by shock at the frailty of this aged figure. All anger and bitterness dissipated with the sight that greeted her. She whispered,

"It's me Mary, Hannah Elliot." Mary's head spun round; she then composed herself as though this very head movement had caused her pain.

"What are you doing here? I don't receive visitors." Hannah came around to the front of Mary's vision, and carefully lowered herself with a ladylike grunt, into the chair opposite Mary. She surveyed the picture before her, an old lady, smartly dressed, although dated, Hannah could still make out a bustle at the back of Mary's dress and she smiled at her one time albeit incomprehensible adversary.

"Getting old, not a bed of roses is it Mary?" Mary gave a half smile in response as though Hannah's suffering had eased her own.

"Why are you here Hannah?" Mary's eyes fluttered to the floor as she spoke. Hannah had forgotten this trait of no direct eye contact that had always suggested dishonour, deceit and deviousness to her, especially latterly.

"Mary," she peered towards the open door of the drawing room and stopped, when a noise of a brush sweeping energetically in an adjacent room reassured her and she continued, "I once hinted to you that our foundling daughter, Eliza, was actually your grand-daughter through Beatrice." She looked for a reaction from Mary, who inclined her head to affirm that had been the case.

"I want you to know that I was absolutely wrong, Mary. And I apologise profusely. I trust you have never approached Beatrice with this. That would have been an inexcusably wretched situation, and I would have been completely to blame. They are a lovely family, not that Eliza is not also a delight, and has been our pleasure to raise, make no mistake. However, Peter has proved to be a wonderful husband, and father to their two adorable children, and Abigail is the absolute image of you, more so as she has grown. It's sad that Edward and Betsy have not been blessed with any children in their marriage. Did you know about the miscarriages being due to a blood condition that usually allows one healthy child?" Mary fiddled with the fringes of the bookmark she had placed in the middle of the leather bound volume on her knee, as though carefully formulating her reply.

"Hannah, I have neither opinion nor interest in Edward and his wife's procreation history, and I have not been in touch with my daughter since her unfortunate marriage into such a lowly family. So of course that regrettable matter has never arisen. However I am pleased you have come to your senses and at least had the decency to apologise. A grandchild of mine, a foundling? What a preposterous suggestion! I can't believe you seriously thought I would have taken any notice of such a scandalous notion Hannah." Hannah's initial sympathies with this woman now a shadow of her former self, a one time friend, mother of her beloved son-in-law, evaporated. It was as though the delivery of each syllable of Mary's final sentence dispatched all empathy.

"Mary, I'm apologizing for accusing Beatrice of being Eliza's real mother, and that is all, make no mistake." She straightened herself up from the chair, and made to take her leave, then paused and looked at Mary, "You know Mary, I feel so sad for you that you allowed dear little Henry Joseph's death to ruin the rest of your life. And that of dear John's. Thank goodness Beatrice and Edward are strong enough to not allow you to ruin their lives. Good day to you Mary. Joseph and I return to Dorset next week, you will not see us again. Thank you for your friendship when we first arrived here. We will never forget your dear husband, he was a wonderful man, and he would be so proud of his children. And his grandchildren, all three of them."

"Hannah, are you sure about this, it's not too late to change our minds you know." They were getting ready for bed the night before their departure, and Joseph was rubbing his eyes anxiously.

"I think it is Joseph. I'm not giving you back word now, not so soon before we leave. The new tenants move in the day after tomorrow. All our belongings are already on their way down to the cottage, and everyone is expecting us. No, I'm really looking forward to it. All the children say they'll visit, so it isn't as if we won't see them anymore. More than anything, Eliza and Micky seem to be quite settled living with the Walkers for now. She says his parents have accepted their marriage and treat her well." She put down her hair brush, "I'll never forgive her for not telling us about their wedding though, Joseph. She didn't need to keep it from us. She said she didn't think you really approved of Micky either." She eased herself onto their high bed and waited for his response.

"Well I expect she was right in a way. But I would never actually stand in the way of any of our children's happiness Hannah, surely she knew that?"

"I'm sure she did really, my dear."

"I know you think Betsy will look out for her, Hannah, but she also gets on so well with Lottie, that I think her and Albert will always watch over her too. She loves little Bertie so much, they have the same sense of humour. We must stop calling him 'little Bertie', he is quite the young man now."

She lay down beside her husband. "Hmm, I think he'll come and visit us soon, he so enjoys the company of his Dorset cousins. I'm sad though, that you won't get to see Henry's mother, Joseph, just two weeks too late. I never really knew her. She'd a good long life though, over eighty wasn't she? But at least we'll be there for Henry. You and Charlotte are all he has now, he really counts you as a brother you know."

"I know Hannah." Joseph turned to kiss his wife goodnight, "I didn't really know his Mama that well, but it's sad for Henry so soon after loosing his wife. Charlotte and her family all live at the house now, their son of course will inherit. But it's company for Henry too." Joseph rolled over to extinguish the oil lamp. "Kathy said in her letter that Benjamin was almost bald now, imagine that!" They indulged an immature giggle at such a vision.

"And Louiza has got very plump, Joseph, don't forget Kathy also said. I'm quite content about that, I won't seem quite so 'rounded' myself!" Joseph chuckled,

"It's wonderful that Rose has decided to retire too, maybe she would like to live with us in the cottage, I wouldn't mind Hannah, would you?" He continued after Hannah's concurrence, "Perhaps we'll find out the truth about what happened with that young man of hers. She shouldn't have remained a spinster, she was born to be a mother if anyone was."

"That's true. Good night Joseph. This town has given our lifetime a wonderful summer and autumn, but it will be good to spend the winter of our lives back where we spent the spring. I'm looking forward to going home Joseph. Good night my dear."

✳ ✳ ✳

"It doesn't seem five minutes since we were all down on Sandside to watch the foundation stone being laid for the Marine Drive, yet that's more than a year ago now Betsy. Ma and Pa were still here." Now we're here on the North Bay for yet another monstrosity.

"And where is that drive Eliza, no sign of it being finished for a long time yet. I've heard they've run out of money. Pa said from the beginning it would cost much more than the £70,000 they thought, it looks as though he was right. Imagine that sort of money? Pa'll have a sneaky smirk when he reads my letter telling him about the lack of progression!"

"I must write too Betsy, I just never seem to get time, I still get so tired sometimes. I want to be with Micky all the time, but I love coming out with you to have a break from his family, they're so different to ours. Micky isn't comfortable either. He really wants to get away. But until he can get into another line of work, what can we do. He can't look for work while he's so busy fishing."

They walked a little way down the hill through Clarence Gardens and towards Warwick's Tower. At over one hundred and fifty feet high and fifteen feet in width, it dominated the panorama of the North Bay. The observation car was thirty feet in diameter and able to accommodate two hundred people hauled to the top by four steel cables driven by a seventy five horse power steam engine. Eliza continued, still thinking about their life with the Walker's on East Sandgate.

"You know, when Micky's Pa eats, he sort of unhinges his jaw to fit as much food in as possible, then proceeds to chew with his mouth open so you can see it all going round and round. Ugh, it quite puts me off eating!" Betsy had started to giggle with the vision of Richard Walker's mouthful of food. Eliza prolonged the amusement by mimicking the action, and both ladies had to halt their progress to catch their breath from their laughter. Feeling disloyal, she added, "he's a very nice man really though, Betsy." Recovering, they proceeded slowly towards the Tower, then gasped in amazement as the observation carriage began to rise up into the air.

"Do you know what Eliza, when I was your age, I was so adamant that this sort of thing should not be built, blotting the beautiful natural landscape with ugly man made structures. Now, I don't have the energy or the inclination to complain. The town relies on visitors to bring in money. If these new spectacles attract the visitors, then so be it. Oh, did you see, it's such a shame, but the storm last week damaged the sails of the old windmill on Mill Street, beyond repair it's said?" Betsy paused to reassure Eliza's enlightenment. "Now there's a lovely old structure, man made I know, but at least it serves a useful purpose." She turned back to stare at the monstrosity that was 'progress'. "Well, you'll never get me up in it. What if that thing falls when you're up there?"

"Hmm, I don't suppose you would know much about it Betsy. It would be a swift end!" Quiet in their own thoughts about the trauma of such a demise, Eliza continued, "Why do you suppose Edward's mother died Betsy. Did she really just go to bed and refuse to get up until she died as you said, can you make yourself do that?"

"Well Edward says you can. He says she just lost the will to live and gave up the fight." She looked at Eliza, she didn't know how much she knew about little Henry. "I don't know if you knew, but life had been a fight for her since the day her youngest child died of cholera. Funnily enough though, she asked to see Edward before she took to her bed. She told him she had come across some information that was too painful to live with, and she was too tired to fight anymore. I wonder what that was? She asked the solicitor to visit her though and she put Beatrice back into her will. That was so nice for Beatrice, although she never got to see her mother, she felt that in including her, she had reconciled in a way. I'll always picture her, seated at the Secretaire Pa made for Doctor Hetherington when I was little, writing letters to her own Mama in Harrogate, and offering all of us children iced lemonade." As though realizing for the first time, Betsy reflected, "She must have just moved here upon her marriage, as Doctor Hetherington's family all hailed from this town. She was so nice when we were little."

Eliza was standing in front of the large looking glass in the hallway of Betsy's elegant home. She swept her right hand over her belly and felt the gentle roundedness beginning to show. She was waiting for Betsy. Together they were travelling to Whitby by train to meet up with Thom and his family and see an exhibition of paintings which was to include one by Thom and two by little Joe. The whole family was very proud, and they had all promised Joseph and Hannah detailed accounts of the whole affair.

Eliza, caught in the moment, had not heard Betsy come out of the drawing room, when she sensed her presence, she spun round, but the look on Betsy's face was transparent. She had seen.

"Oh Betsy, please don't say anything, I haven't told Micky yet." Betsy rushed forward and embraced her.

"Of course I won't say anything. Are you well, how far along are you?"

"I'm well Betsy, thank you. About four months I think. Due early January."

"Well I never, that'll be in 1900, Eliza. A new baby for a new century. We must get Edward to look at you. Oh this is such good news. The day out is a success already!"

"Eliza, that has decided everything for me. I have to earn enough money to get us out of my parent's house and into one of our own. I've been thinking about it for a while. I'm going to join the army!" He restrained Eliza's hands that had flown up to her shaking head in horror.

"Eliza, listen please. The pay is so much better than I can ever earn on the fishing boats, and I'll get paid immediately. We can rent a small house and when I'm home we can lead a normal life, not the chaotic one with my family." They both smiled at his attempt at humour. I'll not consider your sister's offer of money Eliza. I must support my own wife and children. I want us to have Charlie too, not just this one." He gently stroked over her now swelling skirt front. "I don't need to stay in for long, but I can learn a trade ready for when I get out. All will be well Eliza, I promise."

Part 4

Beth

1899 – 1923

Chapter 31

Dorset / Scarborough,
December 1899 – January 1900

"Joseph, that's Henry's motor car hooting at you. Come on, I don't want him to wake the whole neighbourhood, even if they are miles away!"

"Coming my dear. Are you sure you don't mind me going out to the Inn tonight?" "Of course not, Joseph. It seems more respectable these days for men to meet for a sociable drink in an Inn, and you are welcoming in a new Century. That doesn't happen more than once in a lifetime."

"That's true, my dear. Why don't you wait up for me, and we can have a glass of port together? Toast the new Century. 1900, eh, that will take some getting used to saying." Hannah smiled up at him from her book. She had the volume very close to both her face and the oil lamp. Reading was becoming more difficult for her, but she was going with Kathy to a new Ophthalmologist next week to try some spectacles to see if they would help. "Try not to let Henry drink too much though Joseph, Charlotte is concerned about him, the doctor has told him to ease up on his drinking, he's told him the heart doesn't appreciate a diet of too much ale." Joseph was already closing the door behind him, but threw over his shoulder,

"I will Hannah. Have a good evening yourself."

Joseph scurried out to Henry's motor car, easing himself gently into the passenger seat, keeping his coat collar up against the biting wind. He deposited his cane on the rear seat alongside Henry's silver, duck-head topped one.

"Dare I remind you of the one and only other time we went out into this town for a drinking session Joseph my friend?"

"Actually Henry, if you remember, we didn't end up in the Inn at all, we drank my father's whisky instead!" Henry threw back his head and laughed at the memory, then sobered at the aide memoire of what had become a murder weapon.

"Let's not think of that night Joseph, we are celebrating the dawning of a new Century.""I agree Henry, let's celebrate being back in the same town together for this occasion. Back where we both belong, eh?" Henry nodded his approval of the sentiment.

"Now then Joseph, give me the news of all the Scarborough Elliot's."

"Oh, maybe later Henry. Let's enjoy this atmosphere. Look at the young men over there; they're really getting into high spirits over the affair. Where will you leave the carriage, erm, motor car thing?"

"Well that's the beauty of it Joseph, I can leave it wherever I want, it will still be there when we want to go home, it isn't like a horse that may take off if it becomes loose!" They both smiled at this amazing mechanical advance as Henry pulled alongside the Ferguson Arms, heaving on the huge hand brake to the right of him, and both young men simultaneously reached behind them for their canes, before alighting with the guise and mantle of elderly gentlemen.

"Come along Henry, let's get home, sitting on the monument, continuing to drink, and getting wretched about our lives is a little pessimistic at the dawning of a new era. Not to mention bad for our hearts, according to your physician I believe. Life should become easier for future generations now. All the improvements in mechanisation should assist the dreariest and most arduous of tasks. It's all positive Henry. Come on, let's go home, it's freezing out here tonight, and Hannah was going to wait up for me."

"But we won't live to see it all Joseph will we? And I have no offspring to enjoy it. That is a luxury you were permitted, but I was denied. God certainly punished me for loving Lizzibeth, Joseph, didn't he?" Henry paused to savour the disbelief on Joseph's face. "Yes, it's true you know. I discovered a long, long time ago, she was the best thing that ever happened to me. At first I thought I was glorifying her memory, dying so young you know, but I soon realised, it was so much more than that. I think I began to love her the first day I saw her. She fell off her stilts behind your garden hedge, and there I beheld this most exquisite, endearing amusing and yet so lovely an apparition. I can still see her now."

Henry stared into the distance, transported briefly to another time. "Why did I think it could never be Joseph, we had more love between us that night on the monument, and in the years leading up to it, than I've had in a lifetime since. If only I had known what was to lie ahead." Henry fiddled with the beak of the silver duck impaled on his cane, polishing away an incidental smear. "Oh, Amelia was indeed a good woman, but not a loving wife. I should have opposed my father, let him disinherit me, what good is the House to me now, it will go to my nephew anyway."

Joseph's absolute astonishment at Henry's revelation rendered him speechless. How tragic a figure his friend had been? Never once had he considered the possibility of Henry having genuine feelings for Lizzibeth. He had so erroneously assumed Henry had taken advantage of her devotion and willingness. Not that he had actually been captivated by her. Henry's voice broke into his thoughts.

"Perhaps if you had never gone to her, and put her in the family way, she may have come to me in Kent. We could have made a life together. She could have been here with me now. She would have accepted my affliction, and had a fondness for me anyway. She would have spared me the necessity for my waywardness. She would love me still. Why did you deny her in her hour of need Joseph, why? I have never understood."

Henry, regretfully, yet affectionately lifted his eyes to his friend, begging some words of comfort or explanation. Joseph stiffened.

"Henry. Once and for all, although Betsy must never be enlightened, I confirm to you, I was never improper with Lizzibeth. As you persist in this matter, I have no choice but to tell you a truth I intended to take to my grave. I warn you, you will not like this revelation, Henry."

Joseph proceeded to recount the contents of Kate's letter to Henry. To his surprise, Henry did not remonstrate. He nodded through drunken gasps at each disclosure.

"You knew Henry, you knew, you goaded me into telling you. Didn't you? Didn't you?" Joseph staggered up onto his feet, using his stick to push himself erect; steadying himself, he put the stick under his arm and leant his good hand down to Henry's shoulder and shook it wildly as he spoke.

"No Joseph my friend. I did not know. Yet I feel no shock. I always felt that my father had secrets, and I admit to wondering if Lizzibeth had been one of them. I even wondered if he had… you know seen her off, when she went missing, he was so angry that night. And I had heard the servants speculating. But now of course, it all makes sense."

Joseph leant on his stick, incredulous at his friend's own disclosures tonight. He watched Henry as he continued,

"Poor Mama. She was a little like Amelia though, cold sometimes. Oh Joseph, poor, poor Lizzibeth, what did I do to her?"

Joseph looked around the marketplace. No-one had noticed the two elderly men on the fire monument. His son-in-law Arthur, Bill Buxton's own son, with an innocent irony, was laughing amongst a crowd of his friends outside the Inn. Life indeed went on, but it was obvious now, that a part of Henry had died with Lizzibeth on that fateful, tragic night when he had denied the depth and nature of his true feelings for her.

"If it helps Henry, this makes Betsy your half sister. Hannah has a hunch that our little foundling Eliza, is Edward and Betsy's child. She won't reveal how she has arrived at this notion, something to do with inherited features or something. Now, if she's right, then when Eliza has her new baby anytime soon, it will be Lizzibeth's great grandchild, your great-niece. Lizzibeth would want you to look out for her family; she would consider it your duty. It's your family too."

Henry forced a smile through his despair.

"Must be the indentation in the ear Joseph, remember how much teasing Lizzibeth gave me over that! I have always felt a part of your family Joseph, perhaps subliminally I have always felt the connection." He then looked up at the clear ageless inscription on the monument.

"Joseph, is this myth Greek or Egyptian? Lizzibeth asked me all about it that night, and I couldn't remember which it was. Tell her now, I know she's here with us tonight." Joseph was about to answer when a great cheer rose into the air, much back slapping, revelry and camaraderie heralded the stroke of midnight and the new century. Passers-by shook Joseph's hand. The joyous jubilation and hope for this new age was infectious, and Joseph laughed at the antics of men climbing the gas lamps and jumping on and off the flower barrels, hooting, whistling and shouting good wishes to one and all. Joseph reigned in his amusement to answer,

"It's Greek Henry, did you never read any of your school books before you passed them on to me? Henry, Henry. No, Oh, Henry no, don't go to her yet, please, Henry, not yet, I've only just come back."

The group approaching the monument, headed by Arthur, intent on greeting his father-in-law, pulled back as though watching the scene from a distance in slow motion. Joseph and Henry, once again slumped and intoxicated on this Dorset fire monument. But in a tragic twist, this time, Joseph was attempting to rouse Henry, but unlike his own reversible indulgence nearly fifty years earlier, Henry's soul would not turn back. Mayhem broke loose as the crowd registered not only the unfortunate event, but also the identity of its victim.

"It's the Master from Bramble House."

"Go for Doctor Halliday."

"Give him some air."

"Get him into a carriage, quickly."

Joseph moved away from Henry's lifeless body, a heart fatally wounded almost fifty years before, had finally succumbed to its lesion, and ceased to beat. Distraught, and yet resigned to this poignant, almost predictable end to his dear friend's tragedy, Joseph's fist succumbed to its lifetime's habit, and sought his right eye socket, troubling its contents unmercifully. Not least, did he face the realisation that it was he himself who had crowded their threesome. For, Lizzibeth had not loved him as everyone had assumed at all, and he felt a bewildering sense of deflation with this revelation. Indeed his own platonic companionable feelings for her were all that had been reciprocated. She had loved Henry, and he her. Dear Henry. Released at last, to join his childhood companion and lover, for their long awaited eternal and everlasting life together.

Betsy rocked Beth in her arms as she re-read Kathy's letter again and again. She was seated in their stylish drawing room. The winter sun was streaming through the windows between the heavy ruby damask drapes. It illuminated particles as they danced effortlessly in the warmed air from the crackling fire, glowing from within its elegant surround. Eliza was asleep upstairs. She had moved temporarily in with Betsy and Edward following her confinement. Little persuasion had been required, despite Eliza now enjoying relative comfort in the little house Micky had rented in Sussex Street with his soldier's pay. She had Albert and Lottie nearby, and even Thom and Annie were not far away in Belle Vue Street. She had not missed the overcrowding in the Walker's home, albeit a larger house 'down street'. But Eliza had wanted to ensure she recovered her strength this time around. She wanted to be the perfect mother to little Beth, so she had accepted Betsy's hospitality and care. Thus far, she had coped well with the night feeding, but indulged at Betsy's insistence, in an occasional afternoon nap.

Tears rolled weakly down Betsy's cheeks when she thought of the man she had always known as 'Uncle Henry'. Kathy reminded her, he had been sixty four years old, a good age to reach, yet somehow Betsy felt sad for his life. She had never known him appear truly happy. She empathised with his childlessness, had that been the cause of the sadness behind his eyes? Or, the thought suddenly occurred to her, could it have been that he had unrequited feelings for her mother. Surely her mother had loved Joseph – her father, but if that was the case, why had she treasured this coat of Henry's so, to insist on swaddling her new born baby in it as Hannah had told her? Betsy had never understood. She fingered the same cashmere now, enveloping little Beth, and wished she could unravel the uneasiness these feelings tied in the pit of her stomach. The poignancy of Henry's passing, at the very moment of Beth's delivery into this life had not escaped them all. But for Betsy and her secret, there was a greater significance knowing Beth's connection to Lizzibeth and the significance of the legend of a new Phoenix, arising from the old. She was sure Henry in his childlessness, would have taken comfort in a new life symbolically emerging from his own. How fitting for such an ending too, that his last moments were on the monument that her mother Lizzibeth, and his friend Joseph, had felt was so special to them all.

Beth stirred, Betsy flicked away her tears, and turned her attention to her charge.

"Shhh, little one, shhh."

The large double doors into the drawing room creaked open, and Eliza appeared, softly and slowly closing the doors behind her when she realised her baby daughter was asleep.

"She's still asleep then Betsy?"

"Yes, she stirred a moment ago, but she's gone back off again now."

"She's so beautiful Betsy isn't she, so angelic, what do you think Micky will think to her?"

"He'll think she's absolutely perfect Eliza, as we all do. What a shame Ma's not here to see her. You must get a portrait done to send to Dorset. I'd be happy to pay Eliza, if only because I'd like one too."

Eliza looked dreamily at her baby daughter.

"Yes I suppose so Betsy. I just so want Micky back home safely. Lottie said she would be round to see us today. She's been so wonderful to me Betsy, you all have. Even young Bertie. I hear he's sweet on a girl that lives close to them on Victoria Street." She stroked the beige cashmere over the top of Beth's arms, and noticed Kathy's letter. "Have you been reading about Uncle Henry's death again Betsy? Such a sad man. But Ma told me that when they were all young together in Dorset, he was such a fun and happy child." Betsy looked up curiously at Eliza.

"When did Ma tell you that? I've never heard anything about what he'd been like as a child."

"Oh, years ago, when I was a little wayward, Ma said that I was just like Henry had been, especially when together with your real mother Lizzibeth. She said that they all had so much fun together as children in Dorset, but that her and Pa were the sensible ones, and that they really just basked in the antics of Lizzibeth and Henry." Eliza had innocently tightened the inexplicable knot in Betsy's stomach, ensuring it would not now easily come loose. Eliza broke into her turmoil. "Did you read the paper yesterday Betsy, the one Edward brought home?"

"Oh I'm sorry Eliza, I've asked Edward to leave them at the hospital. I don't want you getting upset by what's written in the papers." She scrutinised her foundling sister's face to read any signs that the news had not been good. "What did it say?"

Eliza looked up into Betsy's questioning eyes, naked fear

exposed in her own.

"It just said that Kruger had wanted an early start to the war so that the Boers out-numbered the British troops already present there. And that their victories at Stormberg, Magersfontein and Colenso last month have become known as Black Week for the British. At least we know from today's letter that he's survived those battles Betsy." She smiled to herself as she recalled his words, "Indeed 'in splendid condition after the battle of Colenso' he said Betsy." Eliza looked pensively down at her baby daughter, "I must go back home soon, I want to have a perfect family life set up for Micky, this little one must know where she belongs and who she belongs to. I can't tell you how empty it feels to not know who your parents are." She stopped to concentrate on uncurling Beth's fingers, then added, "I know your mother tragically died when you were born Betsy, but at least you know who she was, so you know who you are." She broke off to allow Betsy to concur; in her innocence she did not notice the slight hesitation in that consensus, exposing Betsy's own anguish. "Anyway, let's hope this war will be over soon, and Micky will be home to fuss over this little beauty here. Won't he? Yes he will." Eliza's tone morphed into adoring childish intonation mid-sentence, as Beth opened her eyes and smiled her toothless delight at her animated nodding mother whose fingers lovingly tickled the velvety soft chubby cheeks and chins.

Chapter 32

Scarborough, February 1901

"Edward, Eliza. I've asked you to be here at this time today to tell you both something that you should have known a long time ago." Betsy paused, and twiddled her gold wedding band around her finger. They were all seated in the drawing room on Prince of Wales Terrace. Edward had taken a break from work in the middle of the day at his wife's request. The atmosphere was leaden with curious yet anxious anticipation, for Betsy had been most serious in her invitation. Her audience were now sitting forward, fearfully in their seats, adrenaline pumping, prepared for fight or flight.

"I'm so sorry that I asked you to leave little Beth with Lottie, Eliza, but I didn't want to be disturbed by her running around our feet when I'm trying to tell you this. I need you both to understand everything, and I mean, everything." She paused again, and looked at the two pairs of eyes she loved most in the world, both apprehensively trained on her at this moment, uneasy as to this mystery, and what was to unfold. Betsy continued,

"The death of our beloved Queen last month has prompted my disclosure. I don't truly understand why, but maybe it's the realisation that nothing is forever, and we must all come to terms with our own mortality. Most of us alive today, only know how to be Victorians, that's all we've ever known, but we must now learn to adapt to a change in our society. Perhaps that's my reasoning in deciding that now's a good time to learn to adapt to another change amongst ourselves?"

"Betsy, my dear, you're not ill are you? Why have you not told me, If anyone can help, I can. Oh, please tell me you are not ill my dear." Edward had left his seat and was on one knee at Betsy's feet.

"Edward, don't be ridiculous, of course I'm not ill, I would have told you that. Sit down please. This is very difficult for me. Please, return to your seat with Eliza, where I can see you both." Betsy pulled herself up straight in her chair, smoothed the material of her fashionable skirt over her knees like a school ma'am, and adjusted the black arm band that she wore in deference to their monarch's recent passing.

"Edward. My beloved husband, I love you dearly with all my heart. You were worth the long years of waiting before you realised that you needed me." She smiled at her own words, and raised her hand to silence Edward's protest. "I have never been happier than since becoming your wife. However, the wait I refer to, is on account of our liaison many years before, prior to your studies for your surgical examinations. You were a different person then. After your father died, you were fun and carefree, and we recklessly indulged, just once, in the pleasures of the flesh. Inhibitions spirited away by the festivities of the Christmas season, and the elation of a carol service." Betsy paused, her arm mid air having indicated the desertion of her inhibitions.

She sensed Edward's palpable embarrassment, not only on account of Eliza's shocked presence, but also that this single indiscretion had never before been raised between them. "Edward, I'm so sorry if I embarrass you, but such indiscretions are often not without consequence." She considered for a few moments how to speak the words she needed to divulge. "Well. Neither was ours." She exhaled her own relief as she watched the words bounce above the heads of her loved ones. She absorbed the shocked and shaken, sharp intake of breath from each of her listeners, then used their stunned silence to continue. "There is your answer, Edward, as to why our 'first' child was not spared the deadly blood disorder. Because he was not indeed, our first child. Our first born sits beside you now my dear. Yes Eliza, you have always belonged in this family. You not only have Elliot blood in your veins, but you also have Hetherington blood too. I was so saddened when you spoke last year of having a sense of not belonging. You most definitely do belong Eliza, for Edward and I are your true parents."

Edward slowly rose from his chair and paced towards the window. Betsy watched him nervously, Eliza stared at the pattern along the carpet on the hypotenuse formed by their three positions. After what seemed like an age, Edward awkwardly broke the silence.

"Why, Betsy, why? Why didn't you tell me?"

"Edward, you were away for most of the time. Can you imagine the shame that your dear Mama would have felt. She would never have allowed us to marry then. Her aspirations for you were either to marry up, certainly not down, or failing that, to stay with her forever as her doting son. You would have been helpless against her." Betsy watched as Edward shook his head in despair.

"Edward, you were also just getting a reputation as a respected physician, it would have ruined you. I couldn't do it to you. I had to hatch a plan. It so nearly went horribly wrong; I had nightmares for years afterwards. We owe so much to Thom, if he hadn't broken into that Ticket Office, then our beautiful first child here, could also have perished." Betsy shivered at the thought. Edward turned slowly back towards her.

"That's why you had me buy Thom's painting at the auction, and it has stayed hidden in our attic ever since."

"He must never know it was you that bought it Edward, we owe him so much, and it gave him such a boost of confidence as a painter." She allowed her brother to creep into her thoughts for a minute, and offered, "There's to be an exhibition soon of all the painters works from Staithes you kn….."

She broke off realising the futility of such information at this time.

Edward turned back to the window as a small forgotten voice spoke quietly to the floor.

"So what was this plan, where exactly was I born? Not a nice clean hospital bed like Beth, I suspect." Betsy turned from Edward, and allowed herself a glimpse, not of her sister but of her daughter Eliza. She quietly and empathically outlined the plan for her daughter's birth nearly twenty five years earlier, to that very child herself.

"I had had pains for most of the day, Eliza, so I knew you were on your way. I prepared a basket for you and made my way down to the sea front at the Spa. I knew Thom was meeting Annie there that night as I'd heard him talking about Kathy leaving him the key to the ticket office. I intercepted it from Thom's bedside table. Quietly I slipped onto the sands, and you came quietly and easily into this world. You were so perfect Eliza. What I did next was the hardest thing I've ever done in my life. I laid you in your basket, filled with soft leaves of different herbs and spices, and left you in the ticket office for Thom and Annie to find later that evening. My mother apparently called her birthing bed, her nest of spices. It's to do with the story of the phoenix bird in greek mythology. I wasn't to know how true to the story your deliverance from the Spa flames would be." She realised her digression was impatiently unappreciated, and she hurried on with her tale. "I was sure in the knowledge that Ma would never let you go, and I was right. She was convinced you belonged to the family in some way, I think Thom and Annie were her chief suspects initially; but then something made her realise, she would not tell me what. I only know it was on the day of the foundation stone being laid for the Marine Drive, she'd met you with some of Micky's family. She said she had made the right decision in keeping you, as she now knew for certain that you couldn't belong to anyone but me, and she was glad that I had played such a large part in your upbringing. I had no idea what she was talking about, and I said nothing, but she knew." Mother and daughter contemplated the floor silently in deference to the wise woman who had lovingly nurtured and fostered them both as her own. Betsy broke the stillness.

"But Eliza, I had to keep gossip away from Edward, your father. You do understand that don't you? Eliza?"

Eliza had never looked up, she could not after all these years of wondering and waiting, lay her eyes upon her true parents. Betsy looked appealingly over to Edward; she was overcome to see tears rolling over his cheeks as he stared unseeingly ahead of him into the dreary February frost.

"Edward, Edward, what was I to do." Betsy was beside him, her arm comfortingly across his back. "I know now it seems quite shocking to put your medical reputation and your mother's feelings above those of a child, but I thought I was doing the right thing for everyone. Ma was the best mother any child could have, surely you see that?" She recessed her speech, hoping for reassurance, when none came, she defended herself again. "Edward, you must concede, my decision was vindicated on your return, when you showed neither memory of our union, nor any interest in our having a future together."

Edward turned then and looked piercingly into his wife's eyes.

"How have you kept this to yourself Betsy? The mental anguish over the years, watching our child struggle with her life. A confinement on a beach. Oh, Betsy, what have I done to you? You needed me, where was I? Pandering to a spoilt selfish woman, instead of providing a home for my wife and child." Betsy moved forwards into his arms, and Edward held her tight, dropping a kiss on the top of her head that sang more evocatively into the room than his wedding vows had done years earlier.

Calmly and quietly, Eliza rose to her feet.

"Hmm, if you will both excuse me, I'll be going now, I can't expect Lottie to keep Beth forever. I'll never understand why you have kept this to yourself for so long, so don't expect me to. Good day to you both."

Edward and Betsy shared a split second glance, then simultaneously jumped forwards to apprehend her exit. She dodged them both.

"I'm sorry Edward, but I can't be so forgiving of her." She spat her words towards Betsy. "Why now? Why not when you married? What could have upset the apple cart then? Your mother was already being flouted. That was about the time I was beginning to struggle with being a 'foundling', and she knew it!" Eliza's quiet soft voice had become harsh and vehement as she spat her last words towards her mother. Betsy pleaded with her daughter,

"I know Eliza, and I wanted to, many times. But by then, Ma was your mother; I couldn't take that away from her. She loved you as her own. I was there for you always. Defending you at every turn."

"But as my sister!" Eliza shook as she shouted, Edward ventured closer to her. When she did not move away, he placed a hand on her shoulder. When she did not flinch, he pulled her to him. He held her as she sobbed her varied emotions into her father's tweed. Betsy looked helplessly on, she wasn't sure how much her revelations had damaged her own relationships, but if she had given Edward a child at last, and her daughter a father to call her own, then she had to believe it had been worth it.

As Eliza's sobs subsided, Betsy remembered a comment from Hannah before she had left for Dorset. She handed Eliza a cotton handkerchief,

"Eliza, I've just remembered what Ma actually said as she left, and told me she knew for certain I would take care of you. I had appeared puzzled, so she said, 'blood will out Betsy, I've met Micky's sister's family, Eliza too has a secret, only you and her hold the key.' What did she mean Eliza?"

Eliza shrugged her shoulders, pulling down the corners of her mouth in denial between her tearful breaths of recovery.

"You know though Betsy," she gasped "having kept this to yourself for Edward's sake all these years, I think we should continue the secrecy, at least until he retires, don't you? It would be a shock to the rest of the family too, not to mention Beatrice's family. And I need time to take in all this, and talk to Micky when he gets home. You owe me that!"

Betsy had gazed out of the front window from their chic chaise longue in the drawing room for over an hour. Edward had taken Eliza home, and the carriage was just returning now outside their house. She rushed to the front door.

"How is she Edward? Do you think she'll ever forgive me?" Edward took his wife's hand and tucked it into the crook of his elbow as he led her back into the drawing room.

"Will you ever forgive me, Betsy? I feel if there is hope for one, then there must be hope for the other."

"But I never blamed you Edward, it was my decision and I was sure the death of our babies, was God's punishment for what I had done, even when we knew the reason for it."

"Oh, my poor, Betsy. Despite my overwhelming anger at my mother's intolerance, and at my own weakness, I have never had more admiration for any human being as I have for you tonight. You were so brave, you could have died on the beach that night. I behaved abominably towards you Betsy. I'm not worthy of your love and devotion, please forgive me." He raised her hand to his lips without taking his eyes away from hers. "Thank you for my wonderful daughter. No wonder she resembles my mother so much, in looks only, be assured, my dear. Oh, but I have a lifetime of attention to heap onto her now, she needs spoiling, not to mention our little grand-daughter." Betsy smiled guardedly, her relief at Edward's reaction balanced by her fears from Eliza's.

"Edward, I do think Eliza is right though in keeping this to ourselves. At least for a little while. We need to put our daughter first now. Besides," Betsy playfully slapped his chest, "what do you mean, you have always spoiled her anyway. Indeed, I often thought you must've known because of it." Edward released his wife and wandered to the fireplace, he put both hands upon the mantle, his head bowed to the flames.

"I wish I had Betsy, I really wish I had." He turned to face her, "But I have no doubt in my mind now, that this was the information that ultimately killed my mother. How sad that she was so unforgiving of everything. Stangely, though, she always spoke highly of your Uncle Henry," In reponse to Betsy's questioning expression, he explained, "we met him often on the Esplanade at Sunday Church Parade whenever he stayed in this house, and I used to walk with her. Yes, she approved of his friendship with your family." He seated himself by the fire, pensively reminded of his mother's demeanour, he added, "Never comfortable around any afflictions, she used to say of him, 'crippled though he is, he seems a really nice fellow'!" Edward smiled at this memory that illogically illustrated his mother's lack of tolerance so well. "She did not begin life with such vitriol you know, Betsy. She just could not cope with tragedy, and yet she was dealt so much.

Chapter 33

Scarborough, April 1904 /
Dorset, May 1904

"You look very handsome in your finery today my dear, no-one would guess you were approaching your sixth decade this summer!"

"Why thank you kind Sir." Betsy bobbed a good-natured curtsy towards her husband. "Gosh Edward, that makes me sound so old. I'm still only forty nine you know. Actually, you still look quite handsome yourself for an old man!" Edward smiled affectionately at her as he made to playfully punch her shoulder with his leather fist.

"You know Edward, I think the whole world looks smarter and younger these days. Just look at the sea of people at Church parade this Sunday morning, befit for any royal occasion here on the Esplanade." Edward paused at the railings that effectively penned the middle class into their niche, and leaning against them, turned and gazed left and right to take in their fellow promenaders.

"I think my dear that whilst you are perhaps right in what you say, you must remember that we have a slightly distorted view from up here. I'm not so sure that Micky's family and friends down there, look younger than their chronological ages. The war has taken its toll on Micky though, he'll get better still, but he is so weary. Sometimes I think it's just as much having to return to fishing as much as the war itself. Life is still very hard for some people." Edward pensively turned his conscience towards the old town, nestling serenely in the spring sunshine neath its medieval battlements. Betsy, quick to defend and explain her statement, linked Edward's arm snuggling closely into him.

"Oh I know that Edward. All too well; but improvements in health and well-being are becoming noticeable. You must take some credit for that, in this town at least."

"Nonsense Betsy, my contribution has been diminutive, but the fact that I have been a contribution at all, is enough for me."

Edward looked over towards the castle promontory,

"I wonder will that roadway ever be completed. It would be nice to think in our lifetime, we would be able to walk from one bay to another on this 'Marine Drive', but it's taken seven years so far. Whilst it seems that the last stone has now been laid this year, I've heard it could be another year at least before the roadway is ready. What a financial and legal disaster it has turned out to be. I only hope that in the end, it proves to be an asset to the town and to all of us."

"And of course, is effective against erosion of the coastline which was its initial purpose." Betsy added, dutifully concurring with her husband.

Mesmerised by the elaboracy of the townsfolk beneath them undertaking their weekly constitutional on the Spa complex, they both fell silent for a few moments.

Edward was the first to speak.

"Do you know what I always think of when I stand here Betsy?"

"Not until you tell me Edward, what do you think of?"

"Well I always get that feeling of falling backwards. Just like I actually did that night many years ago, - off the wall over there." He stiffened as if steeling himself against a fall. "Then of course, that makes me think of your father, and how much I'll always be indebted to him, not only for saving my life that night, but for giving life to you, and so giving me the best wife in the world." Edward turned his head in time to see Betsy avert her eyes from his. He knew she struggled with her own worthiness in view of her deceit regarding their daughter, Eliza. Despite his frequent, and emotional declarations, which often appeared to augment, not lessen her distress. He continued smiling, "But then do you know what picture comes into my head?" Betsy looked up into his amused expression.

"Well, when we were all standing on the wall, we had already noticed your Pa – Joseph, because he was being propositioned by old Millie, and was so politely and innocently trying to get rid of her." He smiled broadly at Betsy's open mouth, horrified at her father's predicament. "You obviously remember her too; well, I'm ashamed to say, that all of us boys knew exactly who and what she was, even at that age, and we found your father's dilemma highly comical. Does that shock you my dear?" He smiled loudly. "Knowing your father as I came to know him over the years, I did feel some remorse at finding amusement in such an awkward situation, however, even now, that vision puts an involuntary smile upon my face."

Betsy smiled in response to Edward's narration, though empathised with her father's experience by pulling her bottom lip behind her top teeth within her grin.

"What's most horrifying Edward, is that you can be amused by anything that happened on the night you nearly drowned!"

"Oh, that was a long, long time ago now my dear." He savoured the word 'long', as if watching the years peel away in front of his eyes.

They turned to walk further along the path, nodding at distinguished neighbours and acquaintances as they passed, all keen to be seen and acknowledged in their finery at Sunday church parade. Most were readily prepared to politely avoid eye contact with those they knew had more interesting news than their own. Nothing was considered worse in a personally boring domestic year, than to have to listen to the foreign exploits of a well-to-do family newly initiated in the pastime of travel and expeditions. Mostly these adventures would be to the French Alps, but occasionally were further afield, even as distant as the Far East. Many even carried photographic evidence of their endeavours to illustrate their descriptions. Betsy had often commented to Edward when being subjected to such boastfulness, that there was something comical about ladies clambering around snow covered mountains in their full regalia of many layers of skirts, and fancy hats. Today they had been spared such ordeals.

"I wonder if any of the family are up here this morning, Edward."

"Well perhaps Albert, he sometimes drags Lottie and Bertie up here on a Sunday morning, but you know Eliza won't be here, Betsy. She won't join us on principle. You can't blame her, she lives in a cleft between the two divisions of the town. And Thom does not bother himself with such traditions."

His voice had softened with discretion as they passed an elderly couple enjoying the ambience of the morning, Edward doffed his cap, then lifted his tone as he switched the topic. "They had all thoroughly enjoyed the circus though last week. Eliza and Beth had gone with Thom and all their family. I saw the procession heading into town when I was visiting an old gentleman on Prospect Road. Very grand it all looked. A brass band was playing atop a very precarious, if ornate wagon. I kept expecting the whole thing to topple over if the wheels caught in those new electric tramlines." Edward coughed politely, naturally suspending the conversation, swiftly and purposely digressing when he realised his insensitivity. Betsy was still excluded by Eliza from many things. He wished his daughter could find more forgiveness in her heart.

"Anyway dearest wife, we were supposed to be making a decision about your trip to Dorset on this morning's walk. I know you worry about your Pa. Kathy's mentioned his ill-health in her last two letters, yet your Ma never writes anything other than that they are all well. You haven't been down for a while Betsy, so why don't you go for a visit anyway. You can see things for yourself. If he's become a spendthrift in his old age, then there's definitely something wrong with him, eh?" He smiled decisively at her, amused by his own attempt at humour, and she nodded, relieved at his decision. She knew in her own heart that she really wanted to go, much as she hated the long journey.

"Shall we go down the funicular to the Spa today dear, or have you walked enough?"

"It's up to you Edward, I don't mind really." As Edward steered them into the lift top station, she added, "Though I hope the miserable attendant isn't on duty today. The one with the full beard, he's positively rude sometimes, everything's too much trouble, I'm surprised he keeps his job."

"Maybe he's fine with everyone else Betsy, he just doesn't like you!"

"Well, thank you so much, husband of mine, I love you too. Oh look, he is here today, you see for yourself how rude he is."

Edward bought their tickets with routine politeness, but both failed to notice the glance at Betsy that could have felled a lion at twenty paces. They took their seats on the inside bench that would pass the other carriage as it travelled upwards, and were discussing when they last remembered seeing 'old Millie' around the town, guessing at when she must have passed away. The doors closed and the carriage jerked away from its station a few feet, before slowing to a halt almost immediately.

Edward pulled a puzzled face at the other six passengers, and in an unspoken consent, he and an austere, top-hatted gentleman got up and walked cautiously to the far end of the carriage to see that the upward bound one had also stopped in the corresponding position. They returned to their seats, but as Edward was lowering himself, he spotted a powerful spray of water coming from the pipe lying between the two tracks, just below the position of their carriage. He knew the steam pumps pushed sea water up to the top carriage to facilitate its descent through weighting it more so than the bottom carriage, loss of water pressure would undoubtedly have been what had stopped the mechanism.

The bearded attendant was frantically busying himself with all the levers and controls at his disposal. Banging on the glass of the door to catch his attention, Edward signalled towards the leak.

A few minutes passed, then astonished, Edward saw the attendant edging his way down the rails towards the leak. Thumping on the window, Edward yelled at him, "You can't stop that on your own man! Just open the door, we can stride across the rails and get back out, it's only gone a few feet!" The attendant looked up at him,

"It's no problem Sir, I only need the pressure to build a bit, then gravity will take over and I'll 'ave you at the bottom in no time."

Edward raised his hands in despair, "Sheer lunacy! Look, all the passengers at the bottom have just walked out." They watched as the man, now soaked through from the spray, pressed something down over the leak, but his feet were slipping on the wet and muddy rails. He held fast his position, the carriage began to groan as though a clockwork mechanism had sprung to life. A sigh exhaled in the spartan wooden cabin as its passengers sensed their sunny Sunday constitutional could soon continue along the Spa Promenade.

Suddenly everyone turned to Betsy as she gasped, her hands covering her mouth. Having started the mechanism, the attendant had now produced a knife and was sawing wildly at the thick rope responsible for controlling its descent.

Edward, having processed the consequences in sheer disbelief, yelled through the window. "What do you think you're doing man, we'll all be killed?" When his question did not halt the man in his task, Edward attempted to open the carriage doors. He turned to the other passengers, "we need to get out quickly, help me with this." The top-hatted gentleman, bewildered by this inexplicable turn of events, began to tug at the doors with Edward.

Betsy had never moved, she was nailed to her wooden seat, watching this mystifying adversary in his irrational and undeserved deed. She mulled swiftly yet in measured motion, all events in her life that could warrant such hatred. Her hands flew to her face as she gasped again, this time with a harmonic chorus of now screaming ladies sharing this scenic coffin. The attendant's foothold had failed on the wet steel and before completing his task, he was sliding the rails between them as the carriages picked up speed, any decrease in water pressure could not halt the momentum now. Through openings in her fingers, Betsy stole a look at the victim of surely impending disaster; he was grabbing hopelessly at the slippery rails, blood was already coursing down his face from a wound on his forehead as he bounced out of control alongside the carriage. Betsy gasped again as she saw the approach of the upward bound carriage, where could he go? He must have sensed her gasp, he looked up at her, and as though forgetting his predicament for a second, he gave her the look of loathing she had come to expect from this stranger. Then he was gone. Replaced by the swish of the other carriage sweeping its way up onto the Esplanade station, counterbalanced by the Spa bound, thankfully still roped, descent of their own.

At the bottom, the door rattled open, Edward yelled at the lower attendant to close the funicular as he barged out of the door. He ran around the back of the station, and began running up the rails towards the man's lifeless body.

Betsy joined him a few minutes later, having noted the frayed, almost severed rope on her way up. Edward, head bowed, was cradling the man's head, remarkably untouched other than one forehead wound, but she could see his torso and limbs were cleaved beyond any possible repair.

"Betsy, don't, it's…"

"I know Edward, its Johnny Robinson isn't it? I saw his face clearly just before…."

"Kathy, I made up my mind to come down here two weeks ago. Now having seen Pa for myself for just a few days, I understand both your own concerns, and also Ma's denial. He's sometimes Pa just as we know him, but then some days he's not in this world. More in a time long since past, with people long past. Yesterday he asked me how Henry was, and to get him to come and see him."

Betsy and Kathy were walking the country lane from the town square towards Bramble House Lodge. It was a beautiful spring day, with the sights, sounds and smells of Betsy's early childhood all around them.

"I know Betsy, it took me ages to pen your letters because I wanted you to know how things were, but Ma has been so insistent that there's no problem. I used to worry about her memory, but she seems to be doing fine, at the moment anyway. She certainly wasn't pleased when you wrote to say you were coming, she says Pa may say something he shouldn't. I think there may be things about your real Mother or her family that wouldn't be nice for you to know."

"Oh, Kathy, for heaven's sake, next month, on my birthday, she will have been dead fifty years. What could possibly be disclosed at this late hour that could cause offence now? "

"Well I don't know, but she does get sharp with Pa when his mind wanders. You can see panic rise within her, she's afraid. I suppose Pa's her very reason for being, she can't imagine life without him steering it. She's not strong enough to lead. Or doesn't want to be. They have set roles within their marriage; she's no desire to see them change. You can understand that. She's clinging desperately to the lucid days, and ignoring the rest."

"I can see that Kathy, and I think I understand it too. It's hard enough for us his children to witness, but imagine when it's happening to someone who has been a part of you for most of your life, shared everything with you, even their own childhood. We can't begin to imagine Kathy."

They walked in silence for a few hundred yards, then Kathy

linked her sister's arm,

"What do you think to the new Chancel in the East End of the Church Betsy, you haven't been in it since it was moved, have you?"

"No I haven't Kathy, I think it looks absolutely splendid, but I'm not so sure about the position of the Organ, it didn't sound as good as I remember. I mean, St Peter and St Paul's must have a good organ sound to match its famous bells." They both laughed aloud, then Kathy sobered and changed the subject back to their dear Pa.

"I've spoken to the Doctor, Betsy. Ma doesn't know. He's told me there's no treatment to help with Pa's condition, which he describes as mild apoplexy. He says this may go on for quite some years before he has an episode of such severity that recovery is impossible." Betsy nodded. It was as she had suspected, she had seen it many times in her nursing days, but a light sob escaped as she faced the truth rather than speculation about her own dear Pa. Kathy squeezed her arm gently. "You'd better stop that before we reach the house, or Pa'll want to know what's amiss!"

"I know Kathy, I'll be fine with him, don't worry." She glanced up at Kathy's face. "Are you happy here Kathy, with Arthur I mean, do you ever regret not marrying Johnny Robinson?"

"Whatever makes you say that Betsy. I never loved Johnny; you know that, it would never have worked. And yes I am happy; Arthur's a wonderful husband and father. I often regret that you didn't have any children Betsy. As Arthur's cousin, your children and ours would have shared great-grandparents on the in-law side of the family, as well as Ma and Pa as grandparents. Wouldn't that have been something?"

"It certainly would Kathy." Almost too quickly, Betsy brought the subject back around to Johnny, but spoke slowly. "You should know dear sister that I also brought distressing news down here with me." She took a deep breath. "Johnny Robinson is dead." Seeing the sadness in Kathy's eyes, she quickly went on to explain his death and the months leading up to it. He had been living in Leeds, but his childless wife had apparently become very involved with the suffragette movement, always travelling to London for rallies and demonstrations. You can imagine how Johnny felt about that, with his attitude to a woman's purpose in life. Well, she had eventually died through weakness from too many episodes of hunger striking whilst in prison. Johnny felt shame rather than pride in her cause; he saw it as an affront to his manhood that he was unable to keep his wife under control, so he had crept back to Scarborough last year in disguise.

In response to Kathy's curious countenance, Betsy explained, "It was a good disguise too Kathy, I didn't recognise him until the day he died. He was older of course with a full thick beard." Betsy went on to describe the accident, but sensitively omitted the attempted murder of a carriage full of passengers, allowing her to assume he had slipped whilst doing the repair. She added the subsequent and surprising revelations from Thom and Annie, that they had given him a room on his return to the town, and he had been re-united with his parents. Thom had described Johnny's obsession that Betsy had ruined his life in turning Kathy against him, and had begged everyone to keep his identity a secret. She went on, "I have no idea where he got the notion about me turning you against him Kathy, there was no basis for that, except that I think he must have thought I kept putting you up to ask him about the Spa fire. As he died, he had said to Edward, "Tell her she'll never know if it was me!"

Kathy nodded, "I had confessed to it being you who kept pushing me to find out about it. But what tragic irony in his death, Betsy, - fixing the funicular carriage you were travelling in." Her voice wavered as she spoke, and a lone tear plopped onto her sister's arm,

Betsy looked up at Kathy.

"Why so sad sister, I thought you didn't love him?"

"Oh I didn't Betsy, but there's another reason I feel responsible for his torment." Kathy took a lace handkerchief from an

opening in her pretty leg-o-mutton sleeve and blew her nose.
"Over a year ago now, Johnny turned up on our doorstep, I was in the house with little Hannah. He tried to persuade me to leave with him, saying it wasn't too late for us to have a life together. I refused obviously, but I thought he wasn't going to take no for an answer, when thankfully, Arthur arrived home with little Billy – who as you know is not so little anymore. I explained that Johnny was just leaving and that he was a childhood friend from Scarborough, Arthur had never known about my betrothal before we met, and it would not have been the time to introduce them as such! Well, Arthur sat him down with a jar of ale. He told him the whole story of his father's death at the railway station, and about how if it hadn't been for finding out about your existence, his own cousin, then maybe we would never have met at all. He obviously also blamed you for that, whereas, I just assumed he had taken in a mental picture of our happy domesticity and decided an elopement with me was impossible. I had certainly not expected that he would have turned his love for me into such vitriol for you. I shudder to think of his ultimate plans, Betsy. I don't think he was well in his head."

Betsy had taken in this new revelation with astonishment, but as they approached Joseph and Hannah's cottage, she squeezed Kathy's hand, "Well let's not think about that now, he was a good friend as a child, then he had to grieve for the loss of you. Part of grieving is finding someone to blame, Johnny found me. But there could only be one such ending to a life as miserable as his, which was his tragedy. It's so awful for his parents though. They must blame us too."

They paused outside the cottage and Betsy hugged her little sister, aware of just how much she missed her companionship.

"You should also know though Kathy, that I had it on very good authority, from an eye-witness in fact, that Johnny was definitely at the Spa Pavilion the night of the fire. I think his conscience never really let him live with what he'd done there either, and that's why he didn't like me pushing you to find out."

"But who told you? How can you know that for sure Betsy?" She paused, "Was it you Betsy? Why were you there?" Kathy's questioning was interrupted by the creaking of the cottage door.

"What are you two looking so miserable about?" Joseph was framed in the doorway, still an upright proud figure of a man, cloaked happily in the afternoon sunshine. "Aren't you two a sight for old tired eyes, where's Lizzibeth? Have you left her by the riverbank? She does love to sit on the bridge dangling her legs doesn't she? Skirts torn and tucked in her panteloons." He laughed heartily at the vision he conjured with absolute clarity of focus.

"Joseph don't be ridiculous, you don't mean Lizzi…." Hannah clutched at his sleeve, desperate to bring him back to her, and for Betsy to suspect nothing.

"It's alright Ma. Yes, Lizzibeth stayed on the bridge Pa, but she'll come soon with Henry."

Hannah looked from one to the other of her daughters, appalled at Betsy's response to her beloved Joseph. Betsy smiled adoringly at the only mother she had ever known. She loved both her parents so much, Hannah was so dear to her, but her father's position was precious, pure and un-usurped. Knowledge of another mother had somehow inflicted inevitable, if minor flaws within her relationship with Hannah. She had to curtail Ma's methods in this regard, from her nursing experience she knew well that lucidity would more likely return if Pa was kept calm rather than aggravated by denial. She was proved right.

"Oh I know she will, Betsy my dear. She has his heart you know, always has had. He told me that the night he di…" Joseph turned to Hannah, "Henry died didn't he Hannah?" On her almost imperceptible nod, he continued, "New Years Eve, on the Fire Monument, Betsy you do get confused!" He curled his good arm around her shoulder to lead her inside. "Now, you come and tell your old Pa all about what's happening in that beautiful Yorkshire town of ours. How's that old North Bay Pier doing, anymore of it washed away yet? Eh?" He laughed heartily as Betsy's eyes rolled heavenward in mock exasperation for the ill-fated Pier.

"I'll tell you something that's happened Pa. Remember the Beehive Inn on Sandside?" Joseph peered up into the top left hand corner of the room, scanning his memory. On his nod of confirmation, Betsy continued, "well, it lost its licence this year on account of complaints by the clergy for noise and drunkenness!" Joseph laughed aloud, Hannah smiled and added,

"I remember the sign over the door, didn't it say 'within this hive we are all alive, good ale will make you funny, if you are dry as you pass by, step in and taste our honey'." They all laughed at her mimicry of the Yorkshire drawl, then Joseph became serious,

"Now Betsy, after some lunch, you must get yourself back up there as soon as possible. You should be spending your time making memories with the living, not wasting precious days on the dying, isn't that right Kathy?"

"Who's dying Pa?" Kathy moved slowly around the table to face them, her gaze never leaving Betsy. "Oh, but I do agree Betsy should go back soon, I've just begun to realise how much she must miss Eliza when she is away!"

Chapter 34

Scarborough, December 1904

"Good mor-ning, Good mor-ning. Is there anybody there? It's only me, Eliza." Betsy cautiously pushed open the front door of Eliza and Micky's Sussex Street house when no-one had responsed to her persistent knocking. She heard footsteps in the back scullery and a voice shouted out as it approached her. "Come through, I'm just in the back yard beating the rugs. Oh, it's you." Betsy's heart lurched, as the natural smile of greeting ran away from Eliza's face with the disappointed tone in her voice, as she had briefly glimpsed her mother following her back through the scullery.

The last few years had been difficult, Eliza had proved unforgiving of what she referred to as her 'childhood lie', despite every effort from both Edward and Micky to try to reconcile the two women, and heal the rift. Eliza's change in behaviour towards Betsy had thespian subtlety in public, so the rest of the family had largely remained ignorant to the situation, although the loss of their previous closeness had not gone un-noticed.

"Eliza, there's no need to take that tone. I know well you will never forgive me, but that's not why I'm here. Edward appears to have gained your forgiveness, despite years of denial of your very conception to me. He's not blameless as he now well admits. However, I know well we will always forgive him everything because he's,.. well,.. he's Edward, Doctor

Hetherington. Everyone in this town loves and respects him. It's because of him that I am here." Betsy paused to breath deeply and gather her words carefully.

"As you know, Beatrice and her family are spending this Christmas at the house in the Crescent. There are currently no tenants, and Beatrice has said that Peter's parents are now too old to travel to them this year. Edward wants to make this a special time for us, and has invited them and the Robinson's to join us for Christmas luncheon. He wondered if you, Micky and Beth would like to join us." Betsy's invitation had been delivered jerkily with breaks between each lash that Eliza continued to inflict upon the rugs, flung evenly across her washing line. Her large wooden beater never rested until Betsy had finished speaking. Then it idled after its last clout upon the autumnal shades of patterned threads, meandering its way downwards amongst the paisley entwined roses, and coming to rest on the ground as its wielder halted her toil to consider her mother's offer.

"That's very kind of you Betsy, but I think Micky has offered to have his nephew, Charlie, around our table to lesson the burden of mouths to feed at his sister Edith's house. Charlie loves spending time with Beth too".

"Oh, but that's not a problem Eliza, there'll be such a crowd at our house, that one more would make no difference to us."

There was a pause, as Eliza digested the further ammunition she'd been handed on a plate.

"And how insensitive of you to point that out to us of all people, Betsy." Eliza's quiet considered, monotone reply, cruelly underlined Betsy's faux pas.

"Oh, Eliza I didn't mean it like…"

"I'll discuss it with Micky tonight when he gets back. That's all I can say at the moment. We would've had to leave in time to watch the fisherman and fireman's football match, but it's been moved to the feast of St Stephen, instead of Christmas day itself now. Anyway, I'll let Edward know at the weekend when he calls, if that will suit you." She led the way back through the scullery leaving Betsy in no doubt as to whether she should leave, adding coldly as she went, "you must excuse me, I still have to dust and polish the parlour as well as all the brass and copper pipes before Micky gets home, he's not happy if everything isn't gleaming you know."

Betsy stepped out into the bitter cold, fastening her bonnet and buttoning her gloves. Her eyes glistened with the tears eager to join the many she had already wept for her daughter and their lost affection for each other. She asked herself again why she had spoilt everything by making them share her secret. But she knew she would not change any of it. For what she had lost, Edward had gained. Giving him a child so late in life, despite the personal cost, was better than the pain of not giving him a child at all. The despair she felt regarding Eliza's coldness, may have borne a little hope had she been able to witness the copious tears being shed at this moment, on the other side of the blue wooden door.

"Uncle Edward, look over there, there's a horseless carriage." Beth ran up the steps to Edward and Betsy's elegant four storey home, her eyes grew wider as she turned and pointed to the motor vehicle parked outside the house on Prince of Wales Terrace. Its driver was seated proudly at the front, resting one hand on a big wheel that looked as though it should be attached to the lower chasis, not inside the car itself. His other hand and his full attention, was taken up with the task of heaving on the handbrake, a large lever to the right side of him.

"So there is Beth, so there is. I've seen them now and again in the town; it must be an important person though." Edward strained his eyes to take in the details of the motor vehicle as he took Beth's hand to lead her inside. He turned to assure himself that the rest of the family were following behind, when he realised the driver of the motorcar was his brother-in-law, Peter Robinson.

"Goodness me Peter! Just when did you become the proud

owner of one of these wretched things? We won't all have to learn to drive them will we?" He hurried down the steps onto the pavement and pumped Peter's hand vigorously. "Where's the rest of the clan, have they all fallen out of this thing on the way here?"

Peter laughed heartily. "No such luck Edward! Bea and James've gone to collect my parents in a Hackney carriage. I just know they would flatly refuse to step into this beautiful beast, but it's got us here from Leeds in one piece, we wouldn't be without it now! Would we Abigail?"

Edward leant around Peter, to see a very pretty young lady seated demurely in the front seat of the automobile.

"Goodness me, Abigail! What a beauty you've grown into. No shortage of suiters I imagine. None of them good enough either I'll wager eh, Peter?"

Both men laughed aloud. Then they followed Abigail's gaze, and Edward realised Beth was sitting on the step shivering despite her thick coat and wool bonnet, and looking quite perplexed at both men. Edward strode over to the steps and reached down to her, swinging her in the air, he opened his mouth to speak, when an excited voice rang out from along the street and Eliza was running towards the motor car.

"Abigail, Abigail." Abigail climbed excitedly down from the motor car, and the two young women flew together like the long lost cousins they actually were, all social distance concertinaed by their warm embrace.

"Erm, I'd like to propose a toast." Edward pushed his chair away from the table, and rose to his feet. "I'd like to start by saying how proud my father would be if he could see who graced my table this Christmas day." He raised his glass, and swept it around the throng as he continued, "William, my father had great respect for you. He used to say that most journalists did not have the same discretion and respect for their fellow citizens as William Robinson had."

William, now an elderly white haired gentleman, raised his glass in grateful response to Edward's kind words.

Edward Continued. "Peter, he would have been so proud of you as his son-in-law. You've proved yourself an admirable, loyal husband and father." He glanced at his sister, acknowledging her glittery eyes that had never left his face since he had begun to speak, "Beatrice, you gave him two wonderful grandchildren that he never knew, yet he would be so proud of them both. He would be thrilled about James' scholarship to do medicine, and would have delighted in Abigail's sweet-natured disposition as well as having a countenance that so resembles our mother in her youth." He saw a lone tear streak over his sister's rounded cheek as she smiled approval at his sentiments, before turning his attention to his wife. "Finally, he would have loved to see his dear friend Joseph Elliot represented at my table. Not only by his beloved eldest daughter, my wonderful wife Betsy, for whom my father had a great fondness; but also by his beloved adopted daughter Eliza, and her own wonderful family."

Betsy smiled up at her husband, her cup runneth over on this Christmas day, what more could she want. Eliza may not share her affections, but she was here. Eliza smiled at Beth, then looked up at Micky who was raising his own glass towards Edward in response.

Micky was now back to his old self after his harrowing army experiences in South Africa, only now, with a new found vigour and zest for life. He was becoming well respected around the town. Most knew him for the publicity his war decorations had given him, but he had time for everyone, and did his best to help the fisher widows and their children down street. Not to mention helping his own family with the many mouths they had to feed. He had saved well from his army pay, and assured Eliza he would only be a fisherman until he had taken stock, and decided what trade to follow. He was even considering taking the apprenticeship being offered by Albert. Bertie had extolled the virtues of a career with him for the future of the family firm, and Micky was considering it, but he disapproved of Bertie's, albeit youthful dismissal of his time in the army saying he himself would never risk his life and limb for someone else's fight.

William Robinson broke the silence after Edward had re-seated himself at the head of their large elaborate dining table. Never before had they entertained so many, or in such lavish style. Betsy had starched the table cloths and napkins especially for today, and polished the silver and glassware. She had bought new Christmas baubles for their little table top tree in the corner of the Drawing Room. There, they had all enjoyed pre dinner drinks, exchanged small gifts and listened to Charlie and Beth's awkward rendition of 'Away in a Manger'.

"Hear hear, Edward. Nice words. I'm sure we all share the sentiments; indeed all who knew your father had great admiration for him and his work in this town. It's a great shame for us all that he passed away so prematurely, and before his work was done."

The gathering fell silent in deference to John Hetherington's memory, then William continued.

"Why was it Thom and Annie declined your hospitality today, Edward? It would have been nice to have our other child join us on Christmas day. Jane still misses our Johnny so."

"Well William, Thom and Annie have so many friends in Staithes now, I can understand that they wanted to spend Christmas there. Alice and Billy now have families of their own to spend Christmas with, there's only little Joe, and he's as at home in Staithes as his parents are, Thom and Little Joe will paint all day, and Annie will doze by the fireside!"

The company chuckled, including her parents, for Annie was affectionately renowned for falling asleep whenever or wherever she seated herself.

"Does Thom still do any stonemasonry Betsy? Annie doesn't mention his work much."

"Oh, just a little Mr Robinson, mainly gravestones I believe. He needs to earn a little more than he gets from his painting. But Little Joe seems to get by just selling his work." William

Robinson pulled an impressed expression, and turned towards his wife.

"Perhaps we should get him to do one for us my dear, they may be worth a bob or two in a few years time, eh." Jane Robinson shrugged her shoulders showing indisputable apathy for what she saw as her Grandson's 'flighty' career. William turned back to his host,

"And Albert too, Edward, where's he today? And his family? He's really gathered quite a reputation for his furniture now, kept very busy I understand. I know he has a team of apprentices working for him in his workshop now that both our young Billy, and Bertie have become Journeyman Cabinet Makers too. Am I right in thinking he has also now purchased their house in Victoria Street?"

Betsy puffed with family pride at the success her brother had made of their father's business. His smart attire about the town undoubtedly publicised his success and promoted his business. She interjected,

"That's right, Mr Robinson, he has. He's done very well my little brother. Pa's very proud of him of course, but I often wonder what my Granpa would say; he taught my Pa everything he knew, a generation earlier, and now those skills have been passed down further."

"Oh, without doubt, very commendable, yes he's quite the businessman now, eh? Our young Billy says Albert actually only designs and supervises now, as most of his time is taken up with orders and payments. I'll wager he's known by most of your neighbours up here, Edward too?"

"Oh he is indeed William. But for the Christmas festivities, Lottie wanted to go to her sister's in York this year. Albert only takes a break from work and his ledgers if he's completely away from the town. Also, Lottie really needed a rest. She's been doing too much recently and has a problem with her blood pressure. She's making it a holiday and staying for a couple of weeks after Christmas too. Bertie's current young lady is from York anyway, so he was more than happy with the arrangement."

"Hmm. Well Edward, perhaps we can add a toast to absent family?"

"To absent family." Chorused the diners loudly in unison, and waving their glasses of Edward's fine port wine at nothing in particular in the centre of the table, then took a respectful sip. A small voice added sadly, with her glass still aloft,

"To the dearly departed." The many pairs of eyes turned to Jane Robinson as one. She had a transitory glazed expression.

"To the dearly departed." They dutifully replied. With glasses replaced slowly and carefully back onto the pristine white linen, the murmur of many individual, lively and festive conversations rose up amongst the tasteful décor, the odour of a fine feast and well repleted guests.

Charlie and Beth were seated between Eliza and Abigail, they had remained quiet throughout the meal, just as they had been instructed. Abigail, whilst regaling her various and comical exploits with many suitors to Eliza, was twirling Beth's plaits around her fingers. She broke off at the natural end of a tale and turned her attention to her task.

"Oh, Eliza, you have the most beautiful daughter, look at these natural golden curls. She's so appealing with those big sapphire blue eyes. When I have a daughter, I want her to be exactly like yours." Beth turned her head swiftly to stifle a giggle in Charlie's direction. The things grown-ups talked about were so funny to a little girl almost five years old! Her sudden movement loosened Abigail's hold on her hair and pulled it clear of the side of her face.

"Oh Eliza, has she been bitten by something? She has a dent in the outside part of her ear, like there's a bit missing." Micky laughed at the look of horror on her pretty face,

"Of course she hasn't Abigail, but, it must be a trait in my family because Charlie here, my sister's child, has it too."

Abigail, curious, and to the crushing embarrassment of Charlie, insisted on feeling and comparing the auricles of both children.

On the other side of the table, Jane spoke quietly to Betsy, "Do you still do any nursing Betsy?"

"Oh, only occasionally Mrs Robinson. The superintendant will send for me if they are short handed at the hospital. But otherwise I find I have quite enough to do at home. We try to need as little help with the house as possible as I prefer to do things myself. I do wish I was just setting out on a nursing career though, the training offered now is so much more detailed than I ever had."

"That's because there is so much more to know now my dear, I won't have you doing yourself down, Betsy, you're an excellent nurse." Edward had interrupted their conversation. "Advances are being made all the time now, not just in the treatment of diseases, but in understanding the workings of the human body. There is so much more to know nowadays."

Jane Robinson, incredulous that Betsy would actually want to work, changed the subject.

"I called round to see Lottie the other day you know when Annie told me she had not been well. I'll go again next week too. If I'm spared of course."

"Yes, Mrs Robinson, Albert told me, that was very sweet of you."

"Well, she already had company though when I arrived, you know that woman that lives two doors down from them. Walks with a stick, you know. Fancy her calling in. I'd never spoken to her before of course, but she was actually quite nice. Well anyway, I made sure she didn't stay long, how can Lottie hope to rest if every cripple in the street keeps dropping in on her!"

"Just explain to me again Betsy, why are we out walking so early on this sunday morning, even before most good Christian people are rising for church?"

"On account of it being good for our constitution Edward." She smiled at him, and then realized she must give him more explanation to justify rising so early on a Sunday. "But also because we were awake anyway, and I wanted to see the damage to that Pier for myself, before everyone else comes to look."

It had been in the newspaper last evening about the severe north-west gale on Friday night damaging the Pier beyond any economical repair. Experts then blamed the extremely heavy seas and exceptionally high-tide for eventually washing away the pier completely the following day.

It was bitterly cold this early January morning, and they had been lucky in picking up a carriage as they had left home and been dropped on Castle Road just before the turning onto Queen's Parade. Betsy wanted to view the new North Bay vista on foot.

"When it was put up, Edward, I walked along with Pa to see the 'blot' that had appeared on our landscape. I remember that day like it was yesterday. It was just after your father had diagnosed Thom's asthma being down to the dust from the workshop. I was so upset at the construction of the Pier, but so enjoyed the precious time alone with Pa. You have to understand, that didn't happen too often in our busy household. Indeed the next time I remember such precious moments with him was when your mother stopped you taking me to the opening banquet of the Spa Grand Hall with you. I've never told you before, Edward dear, but Pa and I still went." Edward stopped their progress and turned to face her.

"How did you? It was ticket only."

"Oh, I don't mean we got into the hall, but Pa knew how upset I was, how much I had looked forward to it, and of course how long I had taken to get ready for you that night."

"But you told me it was fine, that you weren't upset!"

"How little you actually knew me then, Edward. I couldn't allow you to feel responsible, I knew it was your mother's doing, not yours." Edward picked up Betsy's hands in his own, and looked so deeply into her very soul, that she felt exposed and discomfited.

"My dear wife. I have put you through so much over the years, it is a wonder that you waited for me at all. I'm very fortunate indeed, have you forgiven me?"

"There was nothing to forgive Edward, I've told you, I didn't hold you responsible." She turned away from him to continue walking, keeping hold of one hand just long enough to encourage him to walk with her.

"Anyway, we watched the Mayor's arrival, and the Lady Mayoress stopped the carriage to speak to me. I'm ashamed to say that I enjoyed a moral victory over your mother that night, which was made all the more sweet when I knew you had not even been able to see the dignitaries from your seats." She smiled broadly up at her husband who immediately reciprocated, pleased she had enjoyed some part of the night even if it was in the form of retribution. Betsy added, "As well of course, as enjoying a precious and memorable evening with my beloved Pa."

"He's a very special person, Joseph Elliot, gone from this town, but never forgotten. I hope he knew the mark he left here, not just in his work, but on the people too." Betsy half smiled, then solemnly replied,

"Don't talk about him as if he's already gone Edward, please, he may live on for quite a while yet."

"In body though my dear, not really in mind, I fear."

Betsy ignored her husband's realistic reminder of her father's condition. She knew well herself. She moved ahead of him to the railings on Queen's parade over-looking Royal Albert Drive. Putting her hands on the icy metal, she drew in a deep breath as though inhaling the panorama, this northern bay, once again unspoilt by unnecessary man made features. The unsuccessful Warwick's tower was also due to be dismantled later this year, the bay of her youth was reappearing before her eyes. In the summer, horse drawn carriages would line the sea front, but today, only two carriage drivers braved the bitter morning, optimistic of a fare, yet their charges idle. Clouds of damp air were waved from their nostrils as they whinnied and wiggled their heads to keep warm. She leant backwards to affectionately acknowledge Edward's stance behind her, and tilted her head lightly onto his shoulder.

"Oh, Edward, thank you for coming with me this morning, I so wanted to see the bay returned to its unspoilt glory in the quiet morning light. I just wish Pa was with me to see it too. He didn't resist change as I did, but my angst was always his."

From behind her, Edward put his gloved hands on her wool cloaked arms, rubbing warmth into them as he whispered tenderly under her bonnet.

"I know my dear, I know. Come on, let's walk down the gardens to the sea."

"You know, Edward. I wrote to Ma last night to tell them about it, but it depends on what kind of a day he's having as to whether he will take it in. He can't read for himself."

"Pa, isn't that Aunt Betsy over there with Uncle Edward?" Little Joe was huddled against the biting wind on the rocks underneath the Castle on the promontory between the two bays, his easel propped between the boulders and a paintbrush busy on his canvas. He was destined to always be referred to as 'little' Joe despite his coming of age later this next year. As a child the term had distinguished him from his grandfather Joseph, and it had just stuck with him. He had the handsome dark curls and emerald eyes just like his father and grandfather before him and had much coquettish attention from the local girls which he undoubtedly enjoyed. But Little Joe had no time for anything but his painting.

Thom looked up from his own task to where Little Joe had indicated, screwing his ageing eyes carefully in the dusky wintry morning light to focus on the couple walking towards them.

"Looks like it could be, Little Joe. Wonder what they're doing out this early in the morning? We'll give them a shout when they get nearer." Thom turned back to the large rock he was working on, chiseling expertly into it.

"Pa, why do you think there is bad blood between Aunt Betsy

and Eliza? They used to be so close, always together, in fact, when Beth was born, Eliza lived with them for a while didn't she?"

"Oh, I don't know son, your mother and I have discussed it no end, she's asked Eliza about it and she denies any problem. Betsy will never admit to anything, nor will she be the cause if there is a problem. I can hear her saying, 'A house divided against itself cannot stand!' and 'Life's too short!'" He paused to chuckle at his own attempt at mimickry. "Your mother quite selfishly feels that Betsy's loss, however sad, is her gain. She's become quite close to Eliza recently, especially since Lottie has had to take it easy and Eliza doesn't like to go around with Beth too much. She's a charmer though that little one, and so sweet natured, not the little ruffian I remember Eliza being at that age."

"Maybe Betsy found it too hard having a little one living with her when she wasn't able to have any of her own, Pa? Ma said she had a very difficult few years losing lots of babies."

"Yes, you may be right son, but I wouldn't have said that was like our Betsy, she always made a fuss of you lot, and your cousin Bertie. Maybe she resented Micky's return after the war, and Eliza didn't need her so much. We may never know. They were spending Christmas together though, so that was a good sign." Thom straightened himself erect with a long slow groaning exhalation to illustrate his effort. Then he waved his arm in the direction of Betsy and Edward as they looked out to sea from the railings of Royal Albert Drive.

"Betsy, Edward, over here."

"Edward, someone's waving to us from the rocks over there. Who is it?"

"I can't see dear." Edward put his hand up to his forehead unnecessarily, as though shielding his view from a strong summer midday sun.

"There's two of them now, a second man has stood up to wave. Oh now I see, there's an artists easel, it must be Thom and Little Joe. Do you feel up to clambering on those rocks to see

431

them?"

"Of course Edward. We must wish them all the best for this year, we haven't seen them since before the festivities, I didn't know they were back from Staithes."

"Thom, how lovely to see you. Did you have a good Christmas?" Betsy embraced her brother and nephew demurely. Edward shook their hands.

"We wish you all well in the coming year. Lots of success with your painting of course, you must let us buy one some day Thom."

"Little Joe, why are you out here so early?" He had returned to his painting.

"Oh, excuse me for continuing Aunt Betsy, but I wanted to capture this very early morning light. Then Pa and I are meeting some other artists in The Lancaster Inn on Sandside for a lunchtime ale." He picked up his brush and palette and assessed his progress against the backdrop. He added rhetorically, "Don't you think the colours that accompany this enraged weather, are so unique if you catch them at day break, and there's another exhibition coming up at Staithes. I want to catch the beauty of the coast when it's at its most inhospitable." He added a few brush strokes to his canvas that seemed to add instant life and story to his exhibit in progress.

"Still so poetic Little Joe, I could listen to you paint all day!" Joe's emerald eyes twinkled at Betsy's teasing, the un-whiskered portions of his face and neck beguilingly peppered with swarthy stubble in his haste to capture this early morning coastline.

Edward and Thom smiled at the easy camaraderie.

"When do you think they'll finish this roadway then Thom? It's so far behind schedule now, I wonder it will ever be finished. We should have motor charabanc rides around this coastline by now, shouldn't we?"

"It's slow, but sure, Sir. They have been hampered by unusually extreme waves and high tides, but I think we'll be able to walk between these two bays before too long now."

"I hope you're right Thom." He looked around and settled on Thom's tools and the rock behind him, leaving Betsy to admire Little Joe's painting. "What are you doing here then, Thom? You can't be making gravestones down here, how would you transport them?" He looked quizzically at the indentation Thom had chiseled in the large flat surface of the huge rock behind him.

"No, Edward," Thom laughed as he surveyed his handiwork, "that would certainly not be sensible. No I'm just making a permanent shelter for Little Joe's work. He likes this kind of lighting, which means being here during inclement weather conditions. Rather than pack up and go home, he could wait out the showers if he had somewhere to keep his painting sheltered and dry."

Edward nodded his understanding. "Looks like hard work though Thom. I think you've chosen a rock big enough to keep Little Joe sheltered, never mind his painting!"

"It is a large one isn't it? Perhaps I should chisel a door and a window in it too. You could always sleep here Little Joe, and capture any light you like then!"

Chapter 35

Scarborough, 1908

"Betsy, I'm fine now honestly. It was only a bit of a hiccough. Probably my time of life. I'm really back to doing everything I used to do, and I feel perfectly fine."

Betsy walked into the parlour in Victoria Street, removing her delicate kid gloves and warm cape and placing them on the small occasional table beside the sofa. Underneath, was revealed a beautifully frilled blouse in thick white linen. Two deep frills ran from each shoulder and over her comely bosom, to meet at her waist as though joining forces to tunnel under the high waist of the long dark skirt which just reached and tickled the surface of her shiny leather boots. Another deep frill supported her chin, and was held there by a large oval sepia cameo. The leg–o–mutton sleeves were tamed by the deepest of cuffs, which required a dozen buttons to hold them together along their length before another frill escaped onto the back of her dainty hands.

Lottie was busying herself carrying the prepared tea, bread and butter into the parlour, and was resisting Betsy's offer of help.

"Take this morning, Betsy. I was up earlier than usual, about half past five to get the boiler filled and lit, as well as cleaning and lighting the range. I've done the washing in the dolly tub, rinsed and hung out the clothes; and I'm still lively enough to make afternoon tea for us as well as have Albert's tea on the go, to be ready for the minute he walks through the door. He's not best pleased otherwise. Now will you stop fussing?"

She finished her last sentence as she was returning to the scullery for the tea cups, Betsy smiled as Lottie's hands, now off-loaded, hung loosely from her arms as though the wrists were suddenly boneless, allowing her fingers to drip languidly to the floor. The family had always teased Lottie for this stance of hers, indeed she had heard Beth recently accuse Bertie's intended, Emma, as having 'Aunt Lottie' hands after she had finished washing the dishes one day.

As Lottie returned with the cups, she continued, "To quote one of your favourite expressions, Betsy, it was all 'much ado about nothing'!"

"I doubt that very much Lottie, if Edward said you needed to rest, then there must have been good reason. However I'm delighted that you appear to be fully recovered."

Betsy had made herself comfortable in Albert and Lottie's stylish parlour. For a modest street house, there was an air of opulence about the décor and furnishings. The walls were unfashionably plain, but this allowed the luxurious rugs on the highly polished floor, and the deep burgundy of the damask drapes to flaunt their quality. The paler than usual sofa and chairs were comfortable if somewhat unforgiving, and still smelt of their newness. The chair arms wore chenille covers to match the colour of the drapes, as did the chair backs, each one adorned with a contrasting lace antimacassar. Much of the furniture was from Albert's own workshop and of exquisite design. The mantelpiece was fashionably adorned with Victoriana, each piece of china or crystal queuing to meet the heavy mahogany clock in its centre. A large oil painting hung over the clock. Unlike many of the sombre scenes of the day, this was an uplifting summer seascape in pale colours, and seemed to mirror the ambience of the room. The various small watercolours around the walls, Betsy recognised as the work of either Thom or Little Joe. Ornate lamps protruded from the walls and ceiling in readiness for nightfall and the facilitation of reading or sewing activities in the evening. Lottie was very proud of her home and all wood and silver alike reflected their onlooker as clearly as any glass. Betsy regretted for a moment not doing her own housework anymore. Her home did not seem to boast the same loving care.

"Good-day, Lottie, are you home." Eliza appeared around the doorway, so obviously comfortable in her entrance without invitation, a subtlety not lost on Betsy.

Eliza, at thirty two years old, gave the air of a quietly confident and delicately pretty young woman. She hid well her continued feelings of not belonging, despite now knowing otherwise. This no longer stemmed from her 'foundling' status, but from her marriage. To the fisher folk down street, despite being Micky's wife, and a pleasant, hard working and thoughtful member of the community, she would always be a little 'above herself', not least for living up in the main part of town. To her family, she knew, despite their affection for Micky, they felt she had married beneath her. She tried to dress to please both parties. However, her clothes, despite being from plain and inexpensive materials, were exquisitely made, previously with Betsy's assistance, and more latterly with help from either Annie or Lottie, and she wore them well. As a consequence, she could feel an imposter in either company.

"Oh Betsy, you're here too. Well I shall give you both our news. Micky and I are expecting a little brother or sister for Beth early next year, I didn't say anything for a while because I wanted to be sure everything was alright. After waiting so long, we could hardly believe it ourselves."

"Oh Eliza, that's wonderful news. Have you told Beth, I bet she will be so excited." Betsy had jumped to her feet and had taken Eliza's hand. Their relationship had gradually warmed over time, although Eliza could never resist an opportunity to reinforce her displeasure. Lottie clapped her miraculously re-structured hands together in delight.

"Eliza that's so wonderful, you're both so blessed, I had thought you were going to be like us and only have the one child. Oh I'm sorry Betsy. That was so very insensitive of me, how you would have loved to have such a blessing. Please forgive me, I don't always think before I speak."

"Think nothing of it Lottie, Betsy doesn't mind, do you, it's better than thinking too much, so that you end up saying nothing eh, Betsy?"

"Now you come and sit down here Eliza, it's so long since I've seen you, everyone got out of the habit of popping in when they thought I needed rest. I'll get another cup, you must have time for one before Beth gets home from school. I do wish you would bring her around Eliza, I've missed her company, she's such a treasure."

"Yes please Lottie, tea would be lovely." She looked over at Betsy. She was looking down at her knees, never sure what to say after one of Eliza's subtle scoldings. Eliza knew well her effect, and suffered a pang of guilt. Perhaps this had gone on long enough. She had everything to look forward to now, not back. And didn't everyone need their mother at a time like this?

"I'm sorry Betsy, I am trying to forgive you."

"I know you are my dear, I know you are, and I'm very grateful." She lowered her voice as she heard Lottie returning. "Can I tell your father your news?"

"Of course Betsy. Of course."

Lottie returned, and leant over the tray pouring warming cups of tea, and pressing slices of bread and dripping onto her guests.

"Come on now, you need to get some fat into you before the winter cold is upon us. Remember to get Beth sewn into her brown paper and lard vests again this year Eliza." Eliza pulled a face,

"It smelt so bad though Lottie."

"But she had no colds Eliza did she?"

"Actually, Edward and Betsy have bought her some bodice things for this winter. They're supposed to keep in the heat on very cold days, so we can give those a try first. They seem very cosy, although the rubber buttons are hard to fasten, especially with cold hands." Eliza felt she had absolved herself somewhat in negating the power of her previous punch by this acknowledgement of Betsy's part in Beth's gift.

"Well, you can maybe let me help in altering any of Beth's old clothes to fit the new baby. That would keep me busy over the winter. I should see if I have any of Bertie's baby things left; I kept them all, always hopeful they would be needed again, and you may have a boy this time." There was a pause while the three women sipped their tea in almost comical choreographed unison.

"Is everything sorted now then, Lottie, for Bertie's wedding in the new year?"

"Oh I think so, Eliza, but Emma's mother is making all the arrangements, we just have to turn up."

"She'll make a lovely bride Lottie, she's very pretty isn't she?"

"She is that Eliza, but a hard worker too, she'll make our Bertie a very good wife."

"And does my little brother approve the match, Lottie?"

"Oh Albert thinks she'll do just fine in our family, Betsy. He's such the spruce businessman now though, he just teases Bertie not to rush him into living with a Grandma!"

Betsy and Eliza took a synchronised open mouthed swift intakes of breath to show their mock horror at Albert's teasing, then Eliza appeased her hostess,

"Well what a cheek Lottie, wait 'til I see him next, I'll tell him, maybe his lovely wife is not so keen to live with a Grandpa either!"

They all chuckled wickedly at the thought of their young and dapper Albert, as a Grandpa. Lottie too, had remained an attractive woman; she had rounded over the years, but the fullness of her face added to her charm and under-rated the fine, delicate criss-crossing the years had etched around her eyes. Together they still made a very handsome and well-attired couple.

"I'm glad the family are moving to Scarborough though, otherwise Emma may have wanted Bertie to move to York.

The business is going too well for Bertie to want to leave his father now, I hardly ever see Albert, they're so busy, and I think her family realise that. I'll miss Bertie though when he moves to their little house in Falsgrave."

"I'm sure you will Lottie, you've always been so close. Her father loves the cricket here though doesn't he, they should settle well."

"You're right Betsy, and now there's the festival here, there'll be plenty to watch every season. They were all here to watch Bertie's team become champions of the league four years ago just after Bertie and Emma first met. I can see Emma's father wanting to become a Wesleyan just to join the Nelson Street club!"

They all laughed together, then Betsy made a move to gather her gloves and hat.

"We must all do this again sometime, Lottie, it's been such fun, perhaps that cousin of yours, and sister-in-law of ours, Annie could join us next time? Have you heard from your cousin Peter? Edward was just saying the other day that Beatrice hasn't written for a while, it isn't like her."

"No I don't often hear from them, I get their news from Annie. And yes, she would have loved this afternoon, we must do it again. Or even go for one of these new motorised Charabanc rides to Forge Valley for the aftrenoon? They go from the Station forecourt regularly. We could even pretend to be holidaymakers eh? It's a bumpy ride on those tiered seats I believe, it may just keep Annie's lazy soul awake!" Chuckling at the expense of her sleepy cousin, and watching Betsy pin her ornate hat into position, she continued, "Don't you just miss the old bonnets now Betsy, just when we could do with those ribbons to tie up our double chins, they go out of fashion!" She patted the loose skin underneath her jaw, causing further peels of hilarity from her kin. As they all quieted, she was reminded of another recent amusement, "Oh, Betsy, I must just tell you this. Remember the last time you were here, and Bertie brought home that little terrier, the coastguard's dog for the night because he found it wandering around here."

"Yes, I remember, didn't you keep it overnight on account of Bertie not having time to walk it home?"

"Yes that's right. Well, when Bertie took him back to his cottage the next morning, turns out, the coastguard retired after the opening of the Marine Drive this year, he apparently always intended to retire then, but didn't know it would take a whole nine years longer than the schedule! And was it all worth it? I ask you, monstrosity it is, all those thousands of yards of cast iron work. Spoils a naturally beautiful headland if you ask me, not to mention all those perfectly good buildings they demolished, including the old infirmary, just to make way for it. Anyway, would you believe it, he, the coastguard I mean, now lives two doors down from us!" She paused to enjoy both women's sharp intake of surprise. "Poor man had just let the dog out to do its business for the night. Along comes Bertie. Next thing, the coastguard spent the whole night searching the streets whilst his dog enjoyed supper and a warm night by our fireside!"

All three cackled behind hands clutched to their mouths like guilty witches round a cauldron as they wickedly imagined the poor old man stalking the streets thinking he had lost his faithful friend.

When they recovered, Eliza started to laugh again,

"I heard a funny story the other day, apparently one of the men chiselled a little house in one of the big boulders at the bottom of the cliff whilst working on the Marine Drive; but now it's being called Hairy Bobb's Cave." In answer to their quizzical expressions, she explained, "You know the little man that collects the yellowstone from the cliffs to sell on doorsteps, Hairy Bobb, well apparently, he's using it to shelter from his overbearing wife!"

Betsy started to laugh, and it was a few minutes before she had regained enough composure to explain. "Oh how these rumours start, that is just so funny."

She looked at Eliza and Lottie's blank faces,

"It was Thom. It looked like such hard work. He had all his stonemasonry tools with him and was doing it one day when we were down there. It's just a place for Little Joe to shelter his paintings in. He loves to capture the hue of inclement weather, but needs to keep them dry if it rains and then he waits for the weather to clear up enough for him to continue. Annie did tell me though the other day that Thom had actually put two windows and a door shape in it, just as he had teased that he would. Many a true word spoken in jest, eh ladies, he could always be a joker, our Thom!"

By now Lottie and Eliza were laughing again, Lottie spoke first,

"Oh I haven't laughed so much in ages, my belly aches. We should most definitely have afternoon tea together more often." She gathered her composure, her thoughts and her skirts, and continued, "You know though, I think we should keep the knowledge of this story within the family, the myth is so much more fun than the truth."

"I agree, Lottie. And we are very good at keeping secrets in our family aren't we Betsy?"

"Nel-son-went-to-war-in-the-battle-of wa-ter-loo.
Nel-son-lost-an-eye-in-the-battle-of wa-ter-loo.
Nel-son-lost-an-arm-in-the-battle-of wa-ter-loo."

Beth stopped jumping over the twirling fishing rope, and brought it to a halt with her foot.

"Charlie, Nelson wasn't at the Battle of Waterloo, it was Wellington. So how could he possibly have lost anything? He'd died ten years before then at the Battle of Trafalgar!"

Charlie shrugged his shoulders amid the chaos of Foreshore Road.

"Well, you couldn't catch a cold, let alone a fish, not to mention gut one!" Beth childishly poked out her tongue at her cousin, and scanned the crowd for her friends.

Using fisherman's ropes to skip was becoming a tradition

every Shrove Tuesday. It had begun in a small way with the new Century. But now, children got out of school early to join the fun on the sands as a treat if they were good, and it was as much a part of this February day, as the eating of pancakes. Carriages and motor vehicles were prohibited from the seafront, following an injury to a skipping child two years earlier, and the recent arrival of motor charabancs and their perceived potential hazard on this occasion, had necessitated this edict.

Some children ran skipping races with their friends and their own small skipping ropes. Others were competing to see how many skips they could do with their ropes, before fatiguing co-ordination between limbs mis-timed their jump, bringing them to an abrupt halt, laughing and panting, with the rope limp and snaked around their ankles.

Those with fishing connections however, had the benefit of a large fishing rope that stretched across the whole of Foreshore Road, adults were usually charged with the task of twining the rope so that a whole group of children could evidence their expertise of running in and out of the rope to their own particular chants and games.

Beth was waiting for some friends to join them, but Charlie had not let her down in bringing an esteemed fishing rope, and at nearly fourteen years old, had promised to 'twine' for her. Her mother Eliza, had been chatting to acquaintances whilst twirling the other end of the rope. They had moved away, and Eliza turned her attention to Charlie and Beth. She shouted above the cheerful clatter of childish gaiety and the smack of wet rope on asphalt.

"Don't fight about it you two. Remember Charlie isn't at school anymore Beth. I'm very glad you've stopped for a minute though, I'm exhausted, I don't think I can keep this up all afternoon, this little one here's getting in the way making it awkward, my arm's aching!" Eliza transferred the heavy rope to her right hand and held it loosely, having indicated her bulging belly, burgeoning through the opening of her straining cloak, whilst she circled her left shoulder to ease the discomfort with a telling slow groan on her exhalation.

Beth looked uneasily around her, disappointment in her transparent expression. She looked every inch the angelic nine year old she tried so hard to be. Her calf length pristine white pinafore was none the worse for her skipping, though the jumping up and down had shown the starched frills of her panteloons hugging her knees, to be a perfect broiderie anglaise match for those enveloping her shoulders, cuffs and hemline. Her brown boots were polished, and unlike many of her friends, were of the latest style, with shiny buttons on a fashionable diagonal slope up the outside of the boot. They had been a Christmas gift from Betsy and Edward. She had so enjoyed sitting in the chair to have her feet measured for them in Hopper and Mason's, the new department store on Westborough. They had looked at all the dresses for girls her age in there too, but her Mother had pulled her away saying they could not spend her father's hard earned money on clothes like that. Beth had sensed her mother's disapproval of the boots, but knew she always tried to stop Betsy and Edward from spoiling her; Christmas had been her saviour there. Her mother had started to allow Betsy to make new dresses for her now. She would pick out material from The Rem on Market Street, and Betsy would magic a creation. Some of her friends from down street said that The Remnant Warehouse was to be turned into a Department Store soon that everyone would be able to shop in, not just the well-to-do. She looked forward to that, then perhaps her mother could buy herself some new clothes too.

A familiar voice broke piercingly above the noise, into Beth's thoughts.

"Hey Eliza, let me do that for you. You shouldn't be doing that. Come on then Beth, let's see how good you are at this. You ready Charlie?"

"Annie, how nice to see you down here, and awake too!"

"You watch your tongue Eliza Walker!" She yelled back, "Do

you want some help here or not!"

Both ladies laughed, and Beth's child-like, disappointed, indulgent demeanour disappeared at once. She shouted between her cupped hands at her Aunt.

"Of course we do Aunt Annie, thank you."

Eliza smiled at her daughter's politeness, as Annie added,

"Actually, Eliza, the doctor thinks I may have something wrong with my glands, and that could be why I get so tired, it could even be why I have spread out so much around here." She indicated her thickening waistline, and added, "I hope it's nothing really bad."

"Oh I'm sure it won't be Annie, but it would be good to have a reason for it though. Mind, we would have to stop teasing you then, that'd be no fun at all!"

"Aah, how guilty will you all feel then eh?"

Eliza smiled, not quite sure how serious Annie was being. She changed the subject thankfully,

"Look Annie, you're just in time, here's Beth's friends come to join her. Lottie was going to join us too, with Emma, the new Mrs Elliot! Are Alice and Billy here with all your grandchildren?"

"I think they will be. They'll find me though, I said I would buy them all some humbugs. They love those. Gosh, Eliza, this fishing rope is heavy, no wonder you were tired. You must be a strong lad now Charlie."

Charlie beamed with the pride of a boy being promoted to a man. He was a keen fisherman, already learning most of the skills needed to carry on his family's trade.

"He can haul in a whole trawl of fish now Aunt Annie. By himself! But he smells like them most of the time. My Pa says he has to learn to scrub and clean himself up as well as cleaning the fish."

"Och, I heard you cleaned and graded those herring in the summer just as queeck as ony o' those wee herring lassies frae bonny Scotland! Fufty a minute, is that no' the rate, son?"

Beth giggled as she stopped skipping to greet her friends, but

Charlie and Eliza continued their mirth at Annie's mimicry, oblivious to the comedy in her ridiculously poor attempt at the Scottish twang. Thinking she was providing accurate entertainment, Annie chivvied Beth's friends, with her forearms commandingly scooping her fallen bosom, "Come alang bairns, it's a braw brig't day fa' playin' oot!" Beth smiled, trying to hide her embarrassment in front of Norah, only the most popular girl in their class. Charlie could hardly twirl the rope for giggling, and Eliza was helpless with laughter, tears streaming down her face, her bulge bouncing as the muscles of her abdomen struggled with their load.

Annie smiled, smug with her apparent accomplishment.

All four girls had settled into a routine of skipping inside the fishing rope, but taking it in turns to run out of the rope at one end, only to re-join at the other as the remaining skippers shuffled forwards. Charlie and Eliza were still wickedly smiling at Annie when they caught each other's eye, Eliza mimicking her stance. Each anticipated quietly regaling the hilarity to others, though suspecting it was an amusing tail that had to be experienced first hand to appreciate its full comedic value.

"Annie, Annie. Have you seen Eliza?" Annie slowed her arm to look for the familiar voice shouting for her above the lash of ropes and cheers.

"Over here Thom, she's here."

"She's here Skipper, with our Annie, I thought she'd said she'd be near the Ice House and the West Pier." Thom slowed, and walked tenderly towards his wife. He whispered, "Annie dear, it's Micky, there's been an accident, take the children for some sweets. Bring Beth back later, she'll have to know."

All colour drained from Annie's face as she turned to an unsuspecting, and still smiling Eliza. Then realising her countenance displayed too much, she looked quickly away, and followed Thom's bidding with the delighted children.

Eliza looked curiously from Thom to the retreating Annie, she had assumed Thom had wanted to tell Annie some news regarding his painting, perhaps a sale, or an exhibition. Now she felt panic rising within her. As Micky's skipper came into view behind Thom, she felt her knees begin to buckle. No words were now necessary.

Someone was screaming above the raucous occasion, she could hear it, but she had no idea it was from her own lungs, or that somehow a silence had fallen on the entire Foreshore, and the whole town had heard her pain. Word had travelled along from the fishing Pier like flotsam carried on a wave. Mothers in shock and disbelief, ensured the news continued to ride the crest as they scurried their children away to give dignity to her grief. Micky was a well known, and respected member of the town. His father had been the only survivor of a fishing vessel tragically lost in a storm only last week. Their community were no strangers to disaster, but their respect for Micky and his family, was sincere.

"Where's Betsy. Edward, I need Betsy. Will she come? After all I've put her through, will she come? Please Edward, please?"

"Of course she'll come my dear, of course she'll come. I'll send someone for her. She won't know yet. You lie still, if these pains keep up, it could be too early for the baby to survive. Hush now. I'll get Betsy for you."

Edward was seated beside Eliza's bed. She had been taken straight to the Workhouse Infirmary from the Foreshore when it became obvious that the shock could bring the baby. Thom and Lottie had been with her, but they had gone for Edward immediately. He was praying for his daughter now, he felt so helpless. Not since the loss of his own babies, had medicine let him down as much as it did now. Eliza would need this child more than ever to help her through, but not yet, oh please God, not yet. He raised himself up from his aching posture, and arranged a messenger for Betsy to come immediately. This cloud could well have one of Betsy's silver linings if it brought forgiveness along with its suffering.

"Betsy, she's too tiny, she'll never survive you know that well enough. She was so cyanosed for such a long time after her albeit, easy delivery. I was not expecting her to breath at all, but she was determined to have a try, weren't you little one. It just makes for even more heart ache in the end though Betsy, you know that too. She's very floppy at the moment, but she'll probably end up very spastic, if she makes it for any length of time that is."

Betsy was holding the swaddled infant, trying to keep her warm. Edward had stroked her cheek as he spoke.

"I'm glad our children did not survive, Betsy. Not if they were going to have problems, it's a hard enough life for the fit and healthy. We were at least spared that."

"Were we Edward? Are you saying this little one doesn't deserve a chance, just because she may not be perfect?"

"No Betsy, I'm saying it because I know categorically she will be a cripple, and possibly retarded too. I was there, I saw how she struggled to get air into her lungs. Her brain is undoubtedly and unquestionably damaged."

"Shh, Eliza could wake up again at any moment." She lowered her voice still further. "I can't imagine she'll come good either Edward, but she's surprised us so far, you never know. Maybe her father is watching over her, eh?"

"I wish it were that simple Betsy, but you know it isn't. How many children die every year from early or difficult births and the damage that then happens to the brain? You know it's many, Betsy. Maybe not immediately. But eventually, a few months from now? A year?"

"I know Edward, but where there's life there's hope, isn't that so?"

"Do you think there could be any hope for Micky, Betsy?" They both turned as small weak words came from Eliza's bed. "Is that what you're saying? No-one saw him dead. His skipper just said he got tangled in the net and was pulled overboard whilst hauling the trawl and they couldn't find him, he could have been picked up by another boat. He could still be alive?"

Betsy hurried to Eliza's side.

"Best not get your hopes up, love, you know how cold the sea is at this time of year, and off the coast of Scotland too, it's even colder. The skipper said no-one could survive being in the sea for more than a few moments."

Tears were glistening again in Eliza's eyes.

"But Micky's father survived the capsize just last week, he was in the sea."

"I know Eliza, but their boat had been in difficulty for a while, the lifeboat was already there to pick him up when it went down. Even so he was the only survivor remember."

"But Micky's so strong, Betsy, he's so strong." The last words were lost in the crescendo of sobs that wracked her body once again. Betsy turned helplessly to Edward as she seated herself beside their daughter. She straightened the beige wool coat she had brought to warm her, and soothed her with banal words and an inadequate, repetitive, rhythmic stroke on the back of her hand.

"You know Betsy, we both wanted to have another girl, Beth is such a delight."

"Really Eliza, I thought Micky might have wanted a son."

"Oh no Betsy, we already have a son."

"Nurse, quickly, over here, Edward was wrong, he said she was floppy, but she has just had a really good stretch, look, she's moving her head back and straightening her arms and legs." She softened her voice and cooed, "That's a clever girl, you get those arms and legs moving, do it for your mother, eh?" Eliza's expression slowly changed when she realised Rose's stretch was not abating, she looked up questioningly. The nurse scurried over towards Eliza, her initial smile giving way to grave concern. Taking one brief look at the baby, she snatched her up awkwardly, in a manner that spoke of dire urgency,

"I'll take her, nothing to worry yourself about. The doctor will come and talk to you soon."

"Don't take her away, please, no. Don't take her. Get Betsy for me, I want Betsy here. She'll know what to do. Please, get Betsy."

"Edward, I can't thank you enough for getting me out of there. It's so kind of you both to offer to look after us. I really thought little Rose was dying the way the nurse ran off with her, I can't have her doing that again."

Edward and Betsy exchanged a glance.

Eliza was walking slowly into Edward and Betsy's drawing room carrying baby Rose, with an excited Beth skipping at her skirts, desperately trying to get a better look at her new baby sister. As far as she was concerned, the smaller the baby, the more the appeal, she couldn't wait to hold her.

Edward spoke first, indicating to Eliza to sit down.

"Eliza, sit down. We need to talk to you. Beth needs to hear it too, it will affect her." He paused to allow his daughter and granddaughter to be seated on the chaise longue. Eliza looked up at her father as she adjusted the familiar beige wool around her baby, and with a puzzled expression, interrupted him,

"Don't worry, Edward, we won't stay long, as soon as I'm fit, we'll return to our little house. The fishermen say they will help us with our rent for a little while at least…."

"Eliza, listen to me. This has nothing to do with where you live. Betsy and I would be delighted if you'd all live here with us anyway. We're all one family, and this is a very big house for two elderly people like us." He shared a smile with Betsy, and Eliza's tension and defensiveness eased. Then he continued with what he felt had to be said.

"Eliza, this is going to be very difficult for me to say, especially on account of what you are going through with your beloved Micky's accident, but you must be prepared." He took a deep breath, drawing conducted strength from Betsy as she placed a hand upon his shoulder.

"Rose, will not live for long, Eliza. Her brain was affected by her tiny lungs not being able to get enough oxygen around her body because she was born much too far before her time."

Eliza looked disbelievingly at Edward, then at Betsy.

"You must be wrong Edward, isn't he Betsy. Betsy knows the story Edward, don't you Betsy? Micky didn't know it, but he must have built his nest of spices. Mustn't he Betsy? Rose is his phoenix, the new phoenix doesn't die, the old one does. Micky's dead, so why would Rose die too? Betsy, why would Rose die too, she'll get stronger won't she?" She pleaded with them, her eyes begged them to take back what had been said, to say they must have got it wrong.

Edward turned anxiously to Betsy, drawing the courage to continue, he chose to ignore the myth she clung to.

"Eliza, my dear, when the nurse took her from you, the doctor saw that she was having a seizure, that's a sure sign in these babies. She may have even been having brain apoplexy. I mean a bleed in her brain. She may not even be able to feed well enough, and so could just die from Phthisis, that's….."

"I know that means, Edward, she'll just waste away!" Eliza looked down at her baby as if to reassure that this could not be possible, then she continued, "How dare you refer to her as 'these babies'. Is Rose just one of these babies to you Edward? Are you forgetting she is also your family?" Eliza glanced down at Beth before quietly adding, "Your close family?"

"Of course I haven't, Eliza, why else would this be so difficult for me? I'm just so worried that you're not prepared for what will surely happen." He saw Eliza's anger begin to retreat, and in an attempt to ward off any impending guilt she may feel, he added, "You should also know Eliza, that one of the reasons she has survived so far, is because she's a good size. Had you gone your full time, your confinement would have been difficult. You are so small, and in another two months, Rose could have been too big for you to deliver safely. The outcome for Rose may then have been the same as it is now, but we may also have lost you."

Beth moved onto her knees at the side of her mother. She

had listened intently, now she reached for Rose's hand, the fingers tightly curled. Beth gently opened them, and fitted her own finger inside the palm, all the time smiling into her little sister's eyes unseeing yet dazzling eyes.

"It doesn't mean we can't love her and look after her while she's here though, does it Uncle Edward? Then it will be Pa's turn to have her with him."

Edward looked at little Beth, she had suddenly become such a vulnerable little girl again, yet she possesed a simple maturity the rest of them had lost long ago. He felt Betsy's hand tighten on his shoulder and sensed her wipe away a tear with her other hand. He was about to reply, when he saw Beth, with her other hand, wipe away a tear from her mother's face. The sadness in this room weighed so heavy, and reminded him of when his little brother Henry had died. He sighed deeply, he must not allow that brand of grief to taint the rest of their lives as it had for his own mother.

"Of course it doesn't Beth. We must give her as much love and fun as she can take, so that when her time comes to leave us, she takes with her some wonderful memories of us all to show your Pa. And just as important, she must leave plenty here for us too so that we never forget her."

Forcing a smile, Eliza indicated for Beth to sit next to her so she could hold baby Rose. She glanced at Edward and Betsy who nodded their approval,

"You know Beth, she looks to me as if she has yours and your father's wicked sense of humour. See, she won't let you have your finger back will she?"

Chapter 36

Scarborough, 1910 - 1912

"Betsy. I know you're thinking about Pa. You really wish you'd gone down with Albert don't you?"

Betsy looked up from her sewing as Eliza went on.

"I can manage you know. Beth is such a big help, and Edward would still have been here. Rose is nearly a year now. She's more robust."

"I can't deny I would have liked to have been some help to poor Ma, my dear, but there's nothing can be done for Pa now. He's gone from this world. Praying for his soul in the next can be done just as well from his beloved Scarborough, as from Dorset."

"Then why don't you go and see Ma and help her to get over Pa's passing after Albert comes back. Then you can be reassured that Albert is also around for us."

"Now that's a very good idea, Eliza. Maybe I will. I suppose Lottie would always help out too. It's just that she has her grandchild too now, she needs to spend time with her. Albert and Lottie seem to be enjoying themselves recently, gallivanting on an evening too. Lottie mentioned the other day that they had spent an evening at the new Floral Hall watching George Royle's entertainers called the Fol-de-Rols. They had a splendid evening, enjoyable gay and amusing. Perhaps we could get Edward to take us my dear. It would make a change from the Spa. The last time he took me there, it was a very sombre affair. The band members were dressed as though they should be following a funeral cortege, complete with top hats!"

Eliza had the infant Rose on her knee. She was trying to spoon milk into her, but almost as much was pouring back out onto her muslin cloth, carefully placed over her long ivory cotton pin-tucked baby dress. Betsy watched her daughter's futile, but loving attempts to nurture her child.

"Why don't you tip her head back Eliza, to give her more of a chance to get it down."

Eliza tweeked her daughter's cheek, smiling closely and intently into her face.

"I just have to be patient Betsy. I've learnt what's best for her. Well, to be honest, it was Beth that first realised, if you tip her head, she chokes on it and goes stiff, if you leave it forward, she does manage to swallow better. It just takes longer. Doesn't it, yes it does." The last words were emphasized and exaggerated to try to provoke a reaction from her child. She was never disappointed. Her prize was a beaming smile and gurgle at the recognition of Eliza's directed attention and tone. Her little face engaged the large sapphire eyes as she tried purposefully to focus on her recipient of this most precious of her rewards.

"Did you see that Betsy? One of her best smiles ever, specially for your Mother. Eh little Rose? And those eyes Betsy, she can say so much to me just with one look." Eliza stroked her daughter's white blond curls as she cooed.

Betsy smiled back. How precious these moments were for Eliza. She could not bear to think of how things may end.

"Eliza, I've never asked you to explain 'til now, although I've wanted to so many times over these last months, but you were so fragile. You're stronger now, I have to know. Do you remember telling me after Rose was born, that you and Micky also had a son? Is that the secret Ma referred to when she left? Is it Charlie? I've been driven mad with not knowing. I don't know if now is the right time, but please tell me Eliza, please."

Eliza had not taken her eyes away from her beautiful daughter while Betsy spoke. She put down the milk and was now rocking her to sleep, making shushing noises in time with her motion. Now she slowed her movement, and looked up at Betsy shamefully from under her long straight lashes, her eyes glistening with tears made many years before.

"Betsy, how I have longed for this conversation with you. I'm so ashamed of my behaviour towards you. I'm no better, and yet I judged you."

"But I don't understand how we did not know Eliza? Did Ma always know?"

"No Betsy, honestly. No-one knew. I didn't even realise I was in the family way myself until quite late on. Remember how I was trying hard to fit in with Micky's family and staying with his sister. I was working so hard with them all, I just had not realised I had missed. Then when we realised, we thought we would come and live with Ma and Pa if Micky's family would not agree to the marriage. But I caught an infection after my confinement in their house down street. I was so ill, that Edith started to feed Charlie along with her twins, and it seemed an easy solution at first. We always intended to have him with us when we could. It just got so difficult to explain to him, and Edith cared for him as one of her own. He's a fisherman through and through though, and that always disappointed Micky. He always wanted more for him than that." Eliza's tears, restrained over the years, now flowed, not just for the loss of her son, but for the grief she had inflicted on her own mother.

"I'm so sorry Betsy. Can you ever forgive me? We'll move out if you're too angry with me. I'll understand. I know I behaved dreadfully towards you for doing the same thing. I couldn't blame you if you wanted us to go." Betsy pulled a handkerchief from her sleeve, and blew her nose hard.

"What did we all ever do to deserve such heartache Eliza, what did we ever do?"

Eliza struggled forwards in her chair, and raised herself to her feet. She laid the sleeping Rose in her basinet and walked gracefully over to her own mother. Since living with her parents in their home, she had allowed Betsy to make her some clothes in more lavish materials, and her natural elegance had emerged. She no longer worried about her image down street when she visited Micky's sister and Charlie, for this was the extent of her connection to them now. Many were relieved the cuckoo in their nest, had flown. Indeed Charlie, oblivious to any reasoning behind his invitations, often joined them for their Sunday lunch, and was subliminally educated by his grandfather, posing as an elderly chum.

Eliza placed a tentative hand on her mother's shoulder.

"I don't know Betsy. Perhaps the women in our family are destined to take up with the wrong men or at least at the wrong time." She risked a half smile at Betsy as their eyes locked for an instant.

"And Ma, Eliza, how did she know? When did she know?"

"I really don't know Betsy, she seemed to be able to tell as soon as she met Charlie, she said 'blood will out'."

"Strange. I think Charlie looks like his Grandfather Walker, so I certainly never had cause to suspect anything. But Charlie should be with us now, Eliza, as a family. You and Beth enjoy living with us don't you? Charlie could be here too. Poor Edward, he would have loved a son, imagine how he could have spoiled his grandson. He would have wanted him to have an education, perhaps at the new Scarborough College for boys, you know. He could have had the best of everything."

"But Micky would have been too proud to accept that. You know how he hated you spoiling Beth. He wanted to provide for her. It's taken a lot for me to now accept all you offer us. But I feel now that he's not here, and can't provide, he would approve."

"I always thought it was you who didn't want to accept things Eliza, because you hated me so much."

"I never hated you Betsy. You can't think that. I've always had the deepest affection for you both, and that never changed. I'm sure you knew that really. But I was hurt, and you gave me an opportunity to punish you for what we had both done. I was punishing myself too, in denying myself our close relationship and fondness."

Betsy reached up and covered her daughter's hand with her own on her shoulder, smiling as she did so.

"Edward deserves the truth, Eliza."

She nodded.

"Does Charlie know?"

"Of course not Betsy. After the way I reacted? I couldn't risk that."

"But you were hurt because you weren't told for years, Eliza. If I had my time again, I'd have told you earlier. Just remember that."

"We're all so close as we are though Betsy, and Charlie doesn't know that he doesn't belong, so there's nothing to fix. I really can't risk anything for Beth's sake."

"What can't you risk for Beth's sake?" They both looked up to see Beth taking in the emotional scene in front of her. They had quite forgotten the time and that school would have finished for the day. Eliza recovered first.

"Oh, Beth dear, we were just discussing your Grandma in Dorset, one of us needs to go and help her after your Grandpa's funeral, but I've said I can't risk leaving you."

"Oh, well you could leave me Mother, I would be fine, but if you took little Rose with you, you wouldn't manage without me." She laughed as she said what she knew to be true, and danced over to reassure herself, that little Rose was sleeping peacefully in her basinet. Betsy and Eliza smiled at each other. Beth was always like a breath of fresh air blowing life into the house. She plonked herself childishly now on the arm of the chaise, then slid to the floor using it as a backrest.

"Beth, that was not very lady-like!"

Ignoring her mother's remark, she tucked her pinafore between her legs to ensure the demands of an appropriate decorous posture were met, and continued,

"Did you know there was another new department store

opening up on Westborough, Mother. Rowntrees, I think Norah said it is to be called, near to Sinfields confectioners and the Londesborough Theatre."

"Well, I did hear something actually Beth, perhaps Sinfields had better watch out, they say 'All roads lead to Sinfields', but maybe if Rowntrees also sell confectionary goods, they'll have some competition!" They all laughed at Eliza's teasing, they knew how much Beth's sweet tooth loved Sinfields.

As the laughter abated, Beth jumped to her feet, dragging her school bag behind her,

"Got some homework to do, we have to work in a group, and review a piece of writing. I hate working like that. I like sitting with Norah, but she doesn't want to do any work, it makes us all look bad."

"Well, Beth, it's a hard lesson to learn, but – 'A chain is only as strong as its weakest link', I would think about choosing a 'stronger link' as a classmate. You can still be friends with Norah out of School."

"Hmm, you might be right Aunt Betsy." Beth wandered pensively towards the door at the other side of the room, then turned to add rhetorically, "I'll feed Rose at tea time, Mother. If you get hers ready first, then I can take my time with her to make sure she gets plenty without choking. She's looking healthier now, don't you think Aunt Betsy? She has some flesh on her little legs; and I think she's moving them better. The nurse showed me how to exercise them so they don't get too stiff. I'm going to teach her to sit up next." She skipped out of the drawing room, jumping over the little tin trolley, now always referred to as 'Lizzibeth's trolley', but padded now with blankets for Beth to push Rose around in, and leapt up the stairs two at a time to her own room, yelling down as she reached the top,

"Tell me when Rose's tea's ready, Mother."

"Kathy I'm so glad it was me who found Ma. You'd been

through enough over the last few months, no years really, with Pa's illness. How will you manage now? You'll miss her so much."

Kathy and Albert were standing next to their mother's body. Albert had a comforting arm around Kathy's shoulder. They had become surprisingly close over the last days. They had spent hours sifting through their childhood memorabilia in various boxes in the cottage, trying to reduce the work for their mother. Hannah had enjoyed watching them, they had all laughed through their sadness, regaling stories sparked by each momento. Kathy made them both chuckle on finding a little toy Pierrot. She entertained them with a tale about when she took the children to see the Caitlins Royal Pierrots on the Spa sands on holiday in Scarborough. Little Emily had tried to pull a pom pom off the front of one of the Pierrot's tunics. Hannah had remembered the occasion well. Those hours of sorting had all proved to be time well spent now that they would have to completely clear the cottage. Henry Ferguson's nephew had insisted there was no immediate hurry, but Albert wanted to get as much done as he could while he was around. He did not want to leave it all to Kathy.

Laid out before them now in her own parlour, just days after her beloved husband, was just how Hannah had wanted it. The near smile on her face, belied any sadness at her own passing. She had in death, recaptured some of her youthfulness, the busy, bustling look of a mother had gone, her mouth relaxed, her complexion less anxious. She could at last stop, and warm her resting place, her job was done.

Kathy had always planned to gradually move Hannah in with her own family following Joseph's expected demise. She had been taken aback when her mother had retorted quite abruptly to the suggestion, 'Well, you needn't think I'll be with you long'. She thought of this now.

"Actually Albert, of course I'll miss her, but I think I always knew Ma would not be long after Pa. That's exactly how she wanted it. The mind is very powerful Albert, do you think you can die of a broken heart?"

"Well, the doctor did say it was her heart Kathy, only, we know how it was broken, and that none of his potions could possibly have fixed it."

Albert gently steered Kathy towards the parlour door. "Did you see in the paper today that King Edward was very ill? Let's hope he pulls through. Talking of being ill, I don't like to be morbid Kathy, but I don't think Aunt Louisa's long for this world either, she's very frail, I see a big difference in her. Uncle Benjamin and Aunt Rose look hail and hearty though, it's been nice to spend time with them. Come on big sister, lets go through Pa's papers, there may be bills to pay, or insurances to cancel. He kept everything in the secretaire didn't he?"

Albert put down the letter slowly, then rested his head in both his hands. The strain of the last few days had begun to show, Albert's customary stylishness, was tired and worn. His hair and clothes lacked attention and together with his sombre demeanour, looked incongruous on this naturally agreeable and elegant gentleman.

The emotion he now felt in reading something penned in his Granma's hand, was surpassed completely by its contents.

"I tried to stop you reading it Albert, I told you not to, there was no need for you to know. Betsy must never know, please don't think of telling her. She was so close to Pa, to tell her now he was not her father, would be too cruel. She has enough to concern her with Eliza; what with Micky's tragedy, and little Rose."

"When did you find out about this, Kathy?"

"About two years ago, I'd been quite shocked to discover some other information which Ma had apparently known of, for a while. So, I think almost to appease me, Ma shared this letter with me. She said you had imparted the secret mechanism to her years ago, and she had discovered the letter then. She was most upset that her own mother had not confided in her, but chosen Joseph to receive her story. I always wondered if you knew. You could have opened the secret compartment any time, Albert, when it was in Scarborough."

"I suppose if it's known you can access somewhere, you assume there will be nothing for you to discover. It does explain something though. Lottie always asked me how Betsy could look so much like Ma, when she had a different mother. We could never have guessed they shared the same grandfather. No wonder Betsy inherited that house. It all falls into place now. Why has Betsy not questioned all this, Kathy? Are you sure she doesn't know?"

"I'm sure, Albert, now promise me you won't ever tell her will you? Promise me?"

"I won't Kathy, I promise I won't ever tell her."

"Beth, come on. I definitely saw your Charlie, and Sidney Ramsbottom going up Globe Street before you arrived, I'm sure they'd be heading for the Castle, there's a fleet on its way in. If we're quick, we can scoot up Church Stairs Street, get ahead of them, and bump into them accidentally. Oh, look, Beth there's the new motor fire engine, it's supposed to be able to put out fires very quickly 'coz it can pump gallons of water out. Oo, don't the firemen look smart. Afternoon!"

Norah shamelessly waved and shouted to the boys on the fire engine. They smiled coyly away as though self conscious and yet pleasantly embarrassed at the appeal their uniform afforded them. She headed off resolutely, "Leave the flowers alone. Beth, come on!"

Beth moaned as she followed apathetically behind her friend.

"You can tell we are having a lovely spring, Norah, these are flowering early."

Filling her pinafore pocket with the dancing dollies from the fuchsia bush, she leant into the hill, swinging her arms in an exaggerated fashion as though the effort of putting one foot in front of the other, was almost too much. "But what are we doing this for anyway Norah? I can see Charlie anytime, and Sidney Ramsbottom is very, very, very very boring, I don't know why Charlie hangs around with him."

Norah was now well in front of her as she nimbly headed upwards.

"Beth, how can you say that? He's so dreamy, but he doesn't seem to have noticed me yet. Yes, bumping right into him should get him to know I exist!"

"But what are we going to say we're doing there? They go up to watch the fishing fleet come back when they aren't actually on it, but why would we be up there Norah?"

Norah stopped breathlessly half way up the Steps, and turned towards her friend, resting her hands on her knees to recover.

"We can say we've come to watch your cousin paint along the cliffs. Actually, that's not a bad idea either Beth, he's a handsome fellow too, perhaps he would notice me."

Beth ran to catch up to her friend before she set off again,

"Not a chance, Norah, he's had lots of girls make eyes at him, but I've never known him walk out with one. He's only got eyes for his paintings. Besides, he's old now, I heard my mother and Aunt Betsy say the other day that Little Joe would be twenty eight this year!"

"That's not old, Beth, not for a man anyway, they tend to look better as they get older."

Beth considered this carefully thinking of all the older men she knew.

"Hmm, maybe you're right Norah, my Uncle Albert's still very good looking and he's in his forties. He has a dreamy voice too, really deep, yet gentle. It's like warm molasses, sort of comforting, you know. I suppose Uncle Thom is handsome too, but he's in his fifties, and anyway, they're both Grandfathers!" She thought a little more, staring into the top left of her vision peering at the images she found there, "I don't think I'd say that about Uncle Edward though, he's hardly any hair left!"

Norah laughed aloud,

"I didn't mean you had to start considering every 'old man'

you know. And I don't see how a voice can be like molasses. Come on now, let's go and practise making eyes!"

Beth groaned letting her head fall backwards as she continued to plod past St Mary's Church and up onto Castle Road.

"Beth look, we've got ahead of them, no don't look now you idiot, they'll see you've seen them. They're just coming up to the Coastguards cottages, through Paradise, quickly come on. We can get there first." Norah steamed ahead of her friend until she reached the castle keep, then she turned to motivate the straggling Beth. "Not far now, we'll sit on that mound over there, then we can pretend we've been sitting there, chatting, all afternoon."

Beth looked to where Norah was pointing,

"Oh, all right, Norah, I'm coming. But if you succeed in making eyes at Sidney, what am I supposed to do?"

"Well you can talk to Charlie, he's lovely. I know you're cousins, but that's allowed isn't it?"

"Don't be ridiculous, Norah. I'm not making eyes at my cousin. Anyway he's horrible to me sometimes, he's always teasing me since he grew up."

"No he isn't. He always sticks up for you anyway, so there!"

Beth considered this for a moment, then asked quietly,

"Why does he need to stick up for me? I don't get into fights. Has someone been saying horrible things?"

Norah gulped, she had walked right into this one, but she was never one to avoid confrontation, so she explained herself.

"Beth, lots of people are always having a go at you. They say you've got ideas above your station since you moved in with your Aunt on South Cliff, and that you shouldn't forget that you belong to the fisher folk. Look at your clothes, we're very unlikely friends now. But anyway, Charlie always gets angry with them, and defends you. So he must be at least a little sweet on you. And you are very pretty you know."

"Well, thank you so much Norah! What was my mother supposed to do when there was no money to pay our rent, go on the streets?"

"A'right, Beth Walker, keep your bloomers on! I was only telling you. Other fishing families accept help from the community through, then they maybe marry again to get the support they need."

"Well my mother didn't have to take money from them, they should be glad. And she would never marry again. She still talks about my father all the time, so there!" Beth childishly punctuated the end of her retort by sticking out her tongue at her friend. Norah now wished she had never started.

"You know, Beth, you would probably have been better changing schools when you moved, then everyone would have forgotten about you, and left you alone."

"Then I would have been the odd one out at that school though. And I like our school." She flopped down next to Norah on the grassy mound, and pulled her pinafore over her knees.

"I'm glad you didn't move, if that helps, Beth. But you do have Charlie to thank for stopping people having a go at you, he threatened they would have him to deal with if they did. Hey Beth, look who's here, what a surprise. It's your Charlie, and with Sidney Ramsbottom too. What are you two doing up here?"

Charlie was the first to speak, he had spotted them a little way back, and had his suspicions. He knew well that Norah, despite being only thirteen years old, was very sweet on his seventeen year old friend Sid.

"Hello girls. We come up here to watch the fleet come back in, so what are you doing here?"

"Oh we just love the view from up here Charlie. Don't you Sidney?" Norah made the most obvious attempt at fluttering eyes that any of them had ever seen. Beth found herself covering her mouth to stifle the hilarity which would have required explanation. Charlie caught her eye and smiled. Sidney's colour changed to a glowing ruby, as he cleared his throat, attempting to delay his response.

Charlie saved him from the moment. "I'm surprised you would come here for the view you're looking at Norah." He indicated to the grassed area immediately behind a large stone, but directly in front of Norah, where a young couple, in the throws of passion, were hoping for some privacy on this spring afternoon, nestled as they were near the town's batlements. They were unaware that the castle grounds had not afforded them protection from innocent, yet prying eyes.

"Close your mouth, Beth, stop looking. Come on let's move away before they see us." Charlie offered a hand to each of the two girls. As they arose, he steered them towards the other side of the castle grounds. Norah continued to try to get Sidney's attention as they walked. Charlie fell in step beside Beth. "How's little Rose?"

"Oh she's better thank you Charlie. Mother is just being cautious in keeping her inside a little longer to be sure she doesn't pick up any more germs." She picked the flowers out of her pocket and fiddled with them as she walked. Norah caught sight of what she had.

"Here can I have some, Beth?" On handing her one, Norah begged, "Please, Beth, can I have two?" Beth looked at her questioningly, but handed her another fuchsia. Norah expertly threaded the flower through a split in its own long stalk, and looped it over her ear lobe. She did the same with the second one, then strutted towards Sidney as though the flowers dancing around her earlobes were the finishing touches to the most exquisite ball gown ensemble.

Beth enthusiastically set to work on a pair for herself.

"None for me thanks Beth!" said Charlie as he ran to catch up with his non-plussed, bewildered friend and with one arm around his pal, teased, "Doesn't Norah look a picture Sidney, how could any man resist her, hey, you don't think she's sweet on you do you?"

"Betsy, do you feel like a walk today? We could go along to the North side and feed the ducks on Tucker's field, oops, I mean Peasholm Park of course now. Rose always smiles when she sees ducks, she must see them moving when I hold the bread quite close to her. Do you remember how she laughed when one pecked her, making her suddenly startle and jump, scattering ducks in all directions, wings a flapping!" They both smiled warmly at the memory.

"That sounds like a lovely idea, Eliza. Beth'll be home soon, shall we wait for her to come too?"

"Of course. She wouldn't be happy if we took her sister out without her."

"I'll put some hot water in the stone to warm the perambulator for her as soon as I've finished reading this page. Are you sure she's over her chest problems though before we go out in the cold? You don't want to set the attacks off again with another infection."

"Well she's been well for three days now, Betsy, and if we keep her warm she should be alright. She hasn't been outside since her birthday in February, except to see Bertie and Emma's new baby last week; she must be so bored with us all." Eliza raised her eyes to the right hand corner of the ceiling, and smiled to herself as if recalling a special moment. "Wasn't little Eleanor good with Rose, she kept bringing toys for her to play with, she seemed to sense she couldn't do much, but wanted to include her anyway, I hope baby Edith will have the same disposition and be kind to her cousin."

Betsy smiled her concurrence, setting aside her newspaper.

"She has a good example in Beth though, and she mimics her in everything."

"You're right. She does follow Beth around and copy her. You know, a walk would really do us good Betsy. Spring is here, and we all so loved the new Park when it opened last year. Wouldn't it be wonderful to actually visit places like Japan and China? I wonder if that surveyor Mr Smith actually went, or if he designed it all from pictures of gardens he'd seen in books?"

"I've no idea Eliza, I'm sure Beth would know, she's such a book worm now isn't she? Pa would be so proud of her. I've been the only one of his children so far to be really interested in studies, but it has certainly surfaced again in Beth. I hope she chooses to stay on at school Eliza, Edward and I will be happy to support her to study."

"I know you will Betsy, we'll see. I think Micky would be proud of her too."

Betsy tucked the stone bottle into the blankets of the perambulator as she looked up at her daughter's smile. She walked over to where her Eliza was folding the newspaper she herself had been reading a few moments ago, and took her hand.

"I'm sure he would Eliza, no, I absolutely know he would. He would also be proud of little Rose. Look how well she has done, three years old now, and trying her best to stand up. She bravely fights everything life throws at her. Thanks to her mother and sister's amazing care of course." She squeezed Eliza's hand and went to busy herself with their cloaks and bonnets.

"And her devoted grand-parents of course."

Betsy turned to smile her reply. She had taken Eliza and Beth's lead in loving little Rose. They were all slaves to her endearing captivating smile, and like her mother and sister, were learning to listen to her eyes. But Betsy worried they had all become too fond of her. She knew Rose would never make old bones, and this inevitable loss would be all the greater with each day she spent burrowing into their hearts. Betsy returned with their bonnets, gloves and scarves. Pulling on a leather glove, she stopped when she heard Eliza's sombre voice.

"Betsy. Please, I don't want to know any more about the Titanic disaster. All those people, their deaths must have been so similar to Micky's. Icy seas, cold and watery graves. Please don't get that newspaper out again. For me, and for Beth, please."

"Eliza, I'm so sorry, I never thought. You're right, it must have been awful for them. Probably the fear of knowing what was going to happen to them made it even worse, my dear. I promise, no more Titanic. Come along, lets wake Rose and go and see those ducks and Pagodas!"

Eliza laughed,

"I imagine Beth will want to row around the island, her imagination works overtime in settings like that. We'll have a story by bed time! Oh, here she comes now. We're off to the Park for a walk Beth, want to come?"

"Ooh, yes please, can I row around the lake?" She looked from Betsy to Eliza as they shared a knowing look.

"What is it, what have I said?"

Eliza laughed, "Oh nothing dear, we just knew you would want to do that. How was school?"

"Oh, it was alright, Mother. We had an excerpt of a new book read to us today by our literature teacher. It hasn't been published yet, it's by Mr DH Lawrence; but Mr Jones is a friend of his, and he's allowed him to read some of it. Sons and Lovers it is to be called.

"Are you sure it was suitable, Beth, with a title like that? I've heard tell that his books can be a little erm.. suggestive." Betsy pulled an anxious expression at Eliza.

"Well it was only a small passage anyway. I have some history homework to do though. If I get it done, can I go to Aunt Lottie's on Saturday to see the new baby?"

"Of course my dear, she's adorable, you will love her."

"Well I love going to Aunt Lottie's anyway, but it's even better if Eleanor's there, and now baby Edith too. And Uncle Albert thinks I am a tonic, he's been so sad since he came back from Dorset."

"You're a tonic to us all Beth. But you're right, Uncle Albert bore the brunt of the sadness of Grandma and Granpa's passing in being down there. And your Aunt Kathy too of course. I'm hoping Kathy will come to see us all soon. That might cheer him up too. Don't you think Eliza?"

"Oh that would be something for us all to look forward to."

Beth mooched around her busying mother for a few minutes, then put her head on one side as though wondering whether it was appropriate to speak.

"Mother, did you, or even you, Aunt Betsy know, that if you hang a pair of cherries over your ears when you walk out with a boy, it means you will let him take liberties with you? It's a good thing we learnt that today, Mother, from the passage of Mr Lawrence's book, you know, the one I mentioned earlier. I would never have known that, what if I had done it without thinking?"

Betsy and Eliza looked at each other. Eliza was stunned momentarily that her twelve year old girl knew anything at all about 'liberties'. So Betsy was the first to reply.

"I suspected as much from his books. However, don't worry about it Beth dear. The author uses things like that. Its called symbolism, just to help the reader get the picture of what's happening, you don't need to take it too literally."

Beth looked between the two women.

"So it would really be alright for me to do that? It's just that Norah and I hung the dancing dollies from a fuchsia bush over our ears the other day, up on Castle Hill, they looked like Queen Mary's earrings. You know, like the ones on the pictures of her and King George taken in India? Well, we were there with Charlie and Sidney Ramsbottom, I wouldn't want them to think anything of the sort. That's all this Miriam girl in the book did with her cherries."

"I'm sure that they would definitely not think that Beth. Charlie's your cousin, remember! And while we're on the subject, I wouldn't be going up Castle Hill on your own young lady, you may see more than you bargained for in terms of 'liberties'!"

Beth, smiling guiltily, though very relieved, ran up the stairs adding, "I won't Ma. I'll get Rose. Have you warmed the perambulator?"

Eliza headed for the kitchen to collect some bread, sniggering at her daughter's disclosure as she went. Betsy followed her, struggling with the ribbons of her bonnet.

"Betsy, would you believe my little girl knows of such

things."

"Oh I think you'd be surprised what children know about these days, but I just hope Beth and Charlie don't get too close Eliza, he's a young man now, but she's still an impressionable young girl; remember they're not really just cous…."

"Aunt Betsy, can you come here please?" A weak little voice was calling her from the stairs. Eliza and Betsy hurried from the kitchen, Beth was walking slowly and ethereally down the stairs. In her arms she carried her little sister, limp as a rag doll. All stiffness, spasm and startle, now gone from her lifeless body, her lips, blue as her eyes.

"I think it's Pa's turn to have Rose now Mother. He let us keep her longer than we thought he would." She sniffed as she continued to descend the stairs towards her mother and Aunt. "I hope she was able to walk to him, we were just about there you know, she could almost stand." Beth looked up,

"I'm glad Pa's not on his own anymore, Mother, aren't you?" Eliza listened intently to her daughter's speech, then she gently took her load, lifting her little daughter's cold face up to the warmth of her own. She knew Rose had already left them, but she needed to be sure.

"You're right Beth. Pa's turn now. It's time they met." She rocked her gently in her arms, the movements bigger than she could do in life, for there was no fear of startling her now. "Poor little Rose, Betsy, she had no time to build her nest of spices, no new phoenix from her, it'll be as though she never existed."

Betsy could not answer, instead, she looked helplessly down at the crusts of bread in her hand as they absorbed her large fast tears. All grief, sorrow and heartache for the passing of both precious parents that she had been too busy, shocked, and shaken to acknowledge, now flooded over her; washing her in this unbearable loss of the granddaughter who had taught and given her family so much, and yet lived and taken so little. Beth saw,

"Don't worry Aunt Betsy, maybe Rose will feed the ducks as

she flies over Tucker's field."

Chapter 37

Scarborough, Spring 1914 - Spring 1915

"Hello everyone. I've made some Yorkshire Curd Tart today and I know how much Bertie likes it, so I thought I'd bring one for you all to have with your tea……Albert, I didn't expect to see you working here. You've got one of your best shirts on, do you want me to go and get an old working shirt out for you?" Lottie had bustled into the workshop with a treat for all the men, as she often did at least once during the week. She liked to take them some sustenance as Bertie always teased his father about how hard he worked them all.

Albert handed his plane to an apprentice who had been intently watching him work, austerely he turned on his wife.

"So Mrs Elliot, how often are my cabinet makers halted from their work by my wife bringing them treats? Yorkshire Curd Tart indeed." His tone softened on his last sentence, breaking into a grin that instantly broke the palpable tension in the workshop making them all sigh with relief.

"Go on then lads, make a brew to go with this."

There was a clatter of tools as they all stopped what they were doing. With an air of good natured camaraderie, and almost choreographed as one, they reached for their cigarette packets to make the most of their unexpected break. Albert rolled his sleeves back down as he indicated to his wife to follow him into his office area at the back of the workshop. He turned back to throw over his shoulder.

"Jones, you carry on and try to finish what I started off for you, I'll inspect your workmanship later. Sid, you sweep under that table. Come on Lottie, I needed to talk to you anyway." He winked over at Bertie, "No more than ten minutes mind! Especially if you were all hoping to get down to the beach over lunchtime to see that Daily Mail sea plane you've all been talking about."

Lottie looked anxiously at Albert, "What is it Albert, why were you working in the shop today, don't Bertie and Billy do all the teaching of the apprentices now?"

Albert perched on the edge of his desk, he busied himself with his cuff links and the re-positioning of his pocket watch before donning his tweed jacket. Then he looked up at Lottie.

"That's what I needed to talk to you about Lottie. Things are going to have to change around here. Two things have happened to bring this about." He paused to ensure he had roused her curiosity, then he indicated towards his productive, dusty industrious workshop in its brief recess.

"Firstly, despite making a very good living for many years at this, my dear, we are being squeezed by the big factories making mass produced and hence cheaper furniture." Lottie's jaw dropped, she had never expected that Albert's profession could ever be idle; he was always in such demand.

"But who would want that furniture they sell in all the shops, you could find you have the very same as your neighbour, fancy! And, you are so busy, Albert, look at the number of pieces of furniture in various stages of production here now."

"Oh, we are still busy Lottie, but the order book is only one months turn around now. A few years ago, it could be up to six months for a piece of Elliot furniture. It'll start to have an impact on the business, and I may have had to reduce the number of apprentices." Albert lowered his voice to a whisper as he spoke the last words.

"May have had to Albert? Have things changed back again? Why are you telling me then?"

Albert took a deep breath, he knew his wife often buried her head in the sand in terms of anything unpleasant. He knew too, that it was her way of keeping calm, and so not returning to the same malady that had afflicted her a few years ago.

"My dear, even you must know what's in the newspapers, even if you have avoided reading it. We'll be at war with Germany before long. There's talk of conscripting young men to fight. I'll not have this many apprentices anyway if that happens."

Lottie's pallor faded as he spoke, he was right, she had deliberately not been reading the war propaganda. She cocooned herself well against such unpleasantness.

"So my dear, we'll still need to eat. War or not. I must get back into harness and refresh my own Cabinet Making and French Polishing skills. They may be needed once again. I can't imagine the government will have much use for an old man like me on the battlefield!" He laughed his last words in an attempt at humorously chivvying his wife out of her visible panic.

"Albert, you don't think, …you don't think that Bertie would have to go, do you?"

Albert looked helplessly at his wife; he would have loved more than anything to reassure her.

"My dear, it depends on many things. We don't know anything for definite, do we? But we must be prepared for anything. If conscription happens, then it won't only be Bertie, but Billy too. Most likely all the apprentices, except Sid and Ernie, they're too young. Little Joe would go too, and Charlie, Kathy's two lads, and Peter's young James, although he may well be spared, being a qualified doctor." Albert stopped abruptly when he saw the tears coursing down his wife's rounded cheeks.

"Now now, Lottie, don't take on so, you're immediately thinking the worst."

"But the children, Albert, they need their father, little Hubert's only a baby."

"Of course they need their father, and if he goes, he won't be gone long. It'll be over very quickly, you wait and see. They won't last long against the British Army will they? Don't write our Bertie off just yet, he's only at the other side of the room!"

Lottie smiled up at her wise husband, he was so good at cheering her up and making her think sensibly, of course everything would be alright, her Bertie would be just fine and dandy.

* * *

"Albert! Hurry up in there. I really need to go. I went downstairs to pack you up some lunch first. You've been in there ages."

Lottie was hopping from one foot to the other outside their bathroom door, when it slowly opened, a smartly spruced Albert appeared.

"At last Albert. Thank goodness for indoor plumbing, that's all I can say, if I had been hopping up and down outside in this cold I would not have been a happy woman."

"Alright, alright, there you are, I've finished now. Get in there and stop your moaning."

"Do you know that Thom and Annie still have to go outside to use the privy? I don't think they have a lot of money to spend on altering the house. Can't we help in some way?"

"Lottie, I thought you were desperate, get in there." He patted her rounded behind as she scuttled into their bathroom, then with a smile in his voice, he added, "We'll see what we can do for Thom and Annie, he's very proud though you know, perhaps a Christmas gift, eh, - to Annie of course? You know they should really have got themselves an indoor privy with the little bequest from Uncle Henry, for all his Godchildren. No doubt theirs went on travelling around the countryside to paint pictures!" He started to move away from the door, then shouted over his shoulder, "I'll probably be late tonight as its Wednesday, don't start the tea too early."

Suddenly, the whole house seemed to shake from its very foundations with a booming blast that exploded and belched through their home. Albert was thrown to the floor at the top of the stairs, one more step on his way, and he may have found the bottom quicker and more tragically than he intended. He was brought upright swiftly by his wife's piercing scream.

"It's alright, Lottie, I think the new Territorial Army must be testing guns up near the castle or something. Finish your business, you're alright." He had only just finished speaking when the guns sounded again, he staggered and grasped the banister. A few seconds passed, and an ashen Lottie reappeared, unaware that her skirts were almost comical in their array. Holding tight to the door frame, her voice began small and shaky, but built up towards an hysterical crescendo.

"That was no practice guns Albert. The army wouldn't do that at this time of the morning without warning. The Germans must be here! What are we going to do? Oh, Albert, Bertie might be on his way to the workshop already. What shall we do? What shall we do, Albert?"

Another blast sent Lottie to the floor as she yelled the last word, and Albert sank next to her to comfort and reassure her.

He was still bewildered; he had never heard or felt anything like this in his life. War in his own life's experience, was always fought in distant lands. He wondered what could possibly be happening. He had heard that warships could fire shells of explosives onto land, could this be it?

"I'll tell you what we're going to do Lottie, if they're firing at us, then let them. We'll not easily be quashed." He stood himself up, and helping Lottie, he thought quickly,

"We need to get down Lottie, and shelter under the staircase, we'll be alright down there. They'll run out of fire soon. Then you can get on and do what you were going to do today, weren't you going to make the Christmas cake? There's only a week to go, you've usually got it done by now." He was speaking as he encouragingly chivvied his wife to their shelter.

It was two hours later, when Lottie was calm enough for Albert to leave her and investigate the damage. The shelling had lasted for one and a half of those long hours. He knew it would be bad, the direction of the shells made him worry about the workshop, about Bertie, Billy, and his lads. Not to mention the rest of their family. He turned from Victoria Street onto Victoria Road, and headed towards the workshop.

The sights that met him were worse than he could possibly have imagined. There were smudges of thick black smoke all around him, suspended low in the winter morning sky. It was difficult to walk along the street for all the rubble and glass. Mothers were screaming, school children were running wildly, shouting, looking for parents. Some must have left their homes for the nearby Gladstone Road School before the bombardment started. A little boy, maybe six or seven was seated on the pavement edge; blood was dripping from a wound on the right side of his jaw. Albert stopped; he registered the boy's ragged trousers, dusty clothes and bare feet, and a cap too big for his young head; Albert pulled a starched white handkerchief from his pocket, and gently pressed it against the wound. "Where's your Mother, lad?"

"Don't know Sir, she'd already left our house over there to go to work before it started."

Albert looked behind him at the house the boy had indicated, not much was left. "You were lucky, son."

"Yes Mister, but our little Joseph wasn't. My Granny has him over there." He indicated to a silver haired woman, howling as she rocked forwards and backwards holding a baby. Another woman was trying to persuade her to relinquish her load. Silver lametta from a Christmas tree mockingly peppered her red hair. Albert looked away, this was too much. He inspected the state of the wound under his pressure. The flow had stopped. You hang onto that lad, it'll be right as rain in no time. Albert struggled to his feet.

"Thanks Mist….. Oh there's my mother. Mother, over here."

A young woman dressed as a char, came running frantically across the road, scooping up her young son into her arms.

"Thank God you're alright Danny, where's Joseph?" A hush had fallen over the street, as all waited for her to turn, and for her own mother, and her dead baby to come into her field of vision. Their expectation of her distress did not lessen the impact of her scream, piercing, penetrating and painful. Yet the inflicted pain and suffering she thrust upon them, strangely quelled the guilty relief of their own survival.

Albert, dazed, sick to his stomach, yet intent on his mission, continued on his way.

"Albert, oh Albert. Thank God you're alright." Betsy jumped out of a carriage and embraced him. "What about Bertie and Lottie? I've just come from Thom's, they're all alright, shocked but unhurt."

"Lottie's fine. Just going to find Bertie. People are dead Betsy. This is terrible. Who'd have thought this war would effect us in our own homes. We won't be able to sleep in our beds. What about Edward, Eliza and Beth?"

"They're all fine too Albert. Thankfully, erm, her nephew, Charlie, he's in Hartlepool at the moment, helping his Uncle with his trawler there, so that's a relief. I don't doubt that down street will be in a bad way."

"I'm not so sure that all the shells didn't land much further into the town actually, Betsy. Come on, let's use your carriage to get to the workshop and then to Bertie's house. Then perhaps if Edward has a moment, could you ask him to come and take a look at Lottie. She's in such a state, I think her blood pressure problem will come back with all this."

"Lottie, it's Betsy. I've brought Edward with me. Albert's found Bertie, but he said you weren't too well. What a terrible to do this is, your poor neighbours two doors along, they don't have a roof left." Betsy walked into the house ahead of Edward. She peeled off her gloves, looking into the rooms as she went. When no greeting met her, she hurried into the scullery, panic abating temporarily when she saw the mixing bowl full of dried fruit on the scullery table with a plate piled high with flour and spices. Then she registered Lottie's skirts crumpled around the far table leg, and brown sugar splattered across the dull red of the quarry tiled floor.

"Edward!" She screamed from her knees at Lottie's side. Edward was beside her in seconds. Together they gently rolled her over. Lottie sighed deeply, but the air drifted lazily out of the right side of her lips as her mouth hung loosely to one side.

"She's had a stroke Betsy, this is what I have always feared for her. You go and get Albert and Bertie, if you're quick, the carriage should still be outside. We need to get her upstairs to bed, and in the warm."

Bertie approached the side of his mother's bed.

"I know I've never been a great one for the idea of fighting Pa, especially other people's wars. But this is now our War. The Germans have killed her just as much as if they had fired a pistol at her head."

"No-one's killed her, Bertie. Edward says she may still pull through. We must wait and pray."

"He also said Pa, that if she does, she'll never be the same again. She won't be able to use her right side, and may not even be aware of us or her surroundings, let alone be able to talk. Ma would hate that Pa. She'd hate it."

"But don't be too hasty either Bertie, Ma wouldn't want you to avenge her and be killed yourself. You have responsibilities. What about Emma and the children?"

"Exactly Pa. It could be them next. Young Charlie Walker was so lucky in Hartlepool, they got it even worse than us, they had one hundred and twelve dead, and many more wounded. Our eighteen dead and a mere eighty wounded, almost seems blessed by comparison. So far of course." He added the last two words as he gazed gravely at the woman who had nurtured him with almost too much love throughout his childhood and beyond. "No, they have to be stopped Pa. We can't let this happen again to our town. I don't want to see another sombre funeral procession of that size heading along to Dean Road

Cemetery, ever again. Little wonder the heavens cried that day, and even the horses pulling the hearses walked sadly as though their hearts were breaking." Bertie swallowed hard, one of his friends from Wykeham Street had died that day. He composed himself as Albert scrabbled frantically for words of comfort to console his only son. But Bertie continued,

"It's not only the lives and homes lost, though that's bad enough, but have you seen the town Pa? The Grand, The Royal, The Town Hall, and the final insult was the Lighthouse. Who the hell do they think they are Pa! No, we're all agreed. Me, Billy and the lads. We're all signing up as soon as possible."

"Bye Beth, I hope you have a good day. Send someone for me if anything happens won't you? You're such a blessing my dear, everyday I thank God for you."

"Don't worry Uncle Albert, everything will be fine. Aunt Lottie will be fine with me. You go off and make lots of furniture. I'll have tea ready for you when you get home."

Beth was busy washing Lottie's hands. She had to take great care with her right, the fingers were pulled into a tight fist, and Betsy had explained the risk of soreness and infection in her palm if care in her general hygiene was not meticulous. Gently, Beth eased out Lottie's fingers one by one until she had enough leverage to hold the whole hand open long enough to flannel it clean, then dry it very thoroughly, before allowing it to spring back to its adopted position. When Betsy had first shown Beth how to do this, the reek that could emanate from this clenched fist could cause her to balk, but now it was just a regular part of her regime in caring for this Aunt she had so much affection for. Sometimes Lottie's sunken skewed face would look at Beth in such recognition, that Beth was sure she knew she was there, carefully caring for her progressively degenerating yet forcefully twisted form. She would talk her through everything she did. She had explained to Albert one day when he asked who she was talking to, "Can you imagine waking up to find someone washing you, or cleaning your teeth, or pushing food into you? It would be awful, Uncle Albert. I have to tell her what I'm doing so Aunt Lottie knows what's going on, I'd hate her to be frightened."

Albert had smiled tenderly at this young girl for whom he had always had such fondness, but now to whom he owed so much, and he headed back to work for the first time since the bombardment. As he closed the front door, and stepped out onto the street with his newspaper he was greeted by his sister.

"Morning Albert, how's Lottie today? I thought I'd come and give Beth a hand again. I'm sure Lottie enjoys me reading to her. And I think today's Eliza's sewing circle for dressings at the hospital isn't it? Beth likes to help with that, she can go while I'm here." She looked up at the clouds, "Yes today it's the hospital, and I think it's thursdays that she helps the fisher folk make sandbags for the front."

Albert nodded, despite his return to manual work over recent months in his workshop, luckily unscathed by the bombardment, he continued to dress to and from his work as the successful businessman he had become. He doffed his slightly pretentious and yet somehow befitting bowler hat at his sister, and smiling, he settled into conversation with her.

"She's just the same I fear Betsy. I don't think there's likely to be any change for the better now, do you? I know Edward doesn't think so. That's why I must now return to work. With Bertie, Billy and some of the lads already gone, I'm needed there. They've all been picking up some work from Smith's workshop that was gutted in the bombardment. I've also to assess the damage in the Grand and the Royal. They want me to quote for their repairs. How strange to repair or replace Pa's work from all those years ago, Betsy, eh?"

They both smiled in sadness at the need, yet satisfaction that if anyone should do this, it should be their father's son. Albert made to move off, and then added sadly, "I just wish she could recognise me, Betsy. You know, to know that we're all still here for her."

Betsy put an affectionate hand on his arm, she felt his pain. She knew as well as Edward, that Lottie would never recover now. That she had survived so far was due to the care they all gave her. But it was no less than she deserved, they would all miss her company in their lives. Albert continued, "I shall still read to her when I get back every evening, but I don't know what we would do without young Beth. She's been an absolute Godsend to me. You must miss her not living with you. But you were all right of course, it has been so much easier since she has just stayed here. I'm being spoiled though, she's become quite the little housekeeper!"

"Well, of course we miss her terribly at home, especially Eliza. But Beth's been wanting to do nursing for a long time Albert, and what better way to start than by nursing someone dear to her." She smiled tenderly at her little brother, he was too young to be watching his poor wife suffering in this way. She changed the topic cheerily, "Eliza's been throwing herself into this war work you know. I've never seen her so full of energy and motivation for anything. She's even talking of working for the tramways too. It's better than the lamp-lighting she talked about doing at one time. We're going to be so short of men for these jobs though of course.

Albert averted his eyes. Then he looked back at his elder sister, unexpectedly thankful for the opportunity to share his woes.

"Oh, Betsy, the newspapers are full of such horror and suffering in France, I fear for Bertie when his training is over. If we win this war, we'll owe our young men such a debt of gratitude for what they have suffered in our name.

We didn't have our sons to just throw them at enemy gunfire Betsy. I'll be so glad when he's home again, but I fear the worst. Then what will I have left Betsy? Tell me, what will I have left?"

Chapter 38

Scarborough, Summer – Christmas 1915

"Eliza! Whatever are you wearing?"

Eliza had walked back into their house on South Cliff, and put down her bag on the hat stand in the polished hallway. It was a stiflingly hot summer's day outside and as she entered the drawing room, she undid the tie and top button of her blouse.

"It's my uniform for the tramcars Betsy. Don't you think it's smart? I'm on the number fourteen tram, the one that goes down Falsgrave Road and then along Scalby Road. Did you know you can get around the town ride for only thrupence? It's much cheaper than a carriage."

"That may well be Eliza, but it's the length of your skirt I'm worried about. The whole world can see your legs!"

"Oh, that. Well, everyone's skirt hems are heading upwards Betsy, material is in short supply you know. It's the same as corsets, they're going out, much less material needed for one of these new brassieres. I must try one. Besides, Betsy, the new bathing pool opens this summer in the South Bay, everyone will see a lot more than legs then won't they? Anyway, already I can see advantages. It's pouring down outside, and yet the bottom of my skirt is still dry, I think I'll shorten all my skirts!"

Leaving Betsy aghast in their sitting room, she swept confidently and defiantly up the stairs like an unrepentant child.

Betsy walked over to her window and looked out across the chasm of affluence in their neighbourhood and contemplated all the changes the last year had brought to their town. Not least, the depletion of young men, who had enlisted in their droves to avenge the attacks on Scarborough, Hartlepool and Whitby. She morbidly wondered how many would return. Bertie's children were getting used to a life without their father around, as were Billy's. Luckily, Emma had her parents nearby to help, and Thom and Annie were on hand to help Billy's wife and children. Little Joe hadn't yet gone off, if only to appease his mother; but the Staithes painting group had disbanded, and only the other day, Joe had mooted that painting seemed a frivolous pastime under the circumstance of war. It would only be a matter of time before the power of conscription would allow him to join his brother.

Beth though, had surprised them all with her determination to become a nurse like her Aunt Betsy. Until recently, Betsy thought her future may lie in teaching, she had always so enjoyed reading and discussing the various books she studied at school. When she had offered to help Betsy in caring for Lottie following her stroke, she had taken to all the tasks with such care and empathy for her Aunt, that she had quickly become indispensible enough for Albert to offer her a full time nursing post. They all knew it would not last forever, but that this experience would stand Beth in good stead for her future career. Eliza and Betsy had soon persuaded her to live in with Albert. They did not want her travelling between the two houses in fear of another bombardment, and also felt it was better for Albert to have help at hand throughout the night. Albert had always had such a fondness for Beth too.

As many successful businessmen, he wasn't the easiest of men to live with as Lottie frequently used to testify, and if he was to cope with anyone living with him, Beth would be the one.

She considered Edward, poor Edward. He had been thinking of retiring when the war started, now he argued, he was desperately needed at home. Some of the younger doctors

were off to do their work on the battlefields of France. She
visualised Eliza at work on the trams, standing proudly beside
the driver in his open cab, she could see her nipping up and
down the spiral stairs to the open top, to clip the passenger's
tickets. Betsy smiled to herself, her daughter was alive with her
new found purpose. She considered whether their lives would
ever be the same again as she returned to her seat and her
sewing. She smiled inwardly now to herself, and at the futility
and senselessness of discussing the length of a skirt or corset
in such times.

"Albert, Albert, here." Beth's quiet, calm voice spoke from the
doorway of her Uncle's room. He had reluctantly moved into
Bertie's old room since Lottie's stroke, so that he would not be
disturbed when nursing tasks had to be administered during
the night. She had gradually stopped using the prefix to his
name in her standing as his niece. In the few months since she
had become Lottie's nurse, despite her youth, she had morphed
quite dramatically from a girl to a confident young woman.
She had had every support in her tasks and her learning from
her Aunt Betsy and Uncle Edward. But this morning, a strange
sound from her Aunt's room awoke her. When she attended,
she saw instantly. Her job was done. Intriguingly, she realised
that it had not been a noise that had awoken her, but the
silence. The comforting rattle of mucous that accompanied
every one of Lottie's recent breaths, had ceased. She paused
at Lottie's bedside, forbidding any emotion to escape, before
going for her uncle.
"What is it Beth, do you need some help to turn Lottie?"
His optimistic expectations for the woman that had been his
loving wife for thirty years, undammed Beth's tears, and Albert
was out of bed, and beside his wife in an instant.
"No Lottie, no. Not yet. I thought you'd wait to know Bertie
was home safe." Albert fell to his knees, clasping Lottie's soft
sinewy hand within his own calloused ones, and dropped his

forehead onto them.

Beth quietly withdrew from the room, she went to the bathroom, carried out her daily ablutions mindlessly, dressed, and went downstairs to light the fire and make some tea. They had entered into a second year of war, and now, in late September, it was beginning to be cold in the mornings again. She wrote a note on a piece of paper, and walked outside to see if there were any carriages about that would take a message to her Mother, Aunt Betsy and Uncle Edward. She was still gulping from paroxysms of grief as they sporadically washed over her.

As she came back inside, Albert was walking down the stairs. He was wearing a dressing gown that Beth remembered Lottie buying for him one Christmas. Lottie had said it was for the cold mornings when he sometimes took breakfast before using the bathroom. It was the first time Beth had ever seen him wear it.

He looked now at Beth, putting aside his own anguish, he recognised her genuine grief for her Aunt.

"You need your Mother, don't you? Come here, Beth dear." He put his arms around Beth and she sobbed loudly into his shoulder.

"Shhh, there there. Don't take on so. She's out of it now isn't she? The last months have been a living hell for her, despite having her favourite niece pandering to her every whim eh?" He tilted her chin up to look at him.

"Now we can all grieve for her. We couldn't do that while she was still with us. But we really lost her at Christmas didn't we, Beth? Do you know what I think? That she only stayed around to allow us to get used to her not doing everything for us all, before she finally left. What do you think?"

Beth, pulled away from Albert and fished in her pocket for a handkerchief. She blew her reddened nose and nodded.

"Albert, I don't know what to do for her now. I know we should do things, but I don't know, I haven't learnt."

Albert smiled,

"Neither do I Beth, neither do I, but I know someone who will help us. Were you just sending for your Aunt Betsy?" Beth nodded, "Well , I'm sure she'll know what's to do. Don't you? Now, how about a cup of tea for your old Uncle?"

Beth scurried off to make a tankard of sweet tea for them both. She handed one to Albert. As he half looked up to thank her, she saw his normally handsome, laughing eyes were submerged in deep glistening pools. A sight she had never seen in any man before. It was too painful to stay; she turned away, but placed a hand on his shoulder, and briefly, almost imperceptibly, squeezed her comfort into him, before the opening of the front door heralded the arrival of the cavalry.

"Have you seen Bertie's postcard Beth?"

"No, of course not Albert, you haven't shown me. Does he know about his mother yet?"

"No Beth, I keep putting off telling him. He's suffering enough." Absentmindedly, Albert looked all around him, and then paused in his search as he began to painfully regale some of that suffering.

"Bertie says everyone is so tired before they even go into battle on account of the conditions. He talks of bullets deafeningly raining over their heads like a brutal hailstorm, and of trying to carry on with the groans and screams of colleagues all around them."

"Albert, that's terrible."

"Don't you read the newspapers Beth? You must've heard what it's like? Bertie's last letter talked of so much mud that it sticks to their coats and drags them down, making every step such an effort that they sometimes feel it would be easier to die. Then he says someone will talk of home, and that spurs them all onwards."

"Ugh, Albert, it's awful, will it all be worth it?"

"I don't think the enemy have it any easier. Bertie says they can see the relief on the German soldier's faces when they are captured. He's made some wonderful friendships though Beth, he says they all help each other through the bad times, friends like that will last a lifetime. They have shared more horrors than any of us could bear to imagine. His worst time was when they had become conscious that the difficult terrain they were challenged by in the darkness one night, was the bodies of their fallen countrymen that had gone before. They had all been struck with the stark reality that they themselves could become tricky territory underfoot, for those following."

They fell silent, both shockingly unable to curtail the visualisation of this last appalling scenario. Albert abruptly moved in his seat, pulling at a postcard that had slipped between his leg and the side of the chair.

"Here it is look. He sent it to Emma and the children of course, but Emma brought it in for me to see, and to show the family. Then I must get it back to her. She doesn't hear from him often. She says understandably, that it's such a comfort to see and recognise his hand."

Albert continued with his newspaper as Beth stared at the card. It was hard to believe this had come from another country, where human hardship was so unimaginable. Yet Bertie could think of home comforts enough to write something like this. The depiction on the front was one diamond shape containing a uniformed soldier writing on a card, and a second diamond shape with a mother and two children reading the card. At the top it read 'With love to all my dear ones', and at the side, a verse:-

'It's ages since I saw you now it seems,

but your presence ever in my memory gleams,

Here's my love to all at home, 'til I'm back no more to roam,

I shall always have you with me in my dreams.'

On the back of the card, Bertie's own hand had written personal little messages to all the children and to his dear wife, Emma. Beth felt a lump rise in her throat.

"When will it all be over Albert? I'd like to go as a nurse to the front, but Mother won't hear of it, she says I'm too young."

"You certainly are young lady. You aren't quite sixteen yet. Don't be ridiculous. Besides, what would I do without you to keep my house clean and tidy and cook for me? I need you now." Albert smiled to show he was teasing, although he had come to depend on her help more than he could admit.

"But Albert, I've been out to poor homes here, with some of Uncle Edward's nurses. It can be rough here too, there's still a lot of death and disease. People don't understand about the importance of cleanliness here in our own town, never mind a battlefield. The other day, a dog was sick on a carpet in front of me where I was helping the nurse to clean a newborn, the mother leant forwards and picked the puce, jelly-like vomit up with her fingers and put it on her saucer; then she was going to feed the baby. The nurse shouted at her about washing her hands, but that's how easily babies here often die with infections."

Albert had pulled an appropriately disgusted face, but added, "That's ignorance though Beth, it's very different to the brutality and carnage of man's inhumanity to his fellow man. You are much too young to cope with that."

She sighed as she turned to replace Bertie's card on the secretaire,

"I'll take it to show Mother and Aunt Betsy if you like, then take it back to Emma when I go to see the children tomorrow, Emma's not the easiest of people though at the moment, is she?"

"That's kind Beth thank you. Here, take the children some humbugs or something when you go. Why do you find Emma difficult?"

Albert took a coin from his waistcoat pocket and handed it to her.

"I'm not sure really, but I do think it would be nice if you would accept her invitation to go for lunch one Sunday, even buy her the meat if you would feel more comfortable, Albert. I'm sure it would help if you saw more of her and the children."

"Well maybe I should. Tell her I'll come on Sunday if I'm still invited. I suppose I just feel how much Lottie should be enjoying the children. Especially little Hubert, he looks so much like Bertie did as a boy." Beth felt elated at her success.

"But isn't it better that at least you're enjoying them, rather than neither of you?"

"You are wise beyond your years Beth, do you know that? I think you've been in this life before!"

"Well, Uncle Albert, whilst you're listening to your niece," she began with a guarded sarcastic lilt in her voice, then became more serious, "I think you should tell your son that his mother has now passed." She looked back at his expression before continuing, "He may actually be relieved that she is released from her infirmity. Seriously Albert, it's only fair that he knows." She continued on her way back to the scullery, and added "Your tea's ready when you are, which is actually what I came through to tell you."

"Look, children. Grandpa Elliot's here girls. Move over, come on make room for him to have a seat. Dinner won't be long Pa. Mother and Father are joining us too." Emma made the girls move along on their sofa, then she nervously tucked a stray corner of blanket into Hubert's perambulator as though its very neatness was vital to her father-in-law's welcome.

"Emma, stop fretting, my dear. It's my own fault I've been a stranger in your home since Bertie left. But it could be a long time until he's home again. I couldn't go any longer without seeing my grandchildren could I? But it's been a difficult time for me."

"I know Pa, but it's been difficult for me too." Emma bit her lip and twiddled with her apron as Albert looked quizzically at his daughter-in-law. She continued, "I would've liked to have been more help with Ma you know. But with the three children to look after." Albert started to shake his head,

"Oh, Emma, Lottie would not have wanted you to put her

above her grandchildren, not for one minute, please don't even think it. You're doing the best you can keeping house for all of you, and for Bertie when he returns."

Emma smiled uncomfortably,

"It's just that mother says it should have been my place to care for Ma, as her only son's wife, and not a distant relative like Beth. It's made me very uncomfortable, Pa."

"Well Emma, I'll explain to your mother, that Beth is training to be a nurse as soon as she's old enough to take the exams. It was therefore an appropriate position for her to be given. I'm afraid I must also say, that Lottie knew and loved Beth from the day that she was born, and was closer than she could ever be to any other female family member. She is not, as you describe, a distant relative. As such, my wife could not have hoped for a better person to care for her in her final hours, do I make myself clear Emma?"

"But then why is she still at your house?"

"Emma, my dear, this is really none of your business, but I'm trying to keep a business going for your husband to have some means to support his family when he returns. I do not have time to keep house in addition. Beth has kindly offered to keep doing a grand job of it for me until she can begin her nursing."

He paused as though totting up a difficult calculation, then inspired by the answer, he added with a flourish, "Your inheritance is safe, my dear Emma, if that is what concerns your mother."

Emma vehemently denied the charge with a horrified countenance, which failed completely in its attempt to hide, that this was indeed the exact concern of her suspicious mother.

The room had fallen completely silent, Eleanor and Edith, both holding half dressed dolls, had been halted in their play by the uncomfortable tone of the adult voices. Emma was not appeased, but her father-in-law had made his stance on the situation very clear.

"Now then girls, how about a hug for your old Grandpa then

eh?" The tension was immediately released, and both girls climbed up onto Albert's knee, Edith following her big sister's lead. Eleanor spoke politely.

"Thank you for the sweeties Grandpa, Beth brought them the other day. Father says he'll bring some French ones for us when he comes home."

"Well I'm sure he will Eleanor, I'm sure he will. Now who's the most ticklish little girl in this house?" Albert had both girls helpless with childish infectious laughter in no time, and noticed out of the corner of his eye, that even Emma was smiling loudly at her daughters' enjoyment. He paused for breath, when he became aware of a loud knocking, obviously on account of being unheard initially. "Oh there's someone at the door, is that your Granny and Grandfather I wonder?" Emma looked puzzled.

"No, it can't be them, they wouldn't knock." She disappeared from the front room to open the door, Albert heard a boy's voice, but when he didn't hear any response from Emma, he relieved himself of the girls, and curiously followed Emma out into the hallway. He did not need to ask questions when he saw the telegraph boy's uniform.

He looked at the paper Emma was holding in her hand and snatched it from her. The words blurred in front of his eyes, but he needed no details, 'killed in action' had leapt out at him in the boldest of type. He closed the door on the boy in his smart red and black, and turned Emma to face him, he didn't look at her, just smothered her grief with his chest, so that she could not witness his own. His grief was far too personal to share with his suspicious daughter-in-law. He needed Betsy, and Beth. He knew for sure now, that had been the reason for Lottie's timely passing. She had gone ahead, so she could comfort their son after his brutal demise, ease his passing into everlasting life and mother him once more.

Albert had been completely lost for the first few days after

491

the telegram, and he had closed the workshop. Now he was beginning to pick up the pieces of his life without his wife or son. He had insisted on finding out the full details of the Battle of the Loos on the thirteenth of October 1915. He wanted to know which part of it had claimed the life of his son. He became angry with the use of tired troops in a futile battle that took fifty thousand British lives, yet hidden deep amongst all his other emotions was one of immense pride. When this war was won, and their country was free from threats, it would be thanks to sons like his, who had bravely paid the ultimate price

"Betsy, you can't stay here with me forever. I'll manage now. I know I went to pieces a little. But I'll be fine now. Christmas will be difficult, there is no doubt, after all, last Christmas ruined my life completely, it took away my Lottie."

"But Albert, if the bombardment hadn't caused Lottie's stroke, Bertie's death certainly would have. Things would be no different now."

"Of course they would Betsy, If it hadn't been for what the bombardment did to Lottie, Bertie wouldn't have signed up. There's no conscription yet, so he definitely would not have been at Loos. No, the bombardment has a lot to answer for. Anyway, I'll still have Beth to keep an eye on me, you must get back home to prepare for Christmas."

"What preparations should we make brother dear? We have little to celebrate this year."

"I know, but you must make an effort for Beth's sake."

"Albert, Beth is as distraught as you, or haven't you noticed. Christmas'll be here again next year. We can make more of an effort then."

Beth had walked into the front room of Albert's house. She put her hands on her Aunt Betsy's shoulders, and leant down to kiss her cheek. "I'm fine, Aunt Betsy, don't worry about me. But we must do something, if only for Eleanor, Edith and Hubert. They don't understand what's happened, they're too small. We must take them a little happiness at Christmastime."

She wandered over to the back of Albert's chair, and repeated the same affectionate gesture to seal her suggestion, then returned to the scullery and her chores.

"Erm, and that's another reason why I think I should stay, Albert."

Albert looked up from his book, enquiringly.

"What's another reason, Betsy?"

Betsy put down her sewing, and looked at her brother,

"Albert, before I moved in with you both, you know, before Bertie's telegram, people were beginning to talk about a young girl staying in a house alone with a handsome middle aged gentleman. They don't understand the situation as it is. Beth's reputation is at stake if she stays here alone with you, Eliza and I are worried for her, but Edward is becoming quite distressed and insisted that I speak with you about it."

Albert jumped out of the chair, and rounded on his sister,

"I've never heard such a preposterous suggestion in my life, Betsy, Beth is my niece for God's sake, she's my niece! She nursed her Aunt with such loving care, and this is how the gossips treat her. I have the greatest of respect for Edward, Betsy, and I owe him a great deal; but I thought better of him than to listen to such nonsense."

"Albert, calm down. Look at her, she's no longer a child, she's a woman, and a handsome woman at that. It isn't fair to allow her reputation to be ruined." Betsy lowered her voice, "You must also realise that Eliza is known to be a foundling, the gossips do not class Beth as your blood relative which only adds to the scandal." Albert had crossed the room to the secretaire, he leant onto the edges of it, his hands spread wider than his shoulders. He sighed deeply, and then spoke quietly.

"You know Betsy. Of course Beth must leave with you. I cannot allow her innocence to be tarnished by any knowledge of such tawdry accusations. She's far too precious for that. But know this Betsy, you have just extinguished the only remaining light in my life."

Betsy was beside him, one hand on his arm, the other rubbing gentle comfort into his back. She had hated to do this, but someone had to. They could both call often, still support him, but moving Beth back to Prince of Wales Terrace was imperative.

A small voice broke into both their thoughts from the hallway door.

"I'm sorry Aunt Betsy, but I'm not leaving Albert! I for one do not care what people who have nothing better to do all day than gossip, think of our situation. And I'm not so innocent, Albert, that I was not well aware of it. Aunt Betsy, I have a position here that pays me well for the job I do. As long as my employer can use my help, then here is where I will stay. We are a comfort to each other in our loss. You and Mother have valuable war work to keep you busy, when the time is right, I hope to be able to join you in that. In the meantime, I shall stay here and take care of my Uncle. I do agree with Albert though, Aunt Betsy, we can manage quite well now without your help; thank you."

Chapter 39

Scarborough, June 1918

"I'll be off then Beth, are you sure you won't consider coming with me."

Beth was saying goodbye to her mother on the doorstep of Albert's Victoria Street house, she tilted her head now to one side in exasperation of this subject that constantly came between her and her family. "Sorry Beth, I have to keep asking, you can't expect us to be happy about your reputation being tarnished. I don't know what your father would say about it all, and of course you'd make your Uncle Edward happy if you returned home, he says he could get you into a good school of nursing now you're eighteen."

"And I'd make my Uncle Albert very miserable, Mother. Why should I put Uncle Edward's feelings above Uncle Albert's? Why? He's no more a blood relative than Albert is. And he's only happy to get me into nurse training now the war's coming to an end, I'm sure he could have got me in before."

"Beth! Your Uncle Edward gave us a home after your father died. Don't be so disrespectful!"

Eliza had raised her voice in defence of her secret father, she had wondered many times recently if it would now be prudent to explain her own parentage to Beth, but she feared irreparable damage to their relationship, considering her own reaction years earlier.

"Sorry Mother. But I don't want to stop working here for

Albert, he needs me now. And I like to keep his house perfect, just the way Lottie always had it. Actually, I'll just leave the door, Mother, I'm popping a few doors along to the Bagshaw's house in a moment to see how their daughter Molly is. She's been really poorly you know, she has terrible asthma, you know like Uncle Thom sometimes gets? Good luck with your sandbag sewing on the sea front. It'll be packed with holiday makers now, all ambling around with nothing to do. You wouldn't think there was a war on for some people would you? Perhaps you could enlist them all to help you Mother?"

"Well perhaps Mr Lloyd George should make it compulsory. If he can conscript young men for the front, he should conscript affluent layabouts to help with the sandbags!"

They laughed affectionately together at the thought of holidaymakers lined up to sew sandbags for the front, and Eliza sighed. She didn't much care where her daughter lived, as long as she was happy and their relationship was good.

"Albert, I really don't feel well this morning. Do you think you could get your own breakfast?"

Beth was standing in the doorway of Albert's bedroom quite shockingly in her pretty but flimsy white cotton nightgown, trimmed heavily with broiderie anglaise and white ribbons. Albert raised himself onto one elbow to assess this unusual occurrence. His drowsiness gave way to abrupt consciousness at the sight of the somehow pale, yet flushed Beth, and he was out of bed in an instant.

"Get back into bed this minute Beth. Whatever is wrong, shall I send for Edward?"

A lethargic febrile Beth, allowed herself to be led back into her room and helped onto her bed. Albert pulled the covers up around her neck, patting them awkwardly around her shoulders, his brain thinking quickly, he had never dealt with even Bertie's few illnesses, that was Lottie's domain. He realised shamefully that he had absolutely no idea what to do. The knot in his stomach tightened helplessly, and he realised through the panic he felt, that he had allowed Beth to mean more to him than she should. She was now completely indispensable to his own survival. He ran down the stairs in his nightshirt, lit the range, put some water on to boil, then went outside to accost anyone willing to carry a message. It was only when he had accomplished this task, that he realised he had been in the street in his nightshirt! How Beth would laugh at that.

During the next half hour, Albert had run up and down the stairs many times to ask for a report on Beth's progress. Most times she was fast asleep, and Albert had to feel her cheek with the back of his hand to reassure him of a living warmth as he took in the vulnerable beauty that had pulled him through his darkest hours. He owed her so much. He silently prayed to God not to take her from him, it would not be fair for Lottie to have her as well.

He was just returning downstairs, when Edward let himself into the house.

"Where is she Albert?" He asked as he pushed past him on the stairs.

"First door on the right, Edward. Please, don't be angry, just make her well."

"I intend to. Then I'll take her home where she belongs."

The next days merged together as Edward, Betsy, Eliza and Albert kept vigil at Beth's bedside. She had every possible cure at her disposal, yet it seemed this Spanish Flu that was sweeping the country, would not be hurried as it coursed through the human body. The epidemic had begun it's journey in Glasgow and was travelling the country fast. Albert blamed Beth's friend Norah for her malady. He explained he had never been happy about this friend of Beth's when he had found out that she kept two tortoises, under her rug near the range hearth. They had been given to her by a previous sailor suitor. Albert had been appalled at the potential health hazard this could present. But Beth had merely giggled when she recounted the tale of the moving rug on one of her visits, but it was the only place Norah could keep them hidden from her new husband. She had married a fisherman, and had helped the Glasgow herring girls just recently, she and Beth had tea together the week before she became ill, he had then heard that Norah was also sick.

People had taken to wearing anti-germ masks in the street as more and more people in the town succumbed to the virulent virus. Little Molly along the street, had not survived, neither had Norah's unborn child.

Albert wanted to try every rumour of a cure to help his precious Beth, but Edward had taken charge of her care. Albert had heard tobacco smoke could kill the virus and wanted to smoke over her bed, but Edward insisted it could only hamper her breathing. His only concession to such old wives' tales, was the diet of porridge. Edward pronounced this could only be beneficial, so humoured Albert in his insistence that Betsy and Eliza make porridge incessantly throughout the day. Albert willingly took his turn in spooning this and other liquid sustenance into Beth whenever she was receptive to food.

After many days of what seemed like an eternity, Beth's fever broke, her delirium abated, and she began to take notice of her surroundings again, smiling pathetically at her team of adoring nurses.

"Beth, quickly, get down under the windowsill or behind the curtains, quickly hide here with me."

Albert had rushed in through their front door, closed it quickly behind him, and had accosted her as she was polishing the occasional table in his elegant parlour.

Perceptively grasping the nature of the situation, Beth answered in a whisper simultaneously with the knock on the door,

"What is it Albert, why are we whispering and hiding? Who's at the door?"

Whispering, and holding tight to her arm, Albert replied.

"It's Little Joe, but he's changed since he was invalided out of the army. I always suspected, but now, well! I don't mind seeing him at his father's house, but I'm not going to be seen letting him into mine! He looks as brazen as that scoundrel Oscar Wilde, white silk scarf and all!" Albert pressed his head to the wall, and thought he heard retreating footsteps. "Phew, I think he's gone."

Beth tweaked the curtain, and saw her flamboyant cousin turning elegantly away.

"Albert, I have no idea what you're talking about. But I feel very uneasy about turning my own cousin away from our door. I know from Aunt Annie, that he's had a horrible time in hospital with his leg being completely shattered. His hand injury thankfully will recover enough for him to be able to paint again. But I think you should be ashamed of yourself, you've just been extremely rude. I'm not happy with you Albert, not happy at all. He won't be in Scarborough long either. He's moving to Leeds with a friend and his wife, from the Staithes group, I believe. Apparently he's going to try his hand at inland painting as a change from seascapes and fishing boats."

"Well, that's a relief anyway Beth. I wouldn't like to have to keep hiding in my own home!"

"Albert! I don't understand, but then I don't need to. Little Joe's my cousin. I'm just going to finish this, then I shall visit Aunt Annie for afternoon tea, and then hopefully my cousin and me can catch up."

Beth flung the last words at Albert in good natured defiance of his inexplicable behaviour, and for her trouble, received an apathetic grunt, followed by an irritating correction of her syntax.

"It's 'my cousin and I', Beth. Don't let your grammar slip. That's your friend Norah's influence. What your Grandpa Joseph would have said, I cannot imagine!"

Beth waved her fist and face at Albert, and feigning belligerence, she set about finishing her polishing chores. She was already smiling, when their relationship was effortlessly restored by

Albert's resounding laughter as he patted her on her bottom with his newspaper. They both knew she would heed her grammar in future.

Since Beth's brush with death from the deadly flu in the early summer, there had been a subtle change in their relationship. Albert had made his fondness evident to all when they had faced her possible demise. Beth too, in her insistence in not wanting to recuperate with her mother, Aunt Betsy and Uncle Edward, had laid bare her own strength of emotions for her Uncle Albert. Their worries for her honour and reputation had subsided, but they all in their own ways, remained troubled.

Betsy and Edward could not help feeling resentful. She was their granddaughter, yet it was to Betsy's young brother Albert that she had turned for a substitute father figure.

Eliza felt inadequate; she felt it was all her own fault. She had relied on her elder daughter so much to help her care for Rose, that when she died Beth no longer had a sense of being indispensable. She had substituted first Lottie and now Albert for her baby sister Rose, in gratifying her own emotional needs. She worried for her daughter, should anything now happen to Albert.

"Albert can I talk to you?"

"Of course Beth, especially if you will then make me one of your fried Jam sandwiches." He smiled tenderly at her, and put down his newspaper, "what is it my dear?"

"Yes of course I will Albert, we have some dripping left from Sunday's roast. Anyway,… oh, what's that you're reading about the flu?"

"Just that we were very lucky not to loose you, Beth. They estimate that more than two million people will have died in Britain alone. That's more than any other disease in this country since the outbreak of Cholera in 1849."

"Wasn't it cholera that killed Betsy's real mother, Albert?"

"Erm, yes I believe so Beth. Now what did you want to talk

to me about?,"

"Oh, yes. Little Joe. It's alright, I don't want to invite him here for tea, although I don't see why not. He's wonderful, so many funny stories to tell about the hospitals he's been in." She smiled to herself remembering the afternoon they spent together, then hurried on when she felt Albert was becoming impatient.

"It's just that, you don't have any of his recent works. The paintings in the parlour are years old, and he did some really good ones before the war started. There's one of two little girls playing by some seaside cottages. They had those delightful little Staithes bonnets on. I would really love to buy it from him. The smallest little girl looks just like Rose, and I can see myself as the other one. Two sisters, just how I imagine we could have been. Please Albert, please, can we have it on the parlour wall? It would look perfect where the little miniature silhouette was, you know, the one the glass fell out of. It's not a large painting, but so perfect for me."

"Do you know, Beth," Albert began sternly, "I would have said yes, just yesterday. But today, I went to see what all the fuss was about this new affordable department store down on Queen Street. You've been haven't you?"

Beth worriedly concurred, she couldn't imagine how this would prevent her from having Little Joe's painting.

"It isn't new really Albert, it opened a couple of years ago now, after the warehouse was burned down."

"Well anyway, I was surprised at the very size of it, goes all the way back to Leading Post Street doesn't it? I suppose with the population expanding as it is, forty thousand in our town now I believe, despite the loss of so many young men. We're going to need these big stores in our town."

Again, puzzled, Beth agreed.   .

"Well, whilst I was there, I picked up a new picture for that very spot. I got it as a gift for you my dear. I'll get it for you now shall I."

"But why did you buy me a gift, Albert? It isn't Christmas

yet, or my birthday. And if it's from that store, er, are you sure it will be in keeping with the rest of your home?" Beth tried to hide her disappointment as Albert rose from his chair and went into the hall to retrieve a parcel from the cupboard under the stairs.

"Well, I reckon us men will have to keep on the right side of all women folk from now on, otherwise we could be in for a bumpy ride. First the vote this year, then where will it stop? We could have the same pay before you know it, then we could become the ones at home keeping house, washing and ironing your clothes, while you all go out to work!"

Beth had started to laugh out loud, she had been seated on her heels at the side of Albert's chair, now she rocked back and forth in her mirth at Albert's preposterous suggestion.

"You are so funny, Albert, but if it makes men start buying gifts for the womenfolk, let them think it. That's all I can say!"

Albert came towards her, smiling at her girlish giggles. He straightened his face as he handed her his offering, he didn't want her to laugh at this.

"This is for you, Beth, for fighting so hard to stay in this world with me. I really don't know what I would do without you now." As one hand offered her the brown paper parcel, the other stroked her cheek, just as he had done when she was sick, now so soft and familiar to him. He turned, snapping the invisible filament holding their eyes as one, and walked away from Beth's deep questioning gaze. He stopped in the doorway to the scullery, and when he heard the rapid tearing of the paper, he ventured a look at his niece. He watched her eyes fill and spill over their tears as she recognised the two little bonneted girls staring back at her from the painting, and wished he could suspend this moment to hang on the wall of his heart. What a gift it was, to give so much pleasure to one you hold so dear.

Beth slowly raised herself to her feet, no display of her girlish excitement now, instead a mature controlled demonstration of her gratitude as she crossed the floor to Albert. With a loud smile that reached her glittery eyes, she put her arms around his shoulders, and gently but purposefully, kissed his cheek.

"I absolutely love you for that Albert. I presume Thom told you how much I wanted it."

Albert nodded, smiling; but was soon smarting, when Beth released him and added a sharp playful punch on his shoulder, before heading to the scullery to make his fried jam sandwiches. She shouted over his shoulder,

"And that's for teasing me! Affordable store indeed!"

"What is it Albert, what is it? Beth stumbled out of her room, wrapping a dressing gown around her against the bitter cold." Albert was already on his way downstairs in his nightshirt.

"I don't know Beth, someone's shouting in the street, there seems to be lots of people around. You go back to bed, it's only six-o-clock, I'll find out."

By the time Albert had opened his front door, his neighbour was about to knock,

"Did you hear that Mr Elliot, Armistice at eleven o clock this morning. Can you believe it, it's finally over." He changed his demeanour remembering what he had in common with his neighbour. "Thanks to my lad and yours though, Mr Elliot. They didn't make it through to know what they've sacrificed for us, we just have to be so proud of them eh?"

Albert nodded politely and slowly closed the door. He plodded pensively up the stairs.

"What was it Albert? I suppose I'd better get out of this warm bed, it's Monday, you need to be ready for work. What is it?" She sat bolt upright in her bed when she saw Albert, standing in her doorway.

"Armistice at eleven o clock this morning, Betsy, it's all over." "Oh but that's wonderful Albert." Beth paused as they uncomfortably held each other's gaze, linked together by a vision of their beloved Bertie. If only he could have known. "That's eleven, eleven, eleven, Albert." She qualified her statement upon his bewildered expression, "Eleventh hour, eleventh day, and eleventh month." Albert nodded his understanding, then whispered aloud, the words that levitated heavily above their heads.

"Not so wonderful for Bertie though is it my dear? Or the other million or so dead and almost two million maimed!"

"Oh I know Albert." She jumped off her bed and reached her arms around him, holding him.

"Albert, can I read you something? Sit down here." She indicated to and patted her bed. As he tentatively took up her proposed position, she reached down to the little chest of drawers for yesterday's newspaper.

"You know Rupert Brooke, Albert, the poet that died on a French hospital ship about two years ago?" Albert nodded absentmindedly, ill at ease as a visitor in her domain. "Well he wrote this before he died, and I found it such a comforting sentiment, listen." Beth turned slightly to face him as she began to read so as not to miss his reaction to her words.

"If I should die, think only this of me:

That there's some corner of a foreign field

That is for ever England. There shall be

In that rich earth a richer dust concealed;

A dust whom England bore, shaped, made aware,

Gave, once, her flowers to love, her ways to roam,

A body of England's, breathing English air,

Washed by the rivers, blest by suns of home."

She looked expectantly at Albert. When he said nothing, she lifted his be-whiskered chin in her dainty hand to face her, "Does it help?"

Albert looked at this young girl, not yet nineteen, yet with a maturity to match his own. Her hand on his face felt good, too good. He shifted away from her, but held her gaze.

"Nothing helps Beth, except you." She replaced her hand instinctively on his face, transfixing him tightly yet tenderly with her eyes, then leant upwards tentatively and tantalisingly allowing their lips to meet. Albert jumped backwards on the bed as though scalded by their touch. Beth, herself bewildered and alarmed by her audaciousness, was then simultaneously confused and hurt by his rejection. Her eyes searched his soul for an explanation, and her pain tore into him. He leant cautiously towards her to seal the rend. Slowly and reciprocally, the last years of pain, raw emotion and suffering that had tossed them so closely together, unleashed, surging passionately to become the catalyst for their perfect, fervent, earthly, loving union.

"Albert, wake up, what's that banging? Don't tell me we're at war again?"

Beth was snuggled into the crook of Albert's arm as they lay together in her bed. He opened his eyes, disorientated for a second, then he shot upright in the bed, staring disbelievingly at Beth's naked form.

"Don't take the covers off me Albert, it's freezing. But there was a very loud banging on the door!" She pulled the blankets shyly back up to her chin.

"Beth, Beth. What've we done? This is so wrong! You're my niece! Oh my God Beth!" He swung his legs out of the bed keeping his shameful head in his hands. He donned his nightshirt, retrieved from the floor, and made to leave her room.

"Albert please don't say that. You've just told me this morning how much I mean to you. Have you forgotten? Remember you're not really my uncle, my mother was a foundling. I'm no relation to any of you really. So why is it so wrong? Lots of my friends have married older men. There aren't so many younger ones around now, thanks to the war."

"No I know that, Beth. But your mother, Betsy and Edward, they wouldn't be happy. They'd say we've proved the gossips right all along!"

They paused as a voice drifted up from the street below, "Street party today! Street party today!" They both smiled,

"That's going to be some celebration Beth."

"Hmm, but Albert, what about us? If that's what people think about us anyway, does it matter? My reputation's only ruined if I want to look for a new suitor." She knelt up on the bed, the sheet teasingly displaying the wares he had already enjoyed this morning, and held out her arms to him. He moved into them, his heart, anxiously wanting to agree with her, but his head telling him this would not be an easy choice to make. "And I certainly don't need to do that dearest Albert, for I have all I want right here." Beth kissed his lips again gently before adding and punctuating with kisses, "and I assume, you won't hold, my very recent lack of virtue, against me, will you, my dear, dear, Albert?"

Chapter 40

Scarborough, Winter 1922

"Beth, do you think your Mother and Aunt Betsy have any idea of how we live these days? I know we try hard to hide it in their company, but I do wonder if they suspect."

"I'm not sure Albert, why do you ask?"

"It's just that Edward mentioned to me the other day, that the Royal College of Nursing has had the status of State Registration for three years now, and he thought it would be a good time for you to go and do your training. He says you would make a wonderful nurse. And of course he's right Beth. Do you want to go and do your training?"

"Do you want rid of me Albert? Do I not have my hands full already looking after you and your house?"

"Yes you do my dear, of course you do. I just want you to know that I would never stand in your way, if that's what you want. I would have no right to ask you to stay."

Beth was rolling out pastry for a fresh apple pie, and Albert had interrupted her task. Coming up behind her, he had threaded his arms between hers, and her body, sparing the assault on the pastry momentarily. Beth had tipped her head backwards to him in his easy embrace, and now replied to end this discussion.

"This is exactly where I want to be, Albert. Nowhere else. Thank you." Then, she turned in his arms, and wiggling her floury fingers inches away from his nose, added. "Now if you want apple pie for your tea, you had better leave me to it, before I cover you in flour!"

Albert intimately squeezed her behind, before moving away,
"Hmm, its nice to have something to squeeze now Beth, you have certainly recovered you figure since you had that flu. You were like a bag of bones."

"Well, it was a bag of bones you fell for Albert Elliot. Besides, they're still there, just a little more hidden now."

Their relationship had settled into the same easy and affable one they always had, yet now strengthened and fortified by a passion that neither one had expected of the other. Behind the door of Albert's Victoria Street House, they lived completely now, as man and wife. Their only unease was in publicly maintaining a veil of secrecy around their true feelings in anticipation of total family condemnation.

"Mr Chapman, David, would you excuse me, I need to use the Powder room before the main feature begins."

"Why of course Eliza, can you manage in the dark?"

"Oh perfectly, Sir, thank you."

Eliza had reluctantly accepted an offer of an outing to the cinema with their neighbour David Chapman. Betsy and Edward were delighted. They had often invited him to join them for dinner out of kindness since his wife's passing. He was a local solicitor, therefore very respectable, and they had worried so much about Eliza's lack of life outside of their home. It had seemed a union just waiting to happen, and they had seen no harm in nudging it along. They had both commented upon how stunning and alive she had looked before going out tonight. Eliza had continued to shock in her enjoyment of the latest fashions. Her dresses now were very economical on their material, not only short, but also very straight, skimming her slim figure, yet hiding its very curves in its shapelessness despite the contrasting ribbons and bows that often encircled her hips. More shocking than any of this for Betsy, was that Eliza had cut her hair. She now sported a chin length 'bob', which to tease Betsy, Edward had mused she looked very chic, no more than he would expect from his mother's grand-daughter. Tonight, she had worn a new style cloche hat in amber felt. It was as extreme in its plainness as Betsy's Edwardian style hats were in their ostentation.

Since many, though obviously not all the town's young men had returned from the front looking for work, Eliza had relinquished her position as did many other women, to make way for local heroes in the workplace. She continued to be busy with many voluntary missions, but Betsy worried about her loneliness. For she was such a vibrant, energetic and still relatively young woman, and they were both getting on in years to be her only companions.

David Chapman had decided a visit to the Londesborough Theatre to watch one of the ever popular films by Mr Charlie Chaplin, would be a light hearted approach, for this, their first time alone together.

Eliza made her way carefully in the darkness, to the Ladies room, and mused at the mix of classes enjoying this new form of entertainment, as she passed them en route outside the main auditorium. She for one was pleased at this erosion of the barriers that had inevitably begun during the war. Everyone had pulled together regardless of background, and she felt less awkward amongst both the fisher folk and the neighbours on Prince of Wales Terrace. Indeed she enjoyed a new and privileged sense of belonging to both.

She still visited Micky's sister often, and especially when she knew Charlie was back in the town. He had survived the war, being conscripted at the end of 1916, he spent only a little time in France before being invalided out with severe effects of mustard gas. She and Edith had fussed over him like mother hens, but he was soon well enough to return to the life he loved as a fisherman for his Uncle in Hartlepool. He now often skippered the boat, and had married exactly two years after the Armistice. Jane, was a lively fun loving Hartlepool girl, and her father had humorously warned Charlie to make the most of the two minutes silence that day, for it would be the last two minutes silence he would get for the rest of his life!

Eliza thought of him now as she entered the cubicle, wondering if she could soon be a Grandmother. She knew it could never be acknowledged, but she could still be a part of their lives. How nice it would be to know that herself and Micky would be immortalised for generations to come. She could not see Beth ever marrying, she seemed incomprehensively intent on devoting her life to her the care of her uncle.

"Have you met Beth Walker's young man then Mrs Winterbottom?"

"I didn't know she had one Mrs Bagshaw?"

Eliza froze in her cubicle. Was she about to hear some good news, perhaps Beth had more of a life outside Albert's house than they knew. Her heart lifted in anticipation, at twenty two, it was time she made a life for herself.

"Well, if she hasn't got one, how has she got herself in the family way then!"

A sharp intake of breath from Mrs Winterbottom, accompanied Eliza's heart as it thudded to the floor.

"No, you don't say. Are you sure Mrs Bagshaw. Has she told you? Or is it just that she's just looking more rounded over the last couple of years? She nearly died of that flu you know, she looks so much better now."

"She was very lucky, I wish my Molly had been as lucky. But you mark my words Mrs Winterbottom, Beth Walker has the patter of tiny feet arriving next spring. I can spot these things a mile off!"

Eliza had strained to hear these last comments over the running water as the two ladies washed their hands. Then she heard the door to the conveniences open and close behind them, and the volume of their voices drift quietly away.

She had no idea how long she remained perched on the bowl, elbows leant on her knees and her head heavily on her hands. Tears had rained through her fingers onto her skirt. Her hopes for a different life for her daughter faded in front of her. Why had she not confided in her? First Lizzibeth, then Betsy, then herself, and now her own daughter, all disregarded their families and loved ones in secreting their shame.

She heard the door to the conveniences open, and realised she must have been in there some time, David Chapman must wonder whatever had happened to her.

"Mrs Walker, is there a Mrs Walker in here?"

She emerged from her cubicle, stiffened and composed.

"Oh there you are, there's a Mr Chapman outside he was concerned that you may be unwell." Eliza swilled her hands, quickly shook them, and swept past the usherette, feigning her previously hard won poise and respectable self assurance that she knew, had just been crushed.

"Erm, well I wasn't feeling very good. I'm better now thank you. Oh David, thank you for your concern, but I'm quite well again now, really. Would you mind awfully if we went straight back home? I really need to talk to Edward and Betsy about some information that has just been brought to my attention."

Betsy and Edward had waited up tonight, in high hopes of a successful evening for Eliza. They had been disappointed at her early return, but could not have anticipated the news she was about to share with them.

Eliza had her head on Betsy's shoulder and was shaking with such a mixture of emotions.

"There, there Eliza, it's not the end of the world, we of all people should know that. Edward will know what to do, won't you Edward."

"But I wanted more out of life for her Betsy, she's my daughter."

Betsy pushed Eliza gently away from her to look in her eyes. She stroked some stray hairs away from her daughter's face, and spoke softly, but firmly.

"And you think I didn't for you Eliza? Come on now, let's

think how to handle this. Edward?" Edward moved towards them from the window.

"Well, my first concern is who is it, and will he marry her? My second is, will Albert throw her out? I know we would offer her a home here, but she has made it very clear all along that she wanted to live and care for Albert. I can't see that she would want to stop doing that. So, it would break her heart if he no longer wanted her to live there. Then again, maybe Albert knows and approves of this fellow, and has offered them a home with him. But if that is the case, why has she not told us?"

He had paced their drawing room as he spoke, stopped as he paused, as though his voice and his legs worked in unison, if one stopped then the other must. Betsy and Eliza, listened attentively. He set off towards the window again as though interested in something outside in the grave darkness, "We must invite Beth and Albert to Sunday lunch. Have it out with them then. If she hasn't told him yet, then he must be told. She can then stay here if he prefers, I will return with him to collect her belongings."

"Edward this is really kind of you to have us both for lunch today, we've done well this week, we were at Thom and Annie's for tea yesterday. They wanted us to see some of Little Joe's latest work, he brought it up from Leeds for Thom's opinion earlier in the week. I must say, he's very good, but I still think Thom is actually the better painter. After all, he still holds the record sale for that very first painting of his doesn't he?" Betsy cleared her throat behind her napkin, and Edward muffled, "Hmm, I believe so Albert."

"Mind, Thom is also an excellent stonemason, I think he's given that up now though. He just dabbles with his painting. I'm very proud of my brother and his work, aren't you Betsy?"

"But of course Albert. I wonder what he thinks of the stonemasonry of the ancient Egyptians though. Have you seen it all in the papers about the tomb they've uncovered of the boy king in Egypt. They did amazing things back then, considering the limited tools they would have had. Apparently his tomb was like an underground palace, with such treasures."

"Yes I've been reading about it all actually Betsy, fascinating."

"Did you see Little Joe then, Albert? You know, when you went for tea."

Albert with a mouthful of food, had shaken his head to indicate he had not. She continued, "I saw him last time he was here, he's very fashionable. He wore a pair of trousers that had more material in them than Betsy's skirts!"

"Do you mind, Eliza! We don't all want to be showing our legs to the world you know." The merriment rippled around the table, Beth oblivious to the tension veiled amongst her family.

"Oxford bags I believe those trousers are called, Edward, just in case you should want to buy some, I saw them in a magazine."

"Oxford bags indeed. I think I shall pass on those my dear Eliza. Anyway Albert, how is business at the moment? Has Billy taken back to it all well?"

"Oh yes. It was bitter sweet having him back. I was ready for the break in someone else taking over a lot of the orders, but I don't mind admitting that I would have preferred it to have been Bertie."

"Of course Albert, that's understandable. Incidentally, did you know that the building of the town's monument to those who fell is to be finished by next year. They say it should be visible for miles around. And a fitting place to hold the annual service on Armistice day. Lest we Forget eh Albert? As if we are ever likely to do that."

Albert nodded, trying hard to swallow his beef along with the lump that had arisen in his throat.

A silence followed as they all busied their cutlery upon their roast amid their own thoughts of the suffering the Great War had brought to all their lives, but especially Albert's. Then

Eliza broke the awkwardness.

"Is it true that Emma is remarrying soon, Albert? Mrs Cappleman, her mother told me in the green grocers the other day. She had little Hubert with her, he's grown so much since I last saw him at your house."

"Yes it's true Betsy. I wish her every happiness. You can't expect a very young woman like her to stay true to her dead husband forever. She has already lived without him longer than with him. Her intended seems a nice enough fellow, a lot older than her, but he will provide well for my grandchildren. That's important."

Eliza listened intently, this must be difficult for her brother to accept. She empathised,

"Of course Albert, it is very important, and I fear lots of young women will be turning to older men these days, there are so few young ones left. Do you still see the children as much?"

Beth had been sitting very quietly opposite her mother during this exchange, at the mention of the children, she became animated.

"Oh yes, Mother, they still come to us for a couple of hours every Saturday morning while Emma does some shopping for the weekend. Albert spoils them, taking them to the sweetie shop, and telling them stories about their father." She smiled at Albert with an intimacy only they could recognise.

"That's nice Beth. And do you go off and see anybody while Albert has this time with his grandchildren?"

"Of course not Mother. I like to spend time with them too."

Betsy and Eliza shared a glance. How were they to broach this subject? They had no idea, but one look at Beth when she had arrived, confirmed the overheard gossip, to them all. For she too was wearing the new column shaped dresses to just below the knee, but it did not conceal the telltale shape of her misdemeanour.

"Mother, I forgot to ask. How was your visit to the cinema with Mr Chapman? Will you walk out with him again? He's such a nice man. I hope you liked him, I'm sure he's liked you for years."

Edward, Betsy and Eliza shared a rising panic, if ever there was an opening, this was it. Eliza turned to her daughter, and taking her courage in both hands, allowing an awkward glance at Albert first, she began.

"Actually Beth, the evening was cut very short because I overheard some very distressing news in the Ladies Powder Room at the Cinema."

"Mother, what could be so distressing that you cut short a first assignation with Mr Chapman?" Beth laughed out her first words, they then sobered with anxiety as the reason they had been invited to lunch gradually began to dawn on her.

Eliza cleared her throat.

"I think you know well Beth dear. But we felt that perhaps your employer should know." Eliza glanced at Albert, who had replaced his knife and fork onto his plate, put his elbows on the table and awaited clarification of this confrontation, as Eliza now turned towards him.

"Albert, we're all extremely grateful to you for employing Beth over these last years. She would not have taken well to being idle. And her interest in a nursing career appeared to be short lived. I know we were a little resistant initially, but you have treated her well, she has been happy in her work, and for that we thank you. However, you've always been a fine upstanding pillar of the community, and what Beth is hiding from you is that she now has you harbouring her shame." Albert looked incredulously from Eliza to Beth as Edward added,

"We do not expect you to continue to do this, and we are her family. She can come to us, and we will take care of her. You need have no disgrace in your home." Albert scraped back his chair on the highly polished floorboards of their dining room, and walked towards Beth.

"Is this true?" Beth had stared down at her immobile fork since her mother had begun to speak. Now she couldn't imagine why she had not told Albert of her predicament, it must really now be showing. She nodded meekly in answer to his question.

"Then get your coat, we are going home to discuss this, I'm not having this conversation in public." He had begun gently, but the end of his sentence built to an authoritative command.

Beth made to rise from her chair. Edward felt a loss of his paternal position in his own home, and intervened.

"No Albert, leave her here. This problem is not your responsibility. We will do what has to be done here, and deal with the consequences. Not you. Eliza is her mother after all!"

Albert continued to direct a willing Beth towards the door.

"I can assure you Edward, this 'problem' as you call it, is very much my responsibility. I do regret the way I have discovered that I am to be a father again at this stage of my life, but I would like to be alone with Beth as I become accustomed to this news. Throwing her coat over her shoulders, he turned as he opened the front door.

"Good-day to you all. Thank you for lunch. Come along Beth." Albert cupped her elbow as he led her down the steps of The Hetherington abode, leaving Eliza and Edward open mouthed at their front door, and Betsy alone at her table, silently weeping into her lunch.

Albert walked ahead of Beth into the house. He threw his coat over the back of the fireside chair and turned to relieve Beth of hers. As he walked to the front of the chair and lowered onto it, Beth held her breath as he finally spoke.

"Now we will talk about this my dear. I cannot pretend not to be hurt that I was not the first to know." Beth hurried around the chair to sit at Albert's feet.

"But Albert, I've told no-one. I confess to worrying about the consequences in the beginning of our erm, relationship. You know, if I should end up in the family way, but when nothing happened for so long, I thought nothing ever would. It's only recently that I realised I'd not had a monthly for a while. I can only think it must be showing more 'n I think." She bent now, and smoothed her dress over her visibly rounded abdomen to see for herself.

"More *than*, you think, speak properly please Beth, what would your Grandpa Joseph sa…….Good God Beth, how have I not noticed. Have you seen a doctor?"

"No, not yet. I knew I should, soon."

"I'll take you tomorrow. And remember, the one thing we feared is now over." Albert mimicked a goulish voice and said "The family!"

Beth smiled, everything would be alright, as long as Albert was beside her.

"Albert, you're not upset, really? I didn't know how you'd feel. That's partly why I didn't say anything as soon as I suspected."

Albert looked down at this young woman, it seemed only yesterday since he had bounced her on his knee as a baby, enjoyed her girlish company when she visited as a child, and relied totally upon her as a very young woman in his hour of need. Now he looked at her and saw his lover, his soul mate, and now tenderly, the mother of his child.

"Oh, Beth, Beth. You are the best thing that could possibly have come out of Lottie's death. I loved her dearly, but because of her, I have grown to love you more. She would be so happy for both of us you know. I couldn't be happier. But now we must marry. There should be no dishonour in our love my dear. We have done the worst bit, told Betsy, Edward and Eliza, though why they should disapprove I've no idea. Your mother even said young women were bound to be looking to older men for husbands after losing so many young men at the front. And we are no blood relation, the whole town knows that. I'll book the registry office for as soon as possible." He leant forwards and planted a gentle kiss on the tip of her nose, then he glanced downwards and ran his hand over his child. Speaking softly he added, "It's a good thing I'm such a virile, young looking 'old man'. You wouldn't want an elderly father now, would you?"

Beth laughed, for the first time she welcomed her condition, and felt her excitement fluttering around her child.

"I'll go and make us some tea. You'll have to buy me a new dress for the wedding." Beth added the last words as she skipped into the kitchen, the dress already taking a wistful shape in her dreamy head.

Suddenly, there was an aggressive knocking on the front door. Albert arose from his seat,

"Alright, I'm coming, I'm coming."

Beth had filled the kettle and was placing it on the range as Albert returned followed by a tear stained and distraught Betsy.

"Can you make that three cups of tea please my dear. Betsy is very upset with us." Albert helped Betsy into a chair, and offered her another handkerchief.

Beth came scurrying out of the scullery, and she stood awkwardly to one side of her.

"Aunt Betsy, I knew you would be upset, why do you think we didn't tell you? I know you loved Lottie, but I think she'd be happy for us. She'd have wanted Albert to be happy again."

Betsy looked up from blowing her nose on the crisp white cotton, she glanced from her brother to her grand-daughter, then quietly confessed.

"But not, I don't think, Beth, with my own grand-daughter!"

Albert and Beth plonked themselves heavily upon the two-seater fireside chair, and waited. When she had composed herself enough, they listened intently as Betsy regaled for the second time in her life, her and Edward's story of their daughter, Beth's mother, Eliza.

The next weeks passed without any contact between Prince of Wales Terrace and Victoria Street. This was a lot of news for Albert and Beth to take in and deal with in their own ways.

For Beth, it was that Betsy and Edward had been her real Grandparents all along, yet she had always referred to them as a mere Aunt and Uncle. But the health of her child was paramount, and she became anxious regarding their familial link.

For Albert, that Eliza, always his foundling little sister, was in fact his niece, was difficult to comprehend. He thought back to those times, he had been too young to notice any changes in his sister Betsy, or had he? But how had the others not guessed? His respect for Edward Hetherington was dented. How could he have denied Betsy for so long after what had passed between them. He remembered with discomfort Betsy's disappointment the night the Spa Grand Hall opened, and Edward's mother had usurped Betsy's rightful place beside him at the Ball. In his opinion, if you loved someone, and you had committed to them physically, then nothing or no-one should stand in your way. To this end he was resolute, there was no question that he would stand by Beth. He began to understand the anxiety they had all displayed around his arrangement with Beth following Lottie's death, and yet prior to Beth's illness which appeared to have allayed their very fears. Yet, on the other hand, did it really matter? The relationship was not illegal.

He did understand Beth's perceived concern for their child, she had relayed having heard Edward talk often of the problems that could occur, where familial genes were not sufficiently diluted. He could not persuade her at the moment to reconsider marriage, despite his reassurances. She had insisted they wait until the baby was born. They could always marry later. How all this broke his heart.

For, he alone held the final piece of the complex jigsaw that could eradicate this pain for them all. But to do that, he had to inflict a fresh wound upon his beloved Betsy, knowing it would never heal. He would have to take away the father she had known and loved. The one man she held with such high esteem would no longer belong to her. And he would have to break a promise to his sister Kathy. She may never forgive him.

Chapter 41

Scarborough, Spring 1923

The weeks swept by, hurrying them into the following year. Albert desperately wanted to ease Beth's fears for their child. He tried to tell her he knew for certain that things would be alright, but when she challenged him, he could not justify it. They knew they were the subject of much speculation. Neighbours assumed she had been taken advantage of by some young passing sailor, and Albert was being a very understanding benevolent employer in not dismissing her, adopted niece or not.

He wished Kathy would come up, if he could talk to her she may know what to do. It was not possible for him to travel to Dorset with Beth so near her time.

There was a warmth in the air as spring promised its appearance. Albert sauntered back from delivering a small bookcase to a house on Queen's Parade. As he turned back onto Castle Road, something made him cross over towards St Mary's Church. He walked to the Church wall, and took in the changing skyline as the obelisk set to commemorate the fallen, was now visible on Oliver's Mount. He turned and looked at the church yard, and his memory showed him Bertie, playing leapfrog over the gravestones until Albert's chastisement curtailed his innocent lack of respect. Bertie's death had left him feeling that the war had deprived him of all he held dear. But it could never erase the many wonderful memories. Bertie had been a delight to him, both as a child, and as a man. That would stay with him forever. Now he had a second chance. A chance to make more memories with another child, only this time to leave behind him, as his own legacy. He wanted to earn the same respect they had all had for his father before him, Joseph Elliot.

His focus moved back to the monument, the place where they would be able to pay their respects to Bertie. He would tell his child about his or her brave hero of a brother. Having no place to honour Bertie had augmented his loss. His eyes fell to the deserted sweep of the south bay, the tide was out, and the sand had lost its golden hue under the cloudy April sky. He scanned the rooftops, the foreshore, and over to the Grand where there were men on the roof, no doubt sprucing its grandeur, in preparation for the summer season. Then his gaze was drawn back to the Mount, where he muttered an almost incoherent endearment to his son, then let his eyes fall and settle on the pristine white houses of South cliff which appeared nestled in its forefront.

He visualised his sister Betsy seated in her drawing room with her sewing basket at her side, and knew immediately what he had to do to secure a future for his family.

"Beth, are you here, I want us to go up to South Cliff now. Is that alright?"

Beth came toward him, waddling now as she was so close to her confinement. Albert reassured himself as he did every day on his return from work

"You alright? No pains?" He planted a tender kiss on her forehead.

"No nothing at all, Albert dear, I'm sure I'll know when it happens! Why do you want to go to Mother's?"

"I can't say yet Beth dear, but I can't let this go on any longer. I must tell you all something, now where's the key to my secretaire? I brought a letter of Pa's back from Dorset after he died. It's time its contents were shared."

"Do you want to eat first, or later?"

"Later, my dearest Beth, I have a carriage picking us up in a few minutes."

Edward waited patiently for Betsy to pass each sheet of her Granma's hand over to him after she had finished reading it. When she had finished the last sheet, she looked up at her brother.

"How long have you known, Albert?"

"Since Pa died Betsy, I found it in his secretaire. Kathy already knew, Ma had shown her it after she had found something else out from you. Ah,… she'd guessed about Eliza's parentage hadn't she? I'd never question her on the nature of what that something was."

"Why now then Albert, why now?" Edward passed the sheets to Eliza, he felt his wife's palpable anguish. Finding she was the result of abuse by a powerful man, and not an issue of the love she thought her mother had borne Joseph, must be devastating for her, yet somehow, she seemed very calm.

Albert turned his answer to his sister.

"I'm most truly sorry Betsy, but I had to put Beth and our unborn child above your feelings. We're not blood brother and sister. There's no connection, well a very tenuous one through my mother, but by the time that reaches Beth, the link is enough times removed to be completely insignificant. Our child is at no more risk than anyone else's my dearest Beth."

Albert's eyes moved slowly during his reply, from his sister to his lover, his countenance morphing as he did so to one of complete adoration for his young bride to be.

Eliza looked up from the letter, and slowly and thoughtfully, began to speak.

"Beth, I want to tell you something too. Your cousin Charlie, who I know you love dearly, is your brother. It's a very long story, we'll have afternoon tea tomorrow, and I'll tell you all about it. Then we'll both talk to him when he's next in town.

I cannot keep hiding my own shame in the midst of all this sharing of revelations."

Eliza looked back down at the letter as she saw Beth's jaw drop to the floor, and Albert tenderly lift it with his index finger.

"That is no surprise to me either Eliza, Lottie suspected that years ago!"

They all chuckled awkwardly yet affectionately at the perceptiveness of Albert's Lottie. Betsy arose from her chair, as the ever present and constant knot in her stomach began to slowly unravel and come loose. She moved towards her grand-daughter. She put her hands on her shoulders, and spoke softly.

"Beth, you are a very lucky young woman, I spent my childhood with this young man here, he was like a brother to me." She smiled to herself, remembering. "I actually wonder if for nearly seventy years, I've always instinctively known I was a cuckoo in the nest. Despite Ma's welcome protestations and reassurances whenever challenged, neither Bill's words before he died at the railway station all those years ago; nor Uncle Henry's as he read his father's will, have ever completely left me. But, I could have had no better parents." Betsy turned her head to look at Albert, then softly continued, "of all the men you could choose as a husband, he's the best there is, my dear. Like his insightful father and grandfather before him, he has always respectfully valued the women in his life. He will be no different with you. Today he's given you the best gift of all, the gift of truth. Build your life upon it. For the love of you and your child, Albert alone has set you free from this guilty chain of secrets that has linked your mother, grandmother and great-grandmother, through these many generations. For deception comes at a high price Beth, and carries with it such heartache. 'Oh, what a tangled web we weave, when first we practise to deceive'."

An awkward silence signalled the first time no-one dared to mock Betsy for her sayings. Its message was too moving and poignant. Betsy herself smiled audibly, looking long and hard at her grand-daughter, she hugged her uncharacteristically to her. Beth hugged her back, a puree of relief, happiness and sorrow welling up in her.

Betsy let her go, then corrected her posture as though recovering from a sudden sharp pain, and swept proudly and elegantly out of the room.

"Beth, she's absolutely beautiful. And you were so quick with her, no problems. Betsy said my arrival was just like that, but just as well eh – born on a beach!" Mother and daughter laughed together. Beth smiled proudly as she held her new baby girl. She was relieved the baby was a girl. It would have seemed as though a boy was replacing Bertie. She didn't want that, for no-one could replace him in any of their affections.

"You know Mother, when little Rose died, you told Aunt Betsy that she had left no new phoenix behind, didn't you?"

Eliza looked quizzically at Beth as she nodded.

"That's only a myth, Beth. And I was grief stricken for our little Rose, remember?"

"I know, Mother. But now I know everything, everyone's secrets, lots of things that happened within our family have fallen into place. I think Rose left behind a reconciliation that she alone sealed and consolidated between you and Betsy, your mother. A warm and loving family; a nurturing nest of spices. That was her phoenix."

Eliza could not look at her wise daughter, instead she leant forward to kiss her new grand-daughter's forehead; avoiding her daughter's eyes, she then dropped both a kiss and her tears silently onto the top of Beth's head before composing herself to take her leave.

"I'm sure you're right Beth. Anyway I'll go, I've just heard the door go downstairs, so I think that's the proud father back. Have you decided when to wed, we could make you a dress just like Lady Elizabeth Bowes-Lyon had last month when she married the Prince?"

Beth lowered her voice.

"I think, Mother as we didn't manage it before this little one's arrival, we are going to wait until after the monument is unveiled. Put Bertie properly to rest. Finally let him go. Are you all going to go? They've set a date in September I believe. So I think maybe we'll wed in October sometime." They both nodded, sombrely concurring. Then they heard a sound downstairs, and their mood lightened as they laughed hearing Albert take the stair's two at a time. At fifty seven, he still cut a fine fit figure of a man.

"How's my two best girls then?"

"We've been well looked after by Mother, Albert, thank you. You've only been gone a few minutes!" They both sniggered at his attentiveness, then Eliza took her leave.

"I'll leave you two love birds to it. I have to get ready, I'm dining out with Mr Chapman again tonight, it's becoming quite a regular occurrence you know."

"I'm not sure who will marry first now Mother! Thank you for coming."

Albert took in the snapshot of his beloved Beth staring lovingly at his child, and thought that would be the one memory he would take to his grave. He had never expected to be happy again, all this was more than he deserved.

"Have you had any more thoughts about names Beth? Are you still keen on Hannah or Louisa?"

Beth lifted her loving gaze to this man she had adored all her life, as he tweaked his daughter's chubby cheek,

"I was wondering about names that had shaped who we are Albert. What do you think to Charlotte Rose." Albert's eyes darted back to Beth,

"Are you sure Beth?" As Beth nodded, he continued, "I think it's lovely." He looked again at his daughter, "It suits her too. Morning, little Charlotte Rose, may you be as wonderful and loving a woman as your mother, for I doubt I'll make a cabinet maker out of you!"

* * *

It was a lovely late September afternoon when the motor cavalcade and many carriages set off up the steep and winding road to the top of Oliver's Mount. Many thousands of townsfolk had made the journey to pay their last respects to the young men of the town who had given the ultimate sacrifice in the Great War.

The whole of Bertie Elliot's family were gathered together on the south side of the monument, looking out towards the south bay. Today, as though offering its own respects, it was steeped stunningly in the slanting sunlight of a pleasant early autumnal afternoon, following days of previously wretched weather. Beth jiggled little Charlotte in her arms as she supported Albert in this most grim of tasks, saying a final goodbye to his son. The mount itself appeared to stretch and rise further towards the heavens, with a rousing chorus of 'Oh God our help in ages past'.

The deputy Mayor, Councillor Boyes, who had chaired the War Memorial Committee, then climbed the eleven steps up to the base of the monument, each step purposeful as though dragging with him a heavy heart. A hush fell over the whole gathering as he unveiled the memorial, and arms were simultaneously presented by the Guard of Honour.

Each side of the monument was then separately unveiled with assistance from war widows and armed service representatives. A dedication was then made by the Vicar of Scarborough, the Rev. J. Wynyard Capron, prayers were read, and the congregation was led in a stirring rendition of 'For all the Saints'. The Mayor pronounced the memorial with its vantage point to be a constant perpetuation of the memories of the fallen from all over the town. And that the land on which it stood should be forever sacred to their memory, never to be permitted to be used for the purpose of any commerce.

The last post and reveille were played, followed by the laying of poppy wreaths and the singing of the National Anthem.

The sombrely attired gathering reluctantly began to disperse, people drifting away after the cavalcade. Albert moved towards the monument, then turned to Betsy,

"Will you come with me Betsy, I need to see his name?"

"Of course Albert, of course. Edward, you stay here with Beth. Looks like Eliza's deep in conversation with Mr Chapman again Albert." She winked, and they smiled together, the arrival of little Charlotte had put all previous awkwardness and discomfort behind them. Betsy pulled the large beige cashmere wool she still loved to wear on cold days, tightly around her, and gripped Albert's arm tightly as he led his big sister over towards the monument to confirm what he already knew. That his son had fallen in battle, and died to save his country.

She made them pause at the bottom of the steps, he thought she was girding herself before her ascent, but she began to speak.

"Albert, before anything happens to me, as it surely will, I've almost had my three score years and ten. You should know that it was Edward that bought Thom's first ever painting that sold for decent money after that exhibition, at my insistence. It was such a small price to pay. I will always be eternally indebted to him for rescuing our beloved daughter from the flames of the Spa fire." Albert looked incredulously at his sister as she went on, "It's hidden in our attic. I've told Edward that I want you to take care of it after me. Thom must never know. It's a shame for it never to be hung and viewed, but buying it gave Thom the confidence to paint more and build on his collection."

Albert shook his head in amazement, his open mouth sighing wonder at this disclosure.

"I don't know, Betsy, you've been a guardian angel to all of us in your time. What would we do without you? You can't be going anywhere just yet, we all still need you." He squeezed her hand on his arm as they began to take the steps slowly, one at a time. He shamefully realised, he had not seen her getting old. "You're wrong Albert, my work is done. Now I shall be able to rest." The steps conquered, Betsy straightened herself to catch her breath, he waited with her amongst the many sombre mourners milling around this magnificent communal tombstone. "Come on then Albert, let's look for Bertie." They tentatively approached the base of the monument as she smiled up at this imposing, striking and remarkable man who would always be her little brother.

Facing the austere stone, they let their heads fall back, tracking it upwards to the billowing clouds in the afternoon sky. At their eye level, and above, pressed hard into its stony base, were four separate metal slabs, upon which was embossed an unimaginable number of names. Albert quickly scanned, before realising, the entries where they searched, had surnames begining with 'H' and ending with 'R', they were looking at the wrong side. He steered Betsy to his left.

"Oh Albert, all these young men just from one town! It's too much."

They looked up at this next side of the monument, and there, in embossed letters Bertie's surname and initials sang out to them as though Bertie himself was shouting a greeting.

They stood silently together for a few moments, with their own memories of 'Elliot A. J.', better known to them all, as Bertie.

Betsy gripped the crook of Albert's elbow tightly, and whispered into the monument,

"Goodnight, Bertie, God bless." Then he felt her start to slither to the ground as though her legs had given way.

"Betsy, what are,......Edward, Eliza, over here, quickly."

By the time her family had reached her side, Betsy's body lay comfortably on her beige cashmere coat. Its size now enveloped her aged frame and its fibres cocooned her against the cold crazy paving that flanked each set of steps and sloped away from the monument. She looked around at her family and managed a half smile. They took sharp intakes of breath, hardly daring to hope. But she shuttered her eye lids slowly, taking one last, slow snapshot of them with her. They couldn't know the next image that held that smile; for they had been replaced by the vision she always had of her mother, only now, Lizzibeth was holding out her arms to her, coaxing her onwards. Uncle Henry, smiling, one arm around Lizzibeth's shoulders, beckoned with his free hand. Betsy's earthly smile broadened as she left her lifelong precious cashmere, to fall contentedly into those heavenly, long awaited arms. Lizzibeth Buxton could hold her daughter at last. She had flown her mortal nest, to finally glow celestially as one in theirs.

Epilogue

Beth tried to contain the girlish excitement welling up inside her on this, her long awaited wedding day.

She looked at her surroundings. She had been in here once before to register Charlotte's birth, but now as the registrar rambled, she took in the ornateness of the high coving, the starkness of the whitewash, and thought how inviting some flowers would have looked. She stood tall, smart in her new suit and hat, feigning maturity and sophistication beyond her years to try to equal her tall, proud and handsome husband.

She knew that their family would forgive them for their exclusion. The weighty chains of secrecy and shame inherited from the Ferguson's may have been lifted and eradicated from the Elliot's, but respectability was still paramount within this society. To make a celebration out of a mere event so soon after the passing of such an influential figure in both their lives, would have disrespected them all. Edward and Eliza were still in such deep despair, they would just be grateful Albert had married her at last, and all would be well.

She resented the coyness and embarrassment she felt at Mr and Mrs Bagshaw and their son sharing this private moment as they exchanged their solemn vows. She wondered at the absurd necessity for such witnesses to be present on this day, other than to nurse and amuse their baby daughter for them as they became husband and wife.

Albert, serious until now, sensed her anxiety and smiled down into her eyes.

Restored by that one glance, Beth tried to take in the words of the registrar, but they were inconsequential. She adored this man with all her being, and he knew. She had no need to declare her feelings to this stranger, other than as a means to an end. To be Albert Elliot's wife 'til death do they part.

She shivered, the room was cold in its austerity, and her outfit was impractical for a cold October day. She felt a comfort envelope her shoulders, and for a moment thought Albert had quite forgotten himself in the occasion. The warmth cursed through her body, and she smiled, instantly uplifted in the sure and certain knowledge that her family were indeed represented today, if only in the ephemeral spirit of their beloved matriarch.

Betsy's life story had ended much as it had begun. Out of doors, cold, and on a monument surrounded by loved ones. Fittingly the first, celebrating a re-birth. The last, commemorating the dead.

No phoenix emerged from Betsy's smoldering spicy embers, there was no need. Her life's work had been completed. Instead, as the final fulfillment of her life, she released an ethereal legacy of pride in her truth, kindness, honesty and compassion, which would flutter freely and warmly around her loved ones in a dynasty of generations to come.

Made in the USA
Lexington, KY
01 September 2010